Redsands

IA Mullin

Redsands

Redsands Book 3

By
IA Mullin

Redsands—Redsands Book 3—by I.A. Mullin

Published by Avio Publishing, LLC
PO Box 293, Eaton, CO 80615
Edited by Mark Graham and Ann Tinkham of Mark Graham Communications, Denver, Colorado.
Cover design and proofread by Deanna Estes of Lotus Design, Fort Collins, Colorado.
Cover illustration by Kathy Bornhoft.
ISBN-13 978-1-946023-07-0 paperback
ISBN-13 978-1-946023-08-7 ebook
ISBN-13 978-1-946023-09-4 hardback
Check out Magewood.com or facebook @authorIAMullin for new releases and additional content from IA Mullin.
Check out AvioPublishing.com for more about Avio Publishing, LLC.

Redsands is dedicated to my amazing husband. He is my support, my sounding board, the love of my life. He is my soul mate.

Contents

Redsands

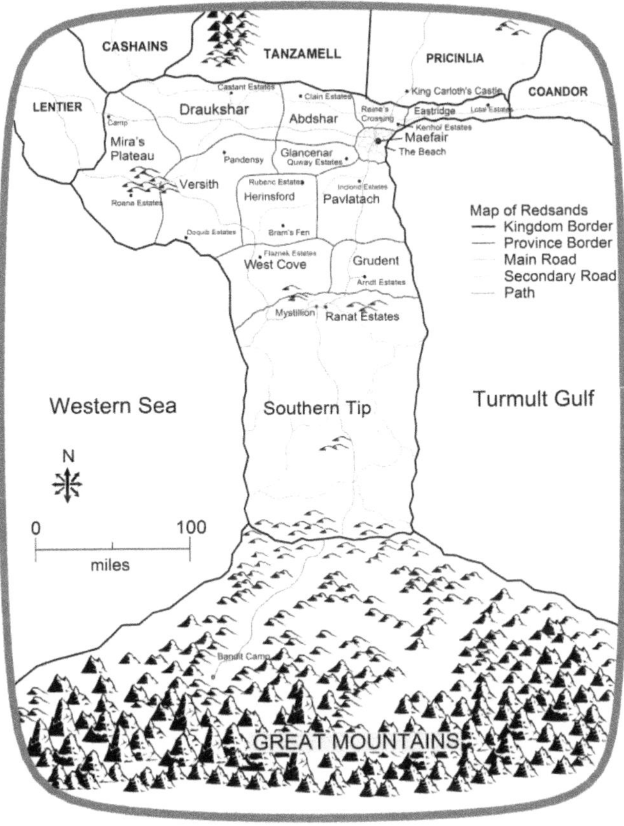

CASHAINS
TANZAMELL
PRICINLIA
LENTIER
COANDOR
Castant Estates
Clain Estates
King Carloth's Castle
Draukshar
Abdshar
Raine's Crossing
Eastridge
Kenhol Estates
Maefair
The Beach
Mira's Plateau
Pandensy
Glancenar
Quway Estates
Versith
Roana Estates
Rubenc Estates
Herinsford
Pavlatach
Bram's Fen
Flaznek Estates
West Cove
Grudent
Arndt Estates
Mystillion
Ranat Estates
Map of Redsands
Kingdom Border
Province Border
Main Road
Secondary Road
Path
Western Sea
Southern Tip
Turmult Gulf
N
0
100
miles
Bandit Camp
GREAT MOUNTAINS

Maefair

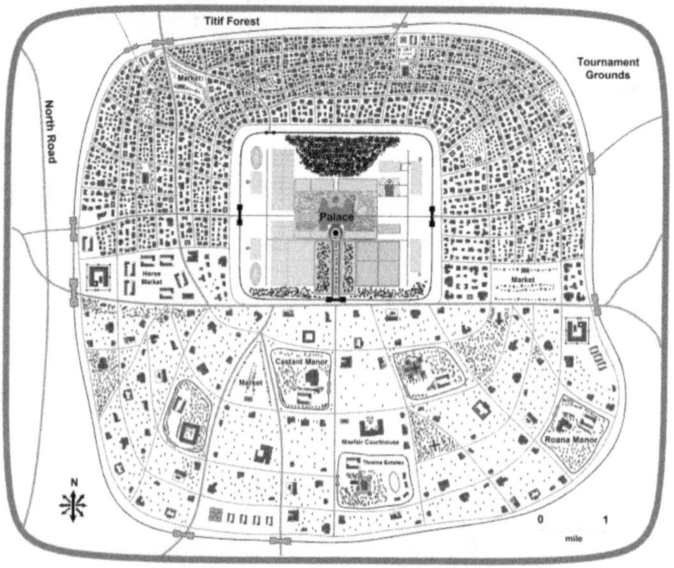

Titif Forest
Tournament Grounds
North Road
Market
Palace
Horse Market
Market
Castant Manor
Market
Maefair Courthouse
Roana Manor
N
0
1
mile

Contenent of Maen

1

The young lion, Marquiese, Crown Prince of Redsands, sat dejectedly in his favorite chair in his sitting room in the Royal Family Apartments in the Royal Palace of Maefair. His father, King Rylan, and his close friend and advisor, Master Castant, heir of Draukshar and Noble-Commander of the Palace Garrison, joined him. They took cups of tea from the pot the servants had left and sat staring into their depths. Marquiese looked away from the older lion and young leopard, choosing to study the tea in his own paws rather than the brooding expressions of his companions. He felt like he was waiting in the dungeon again, waiting for the magistrates' court to decide his fate, only this time he felt there was no bright future to fight for and had no idea how long he would have to wait--fifnights, months, or even years. He felt as if he would be alone forever with this emptiness inside him.

He had been thinking of Marilana and Earek again. It had only been two days since the two greatest friends he had ever known had been escorted out of the palace. Acquitted of treason, they had still claimed to be guilty of aiding the traitor Frishka in his attempt to frame Marquiese of treason to the crown. That confession of guilt had earned their exile, just as Frishka and his mother Prinka had been exiled before them. Marquiese knew Marilana and Earek had one more day inside the borders of Redsands. After that they would officially begin their new lives as heirs to the Southern Tip in Exile. The sting of betrayal shot through him again as he remembered the recent treason trials. He knew Marilana was the greatest of bandit hunters, well skilled in stealth, tracking, and killing—named The Ghost by the bandits who feared her. He had always been proud of her strength, her determination to do what was right even though she had been scorned because of her refusal to act the proper meek peasant female.

Just over one month ago Marilana had accepted the responsibilities and titles of heir to the Southern Tip, and had been adopted by Lady Annabella, her long time warden. Marquiese had been frustrated to the point of anger. He had thought Marilana would change, that she would let go of her past, would become a good leader, and maybe their friendship would grow closer. Instead Marilana had held tightly to her oaths as a bandit hunter and then she had boldly faced torment at the paws of his ill begotten step-brother, Frishka. Admittedly it was due to Marilana's actions that Frishka and Prinka had been banished, but Marilana had chosen to get herself and Earek banished in the process. He knew her plan was to hunt down Frishka and Prinka and kill them before they could try to attack Redsands with force, but he wished she had chosen differently.

"How long do you think it will take Marilana and Earek to find the traitor?" Master Castant asked softly breaking the silence, and echoing Marquiese's own thoughts.

"She is very skilled," King Rylan replied, "and we gave her a good start by sending her out the same route. We should ask the guards that escorted the traitors if they passed Marilana on their return. They may give us some idea about how fast she can travel."

"They will not see her," Marquiese said quietly.

The other two glanced at him. He gazed into his teacup as he spoke.

"She will avoid detection by Frishka's spies by taking to the trees and moving mostly in the twilight hours of dawn and dusk. She will move quickly, never staying in one spot for more than a few hours. If Earek cannot keep up, she will arrange to meet him somewhere later so she can move faster. The Ghost has done this many times and has spent ten years training for this type of hunt. We will not hear of her until she wants us to hear news. As for how fast she can travel, she can move as fast on the road as any scout and almost as fast through the trees."

"What will she do first? Will she try to make contact with local authorities or will she go directly to the point where Frishka and Prinka were released?" King Rylan asked.

"I think she will navigate quickly to the release point so she can pick up the trail; she will watch for signs of the army Frishka claimed to have as she goes. None of our scouts have reported any massing of troops of any kind, but she believed he was telling the truth about it. She believes he will be marching back here soon, but she probably has enough time to infiltrate his ranks before he reenters Redsands. He was sent out only five days ahead of her, how much could he possibly prepare in just one fifnight? I doubt he could be ready to attack for several months yet," Marquiese replied levelly.

"I too doubt his attack is imminent. We have had no reports of large gatherings of men moving in allied lands. He will need time to gather his forces together," agreed King Rylan. Then he added, "However, we must remain vigilant and not underestimate Frishka. I am sure he still has spies in the palace, and we may be able to delay his expected attack if we can quietly root them out. It is a good place to start at any rate."

Lieutenant Ranold rode at the front while the lioness, Marilana, and black leopard, Earek, rode steadily along the road behind him. The escort of fourteen guardsmen maintained a tight formation around them. Lieutenant Ranold was a competent commander, a leopard with a steady confident manner other creatures couldn't help but respect. He had sent scouts ahead and behind ever since the group left the city. He took no situation for granted. Before nightfall, for the previous two evenings, he had made sure to set up an efficient camp. He had sent out two scouts to check the area and immediately established eight sentries. He had directed the remaining men to tend to the horses and set up cook fires. The first night Marilana had offered to care for her own mount, but he said his men would see to the horses. He apologized to her and Earek, and insisted that he secure them, as they were still prisoners. After she acquiesced, he relaxed as if he had been worried that she would resist. He took the lioness and black leopard to the center of the camp, connected a chain to each of their wrist manacles, and drove a long stake though the chain securely into the ground. The stake would not hold long if she and Earek wanted to get away, but it would be obvious to everyone that they were attempting to flee if they tried to extract the stake from the ground. In all consideration, she approved of him and respected his skills.

In the afternoon of the third day after leaving Maefair, they rode surrounded by dense forest. Marilana closely observed the area since they were approaching the western border of Redsands. She would need to know when to turn back from crossing into the kingdom from which she was exiled. She did not wish to have someone hunting her for her mistakes. They passed a cart track leading off the road to the north, and she could see a thin stream of smoke rising above the trees. There was likely a secluded farm at the end of the track, possibly a family group making their living off the abundant wild berries or fruit trees. She had not seen many signs of inhabitants this deep in the forest.

She heard the tinkling of Earek's chains as he adjusted slightly in the saddle. The wrist manacles were merely for show as they rode. None of the guardsmen would have any chance of stopping them if they chose to spur their mounts and gallop away. Not that Marilana or Earek would break the conditions of arrest without sufficient cause. They had been acquitted of treason and banished only because they had plead guilty, forcing the court to either kill them or banish them. She had hoped her adopted brother would stay with Lady Annabella, but his bond of friendship to her was stronger than his bond as second heir to their adopted mother, and so he had followed her in to exile. Now the confident black leopard rode next to her, waiting to follow her orders, and trusting her with his life; the manacles on his wrists confirmed his intentions. To all other creatures who saw them, the manacles were simply a symbol that they were not free, that they were being escorted out, and that it would be within anyone's right to kill them if they returned.

The young lioness turned her attention back to Lieutenant Ranold as one of his scouts came out of the trees ahead, probably bringing word of a camp site for the night. He would want to make camp soon, as it was getting late. This would be the last camp. Tomorrow morning, the guardsmen would escort them over the border and release their chains. The good Lieutenant carried two bundles in his saddlebags that he said he would give them when they parted ways. She knew they were from her adopted mother, Lady Annabella Ranat, and she also suspected what they contained. Annabella knew exactly what she would need in the next few fifnights. Her usual compliment of supplies consisted of a waterskin, a belt knife, a hunting knife, and some dried food rations that could be eaten on the move. She suspected that the bundles also contained some money, probably enough for each of them to buy a small farm. The horses they rode would return with the guards, leaving them to make their way on foot. So, they would need a pair of good horses. She also needed to acquire a bow and a quiver full of arrows. Then she planned to live off the forest, and would not need to enter populated areas for some time. She suspected Frishka's army would be staying away from people to avoid being reported.

They rode on until the sun was touching the treetops; then they turned off the road to the south and moved through a wooded area to a small clearing that had obviously been frequently used as a camp. There were three small stone ringed fire pits; wood was stacked in small piles on the edge of the clearing protected by the low boughs of a pine. The men set to work immediately picketing the horses in two lines, one to the north and one to the south of the clearing. The sentries disappeared into the trees, and two scouts rode off in opposite directions. Marilana dismounted and gave her reins to a guard, then walked to the center area between the fire pits. Earek joined her and Lieutenant Ranold secured their chain, a duty he had performed each night.

"Do you trust your men?" she asked him in a hushed tone as he drove the stake into the ground.

"They are all good men, My Lady, loyal to the King. I do this duty so they can attend to other things. Even good men will grumble if they are asked to look after prisoners, even ones like you," he said.

She and Earek pulled their cloaks around themselves and sat back-to-back on the dry earth as the lieutenant performed his nightly inspection of his men. He had never set guards to watch them after securing their chain, but she had noticed that the men glanced at them every few minutes. She suspected that he had given orders for the men to watch them as they carried out their jobs. It was a good order with such a small group, especially with prisoners that would likely not try to escape. Three men moved wood from the stockpile to the fire pits and quickly ignited the fires. The cook pots and supply packs from the packhorses were brought to the middle and portioned out. There was no need for tents; it was warm at night this time of year, and few rain storms lasted long enough to soak through cloaks. Each man carried his own bedroll, and Marilana and Earek had their cloaks. Lieutenant Ranold had apologized the first night when he realized that no one had packed extra bedrolls for them. Marilana laughed and told him not to worry; she was quite content with her cloak. He was surprised that she slept soundly that night. She told him that, as a bandit hunter, she had slept in worse conditions many times.

She watched the bustle of the camp and listened to the sounds of the forest. The longer she sat there, the more she felt something was wrong. She looked closer at the men's activity; nothing seemed out of place. She had not felt this sense of unease the past two nights. Something was different this night. Something in the sounds of the forest made her nervous. She turned to look along the horse lines. Both lines of horses, to the north and south, were flicking their ears and stamping their hooves. Small signs, but they would sense the mood of the forest before the men did.

Earek twisted around. "What is it?" He sensed her agitation.

"I don't know," the lioness replied studying the treetops. "Something is wrong."

"Something in the forest, like a wild predator?" the black leopard asked studying the horses.

"No, not a wild predator, something else. The forest is restless, watching. We must take turns sleeping tonight, if we sleep at all."

Earek nodded and said no more. Lieutenant Ranold served them bowls of stew and bread. He said nothing, but his brow was slightly furrowed. They ate in silence. Marilana's eyes never left the trees and the horse lines. Her feeling of unease intensified. After they finished eating, Earek lay down, but Marilana remained sitting up. Lieutenant Ranold stood holding his saddlebags and studying the horse lines. He glanced at her, noticing that she was not getting ready for sleep. He approached her and knelt down next to her, keeping watch on the surrounding trees. The last of the sun's light was fading quickly.

"You sense something, too," he said. It was not a question. "My scouts should have returned by now."

"Something is wrong. The forest is agitated, the horses restless. And, yes, your scouts have not returned," she replied.

He turned and frowned at her, "How long have you sensed this?"

"Since we started to set up camp."

He nodded thoughtfully and continued to study the trees. "You must really know forests if you picked up on it that quickly. I only started to notice something was amiss when the sun was fully hidden behind the trees. You may need these," he said setting the saddlebags on the ground beside her. "Lady Annabella sent them. I do not know their full contents, but I was warned they contained knives."

She glanced at him. To knowingly give prisoners knives, he must have been truly worried.

"I can do very little chained," she said.

"I know," he said quietly, "that is why I set the key to your manacles down with the bags. Captain Lorne said I could trust you, and I will trust you to decide what you need to do."

He stood up and walked away chivying his men to be watchful as he circled the small camp.

"He is a good man," Earek said softly behind her.

She said nothing and did not move to pick up the key or open the bundles. She respected the way the lieutenant had given her the key without revealing this to his men. It had also served to prevent any eyes in the trees from seeing his action. She sat watching as the men readied themselves for sleep. The fires were banked to burn low during the night. The men had picked up on their commander's mood, though, and more sentries made rounds inside the camp. Twisting around to watch one of the men pacing, she placed her paw on the ground and picked up the key. Twisting back, she folded her paws in her lap. Working quickly she unlocked the manacles on her wrists, but did not remove them. She sat there a while longer listening and watching. All was quiet. The horses were alert and snorting softly, but they were still; the men in their blankets breathed softly as they succumbed to sleep. She twisted around and placed her paw on Earek's shoulder. The black leopard stirred quietly and raised his paw to hers, taking the key. He sat up and she leaned against his back. She heard the almost silent click of the manacle locks and sighed. She scanned the black line of trees picking out the little details she could see past the dim glow of the campfires. Suddenly she stiffened; the nighttime sounds of the forest had gone suddenly completely silent.

"Attack!" she bellowed into the silence and was echoed by the twanging of dozens of bowstrings loosed in unison.

Lioness and leopard rolled together toward the stake. The unlocked manacles fell from their wrists as they rolled up into identical crouches. Arrows flew silent and deadly threw the air, thudding into targets. Men shouted and horses whinnied. Marilana glanced at the saddlebags pin-cushioned with a half dozen arrows. The attackers must have known the saddlebags contained gifts from Lady Annabella intended for her. The spies in the palace had done their jobs. Creatures of all kinds in crude armor, waving short swords and studded cudgels, metal bits glinting in the dim light, rushed out of the trees on the east and west sides of the camp, shouting wordlessly for battle.

"Quickly, through the horse lines," Marilana called to Earek.

Together they ran toward the southern horse lines, but a blaze of light flared with a rumble at each end of the camp. Two flaming wagons were pushed out of the trees and into the chaos in the camp. Earek was knocked to the ground as a soldier was thrown back by a huge bear in armor. Marilana sprang back as the bear swung his cudgel down on the chest of the soldier. The bear lurched toward her. Not sparing a glance for the men on the ground, she spun and bolted through the fighting men. The darkness was streaked with red light; it flashed on metal and chased dark shadows across the camp making sure footing harder to see. She wove her way toward the east, skirting the flaming wagon. The guardsmen were putting up a good fight, but they were severely outnumbered. Marilana's only thought was to use the chaos of the fight to escape into the forest; away from the firelight she could disappear into the trees. She pushed worry for Earek out of her mind. He was well trained, and assuming this attack was being led by Frishka, that meant she was the main target. Her flight across the clearing would pull attention away from Earek, giving him a better chance to escape. He would know she would head for the trees; he would hide, and she could find him there.

As she wove and dodged through a group of fighters, a guardsman fell across her path and his sword flew out of his paw toward her. She snatched it out of the air and leapt over his body. The wolf he had been fighting lunged toward her and she slid the sword under his up raised arm. The wolf howled in pain and stumbled back. She raced past him and encountered several more creatures racing to block her path. She danced, her blade slashing and darting as she wove her way toward the trees. More men were coming; most of the sounds of fighting had stopped. They would be closing in on her. She pushed forward carving a path toward the trees. Just as she reached the shadow of the forest, she was yanked backward by her neck. She reached up and released her cloak and then swung with her sword. A huge paw grabbed her wrist. The pressure on her neck vanished with her cloak, but the paw grasping her wrist swung her around easily. The sword was wrenched from her grasp as another paw gripped her other arm. She struggled, someone shouted, and then she was thrown backward.

As she landed, she roared with pain; a burning sensation erupted along her back, legs and arms. She hung suspended off the ground, bouncing slightly from her landing. She froze and lay still, realizing what had happened. They had thrown her into a Blackthorn bush. The paw-length, claw-like thorns dug deeply into her flesh, and blood already trickled from the wounds down her back, legs, and arms. She hung panting slightly, watching the dozen or more creatures step back and form a half-ring in front of her. She heard the ringing of blades and several of the men turned to look. Behind them she saw Earek silhouetted by a flaming wagon. Marilana bit her lip to hold in her fear for her brother. He hadn't yet escaped. Brutish creatures approached him from all directions. He was fighting two men at once with a sword, but he was losing ground. Suddenly, he tripped backward and fell under the wagon. Just as he disappeared under the flames, the wagon collapsed. She watched in horror and stifled a sob, wishing she could've saved him somehow, her brother, her dear friend. The beginnings of tears burned the corners of her eyes, but the brutes around her turned their full attention on her and brought her thoughts back to focus on getting out of her own predicament. Her own life hung in the balance. She would grieve for her brother later, if she survived. She shifted her gaze to assess the men in front of her; two men with lit torches stepped into the space around her, and a dark cloaked form stepped forward between them.

"I should have known you would attack here," Marilana snarled, knowing full well who he was.

The traitorous tiger, Frishka, threw his head back and laughed, letting his hood drop to his shoulders and the torchlight illuminated his gaunt face.

"Poor little fool," he said laughing, "Silly little female still thinks she can outwit me. You will soon see the error of your ways. I have planned it all, and I will get what I want. You thought you could ride out and hunt me at your leisure. I knew where you would camp, I knew how many men would be guarding you, and so I planned to take you before you could escape me. I do not know how you got out of your chains, but honestly this was much better. Let it be a lesson to you that I am the better. Did I not tell you that you would be mine to do with as I wish? Once I have taken the throne, you will squirm and scream for me. Pity Earek was killed. I had wanted to capture him. I would have made you watch as he died. It might have taken fifnights for his last breath, and you would have watched every moment of it. You will not defy me again."

He stepped forward and punched her in the stomach. She screamed as the thorns ripped and dug into her flesh. He slammed his fist into her twice more and she screamed each time as the thorns dug deeper wounds. She hung limp, sobbing in burning agony in the clutches of the thorn bush.

"Very nice," Frishka hissed at her, firelight glinting red on his teeth, "I will remember those exquisite screams. I cannot wait to discover how many ways I can cause you agony. But for now we must be moving on. The risk of you trying to warn Marquiese is too great for me to take you back to the palace yet, so you will stay here. I know you are not able to get out of that bush on your own, and there is no one here to help you now, so I will leave you for my second to collect. He is so looking forward to finally getting his paws on you. I am sure he will make your introduction in five hours as memorable as he can. Extracting you from that bush will be a pleasure for him. He loves pain, it seems almost sacred to him, and he takes extraordinary pleasure in slowly drawing it out of his victims. He will be pleased with you." Marilana's hackles rose at Frishka's words, bone deep fear of this second in command rippled through her. Her unspoken suspicion that the creature was one of the feared assassins, one of the secretive Hungdie, turned her insides to ice. That Frishka might be greedy and arrogant enough to ally with one of the pain worshipers made her paws shake with long held fear. Frishka turned to a wolf and a boar. "You will stand guard over her tonight. Tomorrow my reinforcements will find you here."

"Yes, sir," the two young mercenaries saluted, "but what should we do with her?"

"The reinforcements should be here in five hours, by dawn at the latest. Leave her where she is. If she loses consciousness and cannot be roused, pull her out of the bush and do what you can to stop the bleeding. Do not touch her in any other way. She belongs to me. Understand?" Frishka growled.

"Yes, sir!"

Marilana wept in pain and anger as Frishka gathered his men and collected any unspoiled supplies. She saw him pull several arrows loose and throw them aside, then pick up the set of saddlebags meant for her and slung them over the horse brought to him by one of his men. She watched as his men tied the guardsmen's horses together and led them toward the road. She was helpless. She could not touch the ground, and without any leverage, she could not free herself from the thorn bush. Even with help getting out of the bush, the thorns would leave large wounds that would be infected within a day unless cleaned. How had she let this happen? How could she have not thought that Frishka would be waiting for her? She had pushed his anger, made him long to hurt her however he wanted, and she had dismissed the possibility that he would attack her before she could hunt him. She had been so confident in her plan, her own skills. She had thought he would need to gather his forces before attacking, she had not thought he would trust someone else to do it in his stead, but he had.

This attack would have been easy for him. His spies in the Palace of Maefair would have kept him informed. He would have had plenty of warning that she was going to be exiled by her own choice. Furthermore, how had she not considered that Frishka would be liberated as soon as he left Redsands? The allied nations must have not offered to secure safe passage for the banished, and she had known he had a man on the outside. His spies would have informed this accomplice and he would have had ample time to gather a small force to liberate Frishka as soon as he left Redsands. They had all been fools. Now she was dangling at Frishka's pleasure in a thorn bush, waiting for Frishka's accomplice to take her into his tender keeping—a fate worse than death—while Frishka and his advance force moved toward Maefair. She should have assumed that Frishka would be ready to move immediately.

She stopped crying and focused on calming herself. She had to think of her next move. Somehow she needed to return to Maefair and warn Rylan and Marquiese. They would not be expecting an attack so soon. They had fallen into the same trap she had. How was she going to do anything, though? Once she was in the paws of Frishka's second, she doubted she would live to see another day without suffering for it. Frishka had said that this man was more skilled at torture than anyone he knew. Frishka had demonstrated a considerable amount of skilled torture; the greater talents of his teacher scared her. She suspected the man might be more dangerous than even Frishka knew, and she was sure she needed to stay out of his custody. A shudder of dread washed through her, aggravating the wounds where the thorns still pricking her flesh. The boar left to guard her lay down and was soon snoring softly. She studied the wolf standing by her feet. He stood straight and attentive; he was not a sloucher. When he looked at her he snarled his annoyance. He did not like babysitting duty. Maybe she could use that to her advantage.

"Why did you join him?" she asked the man quietly. It was hard to talk; her throat was raw from screaming.

"Don't talk," he snapped.

"Why not?" she asked calmly.

"I said, don't talk!" He kicked her foot and sent a wave of pain up her leg.

Right, she thought, *bad idea. Don't talk to the guard. He doesn't want to be here.*

She forced her breathing to slow again and concentrated on thinking. She was having some trouble with her eyes. The fires had almost burned out and there was very little light now. Her eyes were adjusting to the dim star light, but one shadow seemed to slide contrarily across the dark ground.

Great, I've lost so much blood, I'm hallucinating. I'm going to pass out, and he is going to pull me out, tie me up, and wait for the reinforcements. What a fool I turned out to be.

In an instant, the patch of darkness grew taller behind the young wolf guard, and, with a dim flash of silver, the man collapsed. The shadow dropped and a wet gurgle ended the snores of the second guard.

"Marilana?" a voice spoke softly from the darkness.

"Earek! Oh, Earek," she cried with relief, "I thought I had lost you."

"How do I get you out of there?" he said approaching her; she could barely make out his form in the darkness.

She lifted her arms off the thorns, gritting her teeth against the pain. "Take my paws and set your feet. When you are ready, pull as hard as you can."

He did as she instructed although only using one of his arms. She clamped her teeth and gripped his paw as tightly as she could. He yanked and she pulled and together they managed to get her free of the thorn bush in one try.

She collapsed on the ground breathing hard; he knelt next to her.

"Are you alright?" he asked tiredly.

"I will survive. I'm just wounded and bleeding some. I thought I had lost a lot of blood, and was coming close to passing out, but I was just seeing your movements in the dark. I do not think I have really lost that much yet. How are you?" she asked panting.

"I too, will survive. What do we do now?"

"We have to get back to Maefair as quickly as we can. We must warn them; we have to tell them how badly we underestimated Frishka."

"Neither of us is going very far without stopping our bleeding. I know your back is torn up worse than my arm, but we have lost too much blood—are too exhausted—to go far at the moment."

"What happened to your arm?" she asked struggling to her knees.

"Sword swipe, not too deep, but I bled profusely before I was able to tie it up. It needs stitching I think," he replied.

"I saw you go under the wagon," she said quietly.

"The fools did not think to look on the other side of the wagon after it collapsed. I did not stop rolling until I was in the underbrush on the other side. When they searched the camp they did not see me. I waited until they were gone before taking one of the guardsmen's belts and tying my arm. I took his belt knife too and used it on your friends there. They did not take his knife when they searched him, probably because it is so small, barely as long as my paw and thin as a whip, perfect for stabbing a man in the throat."

"Did you see Lieutenant Ranold?" Marilana asked sadly.

"He slew the man who tackled me, and tried to help me get to the trees," Earek replied softly. "He slew many men before he was taken down by a group. I didn't stop to help him, he told me to run."

"There was nothing you could do," Marilana sighed. "He saved your life, but it cost him his own. We will make sure his loyalty and sense of duty are known if we make it back to Maefair. Now we must concentrate on our own plight."

They helped each other to their feet and stumbled toward the road.

"The farm," Marilana mumbled.

"What?" asked Earek.

"The cart track through the forest to the north. I saw smoke above the trees. We can go there, hide in the barn tonight, clean our wounds and hopefully steal some horses in the morning."

"Alright, but do we follow the road to get there? I seem to remember it was still a ways on horseback."

"No, through the trees will be faster."

"Should we tend your wounds first?"

"We do not have the supplies, and any broken thorns could be driven deeper, doing more damage. I am not bleeding much, and there is already too much contamination to the wounds. Leaving them open will allow some of the contaminates to come out. We need light to do more."

He nodded and together they stumbled on.

2

Marilana shifted where she lay. It seemed soft enough. Dimly she remembered stumbling to a barn and collapsing on a pile of straw inside. But this seemed much softer than a pile of straw. There was pale light behind her eyelids. Was it morning? Her eyes snapped open. She had to warn Marquiese.

"Whoa, there, little missy," said a gravelly voice. A paw rested lightly on her shoulder holding her down.

She blinked the sleep out of her eyes. Early morning light filtered in through an oilcloth window. As she scanned the space, she saw a small neat room with a wardrobe, washstand, and a trunk. Her dress and cloak draped over the chest. How had her cloak gotten there? An old snow white tiger was perched on a small stool next to her bed. His paw resting on her shoulder felt bony but strong.

"Where . . . ," she began, but the old tiger cut her off.

"Now, now," he said smiling, "you jus' relax and drink this before you start askin' questions."

He offered her a white clay bowl; and she could smell a broth laced with remedies she recognized. She took the bowl gingerly in her paws; her arms stiff with bandages. He helped her sit up and then made sure she drank the entire bowl. She leaned back against the wall as the broth soothed her throat.

"I'm sorry 'bout havin' to undress you. It's jus' the two of us men out here. Woulda been jus' me if the young feller hadn' got better. You two young ones made it into my barn las' night an' woulda been there still if he hadn' seen you. He felt somethin' was wrong las' night an' stayed out to watch. He came an' got me when he saw you two stumble into the barn. He rode off to follow your trail right quick an' came back with your cloak. Said it was a killin' field where it was. He had seen light like a bonfire earlier in the night, too. Said a couple of wagons had been torched off. Your friend is sleepin' in the nex' room. We sewed up his arm an' bandaged a few burns, but other than the los' blood, he'll be alrigh' in a few days. When I saw your dress all torn up along the back like tha' I knew you had los' a fight with a Blackthorn bush. Knew we needed to pull out any thorns an' clean you up before too long. So, we had to undress you see an', well, we got you all cleaned up. You'll both be good as new in a couple of days if you keep takin' this broth an' res' here.

"Don' know who did it, but I'm sorry to say all those guardsmen are dead. Whoever their prisoners were, there was no sign of 'em, their manacles were open an' left behind." He trailed off looking at her. She could tell he knew the truth and met his eyes coldly. He shrugged, not pressing her for more information. "Well, tha's the story I'll tell anyone who comes lookin' for you. I won' tell 'em tha' you were here an' tha' I healed you. I mended your dress as bes' I could while I was waitin'. Now don' you worry none. You jus' res' here an' I'll go check on your friend."

He stood up and walked to the door. She let him go without a word. She needed to find out who he and his helper were and if they could be trusted. She waited until the door closed behind him, then got up and tested her muscles. She was sore and weak from losing blood. She could tell the bandages should be changed soon, but she did not have time to wait. She got dressed quickly and fastened her cloak around her neck. When she opened the door she found Earek sitting on a pallet in a corner of a room that looked like a combination kitchen and work space. The old tiger got up when he saw her.

"Now you jus' take yourself back in there an' lay down," he said in consternation, "you shouldn' be up walkin' about yet."

"Please understand, I must leave quickly, good Master. I have grave messages to deliver. If I wait to heal, it will be too late," she said firmly.

"Be that as may be, I don' think you should be leavin' jus' yet . . . ." Before he could finish, a young cheetah entered the door to the yard.

Marilana could only stare. He had the lean look of recent illness about him. The cheetah stopped at the sight of her. He watched her for a moment then hung his hat on a peg and turned to fully face her.

"Guardsman Karndel, what are you doing here?" she asked suspiciously.

"Glain found me dumped in the woods, bleeding and broken, left for dead. He has been helping me heal. I'm not back to full strength, but I think I'm better than you. You both lost a lot of blood last night. Glain said you wouldn't be ready to go anywhere for a few days at the least, My Lady. Perhaps you should go lay back down and rest. And then we can discuss what has been happening," he replied.

"Why should we trust you?" interjected Earek. "How do we know you are not working with Frishka?"

"I am loyal to King Rylan," Karndel said quietly. "Why should I trust you?"

"Peace, both of you," Marilana interrupted. "I trust Karndel for several reasons." She looked down to Earek and said, "He is here where it would have been very unlikely to expect us to find him, and so he is probably not here under orders to wait for us. I can see he is not as well as the last time I saw him. Also, Frishka's men would not have had to knock him out if he was one of them, and I heard a commotion in the hall that morning before we were arrested."

"You say you were arrested," Karndel said cautiously, "so please explain what is going on."

Marilana shook her head, "There is not enough time to tell you the whole story. I will explain what I can quickly, but then I need a horse. I must reach Maefair right away."

"Two horses, Marilana, I am going with you," Earek growled from his place on the floor.

"You need to heal, Earek. This will not be an easy ride," she replied shaking her head.

"I will do what I have to do," he said determined.

"Perhaps you would explain why you want to ride hard when you yourself need healing, Lady." Karndel said.

Marilana took a deep breath and said, "Frishka was banished for treason. He is now returning to Maefair with an army. He and his advance group attacked us last night. I must return to the palace ahead of him to warn King

Rylan and Prince Marquiese. They think they have months to prepare for his arrival, not days."

"Why should you take this message?" Karndel asked. "From the looks of your camp, you two were being escorted out of Redsands, too. Won't they kill you for returning? I could deliver the message."

"No," Marilana said. "You disappeared without a trace, if you show up now without explanation, they will question the authenticity of your word. They will hold you in doubt as a possible trick from Frishka. You are correct that Earek and I were banished as well, but if I return, Prince Marquiese and King Rylan will hear my words as true. The King at least still trusts me. My banishment was my own doing; we were acquitted of treason."

"You won' reach the palace in your condition," Glain asserted. "Surely you can res' a day before settin' out. I could take messages."

"I am sorry, Master Glain. Unless King Rylan knows you, he has no reason to trust you. It would take too long to verify your words as true," Marilana said looking at him and choosing to trust him. "I am grateful for your help, and I am pleased to find Karndel alive, but if I do not arrive before Frishka's army, I am afraid that the King will have no warning that he is there. Frishka is marching his advance force of at least a couple hundred men along the main road, and so I am sure he is trying to intercept anyone attempting to get a warning through. For that matter, you both cannot stay here. Frishka's reinforcement group is supposed to reach this area today. They were expecting to find prisoners at the camp site. When they find we are gone, they will search the surrounding area for us."

"I won' tell 'em anything. You can be sure of that. And my name is Glain; I'm no Master," Glain said confidently.

"I know you will try to hold out, but I have reason to believe that the man leading them is a Master in the art of torture. I will not leave you to his vices. You must leave today."

"I believe you. What would you have us do?" Karndel asked.

"Travel around north of the city and find Lady Annabella camped on the tournament grounds. Tell her what I have told you about Frishka's army. Have her send for reinforcements. Tell her that I said if all goes well, I will ride Storm again soon."

He nodded. "Glain has two horses fit for riding. You two take those and head for the City. Glain and I will take his cart and pony out north." He looked apologetically at Glain. "I know you don't like to see people push themselves too hard or mistreated by others, but I believe her, and, if she is right, we are the only four with the knowledge to prevent our kingdom from falling into the clutches of the worst people I have ever known. Many more people will suffer if we fail."

Glain nodded, "I'm a good King's man. Go get the horses ready. We will pack up what provisions we can."

"Thank you both," Marilana said relieved.

*

The sun was fully above the trees by the time Marilana, Earek, and Glain exited the house. Karndel stood waiting with two short-bows and quivers.

"We have to hurry," he said holding out one of the bows to Marilana. "An elk came into the barn while I was saddling the horses. He started to ask about two people, but then he recognized me and tried to run. I had my bow close and killed him before he got to the forest, but he will be missed. I'm sure he is not the only scout out looking for you. I seem to remember you're a good shot with a bow. We can all head north and try to leave the pursuit behind."

"Thank you for the bow, but we must reach the city before the traitor. The road south of here is the fastest way," Marilana replied taking a quiver of arrows and attaching it to the saddle of a horse along with a pair of bundles Glain had given her.

"They will watch the road closely, and Frishka himself is ahead on the road. You'll be riding right into them," Karndel insisted.

Marilana countered, "I have tracked large groups before. I can avoid them easily, but first I must catch up and then make speed to the city. We are the ones the other scouts are looking for. If we kill some of them to the south, they will focus on us in that direction. That will buy you the time needed to get beyond their range. They may eventually try to find you, but it will not be their first priority. Hide your trail as best as you can. Do not trust anyone until you reach Lady Annabella. Now go quickly."

She turned and climbed into the saddle. Earek was already mounted and waiting. Her legs ached as she settled in, but she ignored the pain.

"Good luck and may The Goddess keep you safe," she said to Glain and Karndel and then turned her mount and led Earek around the little house and into the trees heading east.

She could hear the quiet rumbling of the cart down the more frequently traveled cart path to the north. She dared not use the cart path to the south; she was sure it would be watched where it met the main road. Instead she led Earek east through the trees at a quick trot. She guided the horse with her knees and was pleased to feel it respond well. She let her reins lay on the horse's neck and nocked an arrow to the bow. She scanned the forest constantly and listened to the sounds around them. Their horses made far more noise than she would have liked, but they had to move quickly.

After about an hour, Marilana angled south toward the road. They had no choice but to take their chance and cross the road. The forest on the south was older with denser tree growth and more shade-loving undergrowth. It would provide better cover for them to slip around Frishka's group. She slowed her horse to a walk as the underbrush thickened. As they neared the road, she detected movement to her right. She drew and released out of reflex and nocked the next arrow smoothly. A crashing sound indicated the source of the motion. She guided her horse in the direction of the thud and came upon a horse standing beside a boar on the ground. Her arrow jutted from his chest. She freed the horse's reins from the corpse and turned back toward the road.

"Should we take the horse for a remount? It would speed our passage," Earek whispered riding alongside her.

"No, we will have a hard enough time keeping two horses quiet," she whispered back.

Soon after, she spotted the road through an opening in the trees. Halting her mount, she motioned Earek to stay silent. She dismounted and gave Earek her reins. Taking her bow and nocking an arrow, she crept silently to the edge of the underbrush. Peering out from behind the branches of a bush she studied the road. The surface of the road had seen heavy traffic recently. She could see no one, but she knew if there had been a scout on this side, there was probably a scout on the other side as well, watching both the road and the nearby forest. As she watched, she saw a gazelle on horseback moving slowly through the trees on the other side. He approached the road, looked across, studying the trees and the road, and then moved back into the trees. Marilana waited until he was behind the thicker brush lining the side of the road, then stood and loosed her arrow. As she crouched and moved behind another bush, she heard a resounding thud and the soft snort of a horse. She studied the road a while longer, listening to the sounds of the forest around her. Finally she motioned to Earek to bring the horses and moved to meet him. She grabbed another arrow from the quiver and moved out onto the road. She froze and listened. She motioned Earek to take the horses across. Moving quickly she took quick steps as she faced the east—a combination of running in place and jumping from spot to spot—to cover the hoof marks with boot marks. An experienced tracker who took the time to study the road would not be fooled, but for a quick look it would not be obvious.

As she reached the south side of the road, she heard the sound of a galloping horse on the road. Quickly she mounted and led Earek south a short distance then halted in a patch of thicker undergrowth. She heard the horse galloping closer, then past on the road. It was heading east toward the city. It was most likely a messenger taking word to Frishka of the escaped prisoners. There would be more scouts to dodge to the east. She started her mount toward the south at a quick trot. Frishka's advance group would probably have continued to move during the night and throughout the day. They would be moving quickly to gain control of the roads and stop any messengers from reaching the city with word of the army's approach. She had seen no sign of wheel tracks, but plenty of boot and horse tracks. He could move faster without wagons or carts, but it seemed he did not have enough horses for all of his men. That would slow him a bit and he would have to stop to make camp at some point. Pushing through the night and day would wear out men and horses. He could not push too hard, or his men would not be ready to fight when they arrived at the city.

She angled back east after another hour. The sun was high overhead and the thick trees cast heavy shadows. She rode as quickly as she could, sometimes at a trot, other times slowing to walk, constantly weaving around thicker areas of underbrush and avoiding patches of sunlight. An experienced tracker would be able to follow their trail, but she tried to make it harder by picking her path carefully. With luck they were making good time and leaving a small enough trail that the pursuit would not catch up by nightfall. She planned to gain many hours by continuing through the night. She also hoped that the trackers following would be lazy and stop for the night; not many trackers could track at night and those who could were usually slow.

Her legs were painful and twisting sent sharp pains along her back. She ignored the pain. Glancing back she noticed Earek was looking pale around the eyes. She halted her mount and motioned Earek up beside her. She opened a bundle tied to her saddle and pulled out a pair of waterskins. She passed one to Earek. He took it gratefully and drank deeply. She took a drink from her own and instantly felt better. The skins did not hold water. Glain had insisted on filling each skin with broth and remedies. He claimed that it would be better for them than water and bread. She had wanted to take only water and some dried provisions, but she was glad to have the broth. She had discussed the remedies with Glain and had been pleased to find that he was very knowledgeable. He had not added anything to the broth that might make them drowsy, but had added several ingredients that would sustain them with little extra food. She pulled some dried fruit from the bundle and offered it to Earek.

Earek looked tired and drawn, but he held his reins in a firm, determined grip with his good paw. She could not leave him behind on this run, but she hoped he would survive the pace she set. For that matter she hoped she survived it herself. She did not allow them to stop for long. She kept them moving east through the shadows. Twice more she stopped to listen, trusting the sounds of the forest to help alert her to trouble. As the sun reached the top of the trees Marilana stopped trotting. She let the horses walk at a slow pace. She was sure that Frishka's group would not be far ahead.

Suddenly there was a loud crash and harsh cursing followed by a chorus of laughter. Marilana halted and sat frozen, bow ready. The laughter cut off abruptly and was followed by rustling and minor crashing sounds. The sounds gradually got quieter and faded away. She turned to glance at Earek. He sat erect and alert. The horses shifted their feet and tossed their heads, snorting softly. Marilana dismounted and nodded to Earek. He dismounted and soothed his mount.

Marilana spoke in a hushed tone. "We can stop here for a while. It'll soon be dark. We'll slip around the camp then. I need to scout ahead to determine the location of the sentries. Stay here with the horses; bind their hooves in the rags I brought from Glain's house. Tear strips from the rags and cushion the buckles and joints of the saddles. Loosen the girths and straps so the leather doesn't creak.

I borrowed some nose bags, which will keep the horses from whinnying. Once you're finished with those tasks, eat something. We will lead the horses around the camp on foot, and then we will ride hard."

Earek nodded and immediately set to work. Marilana silently slipped away and wove through the underbrush. She carefully headed in the direction the crashing sounds had come from, and found an area of underbrush that had been disturbed. The ground was scuffed and branches of bushes were broken. She discovered a tree snake that had been stabbed. It must have fallen from a tree branch and surprised one of the men. They were probably gathering firewood. She followed their tracks back to the northeast. She detected sounds emanating from the camp before she spotted any scouts or sentries. She crouched low and studied the forest. There, not twenty paces from her, stood a sentry, turning his head, and scanning the trees. He had not seen her, but was too alert for her to slip past. She turned back, heading north and soon found another sentry out of sight from the first. She smiled at her good luck. The second sentry had dusty boots and dirt on his pant legs, one of the men who had marched all day. He scanned the woods and then leaned against a tree. He was alert, but lazy. She could slip past him easily. She headed south until the man was just in her periphery. Carefully she moved toward the camp.

She slipped between the two sentries and snuck up behind a bush. The camp spread through the trees in front of her. She shook her head in disgust. The camp was disorganized and sloppy, definitely not arranged by a competent commander. Cook fires burned where there was space. Men spread their bedrolls around the small fires and tied their horses to nearby trees and bushes. One tent stood in a clear area in the middle of the camp. She could easily make out Prinka and Frishka sitting on stools at their own fire; an old woman bent over the fire stirring a pot with a long spoon. Three pack horses and three riding horses were tied nearby. Two things stood out. First, the noise level of the camp, while loud, was much quieter than she would expect from a group this size. Second, every creature was well-armed. Not bandits then, but mercenaries. Each man knew his role and was being paid well for it. Frishka probably had a loyal core group of guardsmen, but the rest of this advance group was hired. Likely the reinforcements would contain a sizable percentage of bandits, but this group had been chosen for their skills. Silent and stealthy, Marilana crept out past the sentries and followed the sentry line around to the south and east of the camp.

The sun had already set when she returned to Earek and the horses. She was relieved to find him resting quietly, conserving his energy. The horses stood dozing and relaxed. The horses started slightly as she stepped out of the shadows of the trees, but calmed as she softly spoke.

"I scouted Frishka's camp, and have determined a way around. As soon as it is fully dark, we will set out."

Earek nodded and offered her a waterskin. She took it and drank the refreshing broth. She tested Earek's work with the horses and was satisfied. The cloth would muffle the sounds of the horses and tack.

"I gave them each a drink from the water supply, and let them graze while I worked," he said quietly.

"Good. And I see you have been resting. You will need it." She kept watch on the surrounding forest. She had not seen any scouts for most of the day or any returning to the camp, but she was sure they were still out looking for them. "Are you ready to continue?"

He smiled ruefully. "I will make this run, but you will owe me a fifnight of good sleep. Then you can train me to keep up with you."

She smiled at him. Where he was sitting in the shadows, the darkness nearly engulfed him. His black fur and dark clothes blended into the night. She could just see the glint of starlight reflecting in his eyes.

"Time to go. You can sleep for a month as long as you stay with me."

He got up and took his reins. She turned and led her horse southeast along a slight depression. She moved carefully and stopped every ten paces or so to listen. She had found the depression when she was returning from Frishka's camp and had followed it for a while in both directions to make sure it would work for them. It ran southeast, then curved north toward the road. It would help to hide them from the sentries, and the sound of their steps would be muffled by the sloping earth.

They moved quietly and carefully through the forest. They saw none of Frishka's creatures, and no sounds of pursuit came. They finally reached the road in the calm, deep darkness of early morning. Dismounting, Marilana gave Earek her reins and nocked an arrow. She moved off into the darkness, looking for scouts. She moved out onto the road and cautiously scanned the surface of the road by the dim light of the crescent moon. No recent tracks. She hastened back to Earek and tightened up the horses' saddle girths, removed the cloths from their hooves, and took off the nose bags. She quickly tied the re-bundled supplies to her saddle and mounted. Earek had some difficulty mounting; he was favoring his injured arm. She touched his arm reassuringly and he nodded. They guided their horses to the road and set out at a trot.

Walk, trot, canter, gallop, trot, and walk again. For the rest of the night and the next morning, Marilana set the hard pace and pushed the horses as hard as she dared. She would have preferred to dismount and walk alongside the horses for a time, but she feared that Earek would not be able to mount again. By midday, he had stopped keeping watch and was focused solely on keeping his horse moving with her. By mid-afternoon, Marilana was not sure she could have mounted again herself if she had dismounted to walk. She was nearing exhaustion, and knew Earek was fairing far worse. He did not have her stamina or ability to withstand pain. She took Earek's reins and tied them to her own.

"Just hang on," she told him. He nodded tiredly and gripped the saddle horn with his good paw.

By late evening, she no longer kept her own watch. They had exhausted their food and broth supplies and had nothing to restore their energy. She was losing her adrenaline to the monotonous travel. If their pursuit had been close, she would not have been able to stop an attack in her condition. They had been lucky to have stayed well ahead of any scouts looking for them. All she could do was keep moving toward the palace. Walk, trot, walk. She forced her mind to focus on the pattern and the road. With every movement, the torn and abused skin down her back and along her legs felt like it was on fire. The back of her dress was damp and sticky with blood; she was relieved that her cloak hid her wet dress, and her hood obscured her face from any onlookers. They passed farms and houses and an occasional farmer or peasant heading home. It was pitch black by the time she and Earek rode into Maefair. She had one paw on her reins and with the other she supported Earek, keeping him on his mount. She had touched his injured arm and his coat had been soaked. She knew it was blood. Forcing her mind to focus, she directed the tired horses toward the palace at a walk.

Marquiese blinked sleep from his eyes as his night guard lit the lamp on his washstand.

"I'm sorry, Highness, but Captain Lorne sent a message saying it was urgent that you come down to the west doors," said the guardsman.

It was near midnight according to the crystal timepiece on his bedside table. What could Lorne have thought was so important? He sat up and stretched his limbs. He had not slept well the past two nights. Something about the calm after the tension of the past month left him feeling uneasy, like having a glimpse of storm clouds on the horizon. He slipped on the shirt and pants that the guardsman had pulled out of the wardrobe, then pulled his boots on. He grabbed his sword belt and followed the anxious man out of his rooms. He buckled the belt as he trailed the man through the halls of the palace. The man was nearly jogging and had to restrain himself to Marquiese's brisk pace since the Crown Prince should not be seen running through the palace.

Marquiese frowned as he stepped out of the palace onto the night-shrouded stable lane. In the dim light from the lantern and the palace windows, he could see a figure walking up the road leading two horses surrounded by a group of guardsmen on foot. He could tell the horses were tired, near to collapsing, walking with their heads down, taking slow shambling steps. The guardsmen kept pace with the horses. He could make out two dark figures riding the horses. Apparently some messengers had arrived with an urgent message, and Lorne had sent someone ahead to wake him to hear the message personally. Why were the messengers still riding the horses? They should have dismounted to walk and spare the poor mounts. He stood waiting for the group to approach him. As they got closer, he could discern more details of the dark figures on horseback. It appeared to be a man and a woman garbed in dark clothing and cloaks. He frowned when he realized the woman was holding onto the man.

"Go wake the healers and tell them to be prepared for one, possibly two injured," he said to the guardsman and took the lantern.

He could see now that the man was slumped forward in the saddle and the woman was holding him up. The woman swayed dangerously with the horse's motion. No wonder they still rode the tired horses; likely both the messengers would have collapsed if they had dismounted. Why had these two creatures pushed so hard to get to the palace? Something was clearly wrong. Marquiese wanted to pace, but he forced himself to stay still and keep his face neutral. He had to project strength and control as they approached him.

The woman rode into a patch of light from a palace window. He gasped and nearly dropped the lantern. He moved quickly, passing the lantern to one of the escorting men. He slipped past Captain Lorne who held both horses' bridles and stepped up between the riders.

"Marilana?" he said looking up at her. Her eyes were nearly closed and the skin around her mouth and nose was pale in the night; ashen. When he glanced at Earek, he saw that he was unconscious.

"Take him to the infirmary immediately!" he snapped over his shoulder.

He turned to Marilana as men hurried to do as he commanded. She swayed as Earek's weight was taken from her outstretched arm. She bent toward Marquiese her paw reaching down toward him.

"Marquiese," she whispered.

The faintness of her voice shocked him. Her eyelids fluttered as he moved closer.

"I am here," he said as calmly as he could.

"Frishka brings his army," she forced out in a whisper.

"His army? But—Marilana!"

Her whole body sagged. He realized that she, too, had lost consciousness and barely caught her as she toppled from the saddle, easing her to the ground. He gently turned her in his arms so that he could pick her up, and, as he did so, he realized her dress was soaked.

"Light!" he shouted.

The man with the lantern hurried forward then stopped suddenly as the light shone red and glistening on Marquise's shirt. Marquiese could feel Marilana's heart beating, but her breathing was ragged. He stood, lifting her in his arms, and started toward the palace.

"One of you, go get the stable master. Have him come fetch the horses; do not make the horses move any further until he takes charge. Captain, come with me," he said quickly as he hurried inside.

Captain Lorne hurried to catch up.

"What happened?" Marquiese asked as he carried Marilana through the palace.

"I was making my rounds through the stableyard when I heard a commotion at the gate. I went to investigate and found the lieutenant on duty holding the bridles and demanding what business they had to enter the palace," Lorne said quietly as they walked. "He wasn't bothering to listen to her whispers; he just kept demanding that she speak up. I recognized her as I got closer. I told the lieutenant off and sent a message to the palace to get you down to the lane quickly. I could tell they were in bad shape, the horses too. I decided it would be easiest to just lead them straight to the palace. I gathered an escort and set out as fast as I dared push the horses. I don't know if any of the men at the gate recognized them, but I told them all off for delaying messengers. I didn't want any of them to think about the bounty they would get for killing either of them, and I don't want them to die before you can sort out why they risked death to get back here so quickly."

Marquiese nodded. Captain Lorne was a good man. He had trusted Marilana from the beginning. Marquiese hoped that she had not pushed herself and Earek too hard. He quickened his pace up the last stairs to the infirmary. Captain Lorne held open the door for him.

"Prince Marquiese! You're covered in blood! What happened?" asked Healer Strunt as they entered.

"It's not my blood; it's hers," Marquiese said quickly.

"Yes, yes, of course. The other one is in here. Come quickly," the anteater said and led the way into a small room with two beds. "Put her here so I can examine her." He pointed to one of the beds.

Marquiese gently lay Marilana down and backed away. Earek was on the other bed, his cloak, coat, and shirt in a bloody pile on the floor. An assistant healer was cutting a blood-soaked bandage from his arm. Several other bloody bandages were on his torso and shoulder. Marquiese stepped aside as two more assistants moved toward Marilana's bed. Gently, at Healer Strunt's directions, they turned Marilana face down. The sheet underneath her was bright red. When Marquiese stepped forward again, Healer Strunt spoke quickly without looking away from his examination.

"Please, Your Highness, this room is small and I need to focus on the patients if I am to pull them through this. Please leave us to do our work. I will send word when I know more."

Marquiese started to object, but thought better of it. He followed Captain Lorne out to the waiting room. He eyed a chair, but could not sit. He paced in the small room. Captain Lorne watched him for a while.

"Do you need me for anything else?" he asked quietly. "Should I send a servant with wash water or some tea? Would you like me to wake the King?"

"What?" Marquiese paused to look at Lorne. "Oh, no. Thank you, Captain, I do not require anything. Let the King rest. I will let him know what has happened in the morning. Thank you. Please, get some rest."

Captain Lorne saluted. "I will send a guard for the prisoners. It would not be good if someone decided to kill them. If they are under arrest, though, no one will think the law is being ignored."

"Guards? Yes, I see your point. Very good," Marquiese said absently, pacing once more.

*

Marquiese remained restless in the small waiting room. It had been many hours since Healer Strunt had come out to make his report. He had said that Marilana and Earek were in critical condition. Earek had a cut on one arm that had been sewn up, but the hard journey had broken the wound open and he had needed to resuture it. He had also said that Earek had some major burns that had been bandaged and had likewise broken open and bled during the journey. Marilana had multiple puncture wounds down her back, arms, and legs that had been bandaged, but had also broken open and bled. The main problem with both was significant blood loss. They were very weak and would need lots of time to recover. He had suggested that Marquiese might like to go to his apartments, have a wash, and try to get some sleep. Marquiese had declined and said he would like to stay for a while yet. All but one of the healers had long since gone back to bed. The guardsmen stood guard patiently, and all was quiet. Yet Marquiese couldn't keep still, his boots rhythmically thumping on the rug with each step. His thoughts circled in an endless loop. *She can't die, they can't die. Frishka could attack anytime, she said he is coming, but she can't die!*

The door to the stairs opened, someone entered quietly and stood watching Marquiese.

"Marquiese," said his father's deep rumbling voice.

Marquiese turned to him.

"I would have given you a full report in the morning," Marquiese said quickly. "Captain Lorne should not have woken you. You can go back to bed if you wish, and we can talk in the morning."

"Marquiese," Rylan said gently. "It is morning. It is still early, but the sun has fully risen. I was informed by Captain Lorne of the night's events when I emerged from my rooms, and Healer Strunt has given me a full report."

"I am sorry. I should have met you as well and given you my report. I have lost track of time," he said glancing away.

"Time is not the only thing you have lost track of. I came here because of you. The servants are concerned," Rylan mused.

Marquiese looked at him confused.

Rylan sighed. "Look at yourself; you look as if you should be lying in a sick bed."

Marquiese glanced down at his paws and was startled to see dried blood. His arms and shirt were stained. He had been so worried that he had completely overlooked the fact that he was covered in Marilana's blood.

"Go to your rooms, wash, and put on clean clothes. I know you cannot sleep, but get something to eat before you come back here," Rylan said firmly.

Marquiese hesitated glancing at the guarded door.

"I will stay until you come back if that will make you feel better, but I am ordering you to do as I have said. Now go."

Marquiese nodded reluctantly and left the infirmary. He walked quickly to his apartments and was pleased to find that his menservants were ready for him with warm wash water and clean clothes. They helped him remove his blood-stained clothes. He scrubbed his paws and arms with several changes of the wash water before the men decided he was clean enough and then dressed in clean garments. When he was done, he thought he would just grab a bit of fruit and go back to the infirmary, but when he entered his private sitting room, there was a fully laden breakfast tray. Eggs Benedict, glazed ham, potatoes with peppers and onions steamed on the tray next to fresh sliced peaches. It all smelled so delicious, he sat and ate most of the wonderful breakfast. After he finished his meal, he hurried into the hall and found Master Castant waiting for him. Castant fell into step with him as he rushed back to the infirmary.

Healer Strunt was just walking away from King Rylan when Marquiese dashed into the room followed by Master Castant.

"What happened?" Marquiese asked.

Rylan held his paws up placatingly, "Peace, Marquiese, everything is fine. Did you eat?"

Marquiese nodded curtly.

"Good," Rylan said. "Healer Strunt was just giving me the results of his morning exam. Marilana and Earek are both resting as comfortably as can be expected. They have not woken yet, but the healers have changed their bandages and are pleased that the bleeding has subsided. The wounds while many, are not too serious, and should heal well given time. Due to the blood loss, they may not wake for several days. The healers are giving them a small amount of broth every few hours and will watch them continuously. There is nothing more you can do here. I would speak with you both, however. Come; let the healers do their work."

Rylan started toward the door. Marquiese glanced at the guarded door, then sighed and followed his father.

Once the three men were closed in a private conference room, Rylan turned to face Marquiese.

"Alright, now tell me what Marilana said to you before she lost consciousness. Captain Lorne gave me a full report. He said she tried to say something at the last, but he could not hear her words," Rylan said firmly.

"She said, 'Frishka brings his army'," Marquiese said as he sat down. He had been thinking about those words all morning.

"She rushed back here to tell us what we already anticipated?" Master Castant asked. "That makes no sense. Why would she push herself to the brink of death just to tell us what she knew we already knew?"

"That does sound suspicious. Perhaps she was sent back wounded like that to make us question, to give us doubts," King Rylan added.

"No," Marquiese said shaking his head, "if Frishka had wanted to keep us off balance, he would have sent messages of misleading information, false reports, or conflicting accounts. I can only guess then that Marilana perceived that the threat was great enough for her to risk death." He looked at them gravely. "I think she means that he is bringing his army against the city now. He had his army already waiting somehow, we do not have months to prepare. We have hours maybe days. If she had not thought the threat was imminent, she would not have pushed herself and Earek so hard. She rushed to get here before the threat."

Castant and Rylan exchanged looks.

"What about their injuries? Their injuries had been tended before they got here, and they are so different.

Earek has a slash and burns while Marilana has multiple punctures. I do not understand it," said Castant.

Marquiese nodded. He had thought about the disparity too.

"I think the camp was attacked," he said quietly. "If I were in Frishka's place, that is what I would have done. Marilana made him so mad, beat him at his own game, and got him banished. Then his spies sent word that she was to be banished, so he gathered a force and set an ambush. It would be easiest to attack at night when half the guards are asleep and it is darker in the trees than around the campfires. Also, the prisoners should be chained and secured so there is no chance that they can escape. It sounds good, but somehow Marilana and Earek were not chained and did escape, although they had to fight their way out. They must have found someone—a farmer or another camp of people, bartered for horses and had their wounds tended before they set off, evading Frishka's searchers, and rushing back here."

"I do not know, Marquiese. Why would Frishka risk attacking a group of guardsmen? He could have lost a good portion of his men," said Rylan shaking his head.

Marquiese leaned forward and clasped his paws patiently. "Because of Marilana, he sees the risk as acceptable. He was facing twenty-one guardsmen and two chained prisoners. He could have gotten a force big enough to take that easily. We sent them out on the same route that he had been on. He knew where they would be camping each night. Once the guardsmen had released Marilana though, she would have disappeared. He underestimated her before, but now he knows her reputation as a bandit hunter. Even if he still underestimates her skills, he knows it is much harder to find two individuals who can navigate forests and move quickly."

"I see your point," Rylan nodded frowning. "A force big enough to take on twenty-one guards is not big enough to assault the palace from outside the walls, though. He will need a lot more men for a siege."

"That is what worries me. I was wondering if Frishka had intended to try to bring a small force into the palace grounds unnoticed, a force just big enough to hold the palace from the inside. By the time the guards knew what was happening and got in, we could be dead and the nobles forced to swear fealty to a new king. Now with Marilana returning, we have been warned that something is not right. We can increase the guards on the walls and double posts to prevent one traitor on the inside from letting someone in."

"I have already doubled the wall guards because of Marilana's arrival. I had not known her message," nodded Rylan. "Castant, rearrange the duty rosters, change things up, have the men running siege drills on the practice field, make sure everyone is ready for any kind of attack."

"Yes, Sire."

"I have also sent word to Lady Annabella of her heirs arrival and asked her to remain in her camp. I wanted to spare the healers from her, but it might be a good idea to let her know our suspicions, and keep a ready force of men outside the walls to disrupt a siege. I also sent the maid Altia to her; she was very upset and emotional. I thought it might help if they could wait together. I promised them regular updates."

"That is good," Marquiese agreed, "but something still bothers me. It is not safe to leave Marilana and Earek unwatched."

"What do you mean?" asked Rylan concerned. "Do you think they are helping Frishka somehow? You said before they are not traitors."

"No, no, they are not the traitors," Marquiese said looking up sharply.

"Healer Strunt," Castant said nodding in thought.

"What?" Rylan asked outraged. "Why do you doubt him now?"

"It is something Marilana said just after Frishka's arrest," Marquiese said softly. "Castant offered to fetch the healer because she was acting strangely, and she snapped at him and said that she did not trust Healer Strunt. I dismissed it at the time, because I know she prefers the old remedies and thought she distrusted his methods. After all she had manipulated his diagnosis of her before. Now I am wondering if she might have meant something more. I have no evidence for an accusation, though. I just think it is worth watching them to make sure no one interferes with their healing."

"Very well. What do you suggest?" asked Rylan.

"If I might suggest it, I will select guards personally that I can trust and instruct them to watch everything that passes," Master Castant said. "Captain Lorne personally picked the two watching them now, and I believe they can be trusted."

"That will do, I think," Rylan nodded. "We must be careful not to warn any spies that we are watching for them. We must make it appear that we are making these choices to guard Marilana and Earek, not because we distrust the staff caring for them, but to witness all interactions."

"Leave it to me, Your Majesty, I will take care of it," Castant said saluting with fist to heart and leaving.

Rylan turned to Marquiese as he rose from his seat.

"I know you want to go back to the infirmary, but you have other duties to attend to. I will also warn you against showing too much concern for them until you have decided what their fate is going to be for returning."

Marquiese sat for a long time after Rylan left.

What do I want their fate to be? Not death, certainly, but can I banish them again? If I am correct, the guards did not release them, so technically they never started their banishment. I could send them back out to lawfully start the banishment again. Is that really what I want, though? I have been losing sleep and not eating well the past few days, plagued by thoughts of them, wondering if they were well, and they had not even left the kingdom yet. Can I start down that path again? Even if someone forces me to? Marilana forced me to see it was the right path, but it led to their sudden return, wounded and near death. I do not want that to happen again. I need to know why. Before I make any decisions, I need to know the truth about what happened. If . . . no, when . . . when she wakes, I will hear her story and her reasons. I will wait until then to make any decisions.

Standing up, he firmly focused on his duties and left to go to his study, not the infirmary.

3

Marquiese had busied himself with his duties, determined not to make any decisions until Marilana woke and answered his questions. He had followed his father's advice as well, and had not returned to the infirmary for days. He contented himself with listening to the healer's reports, which had not changed. Marilana and Earek slumbered with no signs of waking. It was just after dinner on the fourth day after Marilana and Earek had returned, and Marquiese joined his father in his study just as one of the assistant healers came to make a report.

"Majesty, Highness," said the middle aged reindeer bowing low to each of them. "I am Assistant Healer Jonwin. I have come with a report from Healer Strunt, if it pleases you."

"Continue Jonwin," Rylan said calmly.

"Yes, Your Majesty. Healer Strunt instructed me to inform you that the patients are continuing to show signs of improvement. Both now have strong vital signs and regular body functions, although both are still moderately dehydrated and unconscious. Healer Strunt is continuing his treatments for prevention of infection and recovery of lost blood," Jonwin said smoothly and then paused. "I do not know why Healer Strunt did not add this to his report, perhaps it slipped his mind, but there is one little thing of note."

"Tell us," commanded Rylan.

Jonwin bowed to Rylan, "Of course, Your Majesty. The Lady Marilana, she seems to be suffering minor delirium. She does not wake, but she has begun to shake her head weakly at times. Healer Strunt is now adding some slight sedation to her medication. Not enough to prevent her from waking, but enough to calm her delirium."

"Thank you, for telling us this," said Rylan. "Do you have anything else to add?"

"No, Your Majesty."

"Then you may go."

Jonwin bowed to Rylan and Marquiese again, then turned and left.

Marquiese stood frowning at the door.

"Do you have suspicions that something is not well? The guardsmen watch inside the room, but I doubt they would suspect the healers of wrong doing," Rylan said softly.

"I am worried. There has been no sign of Frishka and his army. Marilana rushed back here I am sure under the threat of immediate attack. Now there is not a single sign of an army and Marilana lays unconscious. She usually heals quickly. This unconsciousness is not like her, and now delirium. I feel a wrongness hovering over everything, but I do not know enough to know if something is truly wrong. Do you think Healer Strunt meant to leave it out?" Marquiese replied quietly.

"I do not know," Rylan said simply. "It may have just slipped his mind. He has a lot of demands for his time; however, I have never known him to neglect critical patients. The palace is as ready as we can get for any attack. We will just have to wait for something to happen."

*

Marquiese slept fitfully. When he did sleep, his dreams were filled with visions of Marilana lying motionless with dark shadowy forms moving about her. He woke early and paced his rooms before his servants came. Once washed and dressed, he decided to go check on Marilana personally. He strode to the infirmary with determination. When he arrived, he found the sick room to be a bustle of activity, which was unusual so early in the morning. The guardsman standing outside the door saluted and opened the door for him. He joined the second guardsman in a corner of the room. He silently watched as Healer Strunt, assistant healers, and apprentices went about their work. Healer Strunt was examining Earek. The anteater had given him a nod when he had entered, but had continued his assessment without pause.

"Has anything changed?" he asked the guard quietly. The lean eland gave a small sharp nod and was frowning darkly. Before more could be said, Marquiese's attention was caught by a sharp intake of breath from an apprentice, a young dingo, standing by Marilana's head.

"Healer!" called the young apprentice urgently, "She is doing it again!"

"Already?" Healer Strunt turned to see what the boy had noticed.

Marilana's eyelids were fluttering rapidly and she turned her head from side to side. As Marquiese watched, she lifted her arms swinging weakly about the bed.

"Hold her!" Healer Strunt ordered.

Assistants and apprentices moved immediately to force her arms and legs down to the bed. Her head twisted from side to side. Her lips moved as if she were whispering words without sound. Healer Strunt moved quickly to his bag of medicines and began to draw fluid into a syringe. Coming to her side he pierced her upper arm and injected the medicine. Marilana arched off the bed, her head whipping from side to side, her thrashing arms and legs pushed assistants and apprentices with increased strength, and then suddenly she collapsed back onto the bed and lay still. Marquiese swayed slightly with relief as he saw her chest rise rhythmically with her breathing. Healer Strunt approached him wiping his paws on a small towel.

"I am sorry you had to witness that, Your Highness. She seems to be suffering delirium. I administered sedation to try to prevent any injury," he said frowning at Marilana.

"The report we received last night said it was just some head turning of little note. This seems a more significant problem than I was led to believe," he said frowning in return.

"It has gotten worse, I am afraid," Healer Strunt said facing Marquiese. "Her wounds are healing well, but I have had to increase the amount of sedation to stop the uncontrolled thrashing, and the episodes are occurring more frequently. I do not know what may be causing the delirium. Perhaps she was given something when her wounds were first bandaged, but I cannot be sure. All I can do is try to stop her from injuring herself or anyone else."

"Earek seems unaffected?" Marquiese asked.

"Yes," Healer Strunt said, his frown fading. "He is healing well and should regain consciousness in a few days. Pardon, Your Highness, but unless you have any more questions, I should be getting on with my work."

"Yes, of course, thank you," he said absently watching the apprentices reposition Marilana and check her bandages.

He watched for a few minutes more and then left the infirmary. He walked down to the breakfast nook and sat with King Rylan. He did not pay much attention as the servants waited on them. He ate mechanically, still thinking about what he had seen. He looked up when his father touched his arm.

"What is it?" Rylan asked quietly.

Marquiese looked around the room and realized that all the servants had been dismissed.

"I went to the infirmary this morning," Marquiese said quietly, "and something is not right with Marilana. She was thrashing and seemed not in control of her movements. Healer Strunt said her delirium is getting worse although she is healing."

"I questioned him about that this morning," Rylan said cautiously. "He said that she could have been given something to cause this and that we will have to wait for the effects to wear off."

"That does not seem right to me," Marquiese said firmly.

"You are not a healer and have not spent time learning about their ways," Rylan replied.

"I know that, but Father, I know what I have seen," Marquiese interrupted. "Please listen to me. Marilana rides back here, pushing herself to the extent of her abilities, and was coherent on the verge of unconsciousness. She heals fast. You saw her regain consciousness after Frishka beat her. Never have we seen anything like this thrashing from her." He paused, and then continued quietly, "It seemed to get worse after Healer Strunt injected her with a sedative. Her movements were weak, almost as if she were trying to get someone's attention, and then he had her held down and her struggles seemed more urgent but still weak. After he gave the injection, her thrashing seemed different, stronger, out of control, and then she just collapsed, and I thought she was dead until I saw her breathing."

He looked down at his paws. He felt disturbed, harboring a growing sense of worry that he could not quite understand.

"If you think it is something Strunt is doing, then we must stop it," King Rylan said with finality.

Marquiese looked up. "What if he is right, and the sedative is necessary? What if by stopping him we kill her?"

"What if by not stopping him, we let him kill her?" Rylan responded. "What does your heart tell you?"

Marquiese thought for a moment before nodding. "We have to stop him. She distrusted him, and I still trust her instincts and knowledge."

"Then let us go," Rylan stood and Marquiese hurried to join him.

Marquiese followed his father into the infirmary with an air of calm control. The healers were busy with the patients. Teams of apprentices were cleaning tools, rolling bandages, and mixing solutions. Assistant healers were carefully feeding the unconscious patients some broth. Healer Strunt turned away from Marilana with a frown and spoke with King Rylan quietly. Marquiese stepped closer to Marilana and watched with a frown of his own. She appeared to be sleeping soundly yet swallowing the broth reflexively. Marquiese listened to Healer Strunt while he watched Marilana.

"Your Majesty is wise to consider alternate courses of action, but I assure you that I know how to do my job, and that I am doing my best to ensure the continued survival of my patients," Strunt said slightly indignantly. "Whatever this ailment is, I stand firm that we must wait it out and let her body heal on its own. We cannot rush her healing, and we would do her no favors by letting her injure herself."

Marquiese stopped listening as he noticed a pattern to Marilana's movements. Her eyes were moving under her closed eyelids, first one direction and then the other with a distinct pause between. Marquiese frowned deeper. It did not seem like the same fit he had witnessed earlier, but then he had not been watching so close before. The assistant healers laid her back down on the bed and moved away to clean up after her feeding. Marquiese watched as Marilana opened her eyes, looked at him, then closed her eyes again. Marquiese stepped up next to her bed. Had he seen what he thought? Had she looked directly at him?

"Highness, I must insist that you step back," said Healer Strunt approaching Marquiese. "She may go into one of her fits any minute now and could do you harm."

Marilana's ears twitched and her eyelids fluttered slightly at the sound of his voice. "You see, here she goes again. Quickly, hold her!"

Assistants and apprentices moved quickly to take hold of Marilana. She started to shake her head and move her arms as if trying to wave away flies. She whispered. This time, however, Marquiese was closer and could make out one word.

"Stop!" he shouted, the ring of steel accenting his voice as he drew his sword. Healers everywhere stopped moving and gaped at him. Marilana lay shaking on the bed, but had stopped waving her arms. Healer Strunt turned to face him with a fluid-filled syringe.

"If I do not give this to her immediately, there could be serious repercussions, Highness," he said forcefully.

"You will not give her anymore of your medicines," Marquiese said leveling his blade toward the healer.

"Marquiese, what did you see?" Rylan asked cautiously.

"She asked for help, and I am not going to let anyone touch her," Marquiese said menacingly.

"Your Majesty, she is in the midst of delirium! She does not know what she is saying, even if it sounds like she said actual words," Strunt insisted exasperatedly.

"It is not delirium," said Jonwin stepping forward firmly.

Marquiese glanced at the Assistant Healer.

"You know nothing of this!" Strunt spat.

"What do you mean, Jonwin?" Rylan asked.

"After the episodes began to occur more frequently, I watched more closely, Your Majesty. Healer Strunt has been giving something to both patients, something extra. I do not know what it is, but it is in a small black bottle that he keeps in his medicine bag."

"He does not know what he is talking about!" Strunt insisted again.

"Is this causing her episodes?" Marquiese asked. "Why is Earek unaffected?"

"I am sure it is the cause, but I do not know why he is unaffected," Jonwin said shaking his head.

Healer Strunt suddenly hurled the syringe at the guard and fled toward the door.

"Stop him!" shouted Rylan.

The eland dashed toward the door, but Healer Strunt reached it first and slammed into it. It remained firmly shut and Strunt rebounded back into the chasing guardsman. They hit the floor in a tangle of limbs. Having heard the ruckus, the guardsman outside the room stepped in and pulled the anteater off his comrade. Strunt sagged in the guardsman's grip, eyes darting madly around the room, searching for an escape.

"Take him into the next room and make sure he does no harm to himself," Rylan said with disgust. He turned to the reindeer as Strunt was unceremoniously hauled out of the room. "Healer Jonwin, what can be done for the patients?"

"Without knowing what he gave them, I don't know how to help them. I assume because he gave them repeat doses, they will come out of it on their own, but I could be wrong. It is possible they could die without the proper antidote. I simply cannot be sure," Jonwin replied shaking his head.

"Does anyone else have any clue as to what has been going on?" King Rylan asked the other assistant healers and apprentices and was met by sad shakes of heads all around.

"Strunt will not tell the truth if he can help it," Marquiese said quietly. "He knows we do not know the correct course of action, and since Jonwin does not know, it will take time for another healer to be brought in that can help them."

Rylan nodded thoughtfully. The room grew silent, everyone wondering what to do next.

"Red-ring snake venom."

The slow whisper was like a sigh of wind in the silence. The apprentices and assistant healers exchanged glances wondering who had spoken. Marquiese glanced down at Marilana lying on the bed and started with surprise. Truly, her eyes were open and looking at him. He blinked with sudden understanding. It was she who had whispered. He reached out and gently touched her paw. She flinched slightly and closed her eyes.

He looked up at Healer Jonwin. "What do you know about red-ring snake venom?"

The reindeer spoke thoughtfully, "Diluted venom of the red-ring snake is a crude sedative commonly used by bandits. It causes an individual to enter a coma-like state. It is virtually undetectable because all the normal signs of sedation are absent. The individual will simply appear to be in a deep sleep." He glanced at Earek. "It is one of the possibilities that I considered based on Master Earek's condition. I discarded it because Lady Marilana's reaction is unusual."

"Young."

The whisper was stronger this time. Marquiese glanced at Marilana. Her eyes were closed, but her mouth moved like she was trying to say something more. He glanced at Jonwin; comprehension dawned on the healer's face.

"Of course," he said quietly, and sighed, "I had forgotten that the reason most healers do not use the venom is that when given to young children, it has a strange effect. Children will develop an allergy to the venom. If the venom is only used once, it does not matter, but if given the venom a second time, they will have an allergic reaction to it. If given more, the allergy will change. The individual will become resistant to the venom, requiring more frequent larger doses, and the allergic reaction will evolve into involuntary muscle spasms. Just like what Lady Marilana experienced. By giving a second sedative along with the venom, Healer Strunt stopped most of the spasms and decreased the severity of other reactions such as oversensitivity to light, touch, and sound."

Marquiese glanced at Marilana and nodded. She appeared to be asleep again. Her eyes were closed, her arms relaxed, and her breathing rhythmic and slow. He knew what must have happened. She had been a young child when the bandits captured her. She had said she had been given something to make her sleep while she was transported to her release. She must have studied the various sedatives to try to determine which one had been used on her.

"What can we do for them?" Marquiese asked quietly.

"I know someone in the city who might have some of the antidote. We may be able to wake them up in a few hours," said Jonwin with a smile.

"Do it," commanded Rylan, "and I hereby appoint you, Jonwin, Royal Head Healer."

*

Marquiese had been pacing beside Marilana's bed for nearly an hour. Castant and King Rylan had interrogated each of the apprentice and assistant healers. Several had seen Strunt draw fluid from a small black vial when preparing the medicines for Marilana and Earek. More than that they did not know, nor could the vial be found in Strunt's bag or chambers. He had managed to dispose of it or hide it while Marquiese was at breakfast. He must have assumed Marquiese would be back, or decided to change tactics because of Marilana's reactions. Strunt was questioned the longest, but he would say nothing except that they would pay for their crimes. Strunt had been confined in one of the private sick rooms after all the dangerous objects had been removed. He would remain confined in the infirmary until Marilana and Earek were well enough to move to the tower dungeon and all the assistant healers and apprentices were sworn to silence.

They hoped to slow messages from reaching Frishka with the latest spy discovery.

Unable to calm his nerves, Marquiese paced. Marilana had not stirred; she lay as still as Earek with all the signs of deep sleep. He was startled when Jonwin returned escorting a tiny old caracal. She hunched over as she walked, using a gnarled cane for support. She shuffled past Marquiese and between the two beds, set her bag on the floor, and pulled out a long tube.

"Highness, forgive me for taking so long," Jonwin sighed. "She would not give me the antidote. She claims the antidote can be just as deadly as the venom if used incorrectly. She insisted that she see the patients herself."

Marquiese nodded, watching the old woman listen to Marilana's heart with the long tube.

"Why should we trust you, herb woman?" Marquiese asked harshly.

The old woman did not look up nor did she respond. She manipulated Marilana's paws and limbs. When she was done, she turned to Earek and repeated her examination. She finished by smelling his breath.

"Water," she said to Jonwin and he moved to obey. She snatched up her bag and hobbled over to the counter where she pulled pouches and jars of herbs from her bag. Marquiese moved to stop her, but she spoke sharply without looking away from her work. "We must work quickly if we are to save the leopard," she said.

Marquiese started, "The leopard? Marilana had the reaction."

"Yes, she did. There is nothing more I can do for her that she's not already doing for herself. She's wise in the old ways, that one. My niece said as much. The boy, however, has been asleep for too long with far too much poison; he needs the antidote quickly if he's to wake."

Marquiese glanced at the two sleeping patients; he could not see any difference between them.

"Good Mother," he said more respectfully, "they have been getting the venom for the same length of time. I do not understand what you mean or who your niece is."

"Of course you don't understand, Highness. You're not a healer nor an herb dealer. My niece is Altia. I taught her everything she knows of remedies and herbs. She's spoken to me of this Marilana. She's a strong one and will wake when she's ready."

Altia. Her name washed over Marquiese like a balm. One of the most trusted of the palace servants. The one he himself had trusted to assist Marilana when she first came to the palace, and the one that had stood by Marilana's side throughout all the treason trials. He now felt safe with this old herb mother. He still did not understand what she meant about Marilana doing what needed to be done, or that she would wake when she was ready, but he was calmer than he had been for days. Jonwin returned with a bucket of fresh water.

"Mother Gwina, what can I help with?" Jonwin asked respectfully.

She set him to work grinding herbs with a mortar and pestle. She measured herbs and mixed water with some; others she added to the mortar to be ground. She muttered to herself about the freshness of the herbs and the difficulty of getting more with the ache in her bones. Soon King Rylan and Master Castant came in and watched Mother Gwina with suspicion.

"How sure are you that she is not one of Frishka's spies?" asked Rylan quietly.

"Phaw," said Mother Gwina. "Better for all if that one had died."

"You know of the traitor Frishka, Good Mother?" Castant asked.

"Humph," she said, turning and facing them with a heated look. "My niece, she tells me he didn't touch the servants, but the girls of the city were of no account to him. I've given remedies to many of this city. Beautiful girls come to me when they've been taken by men of higher status. They come to make sure they don't carry unwanted children. I tend their cuts and bruises. Girls from the houses see me to cure sicknesses given by men who pay. I see much of this, but I've never seen girls from him. Once he takes a girl, she's never seen again. Yes, we of the city know him. We'd have rejoiced and danced in the street if he'd been executed."

She turned back to the mortar Jonwin was working over. He kept his head down and looked a little pale after her speech. She took the mortar from him with a nod of approval and mixed the various preparations in a little water. Marquiese noticed Castant and his father looked slightly ill upon hearing such harsh revelations. He had expected such was true of this herb mother, and the revelations of Frishka's nature were not new to him. Living in the city she might not have dealt with the victims of bandits as Marilana had in the forests and farmlands, but she had much more insight into the dark side of nobility. He had known the harsh truths that peasants lived with; Marilana had shown him the dangers to the lower castes during the three years he had lived in the Southern Tip.

Mother Gwina shuffled to Earek's side. She opened his mouth and trickled the concoction into it. Jonwin shifted nervously. "Mother Gwina, should I mix more for the other patient?" he asked tentatively. "She is the more critical case."

"No," Mother Gwina chuckled softly.

Rylan, Castant, and Jonwin looked shocked. Castant even reached for his sword, but Marquiese laid his paw on Constant's arm and shook his head.

"She may have had more violent symptoms, but she's not the more critical."

"But he has only slept peacefully," said Jonwin confused.

"You healers think you know so much," Mother Gwina said with scorn. "You would've given her antidote that she didn't need, and let this one slip deeper and deeper into sleep until he couldn't return to the light of day. You call her reaction allergic, but forget that an allergy is caused by the body fighting off the toxin. She's been fighting for days to regain consciousness. While this one allowed the toxins to spread throughout his body, enabling the poisons to penetrate his living tissues until it would've killed him. He's been given too much for too long. This venom has its uses, and they're all short-term. Long-term use is deadly."

"She sleeps now, though, and she has had much more of the venom than he has," Jonwin insisted.

"Yes, and in another, I'd be worried that she would've damaged her tissues. You healers ignore the old ways. You think that because you use needles and blood medicines, the old ways are worthless. She sleeps to heal her body, being well-studied in the arts of herbs and the old ways of healing one's own body. This antidote would cause a reaction the same as the venom in one who had it as a child. Other supportive remedies could help, if she needed them. She doesn't need anything but sleep. She'll wake when she's ready. Don't be surprised if she knows what has passed this day. She's very strong."

She finished trickling the antidote into Earek's mouth and eased his head back down on the pillow. She set about cleaning her bowls and repackaging her herbs. Jonwin watched with a pained expression and paced in front of the door.

"How long will it take him to wake, Mother?" asked Marquiese quietly.

"He'll not wake fully for at least a day. He'll need time to rest and regain the strength that's been leached from him by the poison. It shouldn't be much longer before we know if the antidote worked, however," she said calmly placing herbs in her bag.

They watched in silence as she cleaned her tools. She set the listening tube next to her bag and wiped out her mortar. She wrapped her mortar in toweling and placed it gently in her bag. She picked up her pestle and began to wipe it as well, but she stopped, set it down, and picked up the listening tube. She dipped a rag in the water bucket and moved over to Earek. Marquiese stepped up beside her as she listened to his heart. She moved the tube away as Earek coughed and softly moaned, shifting his paws slightly. Mother Gwina squeezed a trickle of water from the rag into his mouth and he swallowed convulsively. She nodded with satisfaction and returned to cleaning her pestle.

"He'll make a full recovery," she said as she worked. "He's strong too, in his way. He should recover well over the next few days.

There was a trio of sighs as Rylan and Castant echoed Marquiese. Jonwin nodded, then turned to Rylan.

"Majesty, if supportive care could help Marilana, I think I should try. I respect Mother Gwina, but I feel I must do something," Jonwin pleaded.

"I trust Mother Gwina's advice on this," Marquiese interrupted. "She says Marilana will wake on her own, and I believe her."

"Good," said a soft whisper.

Marquiese looked at Mother Gwina who was smiling as she filled a cup with water. She moved to Marilana. Rylan, Castant, and Jonwin gasped. Marquiese smiled with relief as he realized that Marilana was watching him again. She blinked slowly at him, then turned her attention to the cup in Mother Gwina's paw. Mother Gwina helped her sip from the cup.

"Thank you, Aunt Gwina," Marilana murmured when the cup was empty.

Mother Gwina chuckled as she helped rearrange Marilana's pillow. "Altia, was right. You're a good girl."

She faced the royals with paws on hips standing over Marilana, "Now you're not to tire her with questions. She's still weak, and needs sleep to recover fully. And you," she turned to Jonwin, "are to make sure that they both get a good strengthening broth and plenty of water in small quantities. You know where to find me if you need anything else."

"Yes, Mother Gwina. Let me escort you out," Jonwin said sheepishly as Mother Gwina lifted her bag and scuffled for the door leaning on her cane.

After the door closed behind them, Marquiese pulled up a stool next to Marilana's bed. When he took her paw in his, he was stunned to feel how weak she was as she flexed her paw. She did not lift her head or try to move as she blinked slowly from one face to another. She studied them each in turn and returned her gaze to Marquiese.

"How long?" she asked. It pained Marquiese to hear how weak her whisper was.

"You have been asleep for four and a half days."

"No attack?" she asked slightly puzzled.

Marquiese shared a look with Rylan and Castant. "No, there have been no attacks."

She frowned. "I thought he would have already."

Rylan said softly, "We do not need your full story yet, but we need to know the important details. We must know why you returned in haste."

"Yes," she said softly, "Frishka is returning with an army. He had several hundred in his advance guard close to the city. The last camp I saw was a day's hard ride on the road west of the city. They control the road. Reinforcements were a day behind but moving slower. The primary force appears to be mostly mercenaries. Most do not have horses."

"So many," Castant said shaking his head, "already so close. I can hardly believe it."

"I was a fool," Marilana whispered, tears filling her eyes.

"No," Marquiese said firmly, "we all share some blame for this. I want you to put it out of your mind for now, Marilana. You must rest. We know what we need to know for now. We will discuss this after you have recovered."

Marilana nodded, weaker after their short conversation. She closed her eyes and was almost instantly asleep. This time Marquiese recognized the healing trance Marilana had told him about long ago. He suddenly understood what Mother Gwina had noticed and why she had said Marilana was doing what needed to be done. Marquiese released her paw and motioned for the others to leave. Once they were outside, Marquiese found two guards he trusted standing guard on the door. He sent one of them in to keep watch inside the room. Then he led the way out of the infirmary and down to a conference room.

"So, she saw an army only a hard day's ride from the city, and yet there has been no attack," he said as soon as Castant closed the door.

"How could we not know about an army practically on our doorstep?" Rylan asked.

"She said he controls the road," Castant said quietly. "We have received no reports of armies from that direction, but now that I think about it, I do not remember getting any reports from that direction for at least the past fifnight—even before Marilana's return. The lack of reports for a few days is normal, but, if what she says is true, the lack of reports may not be natural. Any scouts using the road to reach us have been stopped."

King Rylan sat down heavily in a chair. "How did this happen? We thought we had months before he could return with an army."

Marquiese sat facing his father. "Marilana said she had been a fool. Frishka must have said something to her during the trial that she did not consider. She may have thought that he was simply boasting, or he might have hinted at something that she did not understand until later."

"Do you believe her?" Rylan asked quietly.

"Yes," Marquiese said firmly. "She is many things, but she is not a liar. She may lie and mislead if there is reason for it, but she never lies to me."

Rylan sighed, "No, I suppose she does not. I trust her too. Even if I wish she were wrong, I do trust her."

"So why has the traitor not attacked?" asked Castant quietly. "He attacks Marilana's camp, he pushes close to the city, and he controls the road. But she is right; I too would have expected him to have already attacked."

Marquiese shook his head and Rylan frowned. Ponder as they might, they had no answers.

*

For the next few days, Marquiese again heeded his father's advice to not show too much interest in the prisoners and stayed away from the infirmary. He received Healer Jonwin's reports with relief, however.

After days of no change in their condition, it was good to hear they were improving and awake for short periods of time.

"I removed Marilana's bandages today and she is healing well, faster than I would expect, but it is a natural healing. She shows no lingering effects of the venom. I am still checking the wound sites daily. Marilana's will be fully healed in a few more days. Earek's arm and burns are healthy with no signs of infection," Jonwin reported the morning two fifnights after they had returned.

"That is good to hear," Marquiese smiled.

"Yes, Your Highness," Jonwin cleared his throat. "There is one more topic to discuss, Your Majesty, Your Highness."

"What is it?" asked Rylan frowning.

"The Lady Marilana," the reindeer said hesitantly, "has requested an audience with you both. She said that Earek is ready, and they must relate the full details of their return."

"Do you think they are ready for such a meeting? I do not wish them to overtax their healing," Marquiese said levelly.

"Your Highness," Jonwin sighed, "I have never had a patient like the Lady Marilana. She says nothing more than is necessary for me to do my job, but it seems she was ready two mornings ago and has been evaluating Master Earek's strength before making this request."

Marquiese laughed. "Yes, that sounds like Marilana. Thank you, Healer Jonwin. You can tell her that we shall discuss when we will speak to them. We are not hers to command."

Rylan chuckled softly as the healer left. "How long will you make her wait?"

"One hour," Marquiese smiled.

*

An hour later, Marquiese followed Rylan into the infirmary with Master Castant. Healer Jonwin looked up from instructing an apprentice as they entered the waiting room.

"Sire," he said surprised, "I did not expect you so soon after the message you sent me with."

"What was her response to the message?" Marquiese asked.

"She simply smiled and continued with her exercises."

"Exercises?" Castant asked.

Jonwin sighed, "She insists on doing mild exercises. She says they are to keep her skin and muscles from becoming stiff. I let her continue them because they are not strenuous."

"That is good," said Marquiese. "Are they awake now?"

Jonwin glanced at the guarded door and nodded. "They should just be finished drinking their broth."

"Very good. Thank you, Healer Jonwin. We will speak with them in private," Rylan said gravely.

Jonwin bowed, and they entered the room. They waited while the assistant healers finished helping Earek with his broth. Marilana sat waiting with her paws in her lap. They were both dressed in the infirmary's white robes, and were sitting propped up by pillows with blankets covering their legs. When an assistant healer, a young doe, adjusted Marilana's blankets, she rolled her eyes and Earek smirked. Castant dismissed the healers and the guardsman.

"Thank you for taking the time to speak with us, Sire, My Lord Highness, Master Castant," Marilana said smoothly with a seated bow once the door closed behind the guardsman.

"You do not seem surprised by our quick response to your request," Rylan commented.

Marilana smiled, "I thought you might be impatient to hear the details of our return."

"Master Earek," Marquiese said quietly, "are you sure you are feeling well enough for this lengthy discussion? I would not risk your health for my curiosity."

"Thank you for your consideration, Your Highness," Earek said also with a seated bow, "but I will be able to cope."

"Very well. You seem to be well cared for," Marquiese said levelly.

Marilana rolled her eyes again. "If we were any better cared for, My Lord, we would be bundled in swaddling and spoon-fed everything, even water."

"You sound tired of your accommodations, My Lady," Castant said levelly.

"My accommodations are better than some I have endured lately, but I am almost completely healed and yet Healer Jonwin insists upon keeping me bedridden. I would like to move about and not have to sit under layers of blankets. If I did not know better, I would think Healer Jonwin was trying the ancient method of sweating out infection," Marilana said with exasperation.

"Why do you say he is not?" Rylan asked.

"He despises the old ways, Sire. He says that the old ways were forgotten for a reason," Marilana said shaking her head.

"It sounds like you and he have had quite a discussion," Rylan said frowning.

"No, Sire," Marilana laughed ruefully, "he tells me his opinions as he works, but I have said nothing. If I ever get the chance, though, he and I are going to have a very lengthy discussion indeed about the old ways and the merits of herbs."

"So, you have kept silent except to answer direct questions pertaining to your health?" asked Rylan.

"Yes, Sire," she nodded and Earek echoed her.

"Very well," nodded Rylan. He pulled a stool over to sit between the feet of their beds and positioned himself so he could see their faces. Castant leaned against the wall behind him and Marquiese crossed his arms standing at the foot of Marilana's bed.

"We will hear your story of events starting with your plan after being exiled," Marquiese said calmly.

Marilana bowed her head in acquiescence. She told them the facts of the journey starting with her plan. She told them how she planned to infiltrate Frishka's camp and get close to him to kill him. She spoke without emotion, and divided her gaze between the three of them. Earek listened carefully, adding what he could. He told them of his part of the fight at the camp and his escape by rolling under the flaming wagon and beyond into the underbrush. They told as many details as they could remember: where the sun was in the sky to mark the time of day, where the scouts were killed, how many horses and how many men. By the time Marilana related reaching Maefair, Marquiese was pacing alongside her bed. He ignored the painful emotional twisting in his chest brought on by her actions, and focused on the evidence of Frishka's intentions.

"I remember trying to urge the horses through the palace gates, but the guard had hold of the bridle. I do not remember what he said; I just kept trying to go through. Then the horses were moving again and I remember focusing on the movement to try to stay awake. Then I heard your voice, My Lord Highness, I heard my name. I could see your face and I tried to tell you that Frishka brings his army. I do not remember anything else until six days ago," she finished.

"What do you remember of Healer Strunt's activities?" Rylan asked quietly.

"I remember pieces of time when I was aware of my surroundings, but unable to make any sense of them. I heard sounds and voices, I felt paws touching me, but I could not wake fully. The awareness occurred more frequently and I remember someone talking about eye movements and ear twitches. Then something poked my arm and pain spread through me. The next time I became aware, I remembered the pain; I tried to stay still to avoid notice, but someone spoke, and it hurt my ears. They saw my ear twitch and the pain came again. I do not know how many times it happened, but every time I became aware of my surroundings something would happen to alert the healers. A loud sound or a touch that would make me flinch and someone would see. I knew someone was placed to watch for the twitching and once the alert was sounded I tried to stop them, but I was too weak. They would hold me down and the pain would come. I remember becoming aware and finally hearing your voice, My Lord Highness. I risked opening my eyes. The light hurt, but I saw you. I thought if I could get your attention you would stop them, but they were too fast and the pain came again."

She paused and looked down at her paws. "The next time I gained awareness, I nearly gave up. I could not stop them and I could not make my intentions understood." She looked up and met Marquiese's gaze; he had stopped pacing and was listening intently. "I heard arguing and risked opening my eyes again. You were there watching me. I tried to ask for help, and this time it worked. You stopped them. I entered the healing trance that I am skilled in and let my body fight the poison. In that state, I am mostly aware of my surroundings. I listened to the discussions and remembered my research in sedatives used by bandits; I realized what must have happened and gave the answers as I could. I was too weak to do more without further healing."

"You did very well, Lady Marilana, to bring us word and to keep fighting," Rylan said gently.

Marilana shook her head. "I was a fool."

Marquiese paced again, thinking about all that had happened. He felt the familiar feeling of betrayal stirring, but he pushed it aside; now was not the time to think about what Marilana had done. He had to focus on stopping Frishka.

"You could not have done any more than you did to stop Strunt," Master Castant said reasonably.

Marilana shook her head again. "That was not what I meant. I had my doubts about him during the trials, but I had no proof that he was working for the traitor. I thought he might have just been inexperienced with concussions and a patient who is trained in the old ways. It is not the first time I have had very experienced healers misdiagnose my healing. I did what could be done here. I meant before. I was a fool to dismiss hints the traitor threw at me."

"I thought as much," Marquiese said as he continued to pace. "When you claimed to be a fool a fifnight ago, I had the feeling you referred to your plan to go hunting. It was a good plan that might have worked if you had had a few months to work with. But he was waiting for you. We thought it would take him more time to gather his army. From what you saw, though, he should have attacked already. Why has he not? Was it just because you arrived here alerting us to his presence?"

"No," Marilana said quietly. "If, upon arrival, we had had the chance to speak with you immediately, his plans might have been disrupted, but he had Strunt drug us. We were not a threat to him as we were; he could have collected us after he had taken the throne and we would not have been able to stop him. Something else must have changed."

"Marquiese," Rylan said with sharp warning, "be sure of what you say. I do not know that this is the right place to speak openly."

Marquiese stopped and gazed at his father, then looked at the lioness and black leopard. They both lowered their eyes in shame. He studied them while he considered his father's warning. He trusted them, but should he discuss everything openly? *Yes,* he thought, *they could provide valuable insight in this matter.*

"Yes, father," he said firmly, "this *is* the time and place for this discussion. Lady Marilana and Master Earek may be able to help answer some questions for us. It would be faster to have the discussion in their presence rather than relaying questions and answers out of context. Your caution is wise, but I think this will be for the best."

Rylan nodded with a hint of a smile. Marquiese paced again, thinking about the last two fifnights. What had changed?

"The guards, maybe," Castant suggested. "We doubled the guards when they arrived, changed up the duty roster, prepared the palace for a siege. I do not think that is much of a deterrent, but if he was planning to slip into the palace undetected, it might have stalled him a few days."

"Yes," Marquiese agreed, "but not for two full fifnights."

"It did not," Marilana said quietly. "I think it did stall him for a few days, a fifnight at most. It is hard for the guardsmen to shift the duty schedule without notice, but a few days out would be easy enough. Then something else changed; his healer was found out."

Marquiese nodded as he paced. "Yes, then we knew your message and took further precautions with scouts and patrols. He would have needed his men on the inside to shift the duty schedule again so that everything lined up for his purposes. So, he should attack today."

"No," Earek said quietly, "there is another point to make him wait." He exchanged looks with Marilana and she nodded.

"We are here," she said simply.

"What do you mean?" Rylan asked cautiously.

Earek answered quietly. "He will take his time to get the duty schedule the way he wants it. That way his men on the inside are not found out the way the healer was, and it keeps you off balance. We rush back almost killing ourselves to get here, and then the healer is found trying to keep us unconscious, both suggesting an imminent attack. However, he has had to change plans several times. Now you are aware he is coming so you take precautions and nothing happens. You begin to doubt us. You question if we brought you false information, or were set up to bring you the message we did. As a result, your vigilance begins to falter; you relax and feel more secure again thinking you have more time."

"The thought has occurred to us already," Rylan said gently. "We trust you are not lying about what happened or what you saw, but you said it yourself, he was waiting for you. How can you be sure he did not set you up?"

"You said you were a fool, you should have expected something. He knew where you would be," Marquiese added firmly, "and he knows how to use you against me."

Marilana sighed, "I know what he said to me. I doubt he had planned to let us escape his grasp. He thought Earek was dead and he truly wants me in the paws of his terrible accomplice. He plans on it happening anyway when he does take the throne, so he would not have risked my life on such a strenuous journey or kept me unconscious if he wanted you to hear the message."

Marquiese nodded. He knew that much to be true. Frishka would not have risked losing Marilana once she was in his grasp. If he had verified that Earek was truly dead, they would not have made it back at all. The odd thing was that he left Marilana for his second in command to collect. The thought made him frown. He met Marilana's gaze and knew she had been avoiding this point.

"Why did he leave you?" he asked coldly. "What do you know of his second in command that makes you afraid to even mention it?"

Earek frowned at Marilana and she dropped her gaze to her paws.

"I was a fool," she repeated in a near whisper.

"Tell me, Marilana. How did you fall into his trap?" Marquiese persisted.

Marilana closed her eyes and spoke quietly, "The traitor taunted me about what would happen once he had the throne. He said that his second in command was gathering his army. I assumed that he was directing the gathering himself. He is not one to let others make their own plans and decisions. I did not realize how much control this second was given. This man made it possible for the traitor to return so quickly. I do not think this second thought the trial would succeed or that even if it did there would be nobles that contested the traitor's rule. The traitor would need an army no matter what. The traitor also taunted me with the threat of another very knowledgeable individual who would be allowed to train me and play with me. He said that this other was his teacher in the arts of torture."

"I do not think this reasoning is very well thought out," Marquiese said when she paused. "As you said, the traitor is not fond of sharing power. This second in command, this torturer, may be a strong individual, but he still answer to Frishka."

Marilana shook her head and said, "That is the thinking that let us fall into this trap—that they answer to Frishka. I have thought about this for days now. I believe that this torturer, Frishka's second in command, has contributed greatly in the planning and directing of events. This individual is dangerous, so dangerous that Frishka gives way to him. Why would Frishka share me? Why would he trust the gathering of his army to someone else explicitly? Why would he leave me for his second in such a condition that might leave me unconscious from lack of blood?"

She sounded desperate. Marquiese thought about her questions. Frishka never trusted anyone that much, not even his mother. Who would he trust to torture someone for him without killing the victim? A thought struck him and he felt sick with it. He looked up and met Castant's own pale gaze.

"His Confidant," Castant growled.

"No," Rylan looked from Castant to him, "It cannot be. That creature has been gone for too long."

"It has to be," Marquiese said coldly, "no one else has ever had the level of trust from Frishka that would make this possible. We never knew truly who he was or his background. He never would tell us how he learned some of the strange things he knew."

"And he knew how to hurt people in ways the healers could not imagine. The healers could not cure some of the conditions and the victims died from it," Castant added harshly.

"One of the Hungdie," Marilana whispered harshly. "One of the assassins trained equally in healing and torture, trained to infiltrate any caste in any culture. They do not just kill their targets but destroy their lives. To success or death, they never stop."

"That ancient cult is just a myth, Marilana," Rylan said curtly shaking his head.

"Of course, Sire," Marilana said bowing her head.

Something in her eyes made Marquiese pause. She was afraid of these Hungdie, deeply afraid, and she did not scare easily. Perhaps she knew more of this myth than was readily known. Whatever she knew or thought, this was not the time to pursue it; he turned back to the matter of stopping Frishka.

"Whoever this second is, he has done a good job of gathering a large force without being noticed," Marquiese said quietly. "Frishka will have to attempt a large-scale attack if he waits too long.

"He may still try to slip in with a small force," Marilana said levelly. "I think his army has gathered over a large area in small groups to avoid notice. The advance force may wait for the second group to hold the road and more reinforcements may be on the way. Then they can make a two-pronged attack."

"That is a rather definite plan. What makes you so sure?" Marquiese asked thoughtfully.

"Frishka knows the inner workings of the palace. He knows the guards and the servants and the nobility. He trusts his second in command with his army, and he still has spies among the guards and in the palace. If I had these connections and wanted to take the throne, it would be a simple plan to execute. Have the spies adjust the duty roster so most of the men garrisoned inside the palace are the traitor's men. Get men stationed on a gate to let in a small force. Slip inside the grounds, make way quietly into the palace, and secure the palace from the inside using the men from the palace garrison. Have your army attack the walls to keep the guards on the walls busy. Collect the nobles in residence, kill the King and Prince, and assume the crown. Announce to the grounds that the royal line has been over-thrown and for the armies to stand down. Anyone who resists is killed. I have had over a month to analyze him and his men. This latest information of army size and composition has just narrowed down his likely avenues of attack," she finished with a shrug of her shoulders.

"It is too easy to forget that you were trained by Lady Annabella and her Captain-General—two of the best. You are a skilled strategist," Rylan said solemnly.

"It was a good move to send Guardsman Karndel to Lady Annabella. She sent word this morning that she had received guests from the northwest. I did not know what she meant until now. I think she will hold the walls well from the outside. If you are right about his plan, the problem will be stopping the small force inside the palace," Master Castant said quietly.

Marquiese nodded. "The best approach would be to ride out and strike his camp, but without knowing where and how many, we risk our men being slaughtered."

"Yes, until we have scout reports to understand what we are up against, we can only defend. Planning a raid based on two fifnight-old information stating that reinforcements were already close is foolhardy indeed. We must have a raiding party ready to go at a moment's notice, however, so we can strike as soon as we have more information. In the meantime, we must remain vigilant and ready," Rylan said meeting Marquiese's eyes.

Marquiese understood. He and his father were the prime targets of Frishka's attack; they could not let themselves be caught unaware. When he looked at Earek, he saw the strain of fatigue in his features.

"We will leave you now," he said quietly. "Get some rest while you can. We will be vigilant, and thank you for bringing us this information."

As Rylan stood, Earek gave a seated bow. Marquiese shifted his gaze to Marilana and studied her face. He could see she was worried and wanted to do more. He gave her a stern stare and a small shake of his head. She dropped her eyes without speaking and gave a seated bow. He followed Rylan and Castant as they left the infirmary.

4

Marilana slipped into a casual, noble style dress, one of the dresses she had left behind. It felt good to be in a nice dress again. Lady Annabella had collected the clothes she and Earek left behind and sent Altia with some fresh garments. Altia kept her eyes downcast and acted calm when she entered with Marquiese's permission to see them properly attired again. Once the healers had left, though, she threw her arms around Marilana's neck.

"We've been so worried about you, My Lady. It was right kind of the King to send me out to your Lady's camp. We got to know each other much better, and it was a relief to know someone else was just as worried about you," Altia said finishing with Marilana's buttons.

Earek chuckled from behind the privacy curtain. "Do you ever go anywhere without picking up strays, Sister?" he teased.

"Altia is not a stray, Brother," she said ruefully. "She is the one responsible for slipping remedies into your food during the trials."

"Well then," he said moving the curtain against the wall and giving a formal bow, "I will hold her in the highest esteem. You do seem to have a knack for picking the best of friends."

"Including yourself?" Marilana asked innocently.

"Well, obviously," he said with unnecessary pomp.

Altia giggled and blushed. Marilana smiled. Earek cut quite a dashing figure in his red shirt and grey pants. He looked considerably more energetic than he had the past few days. The guard smiled as he lounged in the corner behind Earek.

A knock sounded at the door and Healer Jonwin entered the room followed by a pair of servants carrying lunch trays. Altia curtseyed and left looking worried.

"As you are healthy enough, you are going to be moved to new accommodations after lunch," Jonwin said stiffly. "You will eat your lunch here, I will give one last exam, and then turn you over to your new caregivers."

That sounded rather ominous. Marilana knew he did not think they were ready yet, but why did he sound so disdainful about their new caregivers? Had something happened since Altia had arrived? The maid had sounded like everything was fine, but this did not sound so good. She sat down and relaxed a little when the lunch tray was set on her lap. After days of strengthening broth and water, this lunch was like a royal feast. The hearty summer stew, a thick slice of crusty bread, and even a sliced pear spoke more of good tidings than dire events. She ate voraciously, taking pleasure in chewing solid food again. Healer Jonwin sniffed with disapproval.

"Why did you give us such a lunch if you did not think we were ready for it?" Marilana asked, disapproving.

"It is not the lunch I object to, Lady Marilana; it is the speed at which you are eating. I think you are ready for the food, but it should be eaten at a measured pace, not inhaled. You will get a sour stomach," Jonwin said scornfully.

Marilana looked at Earek and rolled her eyes. Earek, who was eating just as quickly, smirked in response.

"Besides, it was not by my order to have you clothed, fed, and ready to move out of the infirmary," said Jonwin more quietly.

Marilana studied the healer as she chewed a mouthful of stew. Jonwin examined her worried expression as if trying to decide how much he should say, then added calmly, "Prince Marquiese sent his orders this morning."

Marilana breathed a little easier. She shared a glance with Earek; his eyes were full of caution, but not fear. If the orders were from Marquiese, they could not be as bad as she first thought.

When they had finished eating, Jonwin insisted on thoroughly examining each of them. When he completed the exams, he sighed and shook his head.

"As far as I can tell, Lady Marilana, you are completely healed and as healthy as a young ox," he said with disapproval.

She raised her eyebrows at his less than flattering comparison.

"Master Earek, you are well, but you will probably tire easily for a few days yet and should not do anything too strenuous. You can follow Lady Marilana's example, if you like, and exercise a little each day to regain your strength. I am sure she would be happy to direct you through her daily routine. I will check in on you each day until I decide you are completely recovered."

Earek nodded as he sat on the edge of his bed. Marilana watched thoughtfully as Jonwin paced. The servants returned and retrieved the empty lunch trays. Still, they sat waiting. A sharp knock on the door startled Jonwin and the guard in the corner grasped the hilt of his short sword. Captain Lorne entered wearing a grave expression. He nodded to the guardsman, who relaxed and saluted with fist to heart.

"Healer Jonwin, are the patients ready for release into my custody?" he asked formally.

"They are, Captain Lorne," Jonwin replied sadly.

"Lady Marilana, Master Earek," Captain Lorne said levelly, "you will accompany me to your new accommodations."

He turned and led them out into the infirmary waiting room where an additional half dozen guards stood at the ready. She and Earek fell into step behind Captain Lorne and the guardsmen formed up around them. Captain Lorne led them out onto the stairs and turned to climb higher into the tower. Now Marilana understood why there was so much formality and why Jonwin was displeased. They were headed back to the confinement of the tower dungeon.

Marquiese watched shrewdly from the tower dungeon observation room as Marilana and Earek were led into the dungeon. The familiar feeling of betrayal had plagued him all night since the discussion in the infirmary about what Frishka might be planning. He had debated with his father over breakfast about what to do with Marilana and Earek. King Rylan had admitted that unless they could revoke the banishment, Marilana and Earek had to be kept under guard or sent back out on pain of death. Marquiese was not ready to face that decision, so they had to be kept under arrest. Healer Jonwin had argued that Earek was not ready to move into a dungeon, and had even questioned if keeping them under arrest was necessary. Marquiese had silently agreed with him, but the law still held them sentenced to exile. Despite wanting them to be free of banishment, he suspected that Marilana had been planning something even as she had lain weak and injured in the infirmary. He decided that locking them in the tower dungeon was the best way to prevent her from acting.

Marquiese watched with a tinge of sadness as Captain Lorne ordered two guardsmen to lock the heavy ball-and-chains to each prisoner's ankle. Marilana and Earek complied, standing straight-backed with heads high. Captain Lorne refused to meet their eyes as he told them that the orders were for them remain in the tower dungeon until other arrangements could be secured. Marilana and Earek stood still as Lorne and the guards left the dungeon, then Marilana turned and slowly walked to the window, dragging the heavy ball on its chain. Watching her, Marquiese could feel the weight of the ball on his own ankle as he remembered his own imprisonment in the tower during the trials. After a moment, Earek moved to join her.

They talked softly, their voices pitched too low for Marquiese to hear their words, but it seemed Earek was trying to persuade Marilana about something. She shook her head and stared out the window. Earek said something more and Marquiese was surprised to see Marilana bow her head. He always thought of her as the stronger willed, but apparently Earek had reasoned well. Earek placed his paw on Marilana's arm and she sighed, then nodded. They returned to the middle of the room and sat on the floor. Marquiese grinned as Marilana instructed Earek in simple exercises, stretching his muscles and working his joints. Marquiese recognized the motions from his own tutelage during their sparring practice in the Southern Tip. She claimed they kept the muscles and skin limber to prevent injury and to facilitate healing.

Eventually Earek continued exercising on his own and Marilana stood up and walked in a circle around the ball at the end of her chain. It was clear she was analyzing her situation. She said something to Earek and he frowned. Stooping she gathered her skirts and tied them up modestly. Curious, Marquiese stepped closer to the observation window. He had seen her do the same thing when working in the stables on Lady Annabella's estates. He watched with amazement as she lifted the heavy ball to the lower windowsill and then scaled the wall to the upper window. The chain was not quite long enough and the ball dangled beneath her as she hoisted herself onto the upper windowsill.

"I wouldn't have believed it if I hadn't just seen her do it," said a quiet voice next to Marquiese.

Realizing his mouth was agape, Marquiese closed it and glanced at the guardsman next to him.

"She has done this before?" he asked crossing his arms and frowning.

"She did it last time, only then she didn't have the ball," replied the guard lightly. "We made bets this morning when we heard you were putting her back in here. We wondered how long it would take her to climb up there, and if the ball would stop her or if she would need help. Apparently, she is a lot stronger than most of us gave her credit for."

"Who won?" asked Marquiese curiously.

"Captain Lorne," the guard chuckled, "said she would be up there without help in the first couple of hours. Excuse me, Highness, but I'd better let the rest know."

"She's up already!" came a strangled yelp from behind Marquiese as the guard related the news.

He did not turn and look as the other guards conversed about Marilana's feat. She finished pulling the ball up to the sill by its chain and looked up at the observation window with satisfaction. She froze when she met his gaze, a look of surprise replacing her smug smile. They remained still, eyes locked on each other for a long time. Her look of surprise slowly melted into wide-eyed uncertainty and then hardened in resignation. Finally, she bowed her head to him and twisted her feet up on the sill beside her; she turned away from him and stared out the window, resting her forehead against the bars. Marquiese blinked several times and glanced at Earek sitting on the dungeon floor. Earek repeatedly glanced from Marilana to the observation window with a worried look. He obviously did not recognize Marquiese silhouetted by the light from the guardroom. Turning, Marquiese strode out of the guardroom and descended to the palace proper struggling to make sense of his tangled emotions.

Several hours after the dinner trays had been served, Marilana finally consented to lower the heavy ball into Earek's raised paws. She dangled from the sill for a moment before dropping lightly to the floor. She took the ball from Earek and followed him over to the pair of straw pallets laid out under the observation window.

Earek sat facing her as she ate her cold soup and bread. He watched her silently until she finished and leaned back against the wall.

"You've been crying," he said gently. When she did not respond, he tried again, "I could not see who it was, but I assume it was Marquiese."

"Yes," she said softly bowing her head and not looking at him, "it was His Highness."

The formal address surprised Earek. He waited for her to continue and eventually she did.

"He just stood there watching. I do not know how long he had been there, maybe since we were brought up. At first, he seemed surprised, but as I looked at him he became colder and his frown deepened. I could not bear to have him look at me that way. I turned away so he would not see my tears," she whispered, tears beginning to form.

He moved next to her and held her as she leaned on his shoulder and cried.

"I do not think he knows what to do with us again," he said softly. "He did not know what to do with us during the trial, and now we are back against the law. He will have to decide soon, but I do not think he wants to send us away. I also think he put us back up here to keep you from doing something about Frishka."

"I will do something, though," she said stubbornly. "At least from here I can keep watch. I am sure the traitor will use the forest gate. It is the smallest, the least heavily guarded, and has the least observed path to the palace. The best vantage to watch that direction is that upper window."

She sat against the wall and studied him. "When the traitor comes, I do not know what will happen. I will do what I must, but you have to swear to me that you will follow my orders."

"Marilana, Sister, I am sworn and honor-bound to obey and protect you," he replied.

"That is not enough, Earek," she said darkly. "Brother, I need to be able to rely on you to do exactly as I tell you and not try to protect me. I will be judging my actions in the moment, and I cannot have you getting in my way. I am also sworn to protect you. Please do not make me choose between you and him."

He bowed his head. "I swear by our Mother I will do as you say and will not place myself between you and danger. I have seen you practice with the sword. You have been training me for seven months. I know I would endanger both of us if I got in your way needlessly."

"Thank you, Earek. In case you were wondering, I was planning to make you swear the same once we started hunting, too," she smiled gently. "When it happens, please stay close to Marquiese and watch his back for me."

He nodded and returned her smile, feeling that he was placing his trust in the best possible individual. He also realized that it meant she would not try to stop him from following her into battle if that was what would come.

"You know of course that the only way we are going to be able to enter the battle ourselves is if someone unlocks the door for us," he said ruefully.

She nodded solemnly. "I shudder to think what will happen to us if we do not get out before the traitor takes the throne."

"I am trying not to think about it," he said darkly.

"No matter what happens, we will only have moments from the time we hear the fighting of the guards to the opening of the door. We will have to move fast."

He nodded his head in understanding and she revealed her plan to escape the dungeon.

Healer Jonwin checked on Earek mid-morning for the third time since they had left the infirmary. Jonwin shook his head when he entered and saw Marilana was sitting in the upper window as she had been when he had come the previous days. Earek watched the healer descend the stairs and got to his feet. Marilana smiled from her vantage point. Earek had been improving quickly since coming to the dungeon. Marilana knew the benefits of solid wholesome food and exercise. She smiled thinking what Mother Gwina would have said if she had known that the healer had continued the strengthening broth and water regiment for days longer than the Herb Mother had intended.

The guards still chuckled to see her sitting in the upper window, the heavy ball under her knees. Everyone took her at her word that she enjoyed the view. Marquiese had not been back since the first afternoon, and neither King Rylan nor Master Castant had come to the observation room that Marilana had seen. Only Jonwin's visits mid-morning, Captain Lorne's morning and evening rounds, and the changes of the guardsmen had marked the hours since they had come. It seemed longer than two and a half days and starting on the third full day since they were locked in the dungeon. She knew Frishka was going for the monotony of being on alert without anything happening. Just when everyone was least expecting an attack, he would strike at their heart.

Marilana turned her attention back to the grounds as Jonwin examined Earek. She scanned the grounds as far as she could see. She had seen several groups of laborers coming from the forest gate this morning, but that was not unusual. Servants and guards moved to and from the forest gate everyday carrying supplies and materials. The forest gate was frequently referred to as the servants' gate, as most of the servants lived in city residences in that direction. She could pick out no one suspicious or familiar in the groups of creatures moving about, yet she was sure Frishka would bring in his men this way.

"Would you come down here, please," Jonwin called to her.

She looked at him puzzled. "You said that you did not need to examine me anymore."

"Yes, I did," he said in exasperation, "but that was before you decided to climb walls with a heavy ball chained to your ankle. King Rylan asked that I check to make sure the manacle is not chafing unduly due to your preference for heights."

She sighed and twisted her legs around, dangling her feet. Jonwin looked highly concerned that she would tumble from her perch. She lowered the ball on its chain until it dangled at full length, then she twisted around and lowered herself until she hung by her claws. She swung the ball just a little and let go. The heavy ball landed with a slight thump on the sill of the lower window, and she landed lightly on the floor as the chain clattered.

"Did you make the ball land there on purpose, My Lady?" Jonwin asked surprised.

"Of course," Marilana said sitting on the lower windowsill next to the ball and raising her chained ankle for him to inspect.

He stepped forward and examined her ankle still looking bemused. "I think if you refrain from dangling the ball from your ankle too much, you will slow the chafing," he said quietly. "If you are held here too long, we may have to deal with sores, but that should not be for many days yet."

"Thank you, Healer Jonwin. I could not have said as much," she replied sarcastically.

He frowned contemplatively, "We do not have to be enemies, My Lady. I am quite impressed with your abilities. I am just doing as I know how, and as King Rylan ordered me. I do not wish you ill."

"Forgive me, Healer Jonwin," she smiled gently, "I do not mean to make an enemy of you. I am just frustrated with my situation, most of which I have caused myself. Please, if we get the chance when this is all over, I would like to discuss my abilities with you. I recognize that while you do not think the old ways are as good as your medicines, you are able and willing to learn more to improve your medicines. I would like to help you with that, but not while I am your patient."

He smiled. "I suppose I should have treated you according to how you actually healed rather than how I thought you should. Forgive me as well, Lady Marilana, and we will start fresh if we ever get to have that discussion. Master Earek, I declare you healed and no longer in need of my attention. My Lady, please send word to me if sores develop on your ankle. Have a good day, both of you."

He stood and climbed the stairs out of the dungeon. Before he reached the top, Marilana had already scaled the wall up to the high window.

After dinner, Marilana sat on her perch and thought that the guards on the walls must be feeling as frustrated as she was. Three and a half days since being confined to the tower, and she could determine nothing—no patterns in the people coming and going, no feints on the walls to give the guards something to do. At least she knew whom they were guarding against. The guards had been posted double for two and a half fifnights with no knowledge of why, except that she and Earek had returned injured. Some had probably figured it out, but for others it was just something to complain about.

She looked down into the dungeon when she heard a muffled curse from Earek. He was attempting her balancing exercises, but was struggling with one of the poses. He resumed the pose as she watched. Balancing on one leg, he extended his arms to both sides with his other leg behind him. He was then to bend forward until his back was level to the floor. He started to bend forward, and toppled sideways, cursing as he fell. Smiling, she turned back to scanning the gardens in the late evening light.

As the sun set, she thought about all the dinners she had enjoyed sitting next to Marquiese in the dining hall. They would have finished dinner by now and the nobles would have retired to their rooms or would be visiting with each other in private chambers. She hadn't seen anyone taking evening strolls through the gardens last night or tonight. She wondered if King Rylan was entertaining anyone or if he and Marquiese had retired to the royal family quarters. She knew they were under as much stress as she was, but they had other duties to attend to. She wondered if she would ever get to talk with them again as nobility to royalty, or maybe even as a friend.

She was thinking it was time to come down for the night. The light was failing and the dark grounds were becoming hard to discern when she spotted a group of creatures moving through the dark gardens from the direction of the forest gate. She watched them as they approached and saw they were wrapped in dark cloaks. There were five figures, three large hulking shapes surrounding one tall slender shape and one shorter plump shape that swayed when it walked. There they were; Frishka, Prinka, and three of their most trusted men. She was sure of it. She inhaled deeply and bellowed the warning into the still night air. "Ring bells! Enemies in the grounds! Ring bells!" she shouted holding onto the bars of the window.

The tower garrison erupted into chaos. Guards in the observation room cursed and chairs toppled as they sprang up to see what was happening. Down below in the dark one of the hulking shapes threw back his cloak and drew a long bow. They aimed to silence Marilana in the tower.

"Get down!" she shouted at Earek and swung out of the window to hang down from the sill by her claws.

The arrow whizzed through the window below her dangling toes and clattered against the far wall. The heavy ball swung wildly from her ankle as it was yanked from the sill above. She let go and landed heavily on the dungeon floor with a loud crunch as the ball skittered on the stones. Earek helped her to her feet. Below them a bell tolled. The tower garrison sounded the alarm. Three tolls, then a pause, followed by three tolls; enemies inside the walls.

"Are you all right?" he asked worriedly.

"Yes, I am," she said standing and moving quickly to glance out of the window.

The group was gone. Guardsmen moved about the grounds running for the palace and initiating search patterns to find the intruders. The guards from the observation room had gone down below and the bell had stopped tolling. No doubt they were deciding what to do next. The garrison had sounded the alarm, but it had been due to Marilana's shout. Was she right or was it a false alarm? They would know soon enough that she was right. She shared a look with Earek; they were as ready as they could be. Waiting was all they could do now.

5

Marilana paced the dungeon. She could not stand being in the dark about what was happening in the palace. The guards had not returned to the observation room and she could hear muffled discussion from the window. She thought the garrison window must be close to the lower dungeon window for her to hear so much of the arguments. Men were still searching the grounds and distant alarm bells could be heard from the walls. Frishka's army was attacking. Earek sat waiting against the wall next to the stairs under the door. He watched Marilana pace in a circle around her ball without moving the weight; she was conserving her strength, but could not sit still. It had been over an hour since she had sounded the alarm. The sky outside was fully dark and all she could make out of the distant walls were the red glows of torches and bonfires.

Suddenly she heard the sounds she had been waiting for. The clash of arms and the shouts of men fighting could be heard from both the outside window and the guard observation window. The tower garrison was under attack.

Marilana snatched up the heavy ball and climbed the stairs to the door. Below her Earek stood and planted his feet; he leaned his back against the wall and raised his paws. He waited and watched the observation room window as she listened at the door. She adjusted her hold on the heavy ball so it dangled from her paws on a length of its chain. The sounds of fighting finally ended and the sounds of stomping boots and murmuring voices grew louder through the observation room.

Turning, Marilana stepped sideways onto Earek's raised paws with her back to the wall. She began to swing the ball, building up momentum. She glanced at the observation room window and saw no one coming to check on them. Keys rattled against the solid wood door as someone inserted a key in the lock. It clicked, and, as it started to open, Marilana heard Prinka's voice.

"Bring them before me, now!" she ordered.

Marilana moved as the door was pushed open by a grizzled grey wolf Marilana had not seen before—definitely not one of the trusted guardsmen who had been assigned to guard them. She stepped back onto the stone of the stairs as she swung the heavy ball into the doorway. It hit the wolf in the snout with a wet crunch. Marilana snatched the wolf's sword from his slackening grip and dove past him into the guardroom. Rolling to her feet, she brought the sword around in an arc, slicing one stunned boar's neck and parrying a gazelle's blade. A hyena, fox, and elk gathered behind the gazelle she fought, and Prinka screeched orders behind them. Marilana assessed the room in a glance, but never stopped moving. She pressed the gazelle hard and spun past him when he lunged forward trying to press his strength. She slid her blade up under his arm as she turned, and he crumpled to the floor behind her. She stepped back to dodge a wild swing from one of the three remaining, and parried the other two, knocking the hyena's sword from his grip.

The three stepped back and worked together. The hyena drew his knife and tried to slip past her as the other two attacked. She parried the two blades and began to press them. The hyena screamed as Earek stabbed him from the open dungeon door. The arrow that Frishka had ordered shot at her jutted out from the creature's thigh. Earek dove sideways as the hyena swung wide with his knife. Earek came up with a sword from a dead man and stabbed the hyena in the neck. Marilana continued to press the two she was fighting, looks of concentration on their faces as they tried to get past her flashing blade. Earek struck from the side sliding his blade up under the fox's arm as he brought his sword around for another attack.

Behind the remaining fighting elk, Marilana saw realization cross Prinka's face. The plump woman turned and started toward the door. Marilana spun, knocking the elk's blade wide and slipped under his arm. She snatched his dagger from his belt and spun past him. Something caught her ankle and she tripped; she flung the dagger as she fell.

Earek helped Marilana to her feet. She cursed the ball still chained to her ankle. It was trapped under the dead gazelle.

"At least you dispatched the elk," she noted.

"It was not so hard since you startled him by slipping past him. He turned to follow you and I stabbed his unprotected side," Earek said with a shrug. "You were the amazing one with that throw."

Marilana turned to see where Earek was looking. She had been sure she had missed, but Prinka lay, face to the floor, the hilt of the dagger protruding from her back.

They rummaged quickly through the dead creatures and found the keys that unlocked the chains from their ankles. Earek tested the swords and quickly found the best two while Marilana let down her skirts and removed a belt of throwing knives from the dead wolf, fastening it around her waist.

"We must be careful and quiet. We have no idea what we are descending into," Marilana cautioned and led the way to the stairs.

The stairs were littered with dead guardsmen. It appeared that they had been taken by surprise; most of the dead guardsmen lay just inside the garrison door. They had not even drawn their swords, still in doubt of the authenticity of the attack. Silently, Marilana crept down the stairs, past the dark infirmary, sword in one paw and dagger in the other. When she reached the bottom, she eased the door slightly and peered out into the hallway. She motioned Earek to follow as she slipped through the door. They stole down the empty passage peering cautiously through open doorways into noble guest rooms, all of them empty.

Just as they reached the door that had been Marilana's for the past few months, she saw movement ahead. Marilana crouched low and Earek struck a ready stance behind her. Ahead at a crossing corridor she detected motion again. A face peeked around the corner and disappeared. Marilana stalked forward silently, balanced on her toes. The face appeared again, and this time the girl in servant's livery slipped around the corner and started toward them. Marilana relaxed slightly as she darted forward. At the next crossing corridor Marilana checked that the corridors were empty and then motioned the caracal to follow them. She led them around the corner and into one of the servant storerooms. They slipped inside and closed the door most of the way. Earek positioned himself so he could peer through the crack and watch the hall outside. The light from the hall dimly lit the room. Heedless of the bare blades in Marilana's paws, Altia threw herself on Marilana and cried.

"Altia," Marilana crooned softly, "you need to control your emotions. We do not have much time, and I need to know what has happened."

Marilana carefully held both blades in one paw and disengaged the caracal. She settled Altia on a stack of crates and calmed her as best as she could.

"Altia," she said more sharply, "what has happened?"

The lithe tawny cat shook herself and wiped away her tears.

"I'm sorry. Of course, you don't know what's happening," said Altia. She inhaled deeply and told them as much as she could. "I was visiting Father Iscoot in his rooms when we heard the alarm sounding—the three chimes of enemies inside the walls. After half an hour I decided I could not stay there; I had to know what was going on. So, I left Father Iscoot and started for the stairs. There were men barring the doors to the outside, but they ignored the servants. Many of us were headed for the stairs, and they just let us go. They were not palace guards. They were rough creatures with crude leather belts bristling with knives and each had a crossbow at the ready. Rather than going down the stairs to the servants' quarters like everyone else, I slipped upstairs, thinking I could glance at the entrance hall or maybe slip through to come get you out. When I came out of the stairs, though," she paused to wipe away fresh tears, "I looked around the corner of the first crossing hallway, and what I saw nearly made my heart stop."

"Frishka was there with a large group of his men. I could see the doors to the royal family quarters; they were closed and the arrow slits were open. Frishka called out for King Rylan and Prince Marquiese to put down their arms and come out. When there was no response, Frishka laughed and said something to his men. They all laughed in turn and some shifted aside. I could see then why no arrows were being shot at Frishka. Six of his brutes stood before the doors and each held a noble daughter in front of them. Some of the young women were crying while others stood with heads high. Frishka called out again, telling King Rylan's defenders to put down their arms and come out or he would harm the girls. When again there was no response, he ran his claw down Mistress Lorlina's cheek. She trembled, but did not cry out. Prince Marquiese shouted, 'Alright, we surrender.' The doors opened and he and King Rylan led the small group of guardsmen out into the hall unarmed.

"Frishka's men moved forward and shoved the King and Prince against the wall tying their paws behind their backs. I was surprised to hear Marquiese speak. He asked, 'Are you going soft, Frishka? You left Marilana alone?' And Frishka replied with a laugh, 'Oh, she will join us soon enough. I sent Mother to collect her. I did not want to risk using her to make you surrender. Since she is condemned to death since she returned, I did not want someone to shoot her and me, so I brought some more innocent persuasion.' The guardsmen were held at sword point and the whole group moved off. I followed them to the entrance hall without being seen. They were taken into the great hall, and from what I could see before the doors closed, all the nobles in the palace have been assembled there under guard."

Altia sniffed and wiped away her tears. "The group of brutes barricading the front entrance did not notice me on the balcony, and the creatures guarding the doors to the great hall never looked up. I didn't know what else to do, so I came looking for you. I had no idea how to stop Frishka from collecting you too, but I thought if I could reach you, somehow you could help. I hoped you could do something to stop him before it is too late," she sniffled.

Marilana gazed thoughtfully at Altia. What could she do? Was she already too late?

"Did you see Master Castant or Captain Lorne? Do you know where they might be?" she asked quietly.

Altia shook her head. "I didn't see them, but if they followed their usual routine, they should have been receiving reports down in the lower dungeon."

"We will have to check on the garrisons and the dungeon first then and assess how they stand," Marilana said with determination.

"But what about the King? Can't you do something?" asked Altia tearfully.

"I am doing something," she replied gently. "Frishka has too many men for Earek and me to take alone. I can cause a distraction and get close to them, but I need reinforcements to take out the rest of Frishka's men. Let us go see what help we can find."

Earek nodded and they slipped out of the room and through the door to the stairs. At the bottom of the stairs Marilana cracked the door open and peered down the hall toward the west garrison and the dungeon. The doors of the garrison appeared to be barricaded from the outside. Further down the hall she could see archers positioned at intersections aiming at the dungeon. Occasional clashing of weapons or arrows skittering along stone indicated that someone inside the dungeon was still resisting. There were too many archers for her to take out. Closing the door, she turned to relate her findings to the others.

"If we could get them out safely, they would probably be able to retake the palace in short order. The problem is getting them out. Even if I had a bow, I could not be sure to reduce the number of invaders enough to release the garrison or the dungeon."

"There is a way," Altia said sounding hopeful. "I've never used it, but there is a secret door from the other stair into the dungeon armory."

"Another secret door?" Marilana asked skeptically. "Sounds too good to be true."

Altia nodded. "The same ancient king who built the door into his mistress' room built this one too."

"Let us get moving," Marilana interrupted. "You can tell us the background as we go."

Altia relayed the story quickly and quietly as they ascended the stairs back to the second level and then moved to the other spiral stairs to descend again.

"When that ancient king was young, the palace was assaulted by a rogue group of guardsmen trying to release a prisoner," Altia said. "The garrison was overrun, and the dungeon was taken. The king rallied the outer garrison and tried to attack the dungeon to recapture it, but the men inside were too well-protected, and because they had the dungeon armory and emergency rations, they survived for days without giving up. When the siege was finally over and the men defeated, the king commissioned a second door into the dungeon armory to prevent it from happening again. He moved the garrison out and isolated the workers. He had them build the door to his mistress' room at the same time. When they were done with both secret doors and the repairs that were needed on the dungeon, he had the architect and all the workers killed. He was the only one who knew of the two doors. He moved the garrison back in showing them the repairs made to the dungeon entrance and the new arrow slits. No one questioned him. Just before he died, he told his most trusted servant about the secret doors, and it has been passed down to only the most loyal servants ever since."

"Let us hope it is still usable," Earek muttered as they descended the last stretch of stairs.

"Here," Altia whispered stopping by an unremarkable piece of wall.

Marilana could see it; it was just like the other door. A thin space where it looked like the mortar had fallen out. She motioned the other two back and unhooked the banister. She slid her claw into the groove and felt the clasp give. She silently cracked the door and peeked through. The room beyond was definitely an armory. Just inside the door was a pair of stands bristling with pikes. There were no people in the room beyond. They slipped in between the pike stands and closed the door behind them.

"Altia, slip out among the guards and find Captain Lorne and Master Castant or whoever is in charge," Marilana said quickly. "Bring them here as quickly as you can."

Altia nodded and crept out the door to the rest of the dungeon.

"Why her?" Earek asked quietly.

"The guards will not be as suspicious with a servant; they have bigger things to think about. If you or I went out there, we would probably be killed before anyone thought to find out how we got in," Marilana said simply.

They did not wait long before the door opened and Altia was pushed gently back into the armory. Captain Lorne came in behind her and closed the door. He froze as he turned to confront the caracal and saw Marilana and Earek standing there.

"I would like to speak with Master Castant as well, if he is here," Marilana said easily.

Lorne nodded his head looking bemused and turned to the door. He opened the door and stuck his head out.

"Castant! You'd better get in here!"

Master Castant appeared a moment later and stepped up to the door.

"Lorne, we do not have time for wild stories from your girlfriend . . . ," he said, but broke off when he spotted Marilana over Lorne's shoulder.

He stepped inside quickly and closed the door behind him.

"What—?" he started, but Marilana cut him off.

"We do not have time for lengthy explanations," she said urgently. "Suffice it to say that Earek and I escaped Frishka's men when they came to get us out of the tower dungeon. Altia found us and told us that she saw King Rylan and Prince Marquiese surrender to Frishka under threat of harm to innocents. She saw them taken to the great hall and saw nobles assembled inside under guard. Frishka's men are holding the doors to the great hall and to the outside of the palace. From what I could tell from the tower windows, Frishka's army is attacking the walls. I have a plan, but I need your help."

Castant and Lorne listened intently as she laid out the details. Their expressions changed from bewilderment to concentration as she explained. When she was finished, they did not hesitate.

"Lorne, go gather the men quietly and free what is left of the garrisons," Castant said, "I will go with Earek and Marilana to the great hall and meet you there."

Lorne nodded and left.

"You cannot go into the great hall with me," Marilana said quietly. "You and Earek will help me get in, but I must go in alone. If you two enter without being under guard, Frishka will know something is wrong, and we will lose the chance to save King Rylan and Prince Marquiese."

"But—" he started to say.

"But nothing, Master Castant. There is only one way I can think of to get close enough to stop Frishka from slitting their throats, which he will do the moment the great hall is attacked. Someone has to get inside first," Marilana said darkly. "You must wait until you hear the clash of blades before you enter in force."

She turned without waiting for his reply and slipped between the pike stands. She found the edge of the door and slid her claw into the groove. Silently she stepped up onto the stairs. Master Castant and Earek followed her lead. She closed the door behind her leaving Altia to open it for Captain Lorne and the men of the dungeon guard. Quickly they climbed back up to the second level, circled back to the other stairs, and descended to the main level.

"Give me a few moments to get to the great hall, and then you take out the men at the stable lane door. I will deal with the others," Marilana said quietly.

She cradled the sword in her arm as if carrying it to present it to someone, opened the door wide and emerged confidently. The creatures guarding the door to the stable lane looked at her with surprise. She nodded to them, closed the door to the stairs, and walked toward the guards further down the hall. They let her go without speaking. The guards further down the hall watched her approach warily. She nodded to the two weasels standing guard on the courtyard door and continued past them toward the pair of wolves outside the great hall. As she neared the great hall, she heard shouts behind her and knew Earek and Castant had emerged and attacked the men at the outside door. The wolves standing guard at the side door to the great hall looked past her with surprise.

She didn't hesitate. She flicked her paw forward, flinging the throwing knife she had held concealed below the sword. She snatched a second knife from the belt around her waist and hurled it at the second wolf. She did not wait to see them collapse; she spun as the two weasels guarding the courtyard door ran toward her from behind. She whipped her sword around as she spun and dispatched the lead weasel with a quick swipe. The second dodged sideways to avoid his staggering comrade and missed his parry of Marilana's strike. Both men collapsed on the floor and Marilana turned back to the side door of the great hall. Frishka's creatures lay dead. Quickly she cleaned her sword, removed the knife belt from her waist and pulled out two more throwing knives. Facing the door, she squared her shoulders and slipped inside hiding the three blades behind her.

Marquiese glared at Frishka from where he was being forced to kneel. The tiger was waiting for something. He had seemed confident at first, sure that everything would go according to his plans. Now he made snide remarks and tried to convince the nobles that his rule would be preferable to King Rylan's. Most of the nobles stood unarmed and under guard along the east side of the hall. The young women used to secure Marquiese and King Rylan's surrender had been shoved back into that group. A small group of nobles stood along the west side of the hall unarmed, but not under guard. They seemed to support Frishka wholeheartedly, but many looked nervous, as if they were unsure of their allegiance. Marquiese knew most were power hungry and not as noble as they liked to portray. Behind that group of nobles, the men of the King's guard who had been in the royal family quarters when the attack occurred knelt with paws behind their heads. Almost twice as many of Frishka's men guarded that small group than guarded the large group of nobles opposite them. It appeared as if Frishka wanted someone to attempt a rescue just so he could give the order to kill someone.

Frishka impatiently paced along the dais. He had ordered the throne brought to front prominence where it was usually situated for the King to sit for official duty. Rylan's crown sat on the seat of the throne waiting for the events of the night to unfold. Frishka paused to touch it every time he passed, as if impatient to complete his coup so that he could finally place it on his foul head.

Marquiese glanced next to him and met Rylan's gaze. Rylan looked calm, but Marquiese could see anger burning in his eyes. They had been brought in past the waiting nobles and forced to kneel just to the west of the dais, visible to everyone in the room. Paws tied behind their backs, they knelt proudly, heads high and backs straight. Two of Frishka's men stood behind them with knives held at the ready. No one dared move against Frishka with his men on the verge of slitting their throats.

Frishka glanced up as some noise arose outside the west side door. He stepped off the dais and paused as the noise stopped. Frowning he waited and watched the door. When the door opened, there was a collective rustling throughout the room, some nobles murmured in surprise, others with dark anger. Marilana sidled through the door. She barely opened the door wide enough to slip through, and nothing could be seen of the hallway outside. She kept her paws behind her back as if they were tied, but she was alone. Frishka's frown deepened as Marilana glided forward, not hurrying, but not hesitantly either. She appeared calm and confident. She glanced around the room once and returned her gaze to Frishka. Marquiese suppressed a shiver. He recognized that look in her eyes—the one that preceded the hunt. She was focused on her target with her whole being, and now she zeroed in on Frishka.

"Where is my mother?" Frishka asked sharply. "Why are you alone?"

Marilana's pace slowed, and she answered calmly. "Your mother is seeing to some minor annoyances. She sent me in. I am sorry to keep you waiting."

Frishka studied her for a moment, but did not seem afraid.

"Where is Earek, Marilana?" he asked coolly. "Is he dead?"

"Oh, no, he is not dead. I am sure he will be along soon enough," she replied lightly.

"Do you really think that I will let you join me freely? I know you have sworn to kill me. Do you still think me fool enough to trust you, girl?" he spat at her.

"Come now, Lord Frishka," she said in a sultry tone, "you have said that power attracts. The trial was deceitful; it did not show strength, but this, taking the throne by force, much stronger. Now that you have won, can a girl like me ignore that? Can I not try to make amends?"

Frishka studied her. He smiled. "I knew it," he hissed. "You are attracted to power just like any other worthless female."

She smiled at him, but did not stop her deliberate advance.

"Look at them," said Frishka waving his paw at the gathered nobles, "too cowardly to try to take the throne themselves. I, however, am bold and strong and have succeeded in claiming my own power."

He turned back to Marilana and smiled at her. She never wavered, her pace was constant and all Frishka saw was her smile.

"Tell me, my dear," he crooned at her, "what shall I do with them? Should I let them live?"

"Oh, every king needs taxpayers," she said lightly still smiling.

"And what of King Rylan and Prince Marquiese," he asked coldly, "shall I make you bathe in their blood?"

Still she did not waver, nor did she take her eyes from Frishka. "You will do as you wish," she replied.

"Yes," he said, his smile turned into a snarl, "I will do as I wish and you will stay right there. I do not know what you are up to, Marilana, but no matter how your opinions have changed, you owe me for the pains you have caused. Once I have secured the crown and forced the nobles to swear allegiance, I will deal with you. You will regret holding out for so long."

He turned and sneered at Marquiese. "You chose a poor girl for a friend, and now you see why she consented to your friendship. Power, Marquiese, it is a girl's only love. Too bad I cannot keep you alive to witness the full depth of her lust for power."

Behind him Marilana continued her steady advance. She was getting close now, not close enough for a dagger strike Marquiese thought, but maybe a knife throw. But if she attacked Frishka, Frishka's men would slit his and Rylan's throats. Frishka glanced at the guard behind Marquiese and frowned at the look on the wolf's face. Frishka spun back to face Marilana and saw that she was still advancing toward him.

"If you take one more step, I will have Marquiese killed," he said menacingly.

She stopped and her smile turned into a sneer. Marquiese frowned; she bent her knees and balanced on her toes in a way he had never seen before. The move was so subtle, he suspected those unfamiliar with her would not have noticed it was out of place. Still, he wondered what she was doing. She continued to hide her paws behind her back.

"Where is my mother?" Frishka asked again, suspicious now that Marilana was up to something to disrupt his plans.

"She is in the tower," Marilana said coldly, "and I expect you will be seeing her quite soon."

"I knew it," he spat. "You would not give up on your precious honor, not after everything I have done to you. Well, I will deal with you my own way. Make no mistake, Marilana, I will have you as my own when I am King. What did you do to my mother; imprison her?"

Marilana's smile was a truly terrible thing, cold and vicious. "I killed her."

Frishka's eyes bulged as he howled in rage. He turned to order Marquiese's death, but Marilana was faster. She flung her paws out, finally looking away from Frishka, and two streaks of silver flashed through the air. With gurgling gasps, Frishka's two men collapsed behind Marquiese. Frishka drew his sword and raised it to charge at Marquiese, but Marilana swung at him from the side with a sword of her own. He barely deflected her strike and then he had to parry again. She was fast and pressed him hard. Marquiese glanced back upon hearing a shout from behind and saw the noblemen trying to take on Frishka's guards unarmed. On the west side the Royal guardsmen had attacked their guards as well. Marquiese returned his gaze to Marilana's fight with Frishka in front of the dais. They were both skilled with swords. Back and forth they fought, circling, defending, and attacking.

"I will make you scream from sundown to sundown for this insolence. When I am King, you will pay. You will not win; my men still hold the palace," Frishka growled as he fought.

"Your mother died like a coward, running for escape," Marilana taunted back.

Frishka howled at her and attacked with renewed ferocity. A resounding crash and shout made Marquiese look away again. Palace guardsmen swarmed in through every door. Marquiese breathed with relief as Master Castant led a group forward and surrounded King Rylan and him. He was only slightly surprised to see Earek at Castant's side. Castant knelt and cut their bonds, then helped them to their feet. Marquiese pushed through the ring of guards so he had a clear view of Marilana. King Rylan stepped up beside him. The guards gave room respectfully. Fighting was ending as Frishka's men were overwhelmed.

"What do you think will happen, girl?" Frishka spat. "I will be banished again and will return with a new army. I will win."

"Not this time," Marilana growled. "This time you face me and you returned on pain of death. I, Marilana, Bandit Hunter of the Southern Tip and Redsands, claim your life as forfeit."

"Even if you do kill me," Frishka growled, "it is not the end of the threat. My second will come for your precious Marquiese. He will die a painful death, and you will watch it happen."

"I will be waiting to defend the crown and your creature will die just like you, a coward," Marilana taunted.

Frishka howled. Marquiese saw the opportunity. Frishka made a back-armed swing at Marilana's middle. Instead of parrying the swing, Marilana spun around Frishka's blade, connecting her blade on the inside arc of his swing and knocked his swing wide. In other fights, Marquiese had always seen her disarm her opponent with the maneuver. This time she continued the spin, swinging her own blade high with both paws on her hilt. Marquiese watched in awe as the moment slowly unfolded. He saw the alarm on Frishka's face and then the spray of blood fly off Marilana's blade. He breathed with relief as Frishka's body collapsed to the floor, his head rolling to a stop twenty paces away.

Cheering erupted throughout the great hall. The palace was theirs, and Frishka was finally dead. Nobles swarmed King Rylan and Marquiese. They beamed and spoke and shook paws in victory. Master Castant stayed at Marquiese's side, and he saw Captain Lorne staying close to King Rylan. A guardsman pushed his way through the crowd calling for King Rylan's attention. The crowd quieted and let the zebra through.

"Your Majesty," he panted, "I just came from the walls where the fighting has ended. Lady Annabella led her forces in defense of the palace and drove the attackers back into the forest. Her men are still pursuing them to the west outside the city."

Another cheer arose from the crowd of guards and nobles. A group of guardsmen advanced. The crowd gave way for them and a clear space grew around them. Inside the ring of guardsmen stood the group of nobles who had been left unguarded by Frishka. A royal family guard presented the King's Crown to Rylan and he placed it back on his head. The crowd grew silent and watched with apprehension.

"I will determine what part each of you had in this blatant act of treason. When I have finished, I will consult with the magistrates to determine if any further action must be taken. In the meantime, you will be held under arrest in your rooms, and will face banishment to your estates until I see fit to summon you back. Be glad it is not more. Now go," Rylan said gravely.

The nobles bowed, but looked terrified as they were escorted out. Everyone knew King Rylan's decree was lenient. Marquiese assumed that the nobles had had very little to do with the actual treason and had probably only agreed to support Frishka's claim for the throne if he succeeded to take the palace and hold it. If it was proven that they had done more, the nobles could be banished from the kingdom or killed. Silently Marquiese agreed with his father's decision to go lightly for now. Rylan turned and met Marquiese's eyes. He nodded and turned gravely toward the dais. The crowd parted and made way for the King and Prince.

Marilana knelt on one knee before the dais, sword point on the stones of the floor and rested her forehead on the pommel. Earek stood a few paces from her, his sword lowered, but ready. They were both splattered with blood, but had cleaned their blades. Together, Rylan and Marquiese approached Marilana. Without looking up, Marilana shifted so that she knelt on both knees and raised the sword toward them on open palms. Earek moved to kneel slightly behind her on the right. He also raised his sword and bowed his head.

"The details of the evening's events can wait," said King Rylan coolly, "but it appears you escaped the tower dungeon, freed the palace garrison, and planned our rescue. I already know that it is due to your forethought and precautions that had Lady Annabella ready to defend the palace from the outside."

He paused to wait for the murmurs from the nobles to die down.

"Regardless, you have returned from banishment on pain of death. A banishment, I acknowledge, that you undertook willingly to attempt to stop the traitor Frishka from returning as he did this very night. I also acknowledge two facts about that journey. First, you were never released from the custody of your guards, you never left Redsands, so your banishment technically never started. And second, that you risked your lives to return to bring word of the traitor's approaching army."

Again, he paused, waiting for the murmurs to cease. Marilana and Earek waited, motionless.

"Marilana," King Rylan said gravely, "what do you have to say?"

"My King," the lioness replied levelly without looking up, "I have pledged my life to the defense of my family, the Southern Tip, Redsands, and the rulers of Redsands. I detected a great threat to the rulers of Redsands, yourself and His Highness Prince Marquiese. I have done what I could to defend your lives without regard for my own life or my future. As I have pledged my services to you, so do I pledge my life. Everything you have said is true, and if it is your will to end my life, I willingly submit myself to your justice."

"Earek," King Rylan continued, "what do you have to say?"

"My King," he replied following Marilana's lead, "I have sworn to obey and protect My Sister Marilana. This

I have done with my whole being to the best of my ability. I have sworn my sword to the defense of my family, my county, my kingdom, and my king. I believe that my skills were best put to use by obeying Marilana to thwart the threat to your lives. I stand by my actions and by Marilana."

Marquiese met Rylan's eyes, smiled, and nodded. They had said what he had expected them to say. Rylan turned to the assembled nobles and studied their faces. Many of them gave knowing nods.

"Does anyone here deny that the actions of these two saved my life and Prince Marquiese's life, and stopped the traitor from taking over Redsands?" he asked loudly.

No one replied, but several smiled.

Turning back to Marilana he continued, "Rise, Lady Marilana. Rise, Master Earek. I pronounce you absolved of any actions that might be perceived as treasonous and repeal your sentences of banishment. You have saved our realm from a traitor, and you have saved our lives."

Rylan paused as Marilana and Earek lowered their swords and stood. Meeting their eyes, he smiled and held his paws out to them.

"Welcome back," Rylan said warmly.

Marilana and Earek bowed. Earek looked relieved and smiled broadly. Marilana however was still serious and gripped her short sword tightly.

"Your Majesty, please do not be too quick to celebrate. Frishka's second in command is still out there. He is even more dangerous than Frishka was. He is a trained assassin. He must be found and stopped before he can get to you and your son," Marilana spoke firmly.

"Marilana," King Rylan raised his paw as worried murmurs swept through the nobles, "I am aware of your concerns, however, tonight is a great victory. Frishka has been defeated. Let us have this moment of triumph. Where ever this second in command is tonight, he may already be dead or have fled. We will look into the matter in due course. For now, celebrate."

Marilana bowed respectfully and forced a smile for the gathering. The nobles cheered again and moved forward to speak with them. Marquiese found himself, once again, surrounded by nobles sharing their stories and relaying the brave deeds of others. He was relieved when King Rylan finally called for a feast to be held the next evening, and retired for the night. It was late, and Marquiese gladly followed him out, Master Castant and Captain Lorne dutifully stayed with them. Once they were back in the royal family quarters, Marquiese turned to Castant.

"What do you have to say about the events of the evening?" Marquiese asked quietly.

Castant smiled slightly and said, "Marilana truly is a remarkable young woman. Without her and Earek, we would not have been able to stop Frishka. I do not know many more details than you do, but I can tell you how she rescued the garrison and the dungeon."

They took seats in Marquiese's study and Castant related the story of Marilana's unexpected appearance in the dungeon armory. Captain Lorne talked about the routing of Frishka's men throughout the palace. Marquiese then told them about Marilana's display in the great hall. When he finished, Rylan met his gaze seriously.

"I would like to publicly announce the victory tomorrow and I would like to name Marilana and Earek as Heroes of the Realm," he said quietly. "I want your agreement to it though."

"My agreement?" asked Marquiese puzzled. "Why would I say differently? They truly did save the realm. And as much as I might be ashamed of it, they saved our lives too."

"At dinner, you still claimed to feel betrayed by Marilana," replied Rylan.

Marquiese reflected on that for a moment. Even after everything Marilana had done, the sting of betrayal remained. It was personal, though. It was something ongoing between them, but he could not pinpoint an incident. He made his decision. "I do feel betrayed, Father, but as I have said before, it is something that I alone have to work out. It is not reason enough to deny what they have done for us. They are heroes and should be named as such," he said determinedly.

"Very well," Rylan said rising. "It is late and has been a very eventful night. Tomorrow will be busy and I would like to get some sleep. Good night to you all."

Rylan left and Captain Lorne excused himself to go check that the guards were back in place and the garrison was in order. Master Castant rose as well, claiming a few other duties that he needed to check in on, and left Marquiese alone.

Marquiese relished the peace and quiet of his study a moment before wandering into his sitting room. He removed his coat and sword belt, setting them on a chair. He walked to the double doors of his balcony and pulled them open. Feeling the warm summer night's breeze on his face, he breathed in the fresh air. It was an immense relief just knowing that Frishka was finally dead. He was worried about Frishka's second, but like his father said, this was a great victory. He walked to the balcony railing and gazed up at the stars. It was a very clear night. After a moment, he decided he really should go to bed, as it was very late. He glanced down into the courtyard below as he turned to go back inside and stopped when he saw someone standing by the fountain.

Marilana looked at the sky with her back to him. Glancing up, he realized that she must be taking in the constellation of the hunter, which was high in the western sky and visible from the courtyard. It was her patron constellation as a bandit hunter. He watched her for a moment and then decided to call down to her. "Marilana, are you all right?"

She started at his voice and turned to look up at him.

"My Lord Highness," she said curtseying, "I did not realize you were there. I just wanted some fresh air before going to bed. Forgive me if I disturbed you."

"You did not disturb me. I also wanted a breath of fresh air. I am sorry for startling you. I just wanted to make sure that the servants were seeing to your needs."

"Thank you, Highness, they have informed me that my former rooms are unoccupied and have been made ready for me. I just needed to see the sky from a different vantage point."

He nodded and replied gently, "You have been under guard for a long time. I spent the whole night after my release out here on my balcony, and I was only a prisoner for a little over three fifnights. It has been much longer for you. I am pleased that you are free again."

"Thank you," she replied softly. "Rest safe, Highness."

He went back inside, closing the balcony doors behind him.

6

Marilana was thrilled to awaken the next morning to servants bringing fresh clothes and bath water. She had taken Marquiese's suggestion and had spent the night on her balcony. It had been very refreshing to sleep in the open air on the soft couch cushions without any guards. Altia was not impressed, but she was glad that Marilana had rested well. Altia supervised her bath and helped her dress. It felt so good to be clean and to not have to worry about the guards or what she was saying to people. She even laughed as Altia fussed about the chafed area around her ankle; it was minor compared to most of what she had endured lately.

When she was dressed, Altia stepped out into the hall and returned a moment later with a line of servants carrying breakfast trays. Marilana watched in amazement as they set food around her modest table for six people. The first of her breakfast companions to arrive was Earek, freshly bathed and appropriately dressed. He walked straight to her and scooped her into a hug; laughing, she returned his embrace. Behind Earek, Master Castant approached her bearing a fist full of flowers. She smiled at him as she took the flowers hesitantly, and then breathed in the sweet scent. He did not hesitate to give her a big brotherly hug.

"I would be dead without you," he said, laughing quietly. "I was right to trust you from the start, and I am very glad to see you finally free."

She smiled and squeezed his arm. She turned and passed the flowers to Altia, and when she turned back, discovered that Lady Annabella had arrived.

"Mother!" Marilana cried and launched herself into Annabella's embrace.

They hugged fiercely, and when they finally parted it was only to arm's length. Tears filled Annabella's eyes as she gazed at Marilana.

"I have missed you, Daughter," Annabella said quietly, "and I am so proud of you."

"No matter what else happens this morning," said a deep voice, "that was worth seeing."

Marilana was startled to see King Rylan and Marquiese standing inside the door. She curtseyed to them, but King Rylan waved it away.

"None of that this morning, my dear," he said warmly. "Come let us eat. I am starving."

She smiled tentatively at Marquiese. He grinned and bowed his head in greeting, then followed his father to the table. Marilana sat beside Annabella, Earek sat at the foot of the table to her right, and Master Castant took the seat facing her. King Rylan, of course, sat at the head of the table, with Marquiese to his left across from Annabella. The food was delicious; lightly glazed fruits and candied nuts accented specially prepared breads and sweet pastries. Marilana had not eaten so well in over a month. No one spoke for a long time except to comment on the food or to ask if someone had tried one of the dishes. The servants scurried about moving dishes and refilling drinks. Finally, everyone had eaten their fill and sat contentedly sipping on a favored drink. The servants gathered the empty plates and dishes and left.

"I would have this contentment go on forever if I could," King Rylan sighed, "but, alas, I must return to more serious topics."

Marilana set her tea cup on the table and waited. Earek brushed her paw with his and she shared a smile with him.

Rylan inhaled deeply, then asked seriously, "Marilana, Earek, I need you to tell us, yet again, the details of unpleasant events. Please tell us what happened last night."

Marilana nodded and told them the events in as much detail as she could. Everyone listened carefully and Earek added what he could.

"You never cease to amaze me," said Annabella when she finished, "you did very well, Daughter."

Annabella took her paw and gave it a warm squeeze. Marilana smiled gratefully at her and returned the pressure. She was still awed by the comfort of a parent's praise and mere presence. Annabella had always treated her as a daughter, she knew that, but there had always been a barrier between them that prevented Marilana from acknowledging the bond and depreciated the comfort that she had received. That barrier was gone and Marilana did not think she would ever take it for granted. Now, she felt overcome with gratitude.

"Yes, very well indeed," King Rylan agreed. "Lady Annabella, would you now please relate your own story? I hear you received some rather interesting visitors some few days ago."

Annabella laughed, "That I did, Rylan. I was in my tent reading reports, trying to think about something other than my heirs, when a commotion in the camp caught my attention. I stepped out to find a tired pony pulling a cart and two men surrounded by my guards. I recognized the young cheetah as the guardsman that had been assigned to Marilana when she first arrived at the palace. I remembered that he had disappeared and could not be found. I suspected a trap from Frishka, but wondered why he would bother sending a false message to me except as a relay to the palace. I demanded what they wanted, and the response was not at all what I expected. The young cheetah looked at me and said that he brought me grave news from Lady Marilana. I was so stunned, I just stared at him. I said to him that the last report I had received from the palace said she was recovering well. He surprised me again by breaking into a grin and shaking the old white tiger's shoulder. 'Hear that, Glain, she's recovering well!' he said with excitement. The old man sagged with relief and he asked about Earek. I said that he was also recovering well, and they both smiled so joyously, I could not help but smile in return."

Marilana shared a grin with Earek. It was good to hear of Karndel and Glain.

"So, I asked them to come into my tent and tell me their news. They relayed some disturbing information about an army and an attack on some prisoners. Then Karndel looked at me seriously and said 'Lady Marilana told me to tell you she said that if all goes well, she will ride Storm again soon. I don't know what it means, but it seemed important to her.' All I could do was laugh. I knew then that the message had, indeed, come from Marilana. I thanked them for believing Marilana, fed them, and gave them a place in my camp to sleep. I set about preparing my men for battle and sent riders off south to bring up reinforcements. When I sent my best scouts out to search for Frishka's camp, they returned with disturbing news. The campsites could be found easily enough, but there were no creatures in the camps. The men were hiding in the forest and covering their tracks."

"False camps?" Marilana asked frowning.

"That is what they thought," Annabella nodded, "but they could not find the real camps."

"My scouts never returned," Rylan said with a frown.

"With all due respect, my scouts are considerably better at tracking bandits and mercenaries than yours, Your Majesty," Annabella replied. "Yours were probably discovered and killed, or were caught inspecting the camp sites. It is generally better to remain hidden with false camps, as bandits tend to use them as traps to capture anyone tracking them."

King Rylan shrugged good-naturedly.

"I missed having my best trackers," Annabella continued with a glance at Marilana, "but my men did what they could. In any event, I started to lay my plans for disrupting a siege and was very glad I did. I do not think the attackers meant to take the walls or even could have if they had wanted to. They were comprised of small groups that moved from spot to spot to keep the guards' attention. They were not well coordinated, some striking at random, others with regularity. It was not difficult to rout them. They ran as soon as they saw the cavalry. I feared they might be leading my men into an ambush, so I had other groups harassing their retreat. I was rather surprised that there were no traps; the men simply fled in any direction they could. I assume they were relying on

Frishka taking the throne by stealth rather than by a successful siege."

Rylan nodded as Annabella finished. Marilana frowned reflecting on Annabella's account. The actual attack seemed inconsistent with everything else she had seen. Yes, the camp she had seen had been disorganized and fractious, but they had taken great care to stop all messengers from the west, had set up false camps and false trails to trap the scouts, and yet had attacked in a disjointed fashion that suggested the groups were acting without a leader. Where had Frishka's second-in-command gone? The thought made her hackles rise. Where was the assassin?

"Very well done, all of you," King Rylan said standing up. "We must be going, but there are a few more things to say. First, Captain Lorne is in charge of interrogating the captured prisoners. He is searching for any information we might have missed, including information about Frishka's second-in-command who is still on the loose. Second, tonight is a feast, and I expect you to present yourselves with style. And third, I am making a public announcement one hour after noon and expect you to be present. Lady Annabella, I would have you bring Guardsman Karndel and this Master Glain as well. Have a good morning, and I will see you all later."

He walked to the door and Annabella and Earek followed close behind. Marquiese and Master Castant whispered to each other as they followed more slowly. Marilana turned away and walked out on to the balcony. She stared out over the expanse of the gardens for a while. She jumped and spun around in surprise when she heard someone clear his throat. Marquiese stood in the open balcony doors looking slightly ashamed.

"I did not mean to surprise you," he said apologetically. "You usually know when people are around, and are much harder to surprise than that."

"Forgive me, Highness," she said with a hasty curtsey, "I thought you had left with the others. I seem to be less aware this morning."

"Perhaps you have just been overwhelmed. Too many people around all the time," he said gently, "too much time spent in confinement."

"Perhaps," she said and waited.

He gazed at her for a long time as if she were a puzzle he was trying to solve. She watched him nervously, waiting for him to give her some clue as to what he was feeling towards her. Finally, he motioned to the chairs in the sitting area inside her rooms.

"Please, come sit with me," he said. "I have a question to ask about an unpleasant topic, and I think it would be better discussed inside."

He moved back inside and waited for her to follow before taking a seat. Once she sat, he waited until she had arranged her skirts and folded her paws in her lap. His unease to broach the subject only made her more nervous. He leaned forward in his chair with his elbows on his knees and clasped his paws together. He studied her face intently before dropping his eyes to his paws.

"Before I ask my question," he said hesitantly. "I wanted to tell you that while you were in the dungeon I inquired with the local magistrates about the petitioner whose daughter had been taken. I know that a lot has happened since that old man was here asking for help from the palace. I remembered your concern that something was unusual in the matter. I received a response from a bandit hunter this morning. He said that he had agreed to consider the matter because he too found it unusual for a ransom to be asked for a peasant girl. He reported searching the area of the girl's disappearance for fifnights without finding any clues. He widened his search, and eventually found a false camp. Fearing a trap, he searched the surrounding area and found a small group of mercenaries. He watched this group for an entire day, but late in the afternoon, the men took up their arms and marched toward the city. He expressed his regret that he did not send warning to the palace of the impending attack, but he did not know it was an attack until it happened. He found no trace of the peasant maid. I wish now that we had acted on your feeling of unease. You thought something was wrong, and we might have been able to stop Frishka before the trials."

"No, Marquiese," Marilana sighed. "We did not have enough time. Frishka's plan was already in motion. Even if we had inquired more into the girl's disappearance, we would have been waiting for the reports to come back, and probably would have planned to go on the shore-side ride anyway because you were supposed to be reviewing the guard. I must say, though, that the girl's disappearance was a masterful stroke that I had not connected before now."

"What do you mean?" he asked sharply.

"The girl and the ransom had a purpose," she said sadly. "News of bandit activity in the area would have spread quickly through the peasant and merchant population of the area. They would have avoided the area where she went missing so they did not happen across the bandits themselves. It drastically cut down the number of people traversing the area, and limited the chances of someone stumbling across Frishka's army. It prevented anyone reporting groups of mercenaries and bandits camping in the area."

"I see," he nodded thoughtfully. "One more way of controlling the flow of information into the palace. It seems the man in charge did consider all of the details."

"That is what worries me most," she said softly. "That man is still out there, still a threat to the throne."

Marquiese looked away from her. She worried that like King Rylan, Marquiese would not take her concern seriously. For moment, they sat in silence. Marilana watched Marquiese stare at his paws and worried about what was bothering him so much. He looked up and studied her eyes again.

Finally, he took a deep breath and nearly whispered, "That is why I want you to tell me about the Hungdie."

Her insides turned to ice. She wanted him to take her warning about an assassin seriously, but she had not expected for him to come straight out and ask. "Why?" she said softly, "You do not believe in them, so why do you ask about them specifically?"

"My father says he does not believe in them, and bristles when the topic is mentioned," he replied quietly. "I did not believe, but what I saw in your eyes when you spoke of them in the infirmary led me to think I should change my opinion. Even now, just mentioning them makes you afraid. When they were mentioned while I lived in the Southern Tip, you became defensive and changed the subject. Marilana, I know you well. You do not scare easily, you do not fear without cause. I want to know why just saying the name terrifies you."

She closed her eyes to calm herself.

"I can see how hard this is for you to speak of," he added gently, "but I would not ask if I did not truly want, and need, to hear your answer."

She swallowed hard and forced her eyes to open. The handsome young lion watched her seriously; concern and sympathy were written on his face. She could not deny him. "I spoke truly of them in the infirmary," she whispered.

"Yes, I had already heard what you said about them. All royalty is told the stories of assassins that never give up. I think you know more," he insisted.

"I was still very young, only six when it happened," she focused on her paws. "I had recovered from my ordeal with the bandits, and I was learning all I could of healing and weapons. I had already learned the healing trance and many of the old ways. Lady Annabella was helping me gather information about the old ways so I could learn as much as possible. She sent word with merchants that she was looking for information."

She paused and took a deep shaky breath, "I have never told anyone the full story of what happened, not even Lady Annabella. She knows part of it. After all, it happened in her castle, but I was alone for much of it."

"I understand," he said.

"An older tiger came to the castle. He said he was a priest and very knowledgeable about the old ways. He said that he had heard there was a young girl who was interested in learning, and that he had brought an ancient scroll with him that he would be willing to let me study for one afternoon with him. We met alone in the library.

Lady Annabella did not think there was any harm in an old priest; of course, she had not met him in person. He asked me why I wanted to learn the healing arts. I told him that life was dangerous and that being able to heal could save lives. He seemed to reserve judgment on my answer, but began to ask questions about how much I knew of the old ways. We spent hours discussing the ways of healing others and one's own body. He was impressed with how much I knew and how quickly I understood the things he told me. He was pleased that I debated with him the merits of the healing trance, and that I could already enter it unaided. He said that childhood was the best time to learn the old ways, before the body hardened into patterns."

"He sounds like a good teacher," Marquiese said when she paused.

She looked up at him and frantically shook her head. The terror of the memory was strong. "No," she said horrified, "I was terrified to be speaking with him. He compelled my attention and participation. I wanted to learn what he had brought, but something about him did not seem right. His manner was cold and his touch sent shivers through me. At first I told myself it was just my imagination, that he was a harmless old priest. Later, I feared meeting his eyes; they were both cold and hungry like nothing I had ever seen before. My stomach turned to ice every time he looked at me. When I stopped meeting his gaze, he smiled strangely, like he enjoyed making me afraid. And he knew much more of my life than anyone else, more than Lady Annabella, more than my parents; somehow, he knew everything I had gone through. I was on the verge of running from the room. I could not stand the feeling of his eyes on me any longer."

"It was then that he asked me if I wanted to see the scroll. My curiosity compelled me to stay and I nodded. He said it was a special, ancient treatise on pain. I asked if he meant the relief of pain or the prevention of pain. He said both and more. He seemed eager to talk about it, like it was the most precious information he had. We studied it for a long time, taking it piece by piece. It spoke of the pain centers of the body and how they affected the patient. It spoke of how to stop the patient from feeling pain and how to alleviate pain. When I realized that above all the scroll presented instructions for causing pain, I pushed back and stared at it in horror. He watched me with his disturbing smile. He asked if I had ever wanted to cause anyone pain. I looked at him in shock. He told me to be sure of my answer. He explained that pain takes many forms both physical and mental, and if I wanted to get revenge on the bandits who took me, I would have to cause pain. I had never considered this. I thought about how I wanted to become a bandit hunter, and how I wanted to stop them from hurting anyone ever again. And he urged me to consider the girls at school, how they laughed and teased me, and how I wanted to make them stop. He said pain was part of achieving my goals and that I would have to decide what was more important to me, not causing others pain or preventing them from causing pain. It was a good lesson; one I had to learn, but I was terrified by the lustful way he spoke of pain."

"He asked me then, as I thought about how to answer, if I had ever heard of the Hungdie. I told him I had not. He said he was a priest of the Hungdie. He said that they considered pain to be sacred. They believed pain is the only true purifier of the body and soul. They saw it as their sacred duty to seek out and stop those that cause the most pain to innocent people. I asked if they hunted bandits, and he laughed. He said bandits hurt innocents for their own pleasure and hurt relatively few. He said the ones they hunt are monarchs. He said a king could cause pain to hundreds or thousands of innocents without thought just by raising the taxes or marching an army through their homes. I said that killing a monarch would not change anything because a new one would be put in their place. He agreed and said that their goal was to avenge the innocents, that they do not just kill the monarch, but destroy their lives, taking away everything they hold dear before they die.

"I asked how they decided whom to target. He said they allow rivals of the monarchs to hire them, to pay large sums for a specific monarch to be the target. I asked what they did if the monarch beat them. He said they respect a worthy opponent, but they would not stop at one defeat, only at death. He explained that the target was assigned to one member of the Hungdie and if the assassin died in the attempt, they would mark the target's family name on a list and for three generations they would not hunt any members of that family."

Marilana closed her eyes a moment and hugged herself tightly to suppress the shivers of fear the memory caused. "He looked at me seriously and said that I could join them, that I could learn the ways of pain and avenge more innocents than I ever would as a bandit hunter. I asked him why he was called a priest. He smiled that horrible smile and said that he had learned to cause pain. He had been given a patient and had given her pain for days unending until she had finally died of it. That he had then been given a target to hunt and that he had destroyed his target's life. And then he had been given the test of pain and had purified his soul. I sat staring at him in terror. This was what he was asking me to become, someone who loved pain, who lived for pain. I could not move. I was more terrified than at any time with the bandits. He smiled sadly at me and patted my paw with his. He said he had thought that would be my answer. He said my wish to heal and preserve life was admirable. He said if I ever crossed paths with the Hungdie when I was grown, I could still be priceless to them. Without another word, he put away his scroll and left me alone. I hid in a corner of the library for two hours before I was able to force my fear away."

She looked away from Marquiese's wide eyes, and tried to control her trembling.

"What did he mean you could be priceless to them," he asked finally in a hoarse whisper.

She closed her eyes again and shook her head. "I have never found out."

"That is why you were searching the library for any references of them," he surmised. "You were trying to learn more about their activities."

"I have searched every library I have had access to," Marilana sighed. "I have tried to find hints of their activities both to learn more about them, and to try to avoid them."

They sat in silence for a long time. Marilana kept her eyes closed and tried to calm her fears.

"I am sorry," Marquiese said still in a hoarse whisper. "I needed to know, and now that I do, I will not forget. I think monarchs would do well to not just remember the old stories, but to believe them. It has been many, many years now, but I remember reading an account of a king who had an unknown enemy. He was plagued by a series of accidents, each time he narrowly avoided his own death, but someone around him died—his wife, his mother, his children—until finally he was left with no one close to him, no one he trusted or loved. Finally, he went missing while on a ride through a forest. When they found what was left of him, the court could not deny it had been an assassination. The account said that all his guards had been slain, the horses too, and the king had been tied to a tree and skinned alive. The culprit was never caught. It is possible the culprit could still be alive, but he would be a very old man."

Marilana opened her eyes and searched Marquiese's face. He lifted his paw, hesitated, and then placed it on her arm.

"I made a vow to myself that day," she whispered earnestly meeting his eyes. "I vowed I would not act like them. I trained hard to be able to make clean kills. I do not cause the creatures I kill to suffer long painful deaths. Even the poisons I use only last a minute or two. I vowed never to use the body's pain receptors to cause pain. I will never forget the things I learned that day, and I never wish to use those methods on anyone. Not even when Frishka tortured me did I want to use those methods on him; a quick death was best."

He nodded and studied the fear written on her face. He gently squeezed her arm.

"I truly am sorry to have had to ask," he said, then stood, strode to the door, and left.

Marilana sat staring at nothing when Altia arrived with the lunch tray.

Marquiese was glad to see Marilana smiling confidently when she came with Lady Annabella to the main gate. King Rylan would address the public from the roof of the gatehouse so the crowd could see. The guards had erected the platform behind the crenellations that the King stood on to make proclamations. Many nobles had gathered on the roof to hear the King's address, and Lady Annabella led Marilana and Earek over to join them. Guardsman Karndel and Glain followed looking awkward. Marquiese caught his father's eye and nodded. Everyone was present who needed to be. Rylan stepped up onto the platform and raised his arms to the large crowd that had gathered outside the palace gate. The people cheered and the royal trumpets sounded.

When the crowd quieted, Rylan called out to them, "People of Maefair, it gives me immense pleasure to address you here today. As many of you know, there was an attempt on my life and the life of my son, Marquiese, yesterday evening by the banished traitor Frishka. I am pleased to announce that the traitor was slain and that we stand victorious."

He waited for the crowd's cheers to die down before continuing. "I would like to take this opportunity to make known those individuals who played key roles in this victory and reward them for their loyalty and bravery. First, I recognize Farmer Glain and Guardsman Karndel who took up the call of loyalty and acted courageously to forewarn Lady Annabella of the impending attack. I award them each the honor of an official family name."

He motioned Glain and Karndel forward. They stepped up and waved at the crowd. Marquiese gave them a letter of rights containing their new family names. The crowd cheered. They stepped aside as Rylan addressed the crowd again.

"Second, I recognize Lady Annabella Ranat of the Southern Tip who used the warning wisely to rally her forces to defend the palace. I award her with a gift of her choosing for her bravery and loyalty."

Lady Annabella stepped up beside Rylan and waved to the crowd. Again, the crowd erupted, and Lady Annabella stepped back to rejoin the nobles.

"Third, I recognize Guardsman Captain Lorne for his unfailing heroism while taking command of the palace garrison and retaking the palace from the attackers. For his loyalty and for gaining the trust of the royal family, I award him with the honor of an official family name and promote him to the post of Commander of the Royal Family Guard."

Lorne seemed in a state of shock as he stepped up to wave at the crowd. The previous commander had unfortunately been slain in the fighting, and Marquiese could not think of anyone worthier of the post. He shook Lorne's paw and smiled as he presented him with his letter of rights containing his new name. Marquiese glanced at Marilana who beamed and applauded.

"Fourth," Rylan continued, "I recognize Master Enton Castant of Draukshar for his quick thought and stalwart loyalty. He chose to trust in others and was proven to have chosen well as those others planned and led our rescue with his help. I award him with a gift of his choosing."

Castant smiled easily as he waved to the cheering crowd. It was not the first time they had heard his name announced with brave deeds, and they loved him for it.

"Fifth, I recognize Master Earek Ranat of the Southern Tip. You have all heard his name proclaimed recently for involvement with the traitor Frishka. I am pleased to announce that he chose to take part in recent events to thwart the traitor's plan. His bravery and courage were vital to our victory last night. For his part in stopping the traitor and for his loyalty, I award him the title and honor of Hero of the Realm."

The crowd cheered loudly as Earek stepped up and waved proudly. He turned and bowed deeply to King Rylan as Rylan hung a medal around his neck. Marquiese smiled as Earek waved at the crowd a second time and then stepped back. Marilana beamed and squeezed his arm, but she looked slightly nervous. Earek just smiled at her encouragingly.

"Finally," Rylan said when the cheers subsided, "I recognize Lady Marilana Ranat of the Southern Tip. Without her willing involvement in recent events, our victory would not have happened. It is she who planned to stop the traitor. It is she who risked her life to ensure that we were victorious. And it is she who slew not only the traitor Frishka, but his traitorous mother Prinka as well."

Rylan paused as the crowds erupted in joyous shouts. He waved Marilana forward and she stood proudly waving to the crowds as they cheered and danced in the street. Finally, the crowds quieted enough for Rylan to finish.

"For her bravery and loyalty and her actions to stop the traitor, I award her the title and honor of Hero of the Realm."

Marquiese smiled and applauded along with the nobles as Rylan hung a medal around her neck. She curtseyed deeply, and, following Earek's lead, waved to the cheering crowd a second time. He watched her step down from the platform and chuckled as noblemen and lordlings instantly surrounded her. She blushed when she met his eyes. Smiling he turned to follow Rylan back to the palace.

7

Marilana had attended several feasts, but never a victory feast that honored her brave deeds. The celebration included dancing and even some friendly competitions. The tables lined the walls of the great hall and clusters of chairs were spaced about. She wore a simple sleeveless gown of the dark green of the Southern Tip. Altia had fussed over Marilana not having a feast gown and had worked hard to find some simple accouterments to add elegance to the ensemble. White gloves encased her paws and extended to her elbows, a white lace fan tied to the simple white belt, and a circlet of green fabric secured a white lace veil. Her silver Hero of the Realm medal hung from its royal blue cord around her neck. She thought the simplicity made her stand out in this crowd of nobles, although she would not have chosen white—which indicated she was seeking courtship. Earek likewise was dressed in a simple dinner suit consisting of a dark red coat over light grey shirt and dark grey pants; he also wore his silver medal with its royal blue cord. She could pick him out from across the room by the eddies of finery swirling around a center devoid of glitter.

She strode casually toward a table loaded with drinks and was not surprised when a young lordling offered her a glass of sparkling red wine. She accepted it with grace and continued strolling around the perimeter of the room. The young bear fell into step beside her. He was not the first this night, nor did she think he would be the last. Most had done a passable job of hiding their horror that she fought as well as any master swordsman. Some had gone so far as to say she would never have to do so again. She wondered how long this bear would last.

"I would be pleased to speak with you, Lady Marilana," he said smiling down at her.

He was quite tall and lean with broad shoulders a dominating presence, a fine young brown bear still maturing. He had strong features, a prominent snout, and kind eyes.

"What would you speak of, good Master?" she asked.

"I am Master Timral Roana. My father is Lord Roana, great-noble of Mira's Plateau. He has a strong friendship with your Lady Annabella," he said with a rumbling voice. "I have heard that you slew Lady Prinka."

He was one of many young men interested in hearing how she had slain the traitorous woman. Most of them had been here in the great hall and witnessed her fight with Frishka, but rumors spread quickly about her fight in the tower.

"I am afraid there is not much to tell of her death, Master Roana," she sighed.

"Please, My Lady, call me Timral."

"Very well, Timral," she smiled. "The traitor Prinka and her men came to collect my brother and myself from the tower. We surprised them and slew the six men with their own blades. When Prinka turned to flee, I grabbed a dagger and hurled it. It stabbed her in the back, a killing blow."

"Really?" he sounded impressed. "But how did you get out of the dungeon and how did you get those men's weapons?"

"Do you really want the details?" she asked amused, most of the others had simply used it to start the conversation.

He blinked a little surprised, "Well, yes, unless you do not wish to relate them."

Smiling she told him the full story as they strolled around the room. He was a good listener and was thrilled to discuss the maneuvers in detail. He confessed that he was a Knight of the Realm and had trained with Master Castant and Prince Marquiese when they were young. He related a comedic incident between Master Castant and an unbroken colt. He was a good story teller, and by the time he reached the climax of Master Castant getting thrown into a pigsty, she found herself giggling and hiding her amusement behind her paw. She enjoyed talking with him and was feeling quite relaxed. They had stopped walking by the east side doors, and she glanced at the dais. It was empty of life. Rylan and Marquiese roamed the room speaking to the nobles and dancing with a few ladies.

"You have not asked me to dance," she mused.

He chuckled softly, "I am fond of dancing, but I have heard you can out-dance anyone. Besides, you have not accepted a single dance yet tonight."

"You are observant," she noted with pleasure. "My previous refusals did not stop the others from asking, however."

He glanced at a nearby group of chairs where some noble daughters sat gossiping happily, taking a rest from dancing. She watched his eyes soften and suspected she knew his answer.

"I would prefer a specific dance partner," he said apologetically.

She smiled mischievously at him. "Does she prefer you as well? Or have you not asked her?"

He chuckled. "She has been forbidden to dance with me tonight. Her parents would prefer her to make the royal courtship. Before the ban, she and I danced many feasts together."

"Would you be willing to introduce me to that group of Daughters?" she asked lightly. "I am afraid I do not know which of them is your lady love."

Laughing he extended his arm and escorted her over to the group of chatting girls. Marilana studied the clouded leopard, elk, yellow leopard, and caribou carefully for their reactions.

"Lady Marilana," he said respectfully, "I would like to introduce you to Mistress Lorlina Quway of Glancenar, Mistress Clidan Inclond of Pavlatach, Mistress Heledia Ruberic of Herinsford, and Mistress Serina Doquib of Versith."

The charming creatures jumped up and curtseyed. Marilana smiled at them and noticed how the clouded leopard, Lorlina, gazed at where her paw rested on Timral's arm. Glancing up at him, she saw that his eyes were locked on Lorlina.

"I am very pleased to make your acquaintances," Marilana said smiling. "Mistress Lorlina, I believe I heard a rumor that said you were quite brave in front of the traitor Frishka."

Lorlina studied her darkly for a moment then curtseyed again. "I was held hostage by the traitor, My Lady, and was used to secure King Rylan and Prince Marquiese's surrender," she said levelly.

"I heard that when he threatened to harm you, you did not cry out or weep," Marilana persisted. "It takes a brave heart to keep control at such times."

Timral shifted. Marilana did not think he had heard the details of that encounter.

"I was terrified, My Lady," Lorlina said coolly. "I am not as brave as you. I am a scholar, not a fighter."

"Bravery comes in many cloaks," Marilana said gently meeting the clouded leopard's eyes. "Often the quiet scholar is overlooked or undervalued but is courageous nonetheless."

Lorlina studied her eyes longer, her look becoming more appraising.

"Perhaps we can discuss some more scholarly subjects another time," Marilana said with a nod. "Ladies, I hope you enjoy yourselves this evening."

Marilana turned away and Timral walked with her again.

"Thank you," he said simply.

"From the account I heard, she acted just as I said. She was obviously terrified, but held her back straight and her head high."

"I knew she had been used by the traitor, but she would not speak of it to me," he paused, then continued more hoarsely. "I was terrified for her. I did not know what to do to make sure she returned safely. When she did come back, she avoided my gaze. I could tell she was ashamed of being used in such a way. She did not want them to surrender, but she was so relieved when they did and ashamed of that as well. She held herself straighter just now after what you said. I don't think she is ashamed anymore. You approved of her actions."

"All terrible deeds take a toll on the innocents forced to participate. It is not those girls' fault that Frishka choose them."

"He said he wanted the most beautiful Daughters and called for Lorlina by name. He said he would introduce them to their darker lusts and would help them to explore the new feelings later."

Marilana sighed, "He was a cruel and terrible individual. He believed that women were nothing, worth nothing; he did not even believe that they could be intelligent. His goal with a woman was to cause pain, nothing else. Those girls had no chance against him. I expect that he chose Lorlina because of her connection with you. He was trying to drive anger and fear in you that he could later use against Marquiese. You are closer to His Highness than most of the young lordlings, and I assume Marquise also knew of your feelings for Lorlina. The traitor used her specifically because Marquiese would have wanted to not only spare her life, but also your heart. The traitor was cruel that way."

"You withstood his attentions," he said quietly.

"Yes, I did," she replied darkly, "and I nearly paid with my life on several occasions. I have trained most of my life to fight men like him. I have trained with all my weapons, Timral, strength, mind, and body. Without that level of control and discipline, one hour with him would have had me groveling on the floor at his feet."

"You make it sound as if he were torturing you," he said surprised.

"You must not have witnessed the trial. He was well trained in the arts of torture and yes he was torturing me, body and mind."

"I only arrived in Maefair a few days ago, but surely your treatment was not so terrible," he turned to face her with astonishment. "King Rylan would never stand for such treatment of a prisoner. It could not have been as bad as you say."

She shook her head sadly. "King Rylan had to be very careful. He was bound by law and had only his suspicions at first. It was not until late in the trial that he found out the truth and then he did what he could and the traitor was banished. By that time Earek and I had both been beaten multiple times and had been fighting a dangerous battle of wits for fifnights. I had walked a fine line with the traitor. If I pushed his temper too far by not obeying his wishes, I was beaten. Sometimes Earek was beaten for my disobedience, and I for his. I had to balance my refusal to obey with humility and courtesy just to remain conscious. He gave me a concussion at the very beginning, and I learned not to push him so far again. I knew that if I pushed too far, he would incapacitate me or kill me, and I would never see Prince Marquiese free. I had to give in to the traitor at times to save Prince Marquiese. Those girls are very fortunate that they did not suffer more."

Timral stared silently down at her for a long moment before offering his arm to her again. They walked on in silence.

"Why did you tell me all of that?" he asked quietly.

"You are a trusted member of the Royal Court. I have nothing to hide from the court, but most will not believe the truth as I say it. If I am ever to feel welcome at court, I need someone to know that I do not lie. You can also spread the truth around and then others will hear and wonder. If they ask the King, he will validate the story, as will Prince Marquiese and Lady Annabella. Some will still disbelieve the details, but it will start to build my reputation."

"For someone who is new to court, you seem to have a very good grasp of the way politics work," he replied darkly.

"I had some very skilled teachers."

He laughed lightly and they stopped walking when Master Castant stepped up to them.

"Ah, Lady Marilana," Castant said with a slight bow, "I trust that Timral has treated you well?"

"Very well indeed, Master Castant. I thank you for sending him to speak with me," she said with a wry smile. "He did a good job of keeping the other ambitious young men at bay, and I think we both learned a thing or two from our conversation."

Timral started in surprise and Castant laughed softly.

"I did tell you not to underestimate her," Castant chuckled. "She has great talent for observation and surmise."

"Hmm, so you did," Timral mused quietly, then continued lightly. "She seemed to enjoy my story about you, a colt, and a pigsty."

Master Castant froze staring at the young bear with a look of disbelief and then shook his head ruefully. "I will get you back for that, Timral. That story keeps coming back to haunt me, although I am glad it helped pass the time. Marilana, Lady Annabella sent me to get you; she says it is time to retire for the night."

"Thank you both. I hope to see you again before I leave for the Southern Tip."

"When will you depart?" Timral asked.

"I do not know. Soon I suspect. I need to establish my position as Lady Annabella's heir and settle into my new home. Lady Annabella is anxious to get us back."

"Of course," Timral bowed to her. "I look forward to our next meeting, My Lady, and wish you a safe journey if I do not see you before you leave."

"Thank you, Master Roana, and a fair fortune be yours," she replied with a slight curtsey to him. Turning, she accepted Castant's proffered arm and let the leopard guide her to where Lady Annabella waited.

"I expect that I shall see you tomorrow, so for now, good night, My Lady," Castant said with a small bow, then he turned and left.

Marilana scanned quickly through the room as she watched him walk away.

"You will not find who you seek," Lady Annabella said quietly. "King Rylan and Prince Marquiese retired for the night several minutes ago. You were in rather serious conversation and missed their leaving."

Marilana faced Annabella and blushed slightly, "I was trying to make Master Roana understand the traitor's nature a little better."

"Yes, of course. His beloved Mistress was rather ashamed of her position as a hostage. I noticed she was more relaxed after your short conversation. You have done well with them, but now we must be off to bed, come."

Marilana and Earek followed Lady Annabella out of the hall and to her rooms.

"Lady Annabella," Marilana asked quietly, "will we be leaving soon to return to the Southern Tip?"

"I thought we could stay for a few fifnights yet, unless you wish to leave sooner," she replied turning to face Marilana.

"The sooner the better," Marilana replied levelly. "I think it would be best if we left on a high note and returned at an opportune time to establish our standings without being here as Marquiese's invited friends. I am also unsure how far that friendship still exists."

"Yes, you might be correct," replied Annabella thoughtfully. "Very well, I shall send word to the camp to break first thing in the morning and start marching south. We will catch them up after breakfast. Sleep well, dears, we ride home tomorrow."

Earek and Marilana bowed as Annabella entered her rooms and closed the door. Earek caught Marilana's arm as she started to turn away.

"Marilana, are you sure you want to leave so soon?" he asked with concern.

"Yes, Earek," she replied sadly, "I think it is time to put some distance between the crown and my emotions. It will be hard, but I do think it is for the best."

He nodded in understanding and gave her a hug before turning to his own rooms.

*

Marilana sat on her couch on the balcony of her rooms and watched the stars. Altia had left a while ago. The girl had taken the news of Marilana's departure poorly. Marilana had wept with the caracal; they had grown so close over the past few months. Before she left, though, Altia had laid out a riding dress and accouterments and then bundled Marilana's few remaining possessions for travel. The work had helped them both get past the sorrow of parting. Altia had not been pleased by Marilana's insistence to sleep on the balcony again, but had helped her get ready for bed insisting that she keep the thick dressing robe on so not to take chill during the night. Marilana had to admit that the robe did help make her more comfortable in the night breeze.

A slight sound from inside the room caught Marilana's attention and was followed by soft boot steps. Marilana calmly slipped her paw under her pillow and grasped the hilt of the dagger she had hidden there. The steps stopped behind her on the balcony. She waited tensely for her midnight visitor to make the next move.

"Are you going to stab me, Marilana?" asked a quiet voice.

Marilana withdrew her paw quickly and clutched the neck of her robe, breathing fast.

She swallowed hard before speaking quietly, "I would never raise my blade against you, My Lord Highness."

"I did not think you would," Marquiese replied.

"Forgive me, Highness," Marilana said and started to rise to face him, "I seem to be a little slow on manners tonight."

His paw pressed softly on her shoulder and stopped her motion. She trembled slightly at his touch.

"Please, do not get up," he said softly. "You are trembling. Are you alright?"

"I am well enough, thank you," she said a little breathily as she turned to look up at him.

"May I join you?" he asked frowning slightly.

"Of course, My Lord Highness," she replied as calmly as she could.

He moved around the end of the couch and sat down. He gazed up at the stars for a long moment. Marilana watched him with her paws in her lap and tried to slow her breathing.

"Is there something I can do for you, Highness," she asked quietly.

Marquiese sighed and looked down at his paws in his lap.

"Master Castant was informed by one of Lady Annabella's servants that you will be leaving tomorrow," he said still looking at his paws.

Marilana waited for him to say more, but broke the silence when he did not.

"Lady Annabella and I think it would be best," she said quietly. "Earek and I have not been back to the Southern Tip since being named Annabella's heirs. We have a lot of work to do before we can truly settle into our new roles. I appreciate everything that I have learned here at the Royal Palace, but my home is waiting for my return."

Marquiese turned to face her. "I understand the reasons," he said with slight exasperation, "but not the timing. You still have a lot to learn about the court and being a noble of Redsands. The best place for you to do that is here. You could at least stay a few days, even a few fifnights to let things settle down again. And this traitor business is not finished. There are traitors among the guards and nobles to judge and sentence. Not to mention Frishka's threat that his second will try again for my life. You said you would be here to stop any attempt."

"I know all of that," Marilana said dropping her own eyes to her paws, "but there is a future now to consider too. If I am correct about this assassin, he will not try to get close to you for a while. His plans have been thwarted to a certain extent. He abandoned Frishka to his death yesterday, he did not even bother to direct the attacking siege forces. He seems to have recognized that the attempt was doomed. He will need to make new plans, and will most likely wait until everyone relaxes again or an opportunity presents itself. It could be months or even years before he reappears. I hope to be here to stop him when he does, but you know about him. Your vigilance will be your greatest protection now. I can only add another set of eyes, another blade."

"You are more than just another line of defense," he retorted.

"Yes," she persisted, "I am Lady Annabella's heir and have accepted a responsibility to the Southern Tip. If I stay here, I would be neglecting my duties. I must return home soon."

They sat in silence for a moment; she did not look up from her paws, although she thought he was still watching her.

"I will stay if you ask me to," Marilana said finally looking up, "but eventually I must go. I believe that the sooner I go, the better for everyone. I came here by your invitation, as your friend. A lot has passed between us since those happy first days. If I leave for a while, I can establish my own reputation as Lady Annabella's heir. No one will forget these past events, but if I return as an established noble in my own right, maybe these events will pass into history without lingering resentment."

Marquiese sighed again and studied her face. "You are too intelligent at times," he said bitterly. "I do not know if I want you to stay or to leave and never come back. But no matter what my emotional state, you have voiced the logic and responsibilities of your position. A position I want you to embrace, but I cannot believe you would go into hiding. You have decided to go, so you will go. There is no strong argument left for me to voice."

"Marquiese, while I am away," Marilana interrupted, "you should spend some time with the noble daughters. Mistresses Ailse and Lorlina could help you, if you let them. Their hearts belong to your friends; you should get to know them."

He looked stunned. "You may be right. I will need to pick someone to enter courtship with, and since you are leaving, it will not be you. Perhaps you are correct that a quick break is best. I do not know if I will be happy to see you return someday, but that day will come when it comes. For now, good night and a safe journey tomorrow."

He stood abruptly and strode briskly back inside the room. Marilana waited for his footsteps to fade before succumbing to her tears.

"Sleep well, Marquiese," she whispered into her paws.

8

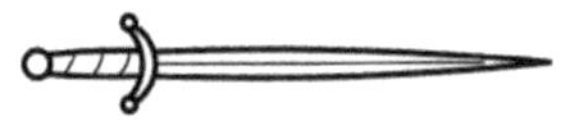

"Should you be down in the courtyard saying farewell, Highness?" mused a deep voice behind Marquiese.

Marquiese glanced up at Timral briefly, then turned back to the scene he was watching from the library window.

"I said my goodbyes last night and have no wish to be jostled by that group of lordlings," the royal lion retorted harshly.

They watched in silence as people milled about the courtyard. Lady Annabella's coach and escort stood waiting. Lords and ladies shifted, all trying to speak with Annabella and Earek. Marquiese frowned with disgust as he watched Marilana being swarmed by the young lords trying to impress her.

"You look like you could chew rocks, Marquiese," the tall bear laughed. "You could have gone down and at least spared Marilana from the vultures. She is quite a remarkable young woman."

"Yes," Marquiese growled, "you and she seemed to enjoy each other's company last night. Are you thinking of giving up your pursuit of Lorlina to chase Marilana?"

"No, never," Timral chuckled. "Marilana is intelligent and beautiful, but she is also bold, willful, and militant. I think she could make a strong ally and a good friend. My father taught me how to read creatures; a person's character, strengths, and weaknesses are all important qualities to evaluate and understand. I need to court someone soft and delicate yet still intelligent. Marilana is different than any woman I have ever met. She will need a strong match."

"You mean someone who can control her," Marquiese growled. "She is much more than you have perceived. She is not easily contained."

"No," Timral replied levelly, "she should not be caged or controlled. She needs someone who can share power with her and share a mutual respect for intelligence and strength. She will make a good leader of people, but she needs a partner she can rely on to work with her, like you, Highness."

"Me! Are you suggesting that I should pursue her?" Marquiese exclaimed.

"Forgive me, Your Highness," the bear replied with a bow, "I did not mean that. I meant that you also need someone who can help you lead the kingdom. Someone who respects the high and the low, and will support your work, not hinder it."

"Yes, well I will consider that at a later time," Marquiese retorted.

They watched the crowd in silence. Earek helped Lady Annabella into the coach and climbed in behind her. Many of the young lords jostled for position to assist Marilana in as well, but she suddenly sprang onto Storm. The stallion shook his head and pranced sideways. The crowd of men appeared startled and a clear space opened up around the horse. Several of the braver ones tried to grab for Storm's reins to calm him down and nearly got bit for it.

"Fools," Marquiese chuckled.

"Someone should do something," said Timral with concern. "Marilana could get thrown from that horse."

Marquiese laughed, "Someone is doing something. Marilana is in no danger. Those fools grabbing for her reins are though."

"What do you mean?" Timral asked puzzled.

"Look at Marilana's paws," said Marquiese pointing at the dancing horse. "Marilana is an excellent rider and trainer. If she were in danger, she would be soothing the horse, not sitting with her paws crossed lazily on the pommel."

"I see what you mean, but why is she letting the horse act up?"

"Storm is not just any horse," Marquiese chuckled. "He is trained as a lady's horse and as a war horse. He would do anything to protect Marilana and would never intentionally throw her. She is his trainer. Apparently Marilana is tired of being pawed and fawned on by the lordlings and is letting Storm create some breathing room."

Timral chuckled appreciatively, "Yes, a very intelligent young woman. No one can say she directed the horse to bite at the young men, but they are at a loss as to how to get close to her."

They watched as the coach and escort moved down the lane. Riding at her ease, Marilana kept Storm at the left side of the coach.

Marquiese sighed, "This is the second time in four years that she will be in the Southern Tip and I will be here."

"A moment ago, you sounded as if you could not wait for her to leave, and now you sound like you want her to stay."

"I do not know what I want. Part of me wants to jump on a horse and chase after her to beg her to stay, while the other part wants to never see her again. She is right, however; she has a duty to do, and so do I. Perhaps when the time is right, I will rejoice in her return, but until then I must focus on my home."

Marquiese watched Marilana ride down the lane out of sight and then turned and walked out of the library with Timral.

9

The bandits gathered around, emerging from the trees on all sides. The road curved around the hills, bending out of sight in both directions. There was no chance of escape. The leader stepped forward with his crossbow aimed at the group of lords in the midst of the trap. Marilana didn't need to see any more. She silently slipped back to her waiting men. It had been three and a half months since she and Earek had returned to the Southern Tip as Lady Annabella's heirs and she had immediately started to teach the soldiers her ways of stealth. Using the paw signals she had taught them, she signed her orders to her captains. The wings of her force would fold in around the bandits while her main force would break through the south edge of the bend in the road. She would take out the leader with her first shot while other archers would take out the remaining crossbowmen. Her force began to move as soon as she mounted Storm.

The lords and guards shifted uneasily as the bandit leader approached. Eyes scanned the forest looking for weak spots and a way to break through the bandits. Before anyone could act, there was a rumble of horse hooves close by, south of their position. A group of horses jumped the brush lining the road. The bandit leader looked to his right and raised his arm to give the signal to kill the lords and run, but, as he opened his mouth, a loud crash of armor sounded and the air was full of flying arrows. A gleaming white horse landed on the road as the bandit leader fell to the ground with an arrow through his throat.

Marilana rode to a halt as her men circled the lords to make a defensive ring. The wings of her force swept through the trees on either side, chasing the now leaderless bandits to the north. It was a perfect rout.

"My Lords, I hope no one has been injured. I received word of your arrival at the same time as a report of the amassing of a large number of bandits on your road. I set out immediately to rout their ambush. I had hoped to be in time to prevent the halt of your passage, but came a bit late," Marilana spoke with nobility, her head high, Storm's reins held in one paw, and her bow in the other.

"Nay, Lady, your timing was perfect. No one is injured," Marquiese responded as he rode forward and lowered his hood.

Marilana stiffened in her saddle at the sound of his voice. Storm tossed his head and pranced a few steps. She had apparently not known he was among the lords riding in her domain.

"Your Highness," Marilana said with a seated bow to him, "forgive me; I did not know this was your party or I would have arranged a proper escort. Please accept these men to escort you to Lady Annabella's estates. She will be pleased to see you unharmed."

"Will you not accompany us?" he asked surprised.

"Please accept my apology once again, Highness, but I must continue the chase with my men. If you would excuse me," she said bowing again and wheeled Storm around.

Marquiese watched her race off into the trees followed by one of her men. Mutters broke out among the lords behind him. Marquiese shared a worried glance with Master Castant before turning to Marilana's captain. With a nod from Marquiese, the guards formed up and the party moved on toward Lady Annabella's.

As he rode, Marquiese listened to the conversation of the lords and wondered about Marilana's strange behavior. He had not seen her in three and a half months. He had expected a more gracious welcome from her. Besides which, it was not like her to leave the protection of important visitors to others. The other lords seemed disturbed by her sudden entrance and the way she commanded her men without speaking. Marquiese knew those things could be attributed to Marilana's discipline and training. Lady Annabella had indicated that Marilana had made remarkable progress with the guard and army commanders in her last letter to King Rylan. Instead, what he worried about was the way she had paled when he spoke, and the way she had rushed off into the trees. She had almost seemed recklessly frantic to get away from him.

*

"Your Highness, Prince Marquiese! How wonderful to see you again. I see Marilana found you. I hope your journey was not too troublesome," Lady Annabella greeted him warmly from the steps of her castle.

"She found us in the midst of a bandit ambush and routed them perfectly. We are unharmed. Thank you for taking the time for our visit. It is good to see you,"

Marquiese replied, returning her warmth and feeling that this welcome was more like he expected.

"Please come in. Your rooms are ready," the noble lioness said bowing them toward the doors.

Marquiese motioned for the lords to precede him and walked slowly with Lady Annabella.

"Lady Annabella," he said quietly, "Marilana seemed not to know who was expected. Did you not tell her of my coming?"

"No, Your Highness. We only learned of your visit this morning. She received word of the suspected ambush at the same time and did not wait to find out who was coming. She left in haste in order to arrive in time. I did not have a chance to tell her, and I also felt it was better this way," she replied apologetically.

"Better?" he asked surprised.

"Yes, Marilana has been rather distracted," she replied hesitantly. "I am not surprised that she did not accompany you back. In fact, I do not expect her to be back soon now that you are here."

Marquiese let that go unremarked as he pursued a different concern. "Lady, I sent word of my visit several fifnights ago. All of the other nobles I have visited had acknowledged my request well in advance of my arrival. Do you have any idea why my letter only just arrived today?"

"I am not sure, Highness. The errand rider arrived on foot, filthy and bloodied. One of my scouts found him stumbling out of the forest. He is in the infirmary, unconscious. Healer Magus is doing everything he can for the poor weasel."

"Rider Bordou is one of my best. I trust Healer Magus to do all he can. I hope he recovers."

They had reached his rooms, so he bowed to her and entered. Marquiese pondered Lady Annabella's words while he bathed and prepared himself for the banquet Lady Annabella had hastily prepared. A welcoming banquet was Annabella's style, but with the short notice of his visit, the formal feast with the landed-gentry of the surrounding lands would be prepared for tomorrow evening. The delay of his message was very disturbing and had obviously led to the bandits' ambush. He regretted not bringing a larger escort and was very concerned for Rider Bordou. Yet, he found his thoughts returning to Marilana. Their first meeting in three and a half months had not gone anything like he had imagined. He had not known what to expect, he had not parted from her pleasantly after all, but he had never expected her to run away.

Marquiese visited the infirmary briefly, but Healer Magus reported no improvement in Rider Bordou's condition. Now Marquiese stood at a window in his rooms from which he could see the main gate and a good portion of the stableyard. He had been watching for Marilana's return. He had not yet seen her and it was getting late. From his count, most of Marilana's men, including Earek had returned already. He had seen Earek riding next to Marilana at the ambush, and he had led the men on after Marilana had stopped to speak with the lords. Marquiese approved of Earek's position as Marilana's Major-General. Earek was intelligent and quick; he would make a fine leader of people and armies.

A movement in the shadows of the gate caught Marquiese's attention. A figure emerged leading two horses toward the stables, one of which was unmistakably Storm. Marquiese studied the horses carefully; they appeared to have been groomed and rested from the earlier activities. He wondered where Marilana had been. He had not expected her to arrive back to her own estates just in time for the banquet and to hide in the shadows. A knock on the door prompted him to turn around, a servant waited to announce him for dinner.

Throughout the banquet Marilana was a silent presence next to Lady Annabella. Marquiese watched her out of the corner of his eye as he spoke with the other attendees. She never looked at him and remained at Lady Annabella's side until late in the evening when she slipped out the garden door. After Marilana left, Marquiese approached Earek for the first time. Earek seemed to have no trouble meeting his eye, smiling, or acting normally.

"Why is it, Master Earek, that you have accepted everything that has passed between us and can be around me without acting strangely, while Marilana is faltering and will not even look at me?" he asked casually.

"Hmm," Earek glanced at the garden door with a sad smile. "I have accepted your position and mine and I have nothing more to trouble my thoughts. I can speak to you without worrying about what the rest of the court is going to say. She cannot. I was her accomplice, fighting for her life and yours. I was a friend to both of you. The court understands all of the motives I could have had as honorable, and I was not in a position to personally benefit from the outcome. Her motives remain suspect. That the matter is still debated does not bother her, but you and she together make people wonder anew. For herself, I do not think she cares. However, she does not want you to be brought down by that suspicion again."

Marquiese frowned. "Thank you, my friend, you have given me something to think about."

"Your friend, Highness?" asked Earek. "I had accepted your formal forgiveness, but I had not realized that I had been returned to friend status.

"Yes," Marquiese grinned, "I have spent a lot of time thinking over the events, and have found that I still think of you as my friend and never really doubted you. If you are agreeable, I wanted to propose for you to be named one of my advisors."

Earek smiled broadly, "Of course, Your Highness. I would be honored."

"I am glad you are so agreeable. I worried your loyalty to Marilana would prevent it."

"Your Highness should know me well enough to know that if you or she tells me something that should not be told to the other that I would not speak of it," Earek replied.

"You would keep secrets from me?" Marquiese asked.

"If she ordered me too, yes. You trust that I will not tell your secrets; it is, in fact, one of the qualities you hold in high esteem. Therefore, you already expected my answer before you asked," Earek said, slightly bowing his head.

Marquiese smiled and returned the bow. "Yes, I do appreciate your loyalty. I hope that I will not put you in too difficult a position between myself and Lady Marilana."

"I will manage," Earek laughed.

"I must also congratulate you for learning so much from her so quickly," Marquise mused. "You have already learned to twist words with finesse."

"I have learned much more than that, as have all of the guardsmen and staff. She has made many strategic changes that have helped improve the efficiency of the castle and the province," Earek chuckled.

"Of that I have no doubt," Marquiese laughed as well. "She is finally able to make all the changes she saw were needed when she was a servant here. I am glad the staff has accepted her elevation to Lady smoothly."

"Smooth is not the term I use," Earek said with a broad smile. "I say joyfully."

*

Marquiese did not see Marilana again until the next evening. He had kept a lookout for her all day as he rested from his journey and prepared for the formal feast. He wanted to spend some time with her talking, perhaps reminiscing about his time in the Southern Tip or discussing the recent changes she had made as Lady Annabella's heiress. He did not catch even a glimpse of her until he entered the great hall for the feast. Marilana looked magnificent dressed in a silver gown trimmed with deep purple. She smiled and talked to the guests and attended Lady Annabella, but he noticed that whenever he got close to her she excused herself or fell silent until he left. Her behavior worried him, but as they both had socializing duties to perform, it did not consume him. As a guest, he was expected to dance and speak with the local nobles, and it was part of her hostess duties to dance with the guests. Marquiese watched, waited, and danced with other ladies. He even danced a graceful turn with Lady Annabella, and beamed fondly while watching Marilana laugh as she danced with Master Castant.

It was late when Marilana had danced with all the lords and visitors that had accompanied Marquiese as well as the local gentlemen; he knew she could no longer ignore him. She spun smiling from her partner just as he bowed to his. She faltered as he turned to face her. Her smile slipped slightly as she inhaled sharply and curtseyed to him. They danced, but it was not graceful. Although it wasn't a difficult dance, she struggled with her footwork. He could tell she was not faking as he had seen her do in school. He helped her as best he could, keeping the foot work simple, but by the time the music ended, Marilana was more embarrassed than he had ever seen her. She curtseyed quickly and spun away. As he watched her move through the crowed, he realized that she had never met his eyes. Not once. Soon afterward she disappeared again and was not seen for the rest of the night.

When Lady Annabella had finished saying goodnight to the guests and Prince Marquiese, she went out to the garden and strode purposefully down the path toward the figure sitting alone on a bench. Marilana did not look up from contemplating her paws when Lady Annabella stopped in front of her. With a sigh, she sat next to the younger lioness.

"All of the guests have gone to their rooms," she said quietly.

Marilana remained silent.

"Will you please explain your behavior?" she asked firmly. "Do you think this will pass for good manners after I am gone?"

Marilana looked up surprised, but speechless. "Well, at least I got a response that time," Lady Annabella frowned. "Daughter, it is time to sort out your feelings. You cannot hide from them any more than you can continue to avoid him. Tomorrow you must attend to his business here. You know that he is not just here for his own pleasure. Royals always have business, even if they cover it up with the appearance of pleasure."

"Yes, Mother, I know," Marilana replied glancing down at her paws.

"Well then, what are you going to do about your little confidence problem?"

"I suppose I need to face it."

"You suppose?" replied Annabella hotly. "Marilana, you face down bandits. You act with more nobility than most nobles. Yet you fall apart whenever he is in the same room, or even when you just think about him. For your sake, I hope you do more than suppose."

"Yes, M'Lady," Marilana whispered.

Annabella sighed. She could see all too well that Marilana was letting her fear of rejection crowd out her confidence and softened her tone. "He leaves the morning after tomorrow. I do not expect you to fix all your issues during his visit, but I do expect you to decide on a plan to fix this before you see him again. I know how hard it is to see the man you love turn down a different path, but your life has much more in it than just him. You must remember to live your life the way you wish. To be seen the way you want. I know you are stronger than this.

"I also trust that you will carry out your duties from now on," she added more forcefully as she stood. A chagrined grimace twisted Marilana's face.

"Goodnight, Daughter," Annabella said quietly and walked away.

10

Marquiese woke early the next morning to the sounds of horses whinnying, hooves pounding, grooms shouting, and hammers clanging—all the sounds of a busy stableyard. Tired as he was, he was determined to speak with Marilana. He knew she would be out there in all that hustle and bustle, so he got up and dressed quickly. He told his servant that he would have breakfast when he returned and promptly left his rooms. Master Castant joined him in the hall and together they left the castle. They did not speak as they crossed the stableyard and approached the training arena. Marilana, Earek, and Lady Annabella's head trainer, Hosten, stood on the raised and railed platform overlooking the track. A young colt raced past as Marquiese and Castant climbed onto the platform. Castant joined Earek lounging against the back rail. Marquiese nodded to Earek, then stepped forward closer to Marilana, but stayed a couple steps behind her where he could see the track clearly without blocking her view. The colt raced past again and Marilana and Hosten watched it critically.

"Nice colt," Marquiese said.

Marilana spun around in surprise, lost her balance, and promptly toppled backward over the railing and onto the track. The four men on the platform leaned over the railing to see her lying in a tangle of skirts on the track.

"Marilana!" Earek called. "Are you alright?"

"Yes," Marilana called back as she sat up and untangled her clothing. "I'm fine."

Marquiese noticed Earek relax as Marilana got to her feet and dusted herself off.

"Hosten, I think I have seen enough for today. Keep up the good work," Marilana called to the older cheetah as she turned to walk out the gap in the track rail.

"Yes, M'Lady. Thank you." Hosten turned his attention back to the colt.

Marquiese followed Earek and Castant down from the platform and was surprised to find Marilana waiting for them. He had expected her to have disappeared again and to have to hunt her down. Instead she smiled and curtseyed to him.

"Your Highness startled me. I was so focused on the colt that I did not know you had joined us," she said lightly.

Marquiese blinked as he realized that she was addressing him directly and meeting his gaze. He studied her eyes; something still was not quite normal about her expression, it was like looking at a mask hiding something deeper, a camouflage she hid behind. "It was not my intention to surprise you, Lady Marilana. Are you sure you are all right?"

"Yes, I am fine. Thank you. You are up early this morning, Your Highness. Did you sleep well?"

"Yes, I slept well. Thank you. I have not yet eaten breakfast. Would you care to join me?"

"That would be quite pleasant. Your sitting room should be well lit by the morning sun, if it pleases you to dine there, and will Earek and Master Castant be joining us?"

"My room would be fine, and of course Earek and Castant may join us," Marquiese replied.

Marilana turned to where a servant and two guardsmen stood waiting. She exchanged several quick gestures with the servant, before the young tigress curtseyed and hurried toward the castle.

Marilana turned back to him and indicated the path back to the castle. She hesitated only slightly to lay her paw on his arm when he offered it to her, and together they returned to the castle. The four of them had a pleasant breakfast discussing horses, weather, the changes Marilana had made, Earek's difficulties gaining the trust of the guard commanders, and the strangely sporadic bandit activity. Marilana told him about her new markets along the southern border that made it easier for the people living in the Great Mountains to acquire the goods and supplies they needed without resorting to banditry. Marquiese felt comfortable among friends, except for Marilana. Something about her mannerisms was still not what he expected. She seemed restrained somehow. Soon after the servant had refilled their cups of tea, a knock sounded on the door and the young tigress servant spoke quietly to Marilana.

"Forgive me, Your Highness, but duty calls. I must leave you now and shall see you later today," Marilana said turning from the door. She curtseyed precisely to him with her head bowed, and then nodded to the others. "Master Castant, Earek, a good day to you."

Marquiese stared at the door for a while after Marilana had swept from the room. Her departure seemed abrupt, but not abrupt enough for a message of urgency. He wondered what it meant.

"Well, I must admit that this morning has been full of surprises," he said turning to look at the two leopards.

"It certainly seems that she is different this morning," agreed the yellow leopard frowning.

"Yes, and no," the black leopard said thoughtfully still staring at the door.

Marquiese met Castant's quick glance, then studied Earek intently.

"What do you mean?" Marquiese asked quietly.

Earek started and glanced at Marquiese apologetically. "Forgive me. I meant there were a few small behaviors I noticed that are consistent with the past few days."

"Go on," said Marquiese picking up his teacup. "As you are one of my advisors now, please, advise me."

"Well," said Earek thoughtfully, "first, her fall off the platform."

"Yes, that was obvious," Marquiese agreed.

"Yes. Then there is the fact that she did not pour the tea herself. Lady Annabella teaches that it is part of Marilana's duty as hostess to serve her guests personally in private settings. I did notice Marilana's paws had a slight tremor during breakfast, and perhaps she did not feel like she should risk pouring the tea. Also, the way she spoke and smiled, she was not relaxed and natural; she seemed to be following a script. She was the perfect hostess."

"I also noticed her mannerisms," added Castant, "a smile at just the right place in a story and precise responses to questions and comments. She was indeed playing the proper hostess."

Marquiese nodded. "I see what you mean, although I did not recognize it at the time. Almost like we were in school again, although without the disrespect from the other students."

"There is one more point to consider," said Earek hesitantly. "She planned the interruption. I caught the gestures she used when she sent the servant to prepare breakfast. She arranged to get a message after the teacups were refilled."

"She arranged that! But why?" asked Marquiese stunned.

"If I may suggest it," said Castant when Earek shook his head puzzled, "she may feel that you do not want her company, that you were playing the perfect guest by asking her to eat with you. So, as the perfect hostess, she arranged to impose her company upon you only as long as necessary to finish breakfast. And she made sure you were not alone with her by inviting Earek and me."

"I sought her out, how can she think I do not want her company?"

"You are known to enjoy watching horse training, and to rise early to walk about in the fresh air," Castant replied ruefully.

"It is possible that she is unsure how deep my forgiveness of her goes," Marquiese said more thoughtfully. "I have given her no reason to believe that I trust her any more now than I did when she left Maefair. I must admit we did not part on the best of terms."

They sat in silence while sipping their tea. The carven clock on the mantle chimed the hour and Earek looked up.

"Forgive me, Your Highness, but it is time for me to attend Lady Annabella," he said standing up and bowing to Marquiese.

"Of course, Earek. If you would, please inform Lady Annabella that I wish to speak with her and her heirs after lunch. We have some private business to attend to," replied Marquiese with a smile.

"It will be done, Your Highness," Earek responded and left the room.

Marquiese turned to Castant after the door closed. "I still find it odd that I can trust Earek so completely and yet still feel uncomfortable with Marilana."

"How can you trust someone you feel betrayed by?" he asked.

"It is true. I feel her betrayal still. I thought I had gotten past that when we left Maefair. I was excited to see her again, but when she rescued us from the bandit ambush, I felt the betrayal all over again. It is as if she is doing something still that I cannot forgive her for, yet I do not know what or why."

"Does her odd behavior make you feel this betrayal?" Castant asked.

"Strangely no," said Marquiese frowning. "Her odd behavior is something else. I felt her betrayal more strongly when she was out chasing the bandits."

"Perhaps you should speak with her. You may be able to narrow down what actions are betrayals," Castant suggested.

Marquiese studied his friend. "You trust her, my father trusts her, and I still trust her to protect my life, but why can I not trust her in other matters?"

Marilana knew she could not escape the after-lunch meeting as easily as she had breakfast. Lady Annabella had said that Marquiese had requested her to attend the business at present. She played hostess well during lunch and directed tea and cakes to be placed in Lady Annabella's private council chamber. She followed Lady Annabella into the chamber, dismissed the servant and closed the door. Marquiese, Castant, Earek, and Annabella seated themselves about the rectangular table in the middle of the room. Marilana busied herself at the sideboard, pouring tea and delivering cups to the room's occupants.

Marquiese spoke as Marilana set the first cup in front of him. "First, I wish to thank you for your gracious hospitality. It is always a pleasure to stay here."

"Thank you, Your Highness. You are always welcome to visit," replied Annabella.

"My father, King Rylan, sent me to invite you and your heirs to the annual tournament next month in honor of our birthdays. I wish to add my own personal request for your presence. As I am turning seventeen, this is my coming-of-age year. Historically, most princes have been betrothed by this year. As I am not, I must follow tradition and dance the courtship dance with all maids for whose favor I ride under during the tournament."

The teapot rattled loudly as Marilana set it on the sideboard. She felt heat rise in her cheeks, but restrained herself from glancing at Lady Annabella. She took the last cup to her place at Lady Annabella's right and sat down quietly. Marquiese continued as if he had not noticed.

"Also, by tradition, I must ask all eligible maids of noble standing to attend if they wish."

He turned from Lady Annabella and met Marilana's eyes. She held his gaze, although she felt the heat returning to her cheeks.

"Lady Marilana, I invite you to attend," he said simply.

"Thank you, Your Highness," she replied quietly.

Marquiese paused for a moment and took two letters from Master Castant. Marilana suspected that this was the real reason for the meeting. She was sure the invitations could have been made in public, although she was glad that her embarrassment had not been seen by anyone else. Marquiese turned a very serious gaze to Lady Annabella.

"As you know, we have been involved these past months in the tracking down the traitor Frishka's conspirators," he said. "We have found several more instances of peasants disappearing in the areas where Frishka's army camped, and have found many of the abandoned camps with the help of local bandit hunters and trackers. We believe that this confirms the theory that the disappearances were used as a means to deter travel in the area and avoid detection."

Marilana stiffened and glanced at Earek's stony expression. She was sure her own expression was equally hard.

"We have also followed many leads and have apprehended and tried many men among the palace guard and the city, even a few women in the merchant caste of the city," continued Marquiese. "Recently we have intensified our search for one man in particular who we have been told is very dangerous. You may remember, Lady Annabella, that Frishka arrived at the palace accompanied by another. He called him simply Confidant. This Confidant was later banished from the allied nations for assaulting me and breaking one of my ribs."

"Yes, I remember," said Lady Annabella darkly.

"We have gathered some evidence from some of Frishka's men that indicate that this Confidant may have indeed been his second in command, as we theorized. It seems that he had left Redsands to gather more forces when Frishka hastened to attack the palace. We have been trying to track this man, but it seems he disappeared with news of Frishka's death." He paused, taking a calming breath. "One fifnight ago, we received a letter from an unconfirmed source beyond the southern border. We have not received any communications from this source in over eight years and had assumed him compromised or dead. The letter includes information about a new bandit leader who is unifying the many different bandit groups. He appears to be gathering individuals with special talents, such as trackers and archers, and training for an attack of some kind. From the information we have, we believe this new leader may be Frishka's Confidant. We felt it necessary to inform you of these developments just beyond your border. We do not think it is time for any direct action against this threat yet, but we would like you to be ready for any unusual bandit activity."

"Thank you, Your Highness. We shall prepare and increase patrols of the border lands," Lady Annabella replied.

Marquiese nodded then dropped his eyes to the letters in his paws. When he looked up again it was Marilana's eyes he sought.

Frowning he spoke softly. "This second letter was included in the first with a request for it to be delivered here to Lady Marilana Lapidis."

Marilana swayed in shock; she felt as if someone had just slapped her. She had not used her father's family name since he had left her in Lady Annabella's custody fourteen years ago. She had only begun to use her father's family crest as her personal seal the past month when she turned seventeen, with King Rylan's approval, and she had never told anyone her father had a family name. Lady Annabella and King Rylan knew, of course, but she had never told anyone what it was. Peasants were rarely granted family names and so no one ever questioned her about it. As Lady Annabella's heir, she had gained Lady Annabella's family name of Ranat rather than continuing her father's family name of Lapidis. Marquiese passed her the sealed letter. She stared at her name scrawled across the paper in writing she recognized from old letters and journals her father had left her.

"I must ask you to tell us everything you can about this letter," Marquiese requested. "It may help us to determine the best course of action."

Marilana nodded, still in shock. She opened her mouth to speak, but could not form the words. She closed her mouth, swallowed, and then tried again.

"Lapidis is my blood father's family name. As you know, family names are granted to people for their achievements. Merchants and nobles pass their name onto their heirs. Royalty pass it on to their children. King Rylan granted my father the family name of Lapidis for services rendered and to give him a recognizable crest to seal letters with. Any reports with this crest pressed in plain wax were directed to the King alone. He did this just before asking my father to undertake a mission beyond the southern border. I was left with Lady Annabella and was given an official copy of the seal for my inheritance."

"Is it possible for someone to have gotten hold of this crest and information to send false reports to the King?" asked Earek.

"As far as I know, there are only two items with this crest. One is my father's signet ring, and the other is my own signet ring. King Rylan recently gave his permission for me to use this crest pressed in the deep green of the Southern Tip for my personal correspondences."

She compared the crest on the letter to the ring on her finger; it matched perfectly. "My father may have been forced to give up this information and his ring, but it is impossible to tell at this point."

"I understand," replied Marquiese, "please continue."

Marilana nodded, broke the seal, and unfolded the letter. As she read, she stood and walked to the window in the corner of the room behind Lady Annabella.

Dearest Daughter,

We hope you receive this letter in private, but we understand that circumstances may require you to share these words with others. Your mother and I have heard that Lady Annabella has chosen you as her heir and adopted you into her family. We cannot express how proud of you we are. We hope that you are happy in your new life and that you remember us fondly as you change your name and grow into your new title. We regret that we could not share in your adventures, pains, and joys, but we hope that everything we did share with you has helped you to become the best person you could, and the great leader we are sure you will become. We think of you often. Fond farewell, beloved daughter.

With Love,

Your Father

Marquiese watched Marilana read and reread the letter. She rubbed her claw gently across the writing. No one said a word. Finally, he got up and moved to stand next to her at the window. Silently she gave him the letter and gazed out at the southern mountains. He read the letter quickly, then passed it to Lady Annabella.

"What are your thoughts?" he asked gently.

"They are out there somewhere. I have no doubt it is from my father. I also do not believe it was written under duress," she replied without moving.

"How do you know?" he asked, pushing aside a small sting of betrayal.

"First, it is written in ink, not the charcoal or pigmented water used by bandits. As a scholar, he knows how to make permanent ink like this. Although it is a lower quality ink than that used by city merchants, it has the proper binding agents to prevent the pigment from separating from the water or rubbing off the paper. I know this because I have read his journals so that I could learn the things he knew. Next, his word choices are specific. He writes with deeper intent. The words express his joy, but also his doubts. He is unsure how I feel about him contacting me after all this time. I received my last letter from him nearly nine years ago when I was eight. He also comments about names and titles, expressing the hope that I cherish this letter with both my new title and my old name. He mentions his pride in me, hinting that I have brought honor to him and our family. He used to tell me in his letters that the most important thing a family could do was to share life with each other. He referred to that lesson several times. Lastly, I recognize his writing from his letters and his journals."

She stopped speaking, still gazing at the distant peaks. Her expression was hard and cold. Marquiese recognized the expression; she was determined and had shut out all further discussion. He sighed, the feeling of betrayal growing stronger, but he tried to ignore it because he knew her emotions were in turmoil.

"Thank you, Marilana. I would not have known to look for all the hidden intricacies. You obviously know your father's writing well. I will let King Rylan know that the letters are legitimate. Again, I thank you, My Lady," he said formally and turned away from her.

He motioned the others toward the doors. Quietly he led the way from the room. Once in the hallway, he turned to find Castant beside him and Lady Annabella closing the doors.

"My Lady, why did Earek remain?" he asked slightly alarmed.

"Forgive us, Your Highness, and peace," she said apologetically. "Marilana needs comfort as much as she needs privacy."

"But why him? Why not you?" he asked forcefully.

"She is my Daughter and I love her dearly, but I do not feel that it is right of me to remain and place pressure on her to choose me over her blood parents. Earek has been separated from his own blood parents and can provide neutral and stable support. Please let them be," Lady Annabella replied quietly.

Marquiese nodded curtly and stormed away down the hallway.

Earek sat quietly sipping his tea, and watched Marilana stare coldly at the distant mountains. Eventually he got up, refilled both of their teacups, and moved to stand next to her at the window.

"They are out there somewhere," she whispered taking the cup of tea without looking away from the peaks.

"And what would have happened if you had gone in search of them?" he asked gently.

"I could have grown up with my parents. I could have lived with a family, my own family," she said, her voice cracking with remorse.

"You could have never found them, you could have died lost and alone, or even worse, you could have compromised them and you all could have been tortured and killed by bandits," he said.

"I . . . I know, but the thought haunts me," she whispered and tears pooled in her eyes.

"There is always a 'what if,'" he said gently.

"They risked everything to send these letters out, Earek. I just want to know if they are safe," she said finally letting the tears fall down her cheeks. "They sent me this letter because they are proud of me, but they don't even really know me. So much of my life has happened without them; I don't know if they even know about my bandit hunting, or my capture by bandits, or all the things that have happened since meeting Marquiese. The converse is also true; I have no idea what they do, how they spend their days, how they have changed . . . or if I have siblings."

"Your father is very resourceful, they have survived this long. Maybe someday you will be able to find them and answer your questions, but right now you have a duty to your people. Lady Annabella needs you; your new family needs you. I do not want to lose my sister," he said quietly.

She smiled sadly at him. "You always know what to say. You will not lose me, Brother. I will not find them. I will not even try. In the last line of the letter, my father bid me farewell. He is on the move again, and will not tell me where. He is making a final break with me, so I will not change my life because of this letter. I have my life to live as I choose and they have theirs."

Earek was at a loss for words. Finally, he comforted her with a one-armed hug. She smiled more warmly at him and sighed. They stood sipping their tea just taking comfort in each other's company and watching the staff working in the gardens. Eventually Earek cleared his throat.

"There is another pressing issue, Sister," he said lightly. "What are you going to do about that certain someone who has been watching us from the corner of the garden hedge?"

Marilana sighed and gazed down at her tea, "I do not know, Brother."

Earek noticed her paws shaking slightly and spoke again. "Marilana, I have never known you to back down from a problem. I have never known you to suffer from insecurity. Even when we were suspected of treason, you stayed focused. Yet these last few months I have seen you become increasingly unstable. I think he is the cause. Am I right?"

Marilana nodded. "I am not the person I used to be. I used to be cold, hard, calculating. I was a very good bandit hunter. Then Marquiese came along and he changed how I saw the world. I still feel driven to protect the people from bandits and injustices, but it is not my only goal. Mother says this is part of growing up. When I was just Marilana the orphaned peasant, I had no reason to think more of my future. My only power was that of the Hunter. Now my world has turned upside down. I must think of our family, I must think of our people, but I must also think of my future. Our people expect me to do certain things in the future. There are so many possibilities to consider and so many ways I can use the power of Nobility. Marquiese opened my eyes to a larger world, and then he helped to shatter who I thought I was. I must now re-forge my thoughts, dreams, and life."

"I have seen these changes, and I have gone through similar changes. I was not a friend to the Bandit Hunter, but I am Brother to the Lady," he said quietly. "You are changing for the better and will be a great leader of people. As a noble you are strong, sure, confident, and determined; however, I think there is more to it."

"I have been seriously thinking about my private life," she admitted. "As the Hunter, I never thought about becoming a wife and raising children; in fact I intended to run from the possibility. I, Lady Marilana, have a softer side. I have come to love to pick out gowns and jewels. I am concerned about how I look and what others think of me. Earek, I truly want to be a wife and mother. I never dreamed of such things before, but I do now."

Earek smiled broadly. "Marilana, Sister, you are becoming a woman."

Marilana giggled and smiled shyly. "There was a time, Brother, that I would have hit you for saying so, but I am no longer so hard and cold."

"And that is the root of the problem; is it not?" he said gently. "I know you love him, but the reason you have trouble keeping your wits around him is that you do not know if he will ever return your love."

"Oh, Earek," Marilana cried, tears forming in her eyes again, "there was a time that I believed he loved me. That is why I hate Frishka so much. The traitor toyed with Marquiese's emotions so much he no longer knows how he feels about me. Since the trials, I have seen Marquiese's hate, anger, sorrow, pity, concern, and polite interest. I have seen him smile and laugh, but there is always something that stops him from showing the warmth I knew as his friend. I am at a loss as to what I can do to regain his trust and possibly his love."

"He cares about you," Earek said gently. "He is always asking about you and he hardly takes his eyes off of you when you are nearby. He was hesitant to discuss his business with you because he did not want to hurt you."

"I see that, but when we are alone, I never know what he is going to do. The night before we left Maefair, he came to see me in my rooms, and it did not go well," she said through her tears.

"No one said anything about seeing him visit you," said Earek puzzled.

"He came secretly," she sighed, "through the secret door. At first, he seemed to not want me to leave, but by the end he told me that he did not want me to ever come back. His concern turned so quickly to anger, I was almost afraid of him. I just do not know what to do about him."

Earek set their teacups on the windowsill and wrapped his arms around her. She pressed her face to his shoulder and cried. He held her gently until she stopped shaking.

"I am sorry," she said eventually, "and thank you."

"I am your Brother," he said firmly. "I am here for you anytime you need a shoulder to cry on or a sparring partner to take out your frustrations on."

She smiled weakly and wiped away her tears.

"I think, Marilana," he said seriously, "it is best for you to relax and just be your natural, beautiful, emotional self, and remind him why you were his friend to begin with. I truly think that deep down he loves you, and being yourself will help him realize that too."

"Thank you, Earek," she replied quietly, "I will think about what you have said. Now though, we had better get ready for dinner."

Together they turned and headed for their rooms.

Marquiese stood at the corner of the garden hedge frowning with his arms crossed. He had come to this place after leaving Lady Annabella and had silently watched the two figures in the window ever since.

"How long do you plan to stand here watching Marilana and Earek?" asked Master Castant from where he leaned against the hedge.

"I should have spoken to her privately," Marquiese said without taking his eyes away from the silhouettes in the window. "I should be there comforting her, not Earek."

"And why do you think you could have comforted her, when you feel betrayed by her and do not trust her?" Castant asked.

"I . . . well I," he stammered slightly surprised, "I should have done something at least.

Castant shrugged. "If you say so."

"Why, Earek?" Marquiese muttered angrily.

"Marquiese," Castant said, "I think you might be jealous."

"Nonsense," growled Marquiese, "I just mean someone else could have done as well."

"It is like Lady Annabella said," Castant said resigned. "Earek is her confidant. Also, he was the only one Marilana would not feel pressured by to choose one path over another."

"That is true," Marquiese said thoughtfully, "however, Marilana knows her duty. She will not abandon Lady Annabella."

"No, not for a private desire, but she needs to choose her path without Lady Annabella's aid, or yours, if she is to be confident in her own heart," Castant said firmly.

Marquiese sighed and glanced at the ground. "You are right. I could not have helped her, not in the way I would have liked. Come on, old friend. We should get ready for dinner."

He glanced once more at the window, now empty of any shadows, then turned and strolled back to the castle with Castant.

11

The leaving feast was an intimate affair. Lady Annabella, Marilana, and Earek hosted Prince Marquiese and his entourage with music, stories, and delicious food. Marilana played the perfect hostess, but was more lively and relaxed than she had been since his arrival. She smiled and laughed with the lords and even listened raptly to Marquiese's stories. Marquiese watched as his entourage bade their hosts a goodnight until he was the last guest still sipping his wine. Finally, he said goodnight to Earek and Lady Annabella and approached Marilana.

"Would you care to accompany me for a walk in the gardens?" he asked, offering his arm.

"What a lovely thought. I would be glad to," she replied smiling and laid her paw lightly on his arm with a curtsey.

As they left through the garden door, Marquiese noticed that his two guards were joined by Master Castant while two other men followed further back. He did not mind as long as no one impinged on his privacy. They strolled in silence for a while, taking in the night. Marquiese tried to be calm, but his emotions were still swirling around from the events of the day. They reached a carved stone bench and Marquiese gestured for Marilana to sit with him. He watched as she mindfully adjusted and smoothed her skirts. He had never noticed her taking such care of her garments. It made him smile. He reached out and took her paws in his and met her eyes. She gazed up at him and waited.

"I wanted to apologize for this afternoon. I did not wish to cause you pain, but I needed to know—," he started.

"I understand, Your Highness," Marilana interrupted quietly. "You do not need to apologize. As you know, I have my own suspicions about the man you are hunting. You needed to be sure the letters were legitimate. Apparently, my father knew that as well. He wrote to me so I could confirm it was his writing." She paused and then added, "I just wish I knew they were safe."

She turned her face away as her voice trailed off. Heat crept up Marquise's neck, his temper flaring at her allusion to her true thoughts; the familiar feeling of betrayal spread through him like poison. He tightened his grip on her paws and her eyes widened in alarm.

"You are a very convincing actress," he spat at her, flinging her paws away. "You can play any part, the perfect hostess, the caring friend, or the grief-stricken victim. Is there any part you have not played? Perhaps you never were a true friend."

He abruptly stood up and paced. Marilana clutched her paws to her chest, leaning back against the bench stunned. Her eyes tracked him aghast.

"There is always something more with you. Some goal you are striving for that you would do anything to achieve. You do not care who you hurt along the way," he raged as he paced, his voice growing louder and colder.

Tears streamed down Marilana's cheeks as she sat frozen on the bench watching him.

"I should have known; I should have seen it from the start. You were always the best at everything. I have never seen such ambition. You will stop at nothing. I believe that you were not in league with the traitor Frishka, but your deceit definitely would have done well in his court!"

"NO!"

Marilana's anguished cry stopped Marquiese cold. There had been a time she would have shouted back at him, demanded better from him, scorned him for his hurtful remarks. Instead, she had slid off the bench onto her knees. She huddled on the ground shaking and weeping into her paws. Marquiese felt ashamed for letting his anger carry his hurtful words. He wanted to take her in his arms and apologize, to say he had not meant it, but the betrayal still burned hotly in his heart. He struggled with his emotions, then turned with a sniff of disgust and strode off deeper into the gardens. Whether he was more disgusted at her apparent weakness or at himself for his own idiocy, he did not know. He just knew he needed to get control of his emotions before he made the situation worse.

Master Castant stood silently on the path watching Marilana weep long after Marquiese had left. Eventually, he moved quietly forward and knelt in front of her, aware of her guard moving closer behind him as well.

"Marilana," he said gently laying his paw on her shoulder, "I know I have little influence in this matter, but I do have a suggestion."

Marilana jumped in surprise and hastily wiped her tears away. "Master Castant," she said hoarsely, "forgive me, I did not realize you were here."

"Relax, Marilana," he said applying pressure on her shoulder to stop her from trying to stand. "I am not here to judge you, and I am not going to report anything to him if you do not wish me to. I just wanted to talk to you—as a friend."

Marilana studied his eyes for a moment, then settled on the ground. Looking away from him she sighed, letting her tears flow freely again.

"When he brought me out here tonight, I thought maybe I was just imagining the suspicion and doubt in his eyes. Apparently not," she said bitterly.

"No, Marilana, there is much doubt in him, but there is also much confusion. I think he brought you out here tonight to try to sort out his feelings for you. He still feels you are betraying him. I do not know what set him off tonight," Castant said gently.

"I have never dreamed of achieving so much in my life. I have ambition, yes, but only to do good, to help people."

"I know that and so does he. He only said those things to hurt you. I do not think he really believes any of what he said. He is confused, unsure of himself or his emotions."

"How can I make him believe that I could never do anything that would hurt him? I did what I had to do to save him."

"Marquiese knows that, but he feels that you did something else and are doing something still that is a betrayal of his trust."

"He will never trust me if he thinks I continue to betray him. I do not know what I am doing to make him feel that way."

"I know. That is why I believe my suggestion will help. He is the only one who can discover the source of this betrayal. I will tell you my plan if you are willing to listen."

"I would do almost anything to gain his trust again," Marilana replied firmly.

Castant smiled. "I want to encourage you to return to Maefair. You must prove yourself to the court. You will have to be confident and controlled. You already act with nobility; you just need to make your presence known. I know Lady Annabella has been encouraging you to decide when to return, but I have some different reasons for it."

"Go on, I am intrigued," she said intently.

"When he is there and you are here, he wonders what you are doing, if you are safe, and feels betrayed. Since we arrived, he has been constantly watching you, keeping track of what you are doing. When he is away from you he is uneasy. When you are near, he is calmer and more like himself—at least until his temper got the better of him. My idea is that if you are close to him, he will be better able to sort out moments that make him feel betrayed rather than feeling betrayed constantly. The tournament provides you with the perfect opportunity to return to court without being ordered there. Yes, you were invited, but so are the other young ladies and noble daughters."

"What you are saying makes sense, but there are many young gentlemen waiting for my return so they can make courtship proposals."

"Well then, post a blanket ban on courtship proposals. Let everyone know that you will not accept any suits, not even from Marquiese, until you feel settled in court life. They do not yet know you, they will want to see if your budding reputation is accurate or not, and they will be glad of any chance to speak with you."

"That way no one will be offended if I out dance them either," Marilana nodded thoughtfully.

"Correct, and they will not push you too hard right now because everyone is waiting for Marquiese to choose his own courtship to pursue."

"Thank you, Master Castant. I will consider all that you have said."

"Please do, Marilana. And if I may make one more suggestion: do not let Marquiese leave the Southern Tip with his last words having been in anger. Your goodbyes the last night you were in Maefair have been a contentious point with him. Sometimes he thinks he did the right thing, and at other times he deeply regrets not sending you off properly. If you send him off better than he sent you, it is more likely he will favorably anticipate your return. Now I wish you a good night," he smiled and stood up.

Marilana remained on the path where he left her, lost in thought.

Marquiese strode angrily down the garden path away from Marilana. He did not know where he was going; he just knew he needed to walk. *How can she treat me like this? How dare she fling hints of her plan in my face? She knows better than to chase after vague hints in a letter. Charging into the Great Mountains to find her family is irresponsible and far too dangerous. What does she think she can accomplish? It's a betrayal, to me, to her people, to her new family. What else is she hiding? How can she betray me like this?* His mind raced with question after question, none answered. As he burst onto a new path, he found Earek approaching him.

"Your Highness, are you alright?" Earek asked as Marquiese strode past him.

"Fine," Marquiese growled.

"You were talking to Marilana," Earek fell into step beside him.

"What kind of question is that?" Marquiese spat.

"More an observation. You were talking to Marilana on a lovely moonlit night, and now you are angrily tearing around the gardens growling at the hedges," Earek said.

"She is deceiving me, Earek," Marquiese said darkly, "and I want to know why. No, I *need* to know why."

"She tries everything to regain your trust or to move on with her life so you can move on with yours. You, however, show her kindness and compassion just to bite off her head."

Marquiese stopped in his tracks and spun around to face Earek. "How dare you accuse me of such actions? I was trying to apologize to her for this afternoon and she put on that act!"

"Forgive me for disagreeing, but I saw no act. She showed you her heart and you sliced it to shreds. I would have thought you of all people would have understood what it meant for her to have found out that the parents she thought were dead were actually alive and in danger."

Marquiese gaped at Earek. "Well, of course I understand. I was apologizing, but she . . . she dismissed it."

"She voiced a wish of her heart that she had already decided she could do nothing about."

"Do nothing about?" Marquiese asked in shock. "I thought she was planning to go look for them. It is what I would have done."

"She knows her position now will not allow her to do so. She accepted the responsibility given to her by Lady Annabella. She will do her duty now just as she did in accepting Master Arndt's courtship," Earek said firmly.

"Courtship? What courtship?" Marquiese growled again.

"You do not know?" asked Earek suddenly wary. "We thought the news would have reached you months ago."

"No, I have heard nothing," Marquiese said coldly. "What courtship of Master Arndt's?"

Earek sighed and glanced downward. "The day before Marilana left for Maefair was the Exhibition Ball at school. The class had an odd number; Marilana was of course told she would not be dancing. Lady Annabella had other plans. She sent messages to Lord Arndt and arranged for Marilana to dance with Master Arndt. You remember that he had been enamored with Marilana since the masquerade; well he agreed to dance the part of Lord Time on the condition that they also perform the courtship dance. Lady Annabella insisted that it would only be a demonstration dance and Master Arndt agreed. Lady Annabella told Marilana to push the limits of the dance but to accept rather than insult him by out-dancing him. So, they danced an amazing dance and the crowds loved it.

"Master Arndt wanted to pursue the courtship for real, but Lady Annabella asked him to wait for two months. If he still wanted to court Marilana after that time, then he could return and arrangements would be made. Of course, Lady Annabella had been planning to name her heirs and then many other events took place as well. When we returned from Maefair, there was a letter already waiting for Lady Annabella. I did not like it, I spoke to Lady Annabella against it, but she was confident that we could be polite and let Marilana take care of herself in this matter. Master Arndt arrived the fifnight after we were back. Lady Annabella asked Marilana to agree to the courtship, and so it started."

"I cannot believe this! She is in the middle of a courtship year, and no one had the decency to tell me of it! I have made a fool of myself—," Marquiese exploded, but Earek interrupted.

"No, Your Highness. Please let me continue," Earek said.

Breathing fast Marquiese waved his paw impatiently and paced across the path.

"Marilana did nothing to encourage Master Arndt. She was pleasant enough, but she took up the task of protecting the Southern Tip from bandit raids, as she had wanted to do. She implemented new patrols and taught the soldiers to communicate silently with gestures. Master Arndt was a bit affronted by her efficiency and tactics, not because they were unethical, but because they were skillful. Still he said that she would move beyond those skills as his wife. He said he was even willing to let her train her own horses in private. When Marilana started to train with her sword again, that was the last straw. He thought it was a joke at first. He did not believe the stories about her fight with Frishka. So, he challenged her to spar against his captain to which Marilana agreed."

"Many of the rumors I hear in Maefair indicate that most of the lordlings do not believe the stories of Marilana's fighting skills. Her reputation is under intense scrutiny," Marquiese mused. "I trust Marilana fared well."

"The fight went as you might expect. The captain approached carefully as if facing a child. Marilana disarmed him on his first attack. She gave him back his sword and told him it was a real match. It made the captain mad, so he attacked with force trying to overpower her. She played with him for a while, parrying and blocking his attacks as she led him around the training ground. He was obviously trying his hardest with lunges and powerful strikes, and she was just as obviously not trying hard as she danced around him. When she disarmed him again, the captain was furious and so was Master Arndt."

"Arndt took Marilana on a walk later that night—much like you did tonight. I trailed them and heard the shouting match. He accused her of lying to him and making a fool of him. She told him that he did not need her help to do that. She also told him that she was not going to act like a shallow, weak girl just because he needed to feel superior. Their quarrel continued a while longer before they stormed off in opposite directions. The next morning Master Arndt met with Lady Annabella and ended the courtship saying that Marilana was too headstrong to make a good wife. The courtship lasted only one fifnight."

Earek smirked slightly at the memory and watched Marquiese pace thoughtfully.

"So, she would not act shallow for him?" Marquiese said with a smirk of his own and stopped pacing. "So brave, bold Master Arndt could not stand Lady Marilana for even one whole fifnight. How very interesting."

Marquiese motioned for Earek to join him and they meandered through more of the gardens.

"I wonder how many other young lordlings are thinking of courting her based solely on her beauty and grace. Those who did not witness the events surrounding Frishka's treason are expressing a disregard of Marilana's bold reputation and alleged bravery. They all have a lot to learn about her," Marquiese commented quietly.

"Quite a few lordlings are looking for her suit, I think," Earek said. "Marilana has received a number of letters asking about her return to the court."

"Really? How interesting. They have no idea what they are walking into. She is not a beast to be tamed as many of them might think. She is intelligent and brave, but I think she takes too many risks," Marquiese said firmly.

"She does what she believes needs to be done," replied Earek.

They walked on for a while in thought. Then Marquiese glanced at Earek. "Am I to understand that you eavesdrop on Marilana's private conversations? Including my own tonight."

Earek grimaced. "I do not eavesdrop, Highness. I protect Marilana in the same manner that Master Castant protects you. I stay within sight of her. I would not have overheard her discussion with Master Arndt or your words to her tonight if there had not been shouting. I was watching behind Master Castant tonight. When he stayed with Marilana, I set off to intercept you."

"Thank you, Earek," Marquiese sighed. "You have helped me to realize my foolishness in assuming too quickly, and to help calm my temper. You did well tonight. I am glad that I chose you as an advisor. I hope Castant has helped Marilana. I hurt her badly. That was not what I had intended to do when I brought her out to the gardens. I just hope I did not inflict too much damage."

"We will deal with what tomorrow brings," Earek replied quietly.

"Yes, we will. For now, though, we should be going to bed. I want to leave early tomorrow. Goodnight, my friend," Marquiese said turning toward the castle.

"Goodnight, Marquiese," Earek said and turned down another garden path.

12

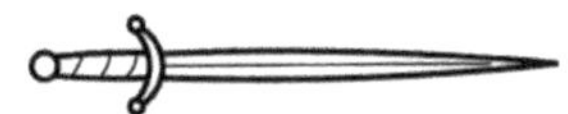

The next morning Marquiese awoke again to shouting voices and stamping hooves in the busy stableyard. He watched from his window while servants gathered his things. He saw Earek lead a group of scouts out through the gate and wondered when he would see him again. He scanned the other people moving around, but did not see Marilana anywhere. Taking a deep calming breath, he left his rooms and walked to Marilana's room. He was determined to speak with her and not let his temper flare up again. When he arrived at her door, a servant was just closing the door on her way out.

"I wish to speak to Lady Marilana," he said quietly.

"I'm sorry, Highness, she is not here," said the young tigress with a curtsey.

"What? Where is she?" he asked slightly alarmed.

"I'm sorry. I don't know," she said.

"Do you know when she left?" he asked.

"She came back early this morning to change her clothing and then left again, Highness," she said curtseying again.

The familiar sting of betrayal rose, but he determinedly shoved it to the back of his thoughts as he headed for the stableyard. Master Castant met him on the castle steps.

"Marilana returned to her rooms early this morning only to change and then left," Marquiese said urgently. "When was the last time you saw her? Was she alright?"

"I left her in the gardens right where you last saw her. She was better when I left her, but still very quiet. Storm was gone by the time I started preparations for your departure," Castant replied.

"I know what I did was wrong, Castant. I wanted to speak to her before we left," Marquiese sighed. "Did you know she had entered a courtship with Master Arndt that lasted only one fifnight?"

"No. I had not heard, not even any rumors," Castant said grimly.

"Earek told me last night. My suspicion is that Master Arndt does not want anyone to know of his humiliation. Apparently, many of the other lordlings have sent her letters too."

"That would make sense; he does not like losing at anything. Marilana also mentioned the young lordlings wanting to court her. They may be thinking that she will be looking for a quick courtship to stay out of your way."

Marquiese shook his head. "She will not do that. She is strong enough to lead by herself, and will only accept a suitor she truly wishes to live with. Earek said she did not encourage the courtship."

Marquiese glanced around the stableyard from the steps. He watched the people moving about, carefully trying to spot Marilana.

"Where is she?" he wondered aloud.

A coyote in the uniform of a Ranat Family guard climbed the steps and approached them.

"Your Highness," he said with a low bow, "I am Major Guardsman Kolt and I am in charge of your escort to the border. You appear to be searching for something. Lady Annabella will see you off momentarily."

"Thank you, but I was hoping Lady Marilana would have returned," Marquiese replied.

"Yes," he said bowing again, "Lady Marilana asked me to inform you that she will be joining you for lunch close to the Grudent border. She departed early to secure your road. Master Earek will also meet you later this morning. We are ready to ride with you, Your Highness."

Kolt bowed again and descended the steps to wait. Marquiese studied him thoughtfully.

"Marilana appears to have put a lot of effort into your safety," Castant remarked quietly.

"Indeed, she has," said Marquiese.

"Ah, Prince Marquiese, I believe everything is ready now," said Lady Annabella descending the steps behind him.

Marquiese turned, exchanging smiles with her.

"I wish you a safe journey and please return if you ever feel the need," she curtseyed to him.

"Thank you, Lady Annabella. Your hospitality is always enjoyable. Shall I be returning the joy in a month?" he said with a slight bow.

"You shall. I would not dream of missing the annual tournament."

"Then I shall see you in a month's time, Lady. Farewell until then."

"May The Goddess keep you, Your Highness. Farewell," she replied.

Marquiese descended the steps to his waiting horse, mounted, and started toward the gates. His entourage fell in behind him, and Lady Annabella's men arranged themselves to either side. He waited until they were well on their way along the road north before calling Major Guardsman Kolt to ride with him. Kolt rode easily, scanning the trees and road ahead as they plodded along.

"You serve Lady Annabella well, Major Guardsman. Your men are quick and attentive," Marquiese said.

"Thank you, Highness. I learned well in service to Lady Annabella, but now I serve Lady Marilana," Kolt said.

"You serve the heiress but not the lady?" asked Marquiese surprised. "Would you please explain this to me?"

"Of course, Highness," the coyote said lightly. "Several months ago, Lady Annabella requested that Lady Marilana choose at least four men to be her personal guards. Lady Marilana consented and chose six men, three for day and three for night. Master Earek also agreed to take on personal guards and chose two men, one for day and one for night."

"That is good news," nodded Marquiese. "Can you tell me why Lady Marilana assigned three for day and night? Would it not serve better to have four for day and only two at night? Surely there is more work to be done during the day."

"That may be true for other nobles, but Lady Marilana is not like other nobles. We laugh that we seem to get more sleep than M'Lady does," Kolt said lightly. "She rises early and retires late so her guards spend very little time just standing at her door."

"You seem very relaxed in her service. Might I ask how she chose her guards? Was it perhaps random, or was there some pattern that she followed?

"It took M'Lady and Master Earek a long time to choose their guards. It was by no means random, Highness, though it may appear that way. They both observed training sessions and conducted interviews with soldiers, guardsmen, and captains all. M'Lady also challenged men to spar with her," said Kolt.

"Archery contests of course," stated Marquiese slightly shocked.

"No, Highness, swordsmanship," Kolt smiled.

"She took only those who refused?" asked Marquiese.

"No, only one man who refused made it in to the final six. She does things her own way for her own reasons, Highness."

"So, you fought her!" raged Marquiese.

"Yes, Highness, we train with her every morning. All six of us together," Kolt said unaffected by Marquiese's tone.

"Every morning!" gasped Marquiese. "She used to only train in private with Captain-General Zariff."

"Yes, Highness. When she trained with you and later with Master Earek, she found that she needed a greater challenge to continue to improve her skills. Also, by training together, we learn how to work as a single unit. It prevents us from getting in each other's way and it prevents accidents. She is very formidable with a sword. It is usually she and Captain Hayden against the rest of us. They are the better swordsmen and so it challenges us and makes us better too," Kolt said with a smile.

"Do you think it is a game, Major Kolt? Will you die for her? Do you owe her any allegiance at all? Or do you laugh when people kill each other?" said Marquiese with annoyance.

Kolt's entire posture shifted. He sat stiffly in his saddle and gripped his sword hilt. Gone was the laughter and smile from his face, a stone seemed warmer and softer than his expression. It seemed to Marquiese that a completely different coyote now rode beside him, all powerful muscle and sinew. Even his voice had become sharp and icy cold when he spoke again in a measured tone.

"I owe Lady Marilana my life, Your Highness. She saved my three sisters and me from horrible deaths at the paws of bandits. It is the greatest joy of my life to serve her. I will obey her every command. I would gladly die for her. I spar with her on the condition that she teaches me to be a better swordsman. She teaches me gladly. I swore my life to The Goddess for her, Your Highness," Kolt growled Marquiese's title dangerously.

Marquiese could almost feel the threat aimed at him from the young Major. He considered calling Kolt down for disrespect, but decided against it as he had pushed Kolt's temper. He took a calming breath and relaxed his posture, reminding himself that he would gladly spar with Marilana every morning, too.

"I am glad to hear it, Major Guardsman," replied Marquiese. "I take Lady Marilana's safety very seriously. Are the others as loyal to her as you are? Does she always have one of you with her?"

"Yes, Your Highness, the others are just as loyal," replied Kolt, and Marquiese was relieved that there was no lingering malice in his cold voice. "One of us is always nearby, however, we respect her right to private conversations."

"You let her speak in private with anyone, without any thought about her safety?" asked Marquiese, his temper rising again.

"No, Highness," replied Kolt with a slight smile, "we alert Master Earek and he does the eavesdropping."

Marquiese could not stop his smile. Earek had taken to his position of Marilana's protector very well if he was collaborating with her guards.

"Tell me one last thing, Major Kolt," Marquiese said gravely. "Does Lady Marilana approve of your telling anyone who asks about her tactics and yours?"

Major Kolt grinned slightly, "No, Your Highness. She said not to tell anyone anything, except for you. My orders were to answer all your questions as best as I could. She said she keeps no secrets from you."

"Thank you, Major Guardsman Kolt. I appreciate your honesty and congratulate you on a job well done. You may return to your post," Marquiese said softly.

"Thank you, Your Highness," Kolt replied with a bow and then turned his horse back to his men.

Marquiese smiled as he thought about Major Kolt's words. He deeply inhaled the warm air, and marveled at the beautiful morning.

*

Marquiese was still smiling mid-morning when Kolt rode ahead to where several large trees lined the east side of the road. Shortly after the Major halted, a group of horses emerged from the trees. Marquiese scanned the group for signs of unease, but did not halt his column. As the column approached, the horsemen turned back to the trees and disappeared. Kolt remained on the road, turning to the west. Two more horsemen appeared from the trees on that side and rode up to meet Kolt on the road. Marquiese was pleased to see that Earek was one of the horsemen.

Earek reined his horse up and approached Marquiese as the column reached the meeting point. Kolt and a vaguely familiar grey wolf took positions with the escort. Marquiese waved for Earek to approach.

"Master Earek, I must say how pleased I am to have you join us," Marquiese said.

"Thank you, Your Highness," replied Earek with a bow. "I hope your morning has gone well."

"Yes, indeed it has," said Marquiese smiling. "I had a very interesting conversation with Major Guardsman

Kolt. I was pleased to hear that you and Marilana have found some loyal guards. Was that one of your men riding with you?"

"That was Guardsman Shaub, a very trustworthy wolf who accepted a position as my personal guard. He is more loyal to Lady Annabella than me, but we work well together."

"I seem to remember seeing him at the castle when I was in hiding. I am sure he believes you will make a good lord," Marquiese said lightly.

"Indeed, he does, and he is very fond of Marilana as well and wants to assist us both as best as he can. My other guard is of like mind."

"That is good. What about Marilana's guards? Are they pleased with how the future looks?"

"I could not wish for six better men to help and protect her. They are so loyal to her that they take any barb aimed at her as a personal insult. They are strong leaders and very proud, but not so proud as to ignore criticisms. They are constantly looking to improve their skills."

"Is it true what Major Kolt said, that they spar with Marilana every morning?" Marquiese asked.

"Yes, it is the most amazing display of skill I have ever seen. I would not dare to challenge even one of them to private battle, let alone all of them together."

"They are that good?" asked Marquiese surprised.

"Yes," said Earek gravely, "you know Marilana's skills. She has taught her men how to fight like she does.

She pushes them to be better. I think they could even give you a good challenge."

"Major Kolt said one of them refused to spar with Marilana. How does that work for practice?" asked Marquiese.

"Captain Hayden refuses to raise his sword against her. He said he would rather she kill him than ever fight her. In the mornings, he stands back-to-back with her as the other five attack. He trusts her to keep his back just as she trusts him with her life."

"And they spar with real swords?"

"No," Earek laughed, "not one of them would agree to that, even though Marilana originally challenged them with her steel blade. She gave all the men who wanted to be her guards the choice of real or practice swords against her real blade. These five accepted the challenge and grabbed the practice swords. When she disarmed the interviewees or if they refused to fight, she placed her sword to their throats and asked if they were ready to die. These six men gave the same response. They knelt in front of her, heads high, and said that if death was what she wanted of them, then they would gladly die for her. She pushed the issue by placing the point of her blade to their skin and prepared to deliver the killing thrust. Again, the six of them did not flinch or show any signs of fear. All the others she interviewed backed out at some point. Some were appalled at her orders, some remarked that she should not bear a weapon, a few laughed at her threat to kill them, and others begged for mercy. She was very careful in choosing; she knows she has a lot of enemies."

"Ah, I see," said Marquiese. "She did not just choose by skill or apparent loyalties. She made them prove their loyalty and resolve."

"Yes," said Earek, "she has made enemies of locals, bandits, rich, and poor. Some are more dangerous and others more cunning. She had to be sure that she could trust these men to protect her at her weakest moments, and that they would trust her enough to obey her without question. In fact, she has given them standing orders that if she dies in battle they are to leave and save themselves. They are not to die defending her body. They all said that they would obey the part about not dying gladly, but the part about leaving her body reluctantly. She prays that she never gives them cause to obey that order."

"Her heart is a most wondrous gift. She thinks of others with no care for herself. Yet she is also one of the most formidable people I have ever known," remarked Marquiese fondly.

They rode slowly in silence for a while. Marquiese studied the country around them.

"What is Marilana's design for my protection?" Marquiese finally asked with a frown. "Did she sleep at all last night?"

"She said she would sleep this morning when she reached the border regions. After leaving you last night, I went in search of her. I found her changed and dispatching orders. She sent out two patrols to scout the areas parallel to your road. She led another group along your road to check for any dangers, and left orders for my group and your escort. I slept before leading my group out early to secure the first half of your road. She is securing the second half to the border," said Earek quietly.

"She seems to think there is great danger for me in these regions," mused Marquiese.

"I only know my orders, not her reasons for giving them. However since your errand rider unfortunately died carrying the message of your arrival, you were attacked on the road south, and you brought news of the bandits rallying behind a single leader, I would chance to say yes, there is great danger to you here," replied Earek nodding his head.

"You sound like a soldier, my merchant friend," said Marquiese lightly.

Earek laughed, "I am Marilana's Major-General, her second in command. If she takes Lady Annabella's place, I will take Zariff's position as Captain-General. I have learned more of what it means to be a solider than I ever thought I would."

"I can tell," Marquiese smiled. "It suits you well. You will make a good Captain-General, or Great-Lord."

"Thank you, Highness," Earek replied.

They fell silent again. The sun rose higher in the sky, and the trees slowly thinned, giving way to farms and hills. As mid-day drew near, Marquiese was still scanning the scenery. No riders appeared and no one entered the road; not even the shadows stirred. Finally, just as the sun reached its zenith, Marquiese called a halt and told the men to rest the horses and break out the rations.

"I thought Marilana would be joining us for lunch," Marquiese said, slightly terse.

"And so, she is," replied Earek pointing. "Look there, Your Highness, on that hill."

Marquiese's gaze followed Earek's finger. A horse and rider had appeared on a low hill where there had been nothing a moment before. They gleamed in the sunlight, almost too bright to look at. Then the rider turned and disappeared again. Marquiese followed Earek's lead and dismounted. He set about taking care of his horse and pulling out his rations. Just as he finished, he heard hooves approaching. He turned to see a pair of riders emerging onto the road ahead and making their way to his party. Marilana dismounted and curtseyed to him. The black bear guardsman that rode with her likewise dismounted and bowed before retreating to where Major Kolt stood.

"Your Highness, I trust you have had a pleasant journey so far," Marilana said politely, but did not quite meet his eye. "Please, let us eat. We do not want you to be late to your destination."

"I am not worried about being late. We left early and ride very slowly to enjoy the day on the road," he replied. Marquiese offered his paw to her and led her away from the group to a low stone wall bordering a field. They sat and ate quietly. Marquiese watched Marilana as they ate, she seemed serene, but in control.

"I wanted to apologize for my behavior last night—," Marquiese began, but Marilana interrupted.

"My Lord, Marquiese, please don't. You are the Crown Prince; you should never take back things that you say." She gazed down at her lap.

"No, Marilana," he continued firmly, "last night I was a man like any other. I made a fool of myself and now I am taking responsibility for my actions. I said things in anger with no other purpose than to hurt you. I am deeply sorry for that. I never wanted to see you hurt, and yet I was the one who hurt you. Now I am asking if you can forgive a fool."

"Thank you for your kind gesture," she replied softly, "I would forgive you anything."

Marquiese cleared his throat and pushed on, "I have been thinking a lot this morning. Mostly about what to say to you."

Marilana glanced up at him briefly then returned her gaze to her lap.

"I really do want you to come back to the palace. You had to interrupt your studies and I would like to see you complete them."

"That would be pleasant. I am sure Sir Libor would be pleased to continue teaching me," she replied.

"Yes, he has mentioned the joys of having such a ready and intelligent pupil," Marquiese said softly. "I also would enjoy your company."

"Your Highness is too kind. Circumstances will be different this time. If I return, it will be in my own right as heir to a great-noble, not as your peasant friend. I will have to play the game properly now," Marilana said.

"Yes," Marquiese smiled ruefully, "but I do not fear for you in that game. I think the other nobles will find you a formidable opponent."

"Thank you, Highness," she said.

"I worry more about the many young suitors waiting for your return. I believe they hope to tame a wild spirit," he said lightly.

Marilana glanced over to where Earek and Castant sat laughing. Her guards stood not far away and the rest of Marquiese's entourage and Marilana's escort tended to the horses along the sides of the road. She watched them for a moment and then a smirk lit up her face.

"A free spirit cannot be tamed," she said finally.

Marquiese laughed, "Only a fool would try to tame or control you. I would never attempt to harness you or put you on display."

Marquiese smiled more for the color that rose in her cheeks. Marilana fidgeted and averted her gaze. He placed his paw lightly on her knee. She took a deep breath and turned back to face him. Still, she did not quite meet his eyes.

"I fear to leave you, My Lady, but I am glad you have surrounded yourself with trusted men. I am also glad that we have smiled together today," he said.

He stood and offered his paw. She took his paw in hers, and they returned to the horses. The men prepared to ride on and soon everyone was mounted except Marilana and Marquiese.

"These men are to escort you to Lord Arndt's estates, where I am told you plan to stop for a few nights," Marilana said.

"Yes, thank you for the added protection. Will I see you again soon?" he asked.

Marilana gazed over the fields frowning in thought. Storm ambled from where he had been sniffing the brown grass to her side and nuzzled her shoulder. She scratched his nose absently.

"I need to think about it," she replied quietly turning and fully meeting his gaze. "Pleasant journey, Prince Marquiese."

He studied her eyes for a moment, then nodded, accepting that he would not get a better answer, that she needed time after his harsh words and subsequent apology. He mounted and she curtseyed to him as he started forward. He looked back for one more sight of her, but she and Earek were already gone.

13

Marquiese paced impatiently at the edge of the tents. The pennants and flags waving lazily in the breeze were tinted golden by the rising sun. The city tournament field was packed with people. Nobles' carriages, people afoot, and hawkers pushing carts streamed past in every direction. The spectator stands were nearly full, yet more people were arriving and crowding around the jousting list. The tents for the combatants were off-limits to most people and more serene, but the relative quiet did nothing to calm Marquiese's nerves. As the Crown Prince, he had received a stream of well-wishers, including most of the other combatants, yet he could not stand still. He finally stopped pacing when he spotted Master Castant weaving his way through the crowd.

"Well, is she here yet?" Marquiese called out when Castant was closer.

"Highness, please be patient. Lady Annabella said she would not miss the tournament. They will come," Castant replied calmly.

Marquiese snorted and began pacing again. "What other news?"

"All the combatants are here. Only a few nobles have yet to arrive. It is time we should finish your arming," Castant raised his arm toward the tents with a slight bow.

Marquiese sighed and cast another look toward the Nobles' Box. "Very well, lead on."

Half an hour later Marquiese and Castant exited the Royal tent. The polished armor Marquiese wore glinted brightly in the early morning sunlight. Castant carried Marquiese's helm under his arm. They walked to the edge of the tents while a squire ran to bring Marquiese's charger.

"Highness, look there," Castant said pointing toward the Nobles' Box.

When Marquiese turned, he saw a dark carriage stop at the platform. The crowds had moved to the stands. Only a few stragglers hurried to find room to see. Marquiese grinned as Earek jumped from his place next to the driver and rushed toward him. Marquiese watched the footman open the carriage door and lower the step.

Earek halted and bowed. "My Lady Annabella, of the Southern Tip, bade me wish Your Highness good fortune today."

"Thank you, Master Earek," Marquiese replied still watching the carriage.

Lady Annabella descended, taking a moment to smooth her dress. It was a beautiful garment of dark green slashed with silver that sparkled in the sunlight, complemented with a dark green veil.

"I was also instructed to give this to Master Castant," Earek said giving Castant a small scroll. "Please forgive my haste, but I must join My Lady."

Marquiese frowned as Earek hurried back to where Lady Annabella and the carriage waited.

"What does it say?" urged Marquiese nervously.

Castant unfurled the scroll, and then smiled broadly.

"It simply says 'I have come'," he laughed. "It is not even signed."

Marquiese sighed with relief as a paw extended from the carriage and the footman assisted Marilana down the step. If he had thought Lady Annabella looked nice, she was nothing compared to Marilana. She was resplendent in a dark green dress with long open silver sleeves, a silver belt, and a shimmering silver veil. She glowed as she followed Lady Annabella to the Nobles' Box.

Marquiese let out a relaxed laugh and clapped Castant on his shoulder as the squire trotted up with his horse.

"Come, my friend, to business. I have a tournament to win," he smiled.

Marilana smiled at Earek as he returned to the carriage. She had waited until Castant had looked down at her note before emerging. It was a planned entrance of sorts and now that she could be seen, she would not look toward Marquiese.

"Hurry up. We must get to our seats quickly," Annabella called.

Earek fell into step with Marilana as they trailed Annabella to the stands.

"They were both relieved to see us arrive," he whispered quickly.

"Good, thank you for telling me," she whispered back.

They followed Annabella up the back of the stands and then down to their reserved seats in the front row. An elderly leopard stood to let them pass his seat. He greeted them warmly.

"Lord Castant, I am truly glad to see you again," Marilana said when she reached the great-noble of Draukshar.

"As am I, child," he said with a bow and kissed her paw. "Please, will you sit by me?"

Marilana glanced at Annabella who nodded. "Of course, My Lord."

No sooner had they taken their seats with Annabella between Marilana and Earek, when a great trumpet fanfare brought them to their feet again. Cheers erupted from the spectators as the curtain of the King's Box was drawn back. King Rylan and Prince Marquiese stood waving to the cheering crowds. King Rylan raised his paws to quiet the uproar. Slowly silence fell.

"Welcome to the annual tournament in honor of my birthday and the birthday of my son. I thank The Goddess for the fine weather. Now for the moment you are all waiting for. Let the tournament begin," Rylan called out to the crowds and threw a rose onto the list.

Marilana could hear his words clearly because the Nobles' Box was directly across from the King's Box, but most of the spectators could not. However, everyone could see the tossing of the rose to indicate the start of the tournament. The crowds roared. Rylan embraced his son, and Marquiese left the King's Box. The crowds cheered even louder for the show of affection between king and prince.

As the King and nobles seated themselves, a rumbling sound emanated from behind the stands. Galloping horses burst into the arena at the north and south ends of the list. Twenty knights, banners fluttering on raised lances, circled twice in front of the cheering spectators before reining into formation in front of the King. As one, the knights bowed to the King, and he bowed his head in return. The knights turned and bowed to the nobles. The great-lords and ladies acknowledged with their own bows. The knights then wheeled their mounts, forming two lines, and cantered back around the arena once and out the gates.

As the last knights exited, squires jumped to their tasks. Poles with rings were set at intervals along the list. Lances were brought in and arranged at both ends. The first group of four knights entered and prepared for their runs.

Lord Castant leaned toward Marilana. "The first round is not an elimination round. After the rings, the jousting will begin. This tournament will not be as elaborate as the last one you attended. That tournament was special because it had a specific goal to win. This one honors an event and is held every year. It marks the end of a fifnight-long festival for the commoners. For us nobles, the grand ball tomorrow night tends to be more climatic. Tomorrow the knights will rest so they are fit to dance with all the lovely ladies. I know you will enjoy yourself."

"I am sure I will, today as much as tomorrow," replied Marilana. "I do love tournaments."

Marilana felt a large paw rest lightly on her shoulder as the knights began their first charge. She turned to look up into a big brown bear's kindly face.

"Come now, Lord Castant, keep to the topics in front of us," he said in a low gravelly voice. "I am Lord Roana, my dear Lady Marilana. My son has spoken highly of you."

"Pleased to finally meet you, My Lord Roana," Marilana replied with a smile to the great-noble of Mira's Plateau. "Master Timral is competing today; is he not?"

"Yes, he is. Now you see here, Marilana," he said indicating the arena, "the rings are a test of skill, much safer than the jousting. The points earned at the rings will determine the jousting order by allowing the judges to pair evenly-matched knights for each elimination round. The highest knights, however, will not be pitted against each other until the Jousting of Champions."

He paused as the crowds applauded for the scoring of the first round. Marilana spoke as the cheers quieted.

"Thank you for the insight, My Lord. The rings are also a good way for the knights and their horses to warm up before the jousting. Properly warmed horses are less likely to sustain injuries at the impact of lance to rider," she smiled kindly.

Lord Castant laughed at Lord Roana's surprise and then said, "You see, Roana, many of these horses are trained in the Southern Tip, and some have been trained personally by Marilana. She has been training horses for Lady Annabella for years. She is very knowledgeable about the different competitions, even highly skilled at some. Although this is only the second tournament she has attended."

Lord Roana recovered from his surprise and smiled. "I had heard that you trained horses, but I did not realize you trained these horses. I will watch them closely. You will point out which ones are yours?"

"I would be honored to, My Lord," she said looking down at the second group of knights. "The chestnut ridden by Sir Graduin, the dapple ridden by Master Clain, and the black ridden by Sir Tavin are three of my five horses here today. The knights of Pandensy are riding the other two."

"I will watch for them. Thank you. It has been a pleasure talking with you, Marilana," he said and leaned back to greet another lord who had come to speak with him.

Marilana turned her attention back to the arena and Lady Annabella leaned close to her.

"That was well done," Annabella said softly, "Lord Roana is a good friend and a wise man. You did well not to embarrass him."

"I do not intend to make any enemies if I can help it," Marilana replied.

"That is a wise choice, my dear."

Marilana smiled as the crowd cheered for the second group. The three knights on her mounts had all scored well. The two knights from Pandensy were in the third group. Master Roatal scored very poorly, but Marilana knew his mount was not best suited to the rings. Master Orthan had scored surprisingly well considering he was young and this was his first time competing at this level. Marilana watched them, but was also attuned to the movements around her. Many lords and ladies moved about the box speaking to each other. Some spoke to Earek or herself, but most spoke to Lady Annabella. She was well-known and respected. Thankfully, Lord Arndt did not approach them. Lord Castant remained in his seat, and like Annabella, was approached by many.

Marquiese rode into the arena with the fifth, and final, group. He performed flawlessly and earned the highest score. The crowd cheered wildly for his score. As he left, the squires swarmed the arena, quickly taking down the poles and erecting the fence for the joust. Servants likewise swarmed the Nobles' Box, offering hors d'oeuvres and drinks. Marilana followed Annabella's lead and took a glass of sparkling cider, but declined the food. Annabella and Earek sampled some of the cocktail meats and cheeses, and Earek took a glass of light wine. The servants retreated to the back of the box as the first jousters entered the list. Lord Roana had taken the vacant seat next to Earek and engaged him in a discussion of jousting techniques. Marilana heard Earek laugh and claim he was not good enough yet to compete in such a high competition; after all, he had only been training for eight months, and for part of that time he had been unable to practice.

Marilana glanced around the box as she signaled for a servant to collect her glass. She noted that the noble daughters had taken up positions where they could watch and be seen by the knights. As she was already in a prime location, she did not move, and turned her attention back to the arena.

"Do you wish to become more prominent?" asked Annabella innocently.

"More?" Marilana laughed. "All of the knights have already seen me sitting here. If I move, they will have to search for me. Besides, I am not looking for a courtship yet. The ban has been issued. This prime position was mine before the tournament began and I will keep it because I am not running away from being seen. Let the other Daughters vie amongst themselves. We will see what comes of it."

"Yes, I fear we will. Look you have already intrigued some poor fool," Annabella grinned as the first two knights approached seeking a lady's color for which to honor. One was Master Arndt, who pointedly did not look at her. The other knight just as pointedly did not waver from her.

"Might I have the honor of riding under your colors, Lady Marilana?" he asked with a bow.

Standing up, Marilana smiled down at Master Roatal of Pandensy. She produced a large kerchief of green and silver and gracefully laid it in his gauntlet.

"My honor to you Master Roatal, and to your mount," she replied.

Lord Castant leaned toward her as she resumed her seat.

"That is one of your horses; is it not?" he asked.

"Yes, it is. A magnificent bay, but a bit too heavy for the rings. He will do better in the joust," she said critically.

They watched closely as the knights faced off. The flag dropped, the horses charged, and the lances dropped into position. Crack! Both lances splintered apart as they each found their mark. Master Arndt hit the ground in a clatter of metal. Master Roatal halted his mount, then turned and rode back to his end of the list.

"I see what you mean," said Lord Castant impressed. "He did not even miss a step when the lances struck. He took the full weight of the impact with both hind feet on the ground. Marvelous."

The ring of steel on steel sounded through the cheers and whistles of the crowd. The two knights fought hard sword-to-sword. Round and round, they circled, this way and that, until with a dull thwack Master Arndt lost his blade. Marilana suppressed a smile. Master Arndt was the first knight to be eliminated. It was not that she wished him ill, but she did not respect his skills as a swordsman. Also, she was pleased that the first knight to ride for her honor, and the first of her mounts, was not eliminated immediately. She applauded along with everyone else.

Both knights stood breathing hard. Master Arndt retrieved his sword, and then they bowed together to King Rylan. The King acknowledged them and named Master Roatal the victor. Master Arndt turned at once, stalking toward his end of the list. Master Roatal, however, turned toward the Nobles' Box and bowed. Marilana nodded to him in acknowledgement. Whispers broke out behind her as Master Roatal strode briskly to his end of the list. The next knights waited to enter the arena.

There were ten matches in the first round of eliminations. The other four knights riding her horses also rode under her colors, and each bowed to her after being named victor of their match. She knew they had planned to honor her in some way for training their mounts, but this was much more honor than she had expected. She would have to thank them later. None of the five wanted to court her, of course; they all had loves of their own and were very loyal. However, they respected her for her skills, and they had acquired their mounts before she had been named Lady Annabella's heiress. They had sent her congratulations on her new title, and all agreed that she deserved it. She liked them, and thought they would make good allies. Two other knights also asked to ride under her colors. By the ninth match she had given out seven of her kerchiefs and was pleased that she had thought ahead and brought extras. She also expected she would be doing a lot of dancing at tomorrow's ball. Only one of the knights to ride under her colors was eliminated.

The last match of the first round was Marquiese's. It was nearly half an hour before high noon when Marquiese entered the arena. He rode easily to the Nobles' Box and—ignoring all the flirtations from the noble daughters—asked Mistress Lorlina for the honor of riding under her colors. The tall clouded leopard smiled at him nervously and gave him her kerchief. He gave Lorlina a slight bow with a warm smile and then rode to his end of the list. Marilana wondered what he was up to. She knew he would not think to court the girl Master Timral loved.

Marilana schooled her features to calm interest and tried to control her breathing during the match. Many noble daughters gasped and swooned every time Marquiese was hit, but not Marilana. She clenched her paws and clamped her jaws shut to stop her winces. Marquiese unhorsed his opponent on the first pass, and quickly disarmed him. Marilana knew that Marquiese could win the tournament—she had trained with him, after all, and knew his skills to rival her own—but she hated the thought that he might get hurt, or lose due to something unforeseen. She also had to admit that some of the other competitors were showing their skills to be just as proficient.

After Marquiese left the list, the servants again moved among the nobles offering trays of finger foods, small bowls of soups, and drinks. Marilana accepted a bowl of vegetable soup and another glass of cider. The nobles milled about, clearly enjoying the light lunch. Most of the noble daughters, including Marilana, remained where they were so someone else did not take their position. Marilana noted that many of the noble daughters were not eating much. She wasn't sure if they were refraining to keep their figures shapely or because of nerves. She could see some looked pale and guessed they also had butterflies flitting in their stomachs. She hoped her discomfort wasn't so obvious.

The second round of eliminations consisted of only five matches, which would leave five knights for the Jousting of Champions. Marilana watched the pairings with interest. Two of the knights riding her mounts were paired together, and the others faced some very tough competitors. Master Clain, riding on her dapple, defeated Master Roatal with difficulty in their match. Marilana could not decide if she was disappointed to see her other mounts defeated, or if she was glad that none were eliminated by Marquiese. She was relieved to see Marquiese defeat the knight facing him, even though the knight carried her colors. Only one other knight, a Master Lotal, had asked to ride under her colors—and this for his second time. She had never met the grey fox before, and Lady Annabella only said that his mother was great-noble of Eastridge. Marilana again wondered what Marquiese was doing when he rode this time under Mistress Ailse's colors. He had another easy victory.

When Marquiese left the list, Lord Castant resumed his seat next to Marilana. He had been engaged in a lengthy discussion with some nobles and seemed exasperated by the effort.

"Some people," he said in an undertone, "should never try to understand skills that they have never tried."

Marilana chuckled, "Too true, My Lord."

Marilana declined the delicate sugar flowers and artful deserts that a servant offered, but took a glass of light wine. Lord Castant took a sip from his own glass then waved a paw toward the arena.

"Five very skilled knights," he said to her. "Prince Marquiese, Master Roana, Master Clain, Master Lotal, and Sir Frauh. These last ten matches will be thrilling. The Jousting of the Champions is a little different in that it is not instant elimination. Instead the knights will face each other for a score, and the knight with the highest score will be named Champion of Redsands. Marquiese won last year, which surprised a lot of people since he had been away for three years. Of course, you know that he had not stopped training during that time. This style of competition is more entertaining for the spectators since there would be so few rounds otherwise."

"I also see wisdom to this arrangement," said Marilana, "as it allows the top five competitors the chance to test each other's skills and compare each to the others."

"Indeed, it does. You are a bright young woman," he grinned and patted her paw as the first two knights entered the arena.

Marilana was surprised to see Marquiese was in the first match since he had just competed, but she supposed it was arranged by the luck of a draw. She sat forward as she recognized the other knight was Master Timral Roana. She had heard that Timral had won the tournament the two years previous to Marquiese's return. She had thought that they would not face off until the last match, but it appeared that luck had placed them in the first match. Timral, of course, asked to ride for Lorlina's colors as he had every round, and Marquiese asked to ride for the honor of Mistress Phoebe. The zebra nearly fainted when he asked and needed help to give him her colors. Marilana did not know the girl, but suppressed a sniff of disdain for her weak countenance.

Marquiese and Timral were indeed well matched in a marvelous display of skill. They each broke three lances before Marquiese succeeded in unhorsing Timral. Marilana leaned forward in anticipation as they fought on foot. Their speed and agility made her catch her breath. Back and forth they fought, neither able to land a blow or to lock blades for a disarming maneuver. Timral was larger and had a longer reach, but Marquiese danced around more, darting in and out. Suddenly Timral swung at Marquiese's middle and Marilana gasped; she knew what was coming next. Marquiese spun around the attack and stepped in close. In the blink of an eye it was over. Marquiese finished his spin and stepped back with both swords in his paws. The crowd erupted. Marilana sat back with her paw covering her mouth, not hiding her shock, but her smile. Marquiese glanced up at the Nobles' Box briefly before returning Timral's sword. Then they turned and bowed to King Rylan.

"Well, I must say," started Lord Castant with surprise, "that was the most impressive move I have ever seen. Well done, well done indeed."

He stood and clapped loudly along with the other lords and even some of the ladies. Mistress Phoebe lay on the floor of the box where she had fainted. Several ladies were working to revive her. Marilana shook her head and watched Timral and Marquiese shake paws before leaving the arena. It had been a match to remember, a very close contest.

Master Clain and Master Lotal entered the arena next and Lotal asked to ride for her honor for a third time. Marilana had the feeling she would be very glad to be done dancing with him at the ball. He was quite persistent in his efforts to gain her attention. Marilana was quite pleased when Master Clain managed to win the intense match. Next was Master Timral against Sir Frauh, another difficult match. Sir Frauh was not a lordling, he was of peasant lineage, but served as a Captain in the Home Guard of Versith and was one of the best swordsmen Marilana had ever seen. Master Timral barely managed to win with a risky back-armed parry and disarm.

The fourth match was between Marquiese and Master Clain. Marquiese unhorsed Master Clain on the second pass, and they fought hard on foot. Marquiese rode under the colors of a Mistress Katrine, and while the slender gazelle paled, at least she did not faint when he won. Marilana was glad when Master Clain shook Marquiese's paw at the end of the match. She did not want them to be enemies. The next match was between Sir Frauh and Master Lotal. Lotal was no match for Sir Frauh's fast sword play and again lost under her colors. Then Master Timral defeated Master Clain.

Marquiese entered the arena for his third joust of the round and faced Sir Frauh. This time Marquiese rode under the colors of Lady Ophelia. Marilana learned that Ophelia was the daughter heir of Lord Castant's cousin,

Lord Ruberic of Herinsford. From the look on Ophelia's face, though, Marilana suspected that the leopard was not pleased with Marquiese honoring her above the other more flirtatious options. Marilana again wondered if Marquiese was picking ladies who truly did not wish to be courted by him. It was another thrilling match, as both fought hard and skillfully. Marquiese succeeded in unhorsing Sir Frauh with his second lance, but they were very evenly matched in the sword. Back and forth they paced, Sir Frauh used his quick antelope speed for several fast spinning jabs, and Marquiese was forced to give ground before attacking back. Finally, Marquiese thrust forward with a series of quick attacks and, with a sharp rap of his blade to Sir Frauh's crossguard, sent the blade spinning across the arena. Sir Frauh seemed jubilant with his loss to the Crown Prince—it had been a well fought match, he gained considerable honor losing to royalty—and, like Timral and Clain, shook paws with Marquiese before leaving the list.

The sun still shone high in the western sky; it was mid-afternoon, and three jousts remained. Marilana anticipated a climatic end. The five competitors were reaching their final scores. Master Lotal had lost two of two matches, Master Clain had won one of three, Sir Frauh had won two of three, Master Timral had also won two of three, and Marquiese had won three of three. If Frauh and Timral won their last matches, and Marquiese lost his, it would be a three-way tie. The atmosphere in the arena was tense. The crowd loved the suspense. Marilana took a deep calming breath. She thought about the matches so far and knew Marquiese's last match was against Lotal. This thought did not make her very happy though; in fact, she dreaded the match. If there were no accidents—and Marquiese kept his focus—the royal lion was sure to win. What bothered her more was this: Lotal would probably ask for her colors again, and so her colors would have been on the defeated side for every match in the Jousting of Champions. Realizing she would have to dance most of her dances with Lotal, she was beginning to dread the ball.

Master Lotal's arrival at the Nobles' Box brought Marilana out of her musings. He again asked for her colors and she gave them graciously, even though she would have rather not. Master Timral faced Lotal and defeated him with his longer reach and greater strength, just as Marilana expected. Master Clain and Sir Frauh faced off for their final match, and Sir Frauh won with spectacular swordplay. Finally, the last match of the tournament was about to begin; the one that would determine if Marquiese would be named Champion, or if a three-way tie would have to be resolved. Marilana closed her eyes and tried to control her emotions. She could hear the creak of armor and clop of hooves as Marquiese and Lotal approached the Nobles' Box. She schooled her face to politeness as she prepared to give Lotal her colors again.

"Lady Marilana," said a warm rich voice, "it would please me greatly if you would allow me to ride for your honor in this match."

Upon hearing his voice, Marilana's eyes blinked open and she smiled, not at Lotal as she had expected, but at Marquiese. His eyes shone with mischief behind his visor and he smiled warmly at her. Marilana glanced briefly at Master Lotal who was claiming the colors of another noble daughter with a forced smile. Marilana stood gracefully and gave Marquiese her green and silver kerchief.

"You honor me greatly, Highness," she replied as he took her colors. "Goddess grant you speed and strength."

He bowed his head to her, and then wheeled his charger and cantered to his end of the list. Lotal glanced at her sourly before turning to his end.

Marquiese showed Lotal no mercy during the match. Lotal was unhorsed with Marquiese's first lance, and did not even break his own lance. On foot, Marquiese pressed Lotal hard. Marilana tensed. She wanted to chide Marquiese, it was clear to her that he was attacking in anger. He could easily make a mistake and lose the whole tournament; this was not the time to be blinded by emotion. Marquiese struck hard locking blades with Lotal. Marquiese started to sweep back and attack again, but Lotal rammed him in the side, using his shorter stature to drive his shoulder plate into the left side split of Marquiese's armor. The crowed howled insults at Master Lotal as Marquiese staggered sideways. Marilana clinched her jaw tighter as Marquiese spun out of Lotal's reach and then attacked. Striking fast and precise he drove Lotal back. Lotal parried well, but stepped back into a furrow left from his earlier fall from his horse, lost his footing, and fell backward. His sword flew from his paw as he crashed to the dirt. The crowd roared. Marquiese and Lotal may not have behaved courteously, but the crowds loved the show. The cheers continued as both knights bowed to King Rylan and Marquiese was named Champion of the Realm for the second year in a row. Flowers rained down onto the list from the stands, and Marquiese raised his paws high to the cheers of the people. Finally, Marquiese left the arena and people milled about, heading for the exits of the stands. Marilana remained seated with Annabella waiting for their coach to come for them.

"Will you accept my hospitality and dine with me at my house tonight?" asked Lord Castant turning to Lady Annabella.

"We would enjoy that, yes," Annabella replied.

"Very good, I shall see you there soon," he said standing.

Marilana watched him say his goodbyes on his way to the door of the box where a servant wearing Draukshar livery waited for him.

"Will we be missing any goings on at the palace?" Marilana asked.

"On the contrary," replied Annabella, "no one will dine at the palace tonight. The kitchens are far too busy preparing for tomorrow. This is one of the few times when the palace does not serve dinner. You will see another in a month's time when the palace prepares for the Winter Council. Instead the lords and ladies with houses in the city host dinner parties. King Rylan and Prince Marquiese travel through the city visiting the various parties and greeting the lords and ladies who have come to celebrate with them. Lord Castant usually hosts a small gathering for a very select group of guests."

"And you are one of his regular guests?" Marilana smiled.

"Yes indeed, as is Lord Roana," nodded Annabella. "We are King Rylan's strongest supporters, and closest friends. This will be the first time we all have heirs. I am hoping that you all can become similarly close allies to Prince Marquiese."

"I think we are well on our way. Will King Rylan and Prince Marquiese visit Lord Castant's party first?" mused Marilana.

"No," laughed Annabella, "Traditionally, it is their last stop before returning to the palace. We will probably follow them back to the palace to retire for the night."

Marilana nodded and reflected on the events of the day. Many lords and ladies came to bid Annabella farewell. The box emptied out slowly. Finally, when they were the last ones remaining, Earek moved to the door and nodded that the coach had arrived.

"Last ones to arrive, last ones to leave," said Earek ruefully.

"I did not wish to throw any more bones to the other nobles than absolutely necessary," replied Annabella. "They will be gnawing on today's events enough without us making a hasty retreat. Come along. Lord Castant will have everything ready by now."

14

Marilana gave her cloak and gloves to a servant, and then followed Annabella's lead by cleaning her face and arms with a damp cloth offered to her by a second servant. When that servant turned to Earek, Marilana took in her surroundings. Lord Castant's house was one of the largest in the city, and quite beautiful. She studied the entrance hall's sweeping arches and dark wood paneling. A door opened behind her and she turned to see Lord Castant smiling at them.

"Family Ranat," he said warmly, "welcome to my humble home."

Annabella smiled and held her paws out to him. He took her paws in his and lightly kissed her on the cheek.

"It is always a pleasure to visit, Withers," Annabella replied. "How are your estates in Draukshar fairing?"

Laughing, Lord Castant turned and escorted Annabella into the lavish parlor. Earek followed smiling and relaxed. Marilana stood for a moment, calming her nerves. This was obviously a gathering of friends, but she was not sure how to behave. She jumped slightly as someone entered the entrance hall from a side door.

"Lady Marilana," Master Castant said warmly as he crossed the room to her, "as lovely as ever."

"Master Castant," she greeted him warmly, "I did not expect to see you so soon."

He chuckled and offered his arm to her. "This is my home away from home. Why should I not enjoy the party?"

"I just thought you would be with Marquiese," she replied.

"It is generally frowned upon for a noble to attend another noble's party uninvited, even as his guard Commander," he chided with laughter.

"Of course," she shook her head, "I should have known. I am just so used to you guarding his back wherever he goes."

He smiled gently. "Do not worry. Commander Lorne is with him. This is a casual party of friends. I shall call you simply Marilana, and you may call me Enton. I can see you are nervous. Come, walk with me."

Smiling timidly, she took his arm as he led her through the house and outside to the private garden. They walked silently for a while as Marilana examined the elegant garden.

"This is a beautiful place, Enton. Do you live here or do you stay at the palace?"

"Both." Enton smiled. "I stay here most of the time with my servants and staff, and report to the palace to fulfill my duties as required. However, I also maintain a room in the officers' quarters that I can use if needed. I stayed at the palace constantly during the treason trials so I could stay close to King Rylan and Marquiese."

"I never properly thanked you for trusting me during those difficult months. We barely knew each other, yet I trusted you, and you took me at my word. You have helped me more than I had right to expect," Marilana smiled up at him.

"I have known Lady Annabella and Marquiese my whole life," Enton replied. "They trusted you, and I trusted them. When Marquiese seemed to stop trusting you, I could see that he was letting his hatred of Frishka blind him. I have been trying ever since to help him rediscover the truth. It was plain to me then, and it is plain to me now that you love him, and that he is pushing you away for some reason only he can feel. I may not tell you my secrets, but I feel in my heart that I can trust you as a friend and ally, especially now that you have taken your place as Lady Annabella's heiress. Our families have a long history as allies. When it came to Frishka, I also had no reason to trust him. I had suffered several times at his or Confidant's paws, and knew that he was not charging Marquiese with treason for any reason other than to claim the crown for his own.

"Frishka seemed to hate you," Marilana said. "Was it just because you protected Marquiese?"

"He hated me for several reasons," Enton said. "I have been Marquiese's friend and companion since his birth. I have spent much of my time at the palace. Frishka was cautious of me because he knew of my deep loyalty to Marquiese. He also hated me, though, because out of all the nobles, I have the best claim to the crown if anything were to happen to King Rylan and Marquiese."

"I have to admit that I have not yet studied your family history," Marilana apologized. "Why do you have such a high claim?"

"My maternal grandparents were a mixed couple," he explained. "They were high-nobles of Maefair; their county lies northwest of the city. They adopted an infant son and two infant daughters from the local orphans, two leopards and a lioness. My mother married into the Castant family, my uncle inherited the family title and is a high-noble of Maefair, while my aunt married Rylan son of Coryan. Aunt Sahry was a wonderful queen. She, Lady Annabella, and Lady Nya Roana helped to raise me after my mother died when I was two. My mother died in childbirth, the child was stillborn. Mother's family blamed my father for her death saying he did not call for the healer soon enough, he had relied on the midwife Herb Mother too much. The healer at the time said he could not have done anything to save her, nevertheless they have distanced themselves from us, and I do not consider them my allies.

"Unfortunately, I have no memories of my mother, but Aunt Sahry loved to tell me stories when I was little. Lady Annabella and Lady Nya watched over both me and Marquiese after Aunt Sahry died. Our families have grown very close with the losses of both my mother and Marquiese's. My family ties to Queen Sahry are the closest family ties to the Royal Family. Marquiese is an only son, and Rylan and Coryan were only sons. To find another with familial ties you have to go back to Coryan's mother who had a sister who married into Family Roana. That gives Timral the next best claim to the throne. Frishka did not attack Timral directly as he did with me, but Prinka worked hard the first few years to alienate all of Rylan's closest supporters, including Family Castant, Family Roana, and Family Ranat."

"Lady Annabella said she and Prinka had their disagreements," Marilana nodded. "Thank you for sharing your history. I feel I know you a little better."

"You seem more relaxed, as well," Enton smiled. "Are you ready to accompany me to the party?"

"Yes, I think so," Marilana smiled in return.

Enton led her back through the garden and into the house. She took a deep calming breath as he opened the parlor door and led her in where everyone was conversing easily.

"Ah, there you are Enton," said Lord Castant as they entered, "and I see that you have found a pretty to dangle on your arm for the evening."

"Nay, Father," Enton laughed. "The only dangling Marilana does is when she hangs young fools out to dry."

Everyone in the room laughed and Marilana smiled ruefully.

"Marilana," said Timral stepping forward, "let me know if you need this young rooster removed, I will gladly toss him out."

"Thank you for the offer, Timral," she replied with a smile, "but as he says, I am well practiced with fools."

Laughter rang out through the room. Enton offered her a chair facing Annabella. She squeezed his arm before settling into the cushions. The walk in the garden and the friendly banter had helped her relax. Enton offered her a glass of light wine and she accepted it with a smile.

"Come now," rumbled Lord Roana, "Timral, Enton, tell us what news there is from the tents. We have waited long enough."

Conversations ceased and everyone became attentive as Timral and Enton took their chairs. Timral glanced at Enton before launching into the events of the day. He mostly relayed the normal news of who had new mounts and new maneuvers. He said everyone was curious about where Marquiese had learned his new disarming technique, but Marquiese refused to say anything about it. Marilana glanced at Earek, and he smiled back. Finally, Timral said that was all that had happened and sipped cider from his glass.

"You missed one bit of news. There was almost a full brawl," interjected Enton lightly.

Timral shot him a dark look. "She does not need to know about that."

"Either she learns of it now from us," countered Enton, "or she learns of it tomorrow at the ball from a less friendly character."

"Come now, you cannot just leave us hanging," Marilana said. "You have hinted enough to pique our curiosity."

"Yes, indeed," agreed Annabella. "You must tell us the details. What was this brawling about?"

"You started it," Timral accused Enton, "you must tell them."

"Very well," said Enton, "the argument was about our own dear Marilana." He shot her a look that she knew was a warning. She nodded in response.

"Master Lotal and his friends were loudly discussing our young lady in a rather unflattering way," Enton continued. "They made the mistake of trying to bring the knights of Pandensy into their discussion. Master Roatal and Sir Orthan were about to ram the words back down Master Lotal's throat when Timral arrived on the scene. Being well-respected, he managed to calm the group down by reminding them that if they broke the peace of the tournament, everyone would forfeit any honor they had won during the day."

"Thank you for keeping the peace, Timral," Marilana said. "Fighting among the tents would have been bad for everyone. You did well."

"I would rather have helped Roatal and Orthan," Timral grumbled.

"Really?" asked Annabella. "You hardly ever let others rile you. What could they have said that flared your temper?"

"I prefer not to repeat such foulness," he growled, "but since you asked, I will relate what I was told." He inhaled deeply before speaking. "Roatal and Orthan said Lotal and his friends were boasting that one of them would 'tame the wild beast'. Two had ridden under the green and silver in the first round and had not yet competed in the second. They said that grace and beauty could be trained, but intelligence could never replace dumb instinct."

The room chilled as disapproving and threatening growls reverberated throughout. Marilana quickly scanned their faces and knew that she was well-liked among this crowd. "I have had much worse said of me," she said calmly. "Do not fear that these men will get along with me any better than Master Arndt."

With her words, the anger dissipated from the room.

"You were right, Enton," Timral said. "She did need to learn of it from us and not dance with these men without warning."

"I will still dance with them," Marilana said, "but I know their kind now, and will not let my guard down." Marilana thought for a moment, then asked, "Is this what prompted the last match?"

Enton glanced at her seriously before responding. "Prince Marquiese did not know of these events. He may have learned of them since leaving the tournament, but I thought it best not to distract him from the tournament at the time. If he has not learned of it by morning, I will inform him then."

"That sounds reasonable," agreed Lord Castant.

Marilana nodded in agreement as well. Stillness fell over the room as everyone reflected on the future ramifications of the events.

Finally, Earek broke the silence. "I was wondering, Enton, why you did not compete?"

Enton laughed and smiles were contagious. "I am older and wiser," he said.

"Perhaps," said Earek, "but you have competed before, and from the stories I have heard, you could have given Prince Marquiese a run for the Championship."

"I have trained with Marquiese and Timral, and know their styles well; it is true. I have even helped Prince Marquiese train since he returned from the Southern Tip. If anyone had a chance to beat him, it would not have been me. He learned a great deal and became very skilled while training under Zariff. It has taken me nearly a year to be able to hold my own against him again, and he still surprised me with that disarm maneuver he used on Timral. Even so, I admit that I would have enjoyed the competition. However, as one of King Rylan's advisors, I have taken on important duties, and while I could still compete, I have chosen to leave that behind in my youth. I may only be two years older, but I feel much older with the weight of my responsibilities," he replied.

"Ah, yes," chimed in Lord Castant, "the maturity that responsibility brings with it. I am sure you will begin to feel much the same way in a few years, Earek."

"I have already begun to feel that way," nodded Earek.

"Well, of course you have," laughed Enton. "You have to protect Marilana. If anyone can cause early aging, it is her. Do you not agree, Annabella?"

Everyone chuckled as Marilana pretended to scowl at him.

"Oh, indeed," agreed Annabella, "she has definitely caused most of my early aging."

"Yes," Marilana snickered, "and I am sure keeping Enton out of trouble led to his father's retirement at such a youthful age."

The room erupted in laughter again. Enton's mouth opened to make a retort, but he seemed to realize he had lost that round. He closed his mouth and bowed his head to Marilana.

"I was warned about your wit, Marilana," he smiled. "I think you will keep me on my toes.

"And I on mine," she replied. "Jousting on horseback is not the only type of jousting I am skilled in."

"Speaking of jousting on horses," Lord Roana interrupted, "your mounts did very well today, Marilana. I was pleased you told me which ones to watch. The knights riding them have good potential for future tournaments."

"Thank you," nodded Marilana, "they are all good men and have practiced hard to excel. I think Master Clain has a good chance for next year, although Sir Frauh will be one to watch as well."

Timral initiated a lengthy discussion about the knights and their mounts. Marilana half-listened, letting the conversation flow past her. She wondered what Marquiese would do when he learned of the argument. She stared into her wine as she reflected and was startled to hear her name. Looking up, she found that Lord Castant was gazing down at her and the rest were making their way through another door.

"Oh, forgive me," she said hastily. "I was lost in thought."

"So, I noticed," he said gently. "Come, dinner is served and I do not want you to miss out on the feast. You hardly ate anything today at the tournament."

Smiling she stood and followed him into the dining room.

Marilana felt like she had eaten too much by the time dinner had finished. The food was delicious, and after she had relaxed, she found she had an appetite. Lord Castant had prepared a full five-course meal for his guests; the theme was hearty winter fare. Thick vegetable soup was followed by garlic-creamed pasta, then a magnificent roast duck and winter squash. To cap if off, rich cheeses and a warm bread pudding with dried currants were served. After everyone had eaten their fill, they retired to a luxurious sitting room with cups of warm spiced cider. It was nearing midnight and the fire crackled merrily in the hearth. Marilana relaxed on a couch and was amused by watching Timral and Enton teach Earek how to play a game of rice-bag toss. Annabella, Lord Castant, and Lord Roana sat quietly discussing politics and watching the young men.

Timral had placed three large jars in a row on the floor where everyone could see and was demonstrating how to toss small bags filled with rice at the jars. The goal was to get one bag in each of the jars in turn starting with the jar closest to the person tossing. It was made more difficult because the jars had narrow openings just big enough for the bag to slide through, although the jars also had wide flat rims and points were given for bags that landed on the rim without falling off.

Earek took the bags from Timral and tossed his first one. It bounced spectacularly off the first jar and knocked the second two jars spinning across the rug. Everyone laughed appreciatively and Enton clapped Earek heartily on the shoulder.

"Now this is what I have been waiting for all night," said a deep voice as Timral went to retrieve the jars.

Everyone turned to see King Rylan and Prince Marquiese entering the room. They crossed the rug to join the others. Marilana and the others started to rise, but King Rylan raised his paw.

"Please, do not get up," he said smiling, "I have dealt with enough formality today. I assume this to be a casual gathering of friends?"

"Of course, Rylan, old friend," said Lord Castant standing up anyway and embracing the King. "Welcome to my little party. Welcome Marquiese. Can I offer you anything to eat or drink?"

"Nothing to eat," said King Rylan, "but do I smell spiced cider? That would be most welcome. It is getting colder outside and the warmth would be good."

"Of course," Lord Castant replied and motioned them toward the chairs.

King Rylan greeted the young men and kissed Marilana's paw, then sat in a chair next to Annabella and engaged Lord Roana and Annabella in conversation. Marquiese had greeted Lord Roana and Annabella first and was exchanging back slapping embraces with the young men.

"Will you join us for a game, Marquiese?" Enton asked.

"No, I have played quite enough of that this evening. I think I shall sit this one out," he said smiling. "Besides from what I saw of Earek's skill, it could be dangerous to be too close."

They all laughed as Earek shot a glare at Marquiese who laughed and clapped him on the arm. Marilana smiled and dropped her eyes to her cup.

"May I sit with you, Marilana," Marquiese asked gently.

"Of course, Highness," she said looking up at him.

"I thought this was a casual party," he said sternly.

"Of course, forgive me, Marquiese," she replied with a smile. "Some habits can be hard to break."

Smiling again, he sat on her couch and accepted a cup of cider from Lord Castant.

"You seem relaxed here among my friends," he said and paused to take a sip from his cup, "that is good."

"The cider is good," she agreed slyly.

"That is not what I was talking about," he said seriously, then looked at her and smiled, "and you knew that."

"Yes," she said, "it is good to relax with friends."

"You and Earek are not the same young people I used to know," he said lightly, "and that is good, too. You and he have both taken to your new positions as if you had been born to them."

"In a way I was," she replied quietly. "Annabella has been training me for it most of my life. All that has really changed is how I view my status."

"That is true," he said sipping his cider. "I recognized it in you after I got to know you better. That was when I first realized that your relationship with Annabella was more than you knew. I am glad she trained you so well. You made quite the stir among the competitors today."

Marilana smiled and paused to watch Enton land all three rice bags on the rims of the jars.

"I did not intend to cause any problems," she said carefully.

"No problems that Timral could not manage," he replied.

"Yes, he said he was not pleased to deal with it peacefully," she said.

"Ah," Marquiese nodded, "so he did tell you of the argument with Lotal."

"Enton did and I am not worried by it. Insults show more the character of the giver than of the receiver," she dismissed the matter lightly.

Marquiese frowned slightly, but let the topic drop.

"Your chargers did very well today," he said.

"So, you remembered them?" she asked.

"Of course," he nodded, "I did not spend three years watching you train horses just to forget about them. I was very interested to see how they would fair. Did you give advice to the knights on how to joust?"

"Not how to joust, just how to learn their mounts. I must say they did a good job of it; they worked fluidly together as a team. Your own steed is a magnificent animal as well," she added smiling.

"Yes, he is well-trained, and I also heeded your advice to learn how the horse moved and how to feel his rhythms. It definitely paid off when facing Timral and Frauh."

"They are tough competitors," she agreed.

"Frauh will do well as Champion in the coming years," Marquiese noted.

"What about Timral? Is he not a worthy Champion?" Marilana asked.

"Indeed, he is, but he has announced that he will not compete anymore. He said he has grown up too much to continue in the sport for young men," Marquiese replied.

"Are you not going to compete anymore?" Marilana asked puzzled.

"No," he sighed, "as much as I would like to, I have come of age and as the Crown Prince, that means I must turn my attentions to my duties. I will continue to train, of course. Men do not follow leaders into battle without feeling confident that the leader is skilled in the arts of war. However, people also want the security of knowing that their King has heirs. I must look to that duty more than knightly sport."

They watched the game and sipped their drinks in silence. Marilana stifled a yawn behind her paw.

"Surely you are not tired, Marilana," teased Earek while waiting his turn. "You usually need much less sleep than the rest of us."

"I am warm and comfortable in pleasant company, and we were on the road well before dawn this morning after traveling hard yesterday as well," she replied easily. "So why should I not grow tired watching you miss your targets."

Marquiese chuckled. "She is right. I grow weary of watching your skills diminish with every toss."

Laughing, Enton gave Earek the rice bags.

"If you think you can do better," rumbled Timral, "Why do you not join us?"

"Yes, Marquiese, if you have had so much practice tonight, why not show us how it is done?" Earek challenged lightly.

"Very well," Marquiese set his cup down on a table and stood up. "Just to show you how it is done."

Smiling, Earek held out the rice bags. Marquiese took the bags and studied the jars. Marilana raised her cup to hide her smile. The room grew quiet as Marquiese took aim. He tossed the first bag and it slid across the rim of the first jar and into the opening. He tossed the second and again it slid across the rim and dropped into the second jar. His third toss landed a little short, did not slide like it should have, and remained on the rim.

"Oh, well done," Annabella congratulated him.

The others chimed in. It was without a doubt the best tossing they had seen all night.

Marilana schooled her face to a slight frown, then said, "It was a good toss, but for all of your boasting, it would seem you need more practice."

Marquiese turned to frown at her with a chorus of laughter from the others.

"If you think you can do better…" he said gesturing her to join the game.

"I do not think so," she smiled and shook her head.

"Are you afraid of missing your boast," teased Enton.

"No," she laughed, "it simply would not be fair."

"Fair?" asked Timral, "You said you have never played this game before, so how could you have such skill at it without practicing?"

"It would not be fair because she cannot do as well as the rest of you precisely because she has never done it before," rumbled Lord Roana.

"Do not underestimate her," smiled Annabella. "She is full of surprises, and the goal is to have fun trying."

"Come on, Marilana," smiled Earek offering the rice bags to her, "show us how to do it."

"Oh, all right, if you insist." She lithely rose to her feet and set down her cup.

She clutched the rice bags in her paws, carefully weighing them and tossed each one up and down a couple of times. Earek and Marquiese exchanged looks of amusement. Marilana took her stance and then tossed all three bags, one after another without waiting for the first to land. The first two fell directly into the openings of their respective jars. Everyone watched with baited breath as the third bag spun high into the air. It seemed to hang just below the ceiling for a moment before falling quickly toward the jars. With a soft whooshing sound it passed perfectly through the mouth of the third jar and made a resounding thunk on the bottom. Earek and Marquiese burst into laughter and Annabella applauded lightly. Marilana spread her skirts and curtseyed to the shocked silence from the others.

Finally, Enton started to laugh. "Well, we did ask her to show us how it was done."

The others laughed as well, and then questions followed. Marilana could not tell who asked which question as they talked over each other. She raised her paws for silence. "Enough," she chuckled, "let me explain."

They settled and waited expectantly. She took a sip of cider.

"When I was first learning the skills of arms, Captain-General Zariff set me the task of practicing my paw-to-eye coordination. He set out targets and gave me stones to throw at them. The better I got with my aim, the harder he made the targets. I learned to judge the weight of my projectiles and how to make them hit any target. That is how he trained me to become so good at many different weapons, including rock throwing. He used to say that anything can be a weapon if you know how to use it," she said with a smile.

"As you said," Marquiese added, "it seems we need more practice."

Everyone laughed again and King Rylan stood up.

"I declare Lady Marilana the winner of this game," he said smiling, and then turned to Marquiese. "As much as I do not want to leave such good company, I am afraid we must. It is late, and tomorrow will be another long, busy day.

"I think I must say the same," said Annabella standing up, "Marilana, Earek, we need to be getting on our way."

King Rylan and Marquiese said quick farewells and left for their coach. Lord Roana and Timral said their farewells as well and went to their waiting horses. Lord Castant and Enton escorted Annabella and Marilana out to the entrance hall where servants had their cloaks and gloves waiting.

"We shall see you tomorrow evening," Lord Castant said smiling. "Until then, farewell, and may The Goddess keep you."

They all waved as they walked out to the coach and climbed in.

"I hope you both enjoyed yourselves," said Annabella as they started toward the palace.

"I most definitely did," nodded Earek.

"Yes, Mother, it was a very enjoyable evening," agreed Marilana.

Marquiese shivered as he slipped through the hidden door into Marilana's bathing chamber. The air inside the room was almost as cold as the night air outside, and he had left his coat behind in his rooms. He walked as silently as he could to the doorway of the bathing chamber and was relieved to see the flickering light of a fire from the hearth around the corner by the bed. He also noticed a lit lamp sitting on the writing desk. He looked toward the balcony and found the source of the chilly air. One of the balcony doors was wide open and he could see Marilana standing at the balcony railing looking at the stars. No longer fearing to wake her up, he walked quietly to the balcony door and watched her for a moment.

She almost seemed insubstantial in the darkness. Her solid white, woolen robe was moving slightly in the night breeze; she appeared to be floating in mid-air. Dim light came from the distant lamp behind him and the stars in the moonless sky offered scant light, so it was difficult to see her clearly. Even so, her eyes sparkled like the stars when she turned to face him.

"I heard you approach the door," she said quietly, and then she frowned as she looked him over. "Marquiese, you will catch a fever if you stand in this cold wind in only shirt and pants."

She approached the door quickly and firmly pushed him back into the room. He winced slightly as her paw pressed against his left side. She closed the door, then turned to face him.

"Have the healers seen that?" she asked sternly.

"Seen what?" he asked innocently.

"How badly are you bruised?" she persisted. "I barely pressed against you and you winced. How will you dance tonight if you are too stiff and sore? Have you done any stretching?"

"I did not come here to have you nurse me," he said stubbornly.

"Nonetheless," she persisted, "you are injured and need healing."

He sighed with resignation knowing that she would not drop the matter.

"I have not yet done the stretching that you taught me and, no, the healers have not seen the bruising. I was going to stretch before going to my bed. I will be fine without healing, Marilana," he insisted.

"Do the stretches," she said walking toward her desk, "and I will make you a tonic."

He sighed again but set about doing the stretches that she had told him once could make the difference between winning and losing a fight. She gathered a cup and her decanter of water. She extracted a pouch from a desk drawer and began to pull out herbs.

"You have at least six dances to perform at the ball tonight and we cannot have you stiff and sore. This will help you just as much as a couple of days of rest, especially since you do not have a couple of days to rest," she said over her shoulder.

He paused to make a retort, but she fixed him with a stern look and he continued the stretching exercises. When he finished the routine, she had a cup of tonic and a clean rag waiting for him.

"Take a drink of the tonic and then have someone massage the bruise with more tonic on the rag. It will improve quite a bit before the ball if you get some rest," she said holding the cup and rag out to him.

"Since you insist." He strode past her without taking the cup or the rag.

He walked to her bed without looking back at her. He could be just as stubborn as she could when he wanted to be. He pulled his shirt off over his head and lay down on his back, crossing his feet and placing his paws behind his head. She followed bemused.

"I did not mean—," she started to say, but stopped when he raised his eyebrows at her.

"Take a sip," she said firmly offering him the cup.

He sat up enough to take a sip, and then lay back down. She moved around the bed so that she could sit by his left side. Carefully she poured some of the tonic on the rag and gently massaged his bruised ribs. He studied her face as she focused on her work, shadows danced across her features from the flickering light of the fire.

"You said this was not the purpose of your visit," she said softly without meeting his gaze. "What else can I do for you this night?"

"I came to speak with you," he said sternly, "to warn you."

"To warn me?" she frowned.

"Yes," he said quietly, "I was concerned with how easily you dismissed the argument between Lotal and your friendly knights. I could not sleep because I was so worried."

Her frown began to fade as she replied, "I take that argument very seriously, Marquiese. I do not like aspersions made on my character, but I did not want a room full of powerful nobles to feel like Lotal and his friends needed to be taught a lesson. I can manage the young fools on my own."

"Marilana, I know Lotal much better than you," he insisted. "I am warning you that he is not someone to dismiss easily. His mother is wise, but also cunning, and he is devious. He will not let any challenge go unmet, and he takes whatever he sets his sights on."

He paused for a moment, then added, "I fear he has his sights set firmly on you."

"Yes," Marilana replied darkly, "he made that quite clear at the tournament. I am sure he will reinforce that idea at the ball by trying to out-dance me at every courtship dance he can. Luckily, I have the ban published so I cannot accept any courtships, and you have helped by claiming my colors for the last joust, so he cannot push too hard until after you have had your dance."

"Marilana," Marquiese said exasperatedly. He reached down with his left paw and stopped her massaging by pressing her paw gently to his side. "Lotal sees you only as a prize. He will not treat you as you deserve to be treated."

"Is that why you fought so aggressively toward him in your match? You could have lost the championship with your loss of focus," she chided.

"He was heaping dishonor on you with all of his losses," he replied with quiet anger. "I know I should not have behaved so aggressively, but I wanted to give you back some of what he had taken away."

"Every match has a loser," she said, "and every loser rides for someone's honor."

"Yes, but you should not be honored only by losers," he sighed. "You will have to dance with Lotal many times and he will try to wear you down. He is a skilled dancer and in good condition. I just want you to be sure not to fall into any traps he may set for you."

"You will have many dances of your own, and you need to rest to be sure you can perform well. Those other five young ladies may not want to accept your courtship proposal, but they will be ordered to accept. You cannot stop the dance too early; you are known to be a skilled dancer," she said directing the conversation back to his plight.

"I will make the dances convincing, but I have to dance with all six young ladies for whose honor I rode before I can accept any courtships. So, the first five can all accept, but I will not accept them," he said slyly.

"So, that was why you chose me for the last match," she said studying his face. "I have banned all courtships including yours, so by dancing with me last, you will be able to leave the night without a courtship."

"Yes, that is my plan," he agreed. "I have not yet decided who to accept a courtship from. This way I satisfy tradition without having to decide. I will have to make a decision soon, but I did not want to do it with this tournament. I am sorry to put those girls through the stress. I only have six dances to face, though; if my count is correct, you have thirteen, five of which are with Lotal."

"And the first five are not for courtship," she interjected.

"No, but that is still a lot of dancing for one person in a night. Are you sure you will be able to contend with it all?" he said concerned.

"I am sure I will be able to out-dance everyone, including you, even though I do not want to," she said firmly.

He frowned and she seemed to realize what she had said. She blushed and looked down at her lap. He felt her paw trembling against his side. She quickly retracted her paw.

"Your bruises should be much better in eight hours or so," she said quietly. "And thank you for the warning."

He studied her for a moment more, then sat up and pulled on his shirt. "It is late and we both need to get some sleep," he said. "I will see you at the ball, Marilana." He strode quickly to the secret door. She did not accompany him. He pulled the door closed behind him and then leaned back against the wall in deep thought.

What did she mean? Does she want to accept a courtship from someone? Perhaps from someone in particular? Could she have meant it the way it sounded? Does she truly want to accept my suit? Is this the answer to the mystery I have been searching for? Was this what my father, Castant, and Earek all hinted at—that she truly loves me? Did she do everything, risk everything, for love, for me? But why would she have? I flirted a little, but I never took it far enough for it to be considered serious or courting. I wanted to, but I could not, I had to stay within the bounds of my position. Could she really have come to love me without anything more than our friendship?

He nearly pushed the door back open to confront her about it, to ask her to give him a straight answer, but he stopped himself. Even if she did love him, the ball had to happen the way he had already planned. She had published the ban and so could not accept his suit. He would wait and confront her after the ball. Depending on her answer, he could then decide on a future course of action. He still had to determine what her purpose had been in her betrayal of him, and why she was still plotting something. He found no answers in his whirling thoughts as he made his way back to his rooms and to his bed.

15

Marilana fixed a smile on her face as she and Earek followed Annabella into the great hall decorated with garlands of conifer boughs and winter foliage. Twenty ceremonial lances were positioned in stands around the dance floor. Each lance was painted brightly in the colors of the knight it represented and from each hung the favors taken from the young ladies during the tournament. Most bore only one or two colors, but five lances bore six colors each. The five lances formed a pentagon with the others spaced evenly in between. Marquiese's lance was positioned directly in front of the royal dais, and Marilana could make out the green and silver kerchief adorning it near the tip.

Still smiling, although she was beginning to feel a little nervous—she still wasn't quite comfortable interacting with large gatherings of nobles, there were too many rules and nuances—she followed Annabella toward the east side of the room. Nobles lined both sides of the room conversing and greeting the new arrivals as they entered. Marilana scanned the room for Enton or Timral, but did not see them. A large gray fox caught her eye and smiled broadly. He said something to the men nearby and they laughed. He never took his eyes from her. She nodded her head to him, and then turned away.

Master Clain hailed her from a group of young men and women. Feeling slightly relieved, she approached them with a warm greeting.

"Lady Marilana," Master Clain bowed to her, "please let me be the first to say you are the most wonderful horse trainer I have ever had the privilege to meet."

"It has been my pleasure," Marilana laughed. "You did not need to grant me quite so much honor though."

"We thought it was the best thing to do, and we all agree that you deserve more honor than you received," Master Clain replied.

The other four knights bowed their heads in agreement.

"My honor will grow with time," she replied, "but I do thank you for starting my rise in such a spectacular fashion."

"We would have done more, My Lady," said Master Roatal.

"We would have stopped Lotal from asking for your colors so many times if Master Roana had not stopped us," added Sir Orthan.

"So I have heard," Marilana replied studying their faces seriously. "I heard what took place among the tents, and I have been warned about Lotal's character. Master Roana was right to act as he did. Let me take care of Master Lotal. I do not want to hear of you breaking the peace tonight and bringing shame to your lovely ladies."

As the knights introduced their ladies, smiles eclipsed their frowns. They chatted about the tournament and the nobles around them until the trumpets blared. They turned to the main doors and bowed as King Rylan and Prince Marquiese entered. Marilana watched them proceed to the dais through her lashes. They both looked magnificent in suits of blue with the royal red sash. The gold embroidery adorning King Rylan's shoulders and sleeves shimmered in the light. Marquiese had less gold in his coat, but Marilana could make out hints around his cuffs and collar. The crowd straightened when King Rylan turned to face the nobles from the dais.

"Welcome to the annual ball in honor of my birth and the birth of my son," King Rylan greeted them warmly. "I have only one wish for you all tonight. Enjoy!"

Laughing, the nobles clapped and bowed as King Rylan and Marquiese stepped down to join the crowds. Servants entered from the kitchens bearing platters and bowls—a never-ending stream of food and drink; the tables lining the walls were laden with a bounty of specially prepared dishes. Music floated from the musicians' corner and couples moved toward the dance floor for the first dance.

Master Roatal stepped forward and offered Marilana his paw. "Shall we start the evening off with a dance, My Lady?" he asked. "I know you have a lot of dancing to do tonight, and I have the honor of being the first."

"Gladly, Sir Knight," she replied and placed her paw on his.

She danced gracefully without hesitation first with Master Roatal, then with Sir Tavin, and then Sir Graduin. Every time one dance ended, the next knight was waiting his turn with her. On the fourth song, she got a welcome break. It was the first courtship dance of the night and so she left the dance floor. Marquiese led Lorlina to the center and they danced. Several other couples joined them. Lorlina looked nervous but danced well. Marilana watched them for a moment, then turned back to the knights and their ladies. Master Roatal held out a glass for her.

"Cider," he said quietly, "I know you will need your wits tonight."

"Perfect. Thank you," she replied accepting the glass and taking a sip.

"So here you are," said a scornful voice beside Marilana.

Marilana turned toward the voice with surprise. Brittia, the merchant daughter who had harassed Marilana through all her childhood, sneered up at her. She was dressed well in the colors of house Arndt.

"Brittia," Marilana greeted her coolly, "I heard that your family felt they needed to move away from the Southern Tip. It appears that you are doing well in your new home."

"Of course, we had to move away," spat Brittia. "We could not bear the shame of living under the leadership of an orphan. Everyone knows I should have been named heiress to the Southern Tip, not some lowly peasant."

Master Roatal started forward, but Marilana placed her paw on his arm and stopped him without taking her eyes from Brittia. "I am sorry you feel that way," Marilana replied. "Your father was well-respected and provided good service to Lady Annabella."

"Yes," sneered Brittia, "Lord Arndt has welcomed his services much better than Annabella ever did. She never showed us proper appreciation. Then she went and named you her heir, and we knew she must be going senile."

Marilana detected a dark figure approaching quickly from her right; she raised her paw to halt the movement.

Brittia looked away from Marilana and glared. "Oh, yes, Earek," she growled, "defend her. You left me for her, and your family disowned you for it. You disgust me. I heard about the trials last summer. You two are nothing more than conniving traitors."

Brittia turned back to meet Marilana's eyes and stepped back in shock. Marilana stood tall and looked calmly down at the young lynx, but seemed to loom over the girl. Power radiated from Marilana. Brittia opened her mouth, but Marilana cut her off in an authoritative voice. "I have heard what you wanted to say to me. Your insults are unwelcome here. You are dismissed from my presence, Merchant."

Brittia looked at Marilana wide-eyed for a moment then bobbed a curtsey and hastily disappeared into the crowd. Marilana watched her go. Marilana noticed an attentive individual close by and discovered Lord Arndt watching closely. He nodded to her, his expression grave. She returned a nod before turning back to Earek and the Knights They all bowed to her and she smiled self-consciously.

"That was impressive, Sister," Earek said. "I have only seen Mother do that a couple of times."

"Impressive indeed," agreed Master Clain, "few nobles I have met can pull off such displays of authority."

"She deserves a good lashing for that much disrespect," growled Master Roatal.

"She is not done yet," Marilana shook her head, "she will run to Master Arndt and seek his assistance. I know her well enough to know that. I had only heard a rumor that he had offered her a courtship. We shall see what comes of it later. For now, I feel like another dance."

"I believe it is my turn," Sir Orthan said stepping forward and offering his paw.

Marilana danced with Sir Orthan, and then Master Clain asked for his turn. Marilana felt relaxed with the first five dances of the night complete. She did not think she would enjoy the next ones as much, but she felt she was making progress. As each dance was completed, the proper kerchief was removed from the lance. Looking around at the lances, Marilana saw that some of them were now bare. The courtship dance music began again, and Marilana spotted Marquiese leading a nervous Ailse through the crowd. Turning away, Marilana excused herself from her friendly knights and headed toward the food tables to select a few items to eat while she had the chance. Taking her plate of delicacies, she moved toward a group of unoccupied chairs. Before she reached them someone lightly touched her arm. Marilana turned to see who wanted her attention.

Mistress Lorlina smiled back at her. "Come sit with us," she said and guided Marilana to a group of chattering noble daughters.

"Lady Marilana, please join us," said Lady Ophelia indicating a chair.

Marilana sat and thanked the girls. They were around her age or a little younger. Lady Ophelia was the highest ranking among them, equal to Marilana as a great-noble heiress. Marilana listened to the conversation while enjoying her plate of food. Several others also had food or drink. She studied them for a moment and recognized all the noble daughters for whose honor Marquise had ridden, except Ailse, sitting in the group along with several others. The music changed to a landler as Marilana finished eating, and a passing servant whisked her empty plate away. Ailse joined them and the young ladies who had not been honored by Marquiese got up and moved toward the dance floor.

"That gown is simply stunning, Marilana," said Ophelia turning to her.

"Do you like it?" Marilana asked smiling politely while wondering what they really wanted.

"Oh, yes," chimed in Ailse, "it is simply lovely."

They all admired the silver embroidered vines accenting the dark green skirt and the curved neckline of the dark green bodice. Marilana adjusted the sheer silver sleeves and belt.

Lorlina noticed the silver fan hanging from the belt. "I thought you did not intend to accept any courtships?" she asked indicating the fan.

"I do not," Marilana replied opening the fan. "However, I will have to dance the courtship dance at least once tonight, and for that I must have a fan."

It was silver silk embroidered with dark green flowers and vines, not the pure white fan of a young girl looking to accept a courtship. She closed the fan and replaced it on her belt.

"Yes, we all must dance the courtship dance at least once tonight," said Mistress Katrine. The young gazelle shifted her hooves nervously.

Marilana studied them for a moment. They all seemed scared or irritated at the thought of dancing with

Marquiese. Lorlina and Ailse shifted uneasily. Mistress Phoebe seemed ready to faint again.

"I would have thought that would have made at least some of you happy," Marilana said with affected surprise. "Is the Royal suit not the goal of every noble daughter?"

"Well, um, yes, it is," said Ophelia hesitantly, unconsciously tracing one of her leopard spots with a claw, "and our families are pleased."

"But?" prompted Marilana.

The girls exchanged nervous looks, waiting for someone else to answer.

"That is what we wanted to talk to you about," said Ailse finally. "We have discussed it, and we think that it would be better for all of us if you would accept the courtship."

"But I cannot," Marilana said seriously, "even if I wanted to, the ban has been announced and it would take several days to retract it."

"Then what can we do?" asked Phoebe weakly.

"You will stop and think," said Marilana.

The girls exchanged puzzled looks.

"What do you mean?" asked Lorlina. "Once His Highness dances with you he will be free to dance again with any of us he chooses, and we will have to accept his suit."

"You are not thinking clearly," said Marilana shaking her head. "If he wanted to choose one of you for his suit, why did he choose to ride under my colors last?"

"He stopped Lotal from riding under your colors in their match," said Ophelia. "Not that any of us can fault him for that. Lotal is less than honorable at the best of times, and is usually a disgusting leech."

"We feel bad that you must dance with him so much; he can be very stubborn and persistent," Katrine added.

"His Highness did you a great favor by stopping Lotal from claiming your colors for the last round," Ailse agreed.

"Was that Prince Marquiese's only goal? Or was that just a secondary benefit?" asked Marilana.

"I do not understand," Phoebe said. "By tradition he must dance the courtship dance with all of the young ladies for whose honor he rode."

"That is true, but I will explain more," replied Marilana. "By riding under my colors last, he has an opportunity to leave the ball without accepting any courtships at all. Tradition dictates that he must dance, but it does not say that he must accept any of the proposals. Usually the last lady he would dance with would be the one he accepted. However, I have announced a ban against accepting his courtship tonight. Do you understand?"

"Yes," gasped Katrine, "he is using your ban to get out of accepting any of the courtships."

"He could, but why would he?" asked Phoebe. "And why would he choose us?"

"He may not know what he wants yet," answered Marilana. "As to why he chose you, I happen to know that you all have something in common that means he will not break your hearts tonight by not accepting any courtships. It is the same reason we are having this conversation."

They all exchanged wary looks.

"What do you mean you know?" asked Ophelia coldly. "I did not even realize that such a commonality could be a possibility until we discussed it this evening. Most people know of Lorlina's preference, but how do you know about the rest of us? You have not been in court long enough to have figured it out. Does the whole court know?"

"No," smiled Marilana, "some of your positions are known to select individuals, but most of the court is ignorant of your connection. I figured it out from information I gathered from others as well as my own observations today at the tournament, and our conversation here has confirmed it."

"How would His Highness know?" asked Phoebe worriedly. "What if you are wrong and it is just a coincidence?"

"Stop and think," reprimanded Marilana again. "Is Prince Marquiese cruel or thoughtless or naive?"

"No," replied Lorlina, "but he has only been back in court for little over a year. He has had his little gatherings these past four months, but I did not think he was using them to plot an escape. I thought he was trying to learn more about us so he could make a good choice. He has not had the opportunity to trace all of the clues that would lead him to the connections we share."

"Nor have I had the time, but others have," Marilana said fixing a look on Ailse.

Ailse blushed and then smiled shyly. "You are correct; His Highness has advisors who could have informed him of the goings on at court.

"And I have made a few friends in my time here as well," Marilana said. "You all need to just relax and enjoy dancing with one of the best dancers in the kingdom."

"It was a lot of fun," giggled Ailse. "However, if he does not accept a courtship tonight, then tradition dictates that he must perform the Royal Courtship Dance."

"What is that?" asked Marilana warily.

"Oh, from the description, it sounds wonderful," replied Ophelia. "It has not been performed in several generations, but as it says it is a dance."

"A very specific dance," added Lorlina. "The Prince has to choose ten possible brides. Two of the women are selected to wear black and direct the dance. The others take part in the dance. The dance itself is the courtship dance, but it is done in turns. As the dance progresses, the Prince will have to choose to dismiss the women one at a time until there is only one left. That lucky woman is accepted into courtship."

"That sounds amazing to watch, but why is it done? Surely the Prince would know who he was going to pick from the start?" mused Marilana.

"He might know who he wants to pick, but all of the women's clothing is done in a way to conceal their identities, gloves, veils, shoes, and even the colors are all dictated to prevent the Prince from knowing who he is dancing with at any given time," answered Ailse. "The last woman is the best dancer, and it was used as an alternative to an arranged marriage."

"Concealing the women's identities does add a degree of suspense," Marilana nodded. "I think His Highness would perform it masterfully. We shall have to wait and see what he chooses to do."

The others nodded and, seeming more relaxed, gossiped about the dresses they had seen in past balls. Marilana joined in for a while, but part of her thoughts were occupied by the revelation of the Royal Courtship Dance. She knew Marquiese wanted to delay courting anyone, but she wondered how soon he would be forced to accept someone, and who that lucky girl would be. Disturbed and restless, she took her leave of the daughters. She intended to walk a bit to calm her thoughts, but she barely got a few paces away when the gray fox she had seen earlier approached her.

"Lady Marilana," he greeted her in a strong voice and offered his paw. "I am Master Lotal. I believe you owe me some dances tonight."

She forced a smile and curtseyed to him while laying her paw on his. Without waiting for more of an answer, he led her out to the dance floor. She glanced back at the group of Daughters she had just left; they watched with disapproval. It was a fast mazurka and, just as Marquiese had warned, Lotal was a good dancer. She kept up with him easily, though, and even had fun. As she turned away from him at the end, another knight stepped up to her. He was the last of the knights from the first round. She danced the next dance with him, a waltz, and glided off the dance floor when the song ended. She was relieved to hear the strains of the next courtship dance without Master Lotal approaching her.

She accepted a glass of white wine from a passing servant and then watched Marquiese and Mistress Phoebe dance a stanza. The young zebra appeared relaxed and danced beautifully. Turning away, she spotted Earek and Annabella talking intensely, and moved toward them wondering what was going on. Suddenly, Master Arndt stepped in front of her and blocked her way. With a sigh, Marilana gave her glass to a nearby servant and folded her paws together, waiting for him to speak first. She did not have to wait long.

"How dare you insult my guest, Marilana," he said angrily. "Brittia may be a merchant's daughter, but she is my guest here and you had no right to insult her before witnesses. You may not be aware, but I am courting her and intend to marry her."

"I think you and she will make a good pair," Marilana replied calmly, "but if you intend for her to attend gatherings of nobles, you would be well advised to teach her some manners."

"How dare you!" he growled. "She has perfect manners."

"You should not protect her without finding out the truth of the matter," said a deep voice behind Master Arndt.

He turned around angrily, but stopped when he found himself face to face with his father.

"Father, what do you mean?" he asked sharply.

"I witnessed the whole encounter earlier. Lady Marilana did not insult the girl, nor did she behave in an unladylike manner. Your lynx, however, insulted Lady Marilana, Master Earek, and Lady Annabella. Even if you do marry her, she needs to learn that Lady Marilana will always stand higher than she does and she needs to show proper respect," stated Lord Arndt.

Master Arndt looked confused and said, "But Brittia told me that Marilana threatened her."

"Marilana dismissed Brittia from her presence as was her right. Brittia was lucky that dismissal was all she got for her disrespect. I may change my mind about letting you continue with your courtship if her manners do not improve," retorted Lord Arndt. "Forgive my son, Lady Marilana. You will not be troubled by him or the girl for the rest of the evening."

"It is forgiven and forgotten," she curtseyed to him. "I do not hold your house accountable for Brittia's manners."

"That is very noble of you. Goodnight," he replied and walked away with his son speaking in hushed tones.

No sooner had they stepped away than Master Lotal approached her. "Time to dance again," he said taking her paw and leading her to the dance floor.

She frowned, but followed without complaint. She had four dances remaining with him and did not want to draw it out all night. It was another fast dance, and she tried to have fun with it, but with each turn of the music, she liked Lotal less. He leered at her throughout the dance and when the song finished he simply walked away from her. She took a deep breath and turned to leave the dance floor in a different direction only to find another knight waiting for a dance with her. She smiled and took up the starting position of the new dance, holding her skirts up slightly with her paws. It was a complex reel that led the dancers all around the dance floor. She reveled in the dance, laughing as she went. As the dance finished, she was breathing harder than she would have liked.

When she made the last turn, her heart sank at the sight of Lotal approaching the dance floor. She quickly wove her way through the milling mass of people and slipped away from the dance floor in a different direction as the musicians started up another dance. She passed a pillar and was startled when someone gently touched her arm. She turned and was surprised to see Brittia nervously curtseying to her.

"I know Lord Arndt said that I would not bother you again tonight," Brittia said in haste, "but I felt like this needed to be said tonight."

Marilana waited as Brittia struggled with her words.

"I . . . I want to apologize," Brittia said finally, "What I said earlier was disrespectful and rude. It is hard for me to think of you as a noble when I have known you for so long as a peasant. I was surprised tonight when your response to my words was not what I expected. You used to heap disrespect on me when I was rude to you in school. I can see now that you have grown into a noble while I cling to my childish ways." Brittia stopped speaking and hung her head in shame. Marilana reached out her paw and lifted Brittia's chin to peer into her eyes.

"You must mature quickly if you intend to marry Master Arndt. This apology is a good start," Marilana said softly.

"I never realized the importance of proper manners. When I almost lost Frederick because of what I said to you . . . ," Brittia shook her head lost for words.

"I am glad that you finally have something worth fighting for," Marilana replied.

Brittia looked puzzled so Marilana explained.

"You have always disregarded my reasons for doing the things I do. I fought against your rudeness and against bandits to protect others. I had a purpose, a reason I deemed worth fighting for. You have found someone who I believe you can love. Your actions nearly caused him to be taken from you; but instead of giving up, you fought back by finding the right words and actions to prevent losing him. You came here and made a difficult apology as another way to prevent that loss. I think you will be more careful with your words and actions in the future."

"I know Frederick courted you for a time," said Brittia sourly.

"Yes, and he, like you, finds my skills and studies insulting. I was not right for him. I am glad that he found you, he thinks he wants someone like you."

"This doesn't mean that I am going to be your friend or agree with what you do," said Brittia coldly.

"No," laughed Marilana, "I did not think so. Nor do I think we will ever be friends or even allies. Although perhaps we can admit that sometimes we are not enemies. Goodnight, Brittia, and I hope you and Master Frederick Arndt find happiness. And one last word of advice; listen to Lady Arndt, she has perfected the art of manners even when facing those she despises."

Brittia frowned with confusion, but Marilana didn't choose to explain. She turned away with the intent of walking some more, but found an angry Lotal waiting for her. He stepped forward, seized her paw, and pulled her back to the dance floor. Marilana followed and sighed softly. She had three more dances with him. As they reached the dance floor, the music changed to the courtship dance. Marilana stopped and Lotal turned to face her.

"I am not accepting any courtships," she said firmly.

"Yes, but it is my choice when I want to dance with you. I say we dance now. Or would you rather lose face and honor by refusing?" he asked slyly.

"I will dance, but I will not accept," she said coldly.

He smiled malevolently as he stepped backward onto the dance floor. Marilana followed and took up the starting position of the dance with her open fan blocking his view of her face. The dance began when Marquiese and Mistress Katrine had taken their positions. Marilana flowed with the music through the twists and turns, slowly at first and then faster and faster. She concentrated on her breathing and Lotal's posture, keeping the fan between them at all times. Finally, Lotal dropped down to one knee, bowing his head and breathing hard. Marilana held the fan between them and curtseyed to him. Turning away with a snap of her fan, she realized that they were the last pair of dancers for the dance. Marquiese and Katrine watched from the side, Katrine with a grin and Marquiese slightly frowning. Marilana smiled and walked off the dance floor.

Lotal followed Marilana into the crowd, and grabbed her arm. Marilana turned to face him with her eyebrows raised.

"You will wait here with me; we will dance again after this dance," he said sharply.

"I will go where I please," she replied coldly, "and you can search me out when you are fit to dance again."

Lotal's scowl didn't prevent Marilana from yanking her arm away from him and walking away. She had no destination in mind; she just had to get away from him. She would not let him dictate where she was to wait his pleasure, they were of equal rank and she would not let him have any leverage over her. As the song neared its final stanza, she turned and started back toward the dance floor. She wanted to finish the dances with Lotal so she could be done with him. She waited among the onlookers. The song ended, and she smiled as she watched Master Timral lead a shyly smiling Lorlina onto the floor for the next dance. Suddenly Lotal gripped her elbow and pushed her forward through the crowd.

Once on the dance floor, Marilana turned and smiled coldly at Master Lotal. His smile was both predatory and angry. This time the song was a waltz. Marilana let Lotal lead her through the graceful steps and sweeping turns. They glared at each other throughout the dance, neither letting their emotions effect their performance, and at the end, she gave him the slightest of curtsies. As she turned to walk away again, he grabbed her paw and held fast.

"We dance again," he snarled.

She turned back to face him for her fifth dance with him, the other dancers left the floor. Marilana's anger flared as the first notes signaled the next courtship dance. Lotal grinned hungrily and took up his starting stance. Marilana vouchsafed him an icy smile before she snapped open her fan and again tried to lose herself in the dance. As the pace of the music quickened Marilana danced as fast as she could. Lotal fought to keep pace with her; his breathing labored and ragged. Finally, Lotal stumbled and dropped to one knee. Marilana spun through several more steps before stopping and curtseying to him still with her fan between them. She was breathing hard, but not nearly as hard as Lotal. Blood flushed his face under his thin fur and his pulse throbbed noticeably in his neck. *It'd serve him right if he passed out from over exertion right now*, she thought vindictively. Looking around, she saw that once again she and Lotal were the last dancers, and again Marquiese frowned as he watched. Lady Ophelia nodded her head to Marilana from where she stood next to Marquiese. Spinning on her heel, Marilana glided off the dance floor having danced her final dance with Master Lotal.

Marilana walked calmly through the crowd of onlookers and headed toward a group of unoccupied chairs. The musicians started up the next song, another fast reel, and people gathered around the dance floor to watch. Even with music playing, Marilana detected the sound of heavy breathing; she knew that Lotal was trailing after her. When she reached the clear area around the chairs, she turned and faced Lotal. He seemed surprised that she had known he was behind her, but his surprise quickly returned to anger.

"You made a fool of me tonight," he growled quietly stepping up to her.

"You did that yourself," Marilana replied without lowering her voice. "My ban was announced a full fifnight ago, so it was known that I would not be accepting any courtships. I told you before the first courtship dance, that I would not accept your courtship. Nothing has changed my mind."

Lotal glanced at the nobles nearby. Some watched their conversation curiously. Others shot covert glances at them. "Lower your voice," he growled. "This is a private matter and I do not want everyone in court to know about it."

"It is too late for that. If you had wanted it to remain private, you should have respected the ban and not danced the courtship dances," Marilana replied heatedly.

"This is not a proper place for this discussion," said the grey fox wincing and trying to push her toward one of the side doors.

"This is the only place to have this discussion," Marilana replied, and pulled back out of his grasp. "You have made a public spectacle of our interactions, so it will remain public. You chose to ask for the honor of competing under the colors of the Southern Tip. I granted your request, and although you lost all your pairings in the Jousting of Champions, you still competed honorably. I thank you for the honor you gave me. I have danced with you willingly in return. You chose to treat me poorly, you disregarded my wishes, and you ignored the ban that Lady Annabella announced. You tried to force me to accept your courtship by attempting to out-dance me. Instead I out-danced you and now, rather than be honorable and accept the outcome you should have expected, you are trying to claim that I insulted you."

"You are a high-spirited female who needs to learn her proper place," he said angrily without trying to stay quiet. "A proper wife should accept quietly, be seen and not heard, and obey without question. Any proper lady of the court knows this and should behave accordingly."

"I must disagree with you," replied Marilana firmly. "Many ladies of this court do not believe as you do, and many young lords would do well to listen to the ladies. Your own mother does not follow your line of thinking. As Lady Annabella's heir, I have no intention of becoming a puppet for a power-hungry boy who needs lessons in manners. I heard of your argument with the knights of Pandensy during the tournament, and they told me of your opinion of me."

"They lied," he snarled. "They were just trying to turn you against me. They have no honor—"

"You will not insult them," Marilana interrupted coldly. "I know them personally, and I know they were defending my honor. You seem to have no concept of honor since you just lied to me. I have no reason to accept any proposals from you in the future. Goodnight."

Lotal seized her arm before she could turn away from him. Marilana glared at him.

"We are not done with our conversation," he growled.

"Yes, we are," Marilana stated flatly.

"You will listen to me," Lotal growled.

"You will release her," rumbled a deep voice.

Lotal turned toward the speaker without releasing Marilana. Three lords stood scowling at Lotal with their arms crossed. Marilana could not identify them. Two were leopards, and one was an oryx with stunning long horns extending above his head.

"This is no business of yours," Lotal replied coldly.

"On the contrary," said the leopard in the middle, "as Lady Marilana said, you turned this into a public spectacle with your actions at the tournament. As a public matter, we have the right to interfere if we want to, and I have decided that I want to interfere."

The other two lords nodded agreement. Marilana glanced past them; many other nobles watched Lotal with disapproval.

"My Lords," said Lotal in a tight voice, "she has made a mockery of the honor I tried to bestow upon her."

"No," replied the oryx with the deep voice, "you used this whole affair to mock her. She took your actions with good grace and was respectful in telling you she would not accept your courtship. Your behavior in trying to push the issue is insulting and despicable."

"Yes," agreed the leopard on the left, "and she was perfectly in her rights to tell you her mind at the end of her obligation to you. You have no right to try to push the issue farther. She has behaved admirably. Your contact with her will be tolerated no longer."

Lotal glared at each of the lords in turn. When they did not back down, he released Marilana and stormed away without looking at her.

"He needs a lesson in manners," grumped the oryx, "and he should have apologized."

"His apology would not have been sincere," replied Marilana quietly.

They turned their attention to her and she curtseyed respectfully to them. The musicians started a new dance, and the crowds shifted about. Most nobles who had witnessed the scene with Lotal resumed their conversations.

"I would like to thank you for taking action," she smiled at them. "I would be pleased to learn your names."

"Of course, Lady Marilana," said the leopard in the middle with a slight bow. "I am Lord Ruberic of Herinsford. This is Lord Kenhol of Reine's Crossing," he indicated the leopard on the left, then turned to the oryx on the right, "and this is Lord Threine of Maefair."

Marilana was pleased to meet Lady Ophelia's and Mistress Ailse's fathers. She wondered how much they lived up to their reputations. She remembered too that Lord Ruberic was Lord Castant's cousin, and that he had assisted Marquiese in Bram's Fen to deal with Demdrake, Brittia's loathsome cousin. She was pleased to see some resemblance between him and Lord Castant. Lord Threine she had heard little about, but knew he was the high-lord who controlled the city of Maefair in service directly under King Rylan.

"I am honored, My Lords," Marilana replied bowing her head.

"My Lords, Lady Marilana, is something amiss?" asked Marquiese walking up to them.

"On the contrary," said Lord Ruberic, "we were just helping the young lady with an annoyance."

"Ah, Master Lotal," said Marquiese frowning. "I am glad you were of assistance to Lady Marilana. I am sure she had her paws full."

"She dealt with the situation graciously and has comported herself with utmost nobility," said Lord Threine gravely.

"Yes," agreed Lord Kenhol with a jovial laugh, "and sent that young whelp off with an earful."

Marilana smiled and said, "I simply told him in no uncertain terms that I would not tolerate aspersions against honorable knights of the realm, nor would I tolerate being lied to or pushed around. These gracious lords helped me keep the peace."

"That sounds honorable," replied Marquiese levelly, a twinkle of mirth in his eyes. "Thank you, My Lords, for lending your authority to such reasonable requests and helping to keep the peace of my father's hall. Now then, Lady Marilana, do you have any other urgent matters to attend to?"

"No, Your Highness," answered Marilana.

"Very well," said Marquiese, "by tradition I must dance only the courtship dance tonight and so I must ask you to dance the courtship dance with me. I am aware of your ban of all courtships including mine, so I will not take offense when you do not accept. I am hoping that you will consider this an exhibition dance and agree to dance with me. Also, as you are such a talented dancer, I would like to ask you to dance High Style."

"It would be my pleasure to dance High Style with you, Highness," Marilana curtseyed to Marquiese, and then curtsied to the lords. "Thank you again for your assistance, My Lords. It was a pleasure to meet you."

The lords were surprised, but nodded approvingly. Marquiese offered his paw to her and she placed her paw on his. With a nod of his head to the lords, Marquiese led her to the edge of the dance floor. Lotal, Timral, and several others were dancing a waltz. Looking around at the lances, Marilana realized that they were all bare except for her green and silver hanging from Marquiese's red and blue striped lance.

Marquiese had been annoyed at Lord Flaznek of West Cove. The old elk had approached him after his courtship dance with Ophelia and engaged him in a lengthy discussion about fishing rights, of all things. Marquiese had seen Lotal follow Marilana from the dance floor and had wanted to go intervene, but he could not be rude to the great-lord of West Cove. When he had finally gotten away, his feeling of betrayal had risen and he knew he had to find Marilana right away to find out what she up to that had his hackles up. When he had found her, he had been relieved, and was now feeling ashamed of thinking she was acting against him tonight.

"I should have been there to help with Lotal," Marquiese murmured softly to her so no one could overhear, and carefully did not look at her. "I was engaged in socializing, as is my duty tonight, and did not see where you disappeared to, I am sorry."

"You do not need to fight my battles," Marilana replied just as softly. "I am confident I can take care of myself. I must say I am looking forward to this dance."

Marquiese chuckled softly—he was excited for this dance as well—and let his worries dissipate. When the waltz ended Marquiese led Marilana out on the dance floor. Murmurs swept through the onlookers as they took up the more grandiose, extended, and difficult positions for High Style. The crowd swelled; everyone wanted to see how this dance would end, and no other dancers came onto the floor. Marquiese focused on his breathing as the first notes of the dance were played. In time with each other, they took the first slow steps, letting the movements flow with the music. As the music quickened, they stayed in perfect unison, dancing faster and faster, until finally, muscles burning and heart pounding, he could go further. In that instant, the dance ended. Marquiese bowed on one knee, and Marilana simultaneously curtseyed still with her fan at arm's length between them. They remained motionless for a moment, both trying to catch their breath. The crowd around the dance floor erupted in applause. With a soft swish, Marilana closed her fan and rose smiling to face Marquiese. He rose at the same time and smiled back at her.

Marquiese studied Marilana's eyes as they faced each other on the dance floor. He felt more alive and everything around them seemed sharper after such a spectacular dance. He did not regret his decision to dance his last dance of the night with her. No one could find fault with his choice to not dance again tonight, not after that display. The applause from the onlookers diminished.

Still gazing into her eyes, he slightly bowed his head to her. "Thank you for dancing with me," he said quietly. "I can honestly say that you are the best dancer I have ever danced with. I am glad that you sorted out your problem with Lotal before we danced and that you did so without breaking the peace. I think it freed our thoughts to focus on the dance."

"Thank you for asking me to dance, Highness," Marilana replied. "I enjoyed it immensely. I also want to thank you for worrying about me; it makes me feel glad that I returned to your court."

"You were right about the tonic too," he teased. "I felt much better after your skillful treatment."

Marilana blushed and smiled shyly at him. After a moment she broke their eye contact and looked past him. He saw concern tighten her features. She looked back at him, and although she still smiled, the joy he had seen only a moment before was gone. She curtseyed deeply to him.

"I am afraid duty calls," she said, "but thank you . . . for everything."

"Of course, Marilana," he replied and walked reluctantly past her toward where Timral stood smiling.

He realized that most nobles had been watching them gaze at each other on the dance floor. He worried briefly, wondering if the nobles thought he and Marilana had stepped beyond duty for the dance, but dismissed the concern. Judging by the many smiles and nods he was receiving, most of the spectators approved of his choice to dance the last dance with such a talented dancer. Once he reached the edge of the dance floor, he glanced back at Marilana to see her gliding gracefully toward Lady Annabella and Earek. Lady Annabella smiled politely, but Earek scowled by her shoulder. He watched as Earek gave Marilana a tightly furled paper. Marilana unfurled it and as she read, she too scowled. The three spoke in haste; then Marilana and Earek quickly disappeared into the crowd.

"I wonder what that was about," Marquiese said frowning.

"I do not know," replied Timral. "What I do know is that you and Marilana were made to dance together. That was amazing, Highness."

Marquiese smiled at his friend. "Thank you, Master Timral, I appreciate your candor."

"Especially since you are about to be showered with enough flattery to last a lifetime," Timral laughed and quickly moved aside to speak with nobles close by.

Marquiese stifled a resigned sigh and fixed a polite smile as noble daughters emerged from the crowd in every direction. They swarmed around him now that he no longer had designated dances to perform. They shoved each other aside to compliment him on his stunning dance. Each batted her eyes, pouted her lips, and hinted that she would like to have the next dance. He made polite excuses, attempting to break free from the swarm. The girls had to make way or risk appearing rude, but still they managed to slow his progress considerably. He sought Master Castant through the sea of veils and hats wondering what had demanded Marilana's urgent attention.

The main doors to the hall stood open, and as he approached them, he noticed a flurry of activity in the entrance hall beyond. Servants hurried toward the main palace doors carrying what appeared to be saddlebags and travel supplies. A group of guards wearing Southern Tip insignia hurried down the stairs from the guest rooms. Marquiese froze. Marilana and Earek, garbed for travel, were amidst the guards. He started toward the doors frowning as Marilana swung a heavy traveling cloak around her shoulders and darted across the entrance hall.

Someone stepped in front of Marquiese. He recoiled quickly to avoid colliding with the man.

"Forgive me, Your Highness," said Master Arndt with a bow. "My guest wishes to greet you."

Marquiese stifled his anger; he could not afford to be rude tonight, even though he wanted to rush after Marilana. He supplanted his impatience and anger with calm politeness.

"Your guest, Master Arndt?" he asked politely.

"Yes, she tells me you are an old acquaintance from your years of silence," said Master Arndt, extending his arm to his right.

Marquiese turned slightly with a polite smile as Brittia approached him.

"Miss Brittia," he said flatly, "I see you have made your way to the royal court."

"Yes, even though my family has only recently entered service to Lord Arndt, I have been granted the high honor of entering a courtship with Master Frederick," she said batting her lashes at Marquiese.

"Congratulations, I hope you will be happy," Marquiese said politely and turned away from her.

"I had hoped to hear from you after you left the Southern Tip," she persisted. "I thought I had been a good friend to you, Marquiese, and I see that your dancing is greatly improved."

"You will address me properly." Marquiese frowned at her. "When I was in the Southern Tip, I was in hiding and therefore was known simply. I am back in my proper place now and you will remember your manners. As for my dancing, the mistakes were intentional. I never danced properly in the Southern Tip to prevent anyone from taking notice of my skills. Now if you will excuse me."

Ignoring Brittia's shamed blushing and Master Arndt's anger, he walked around them toward the doors. He knew he should not have treated them so harshly, but it angered him that Brittia was flirting with him despite having entered a courtship with Master Arndt. And he was annoyed that she remained at the festivities after what had occurred between her and Marilana. He surmised Lord Arndt would get many headaches from the schemes that pair would devise. At least if the courtship lasted, and knowing Master Arndt's quicksilver preferences, Marquiese had his doubts.

Before he reached the entrance hall doors, Master Castant appeared in the doorway and spotted him. Castant quickly wove his way through the crowd and stopped in front of him with a slight bow.

"What is going on?" Marquiese asked urgently.

"Highness, have you spoken with your father yet?" asked Castant cautiously.

"No," Marquiese answered slowly.

"Then you must speak with him without delay. I can tell you nothing more until you do," said Castant quickly.

Marquiese scanned the crowds and spotted King Rylan and Lady Annabella walking casually toward the entrance doors. They smiled and stopped to speak to other nobles as they meandered, appearing in no hurry to reach the doors. Marquiese smiled slightly as he started toward them; they did not act as if they were walking together for any reason other than to enjoy each other's company. When he reached them, he bowed slightly to his father. The nobles, including Lady Annabella, stepped away to give them a moment of privacy. Master Castant spoke quietly to Lady Annabella in their own small space of separation.

"What is going on that I must speak with you, Father?" asked Marquiese in a hushed tone.

"You have a duty to this gathering," Rylan said simply. "You must act as though you are enjoying yourself."

"Of course, my apologies," said Marquiese forcing a smile for the onlookers. "Now, where did Marilana rush off to?"

Rylan motioned for Lady Annabella to join them as he answered. "Marilana was called away by duties to the Southern Tip."

"A messenger arrived several hours ago that required Marilana's urgent attention," said Lady Annabella with a calm smile. "Earek took the message as Marilana was preoccupied and informed me of its contents. I chose to wait for Marilana to finish her obligations before informing her. She had to leave immediately to manage the situation. She asked me to pass on her apologies for leaving so suddenly and her continued good wishes for a happy birthday celebration."

"What situation? Where did she go?" persisted Marquiese.

"Now is not the time for that discussion," stated Rylan. "Suffice it to say for now that she went to do her duty, and you will act pleasantly for the duration of the night as is your duty."

Marquiese sighed and nodded, then looked up and forced another smile. "I will do my duty, but we will speak soon after."

Rylan nodded and motioned for Lady Annabella to continue walking with him. They meandered on around the room, and Castant hurried to Marquiese.

"Tell me this," Marquiese said quietly while attempting a smile, "if I left now could I catch her?"

Castant studied him a moment before answering. "No, I do not think you could even if you rode your horse to death, which I would not recommend. She planned to make the best possible time and push her men to their limits. She had Storm saddled, and he and the other Southern Tip horses can manage the pace better than any of your mounts."

"Thank you, Castant, we will speak more later, but I intend to follow her as soon as possible."

*

Marquiese frowned as he paced in Lady Annabella's rooms. It had been several hours since Marilana's departure and only about a half hour since he had left the ball. Many nobles still occupied the great hall and several young couples had been meandering in the gardens even though it was well after midnight and cold enough to see their breath. Marquiese had retired to his rooms only long enough to give packing instructions to his menservants. Then he had cautiously made his way to Lady Annabella's rooms. She had been waiting for him along with Master Castant, but refused to tell him more until King Rylan arrived. Now she and Castant stood calmly watching him pace.

A light knock sounded on the door.

"Enter," called Lady Annabella.

The door opened and King Rylan slipped in.

"Good, you are here," growled Marquiese. "Now please tell me what is going on."

"Watch your manners, Marquiese," said Rylan darkly, then nodded to Lady Annabella without waiting for Marquiese's contrite apology.

"The messenger brought a ransom letter to Marilana," she said without preamble. "Ten children were captured in raids of several villages the evening of the tournament. The bandits demanded that Marilana bring a ransom to a specific meadow at noon today. She must enter the meadow alone and unarmed to ransom the children. If the ransom is not met on time, or if she is not the one to enter the meadow, or she is not alone, the letter claimed that ten little corpses would be returned to the parents. It further stated that ten children would be collected and executed every fifnight until the demands were met. She had to leave immediately and ride with all her might to arrive on time. I fear that no matter how hard she rides, she might not make it, and even if she does something will go wrong."

Marquiese stared at Lady Annabella's concerned face, his thoughts churning.

"That is almost certainly a trap," he said with quiet rage. "Marilana has said that bandits would never deal with her directly. I have also never heard of a bandit group making such demands before."

"I agree," sighed Lady Annabella, "but what else can she do but try to rescue those children? She said she would do everything in her power to thwart the trap, but she would not risk those children's lives needlessly."

"Just when I was beginning to trust her, she betrays me yet again," growled Marquiese fiercely.

"Betrays you?" gasped Lady Annabella. "You of all people know why she is doing this. She watched two young girls, who she regarded as sisters, be raped and murdered by bandits. She vowed to end such predations. How can you say she is betraying you?"

"I know why she is going to rescue those children," said Marquiese frustrated, "and I understand her vow. However, as soon as I saw her leaving, I felt betrayed. I do not know why or how. I am just certain she is betraying me. I must follow her to find out why; I have to resolve this betrayal if I am ever to be at peace and move on with my life."

Marquiese looked from Lady Annabella to his father. They frowned at him lost in their own thoughts. Finally, Rylan looked at Lady Annabella and she nodded.

Castant moved quickly forward. "I wish to go with Prince Marquiese. I do not like this situation any better than he does, and I have come to view Marilana as a friend. I want to help her and defend Marquiese."

"Very well," Rylan said gravely, "you two will accompany Lady Annabella back to the Southern Tip and you will take a legion of guardsmen with you. If it is a trap, it is possible that Frishka's Confidant is behind it. If he is there, be careful, Marilana may not be the only target. Get some sleep if you can; you leave the hour after dawn."

16

Marilana peered through the branches of a bush and down into the meadow. She understood why the bandit leader had chosen this meadow. Sparse brush covered the ridge she lay on and separated the meadow from the road behind her. The meadow was bordered on the other sides by trees and thick underbrush. The forest extended across the hills beyond the meadow and on, past the distant southern border of the realm. She had scouted the trees herself and had received warnings from her bandit hunter protégé, Child. The trees were full of archers on all sides, and many more bandits were positioned behind the underbrush with horses ready to flee. This was the largest gathering of bandits she had ever seen in the Southern Tip, in the range of two hundred armed bandits.

She did not have enough men to encircle the entire area. If she tried to flank the bandits on each side or to attack from the front, the archers were in prime position to do major damage to her attacking forces and allow most of the bandits to flee. If she attacked the center of the arc from behind, there would be minimal damage to her forces, but again most of the bandits would escape. Any attack left the children completely undefended and there were plenty of archers to spare a few arrows to kill them.

It was a deadly trap, and Marilana knew she was the target. She feared to be caught in it, yet let her mind settle into the bandit hunter focus, blocking out all emotions. Marilana committed herself to the only remaining option. Most of her force was gathered in the forest beyond the bandits' sentries waiting to attack the center of the arc from behind. The rest waited with Marilana behind the ridge. Child was hidden in the trees somewhere close by. She was glad she had chosen to leave Storm at the Estates; she did not want the horse to be shot with arrows while trying to come to her aid.

"I do not like it, Sister," scowled Earek. "You are putting yourself at too much risk."

"You know what would happen if I let someone else enter the meadow in my stead," she replied calmly. "Wait for the children to reach the safety of the ridge before giving the signal to attack."

"At least let some of us accompany you," grumbled Captain Hayden. "You have charged us with your protection, M'Lady. How can we protect you if we are not with you?"

"You have your orders, Captain," she replied calmly. "Would you have those children killed needlessly?"

"I don't want children hurt, M'Lady, but I would rather you be safe," he growled then turned away to issue the orders.

Down in the meadow a cloaked and hooded man emerged from the shadows of the trees and ushered a group of children through the underbrush. He stood to the side of the children and ordered them to kneel in the grass. Marilana counted ten small forms. Closing her eyes, she took a deep breath and released it slowly. It was time to spring a trap and hopefully not get caught in it.

"It is time," she said and grasped Earek's shoulder, "I am counting on you, Brother. I know I cannot order you to not try to find me if events conspire against us, but I want you to think carefully before rushing headlong into action. Protect Mother and be strong. Tell Marquiese . . . everything."

Without waiting for his response, she stood, brushed off her dress, and strode over the ridge into full view of the archers. She focused on the man with the children and strode toward him purposefully. She could see the glitter of his eyes as she approached him, but could not make out his features in the shadow of his hood. She stopped three paces from him. Carefully she detached a large purse from her belt and held it up. "A king's ransom for ten children," she said shaking the bag so that the coins inside jingled.

He casually held out a black-gloved paw.

"Release the children first," said Marilana.

"You are unarmed?" he asked in a calm baritone voice.

"Yes," she replied.

He motioned to the children and they got up and ran for the ridge behind her. He dropped his paw to his side and waited. Marilana watched the man for a moment without moving, then glanced back over her shoulder. The children scrambled up the ridge.

"Your ransom," she said turning back to the man.

He made no move to take the bag; instead he let out a quiet chuckle and took a step backward away from her.

"You are the ransom," he snickered and turned toward the trees.

Marilana dropped the bag and dove to the side as hundreds of bowstrings twanged. Rolling into a crouch she glanced back at the ridge and saw arrows peppering the ridge and the meadow behind her. More arrows arced through the air forcing her to roll out of the way again. Looking toward the trees, the meadow was free of arrows. The man had disappeared into the trees on the left, so she ran for the center of the arc knowing that her forces would be moving toward the same point. A chirping sound caught her attention and she zigzagged to the right as more arrows fell along her path. Suddenly the chirping squawked and fell silent. Marilana suppressed a scream of rage—she could not worry about Child right now—and focused on her own survival. Reaching the edge of the trees Marilana darted back to the left and dove through a patch of dense underbrush. She continued her roll on the other side of the brush and knocked an antelope off his feet. As she had expected, the bandits were waiting for her.

Surprise flashed across the creatures' faces as they adjusted to her position. They had not anticipated her roll through the dense brush and had taken positions around a thinner section. Marilana did not wait for the surprise to pass. She lashed out with her right foot as she rolled up onto her left and swept the nearest man off his feet. The wolf landed with a loud thump on the forest floor. Marilana pivoted over him and wrenched the sword from his grasp. She made a quick swipe across his throat, then spun and stabbed the next creature under his arm as he raised his sword to strike down at her. Spinning around him as he collapsed, she spotted a line of horses and darted toward them only to have to dodge back as someone lunged toward her from the left. Spinning, she parried a blow from the right, and was forced to defend from the men that had been behind her. With her momentum disrupted, more men were running to join the fight from both directions. In a matter of seconds, Marilana found herself surrounded by a ring of spears and swords. She parried and attacked and stabbed wherever she found an opening. Paws reached for her and she stabbed or sliced at them forcing them to withdraw. Several creatures pushed through the ring of steel toward her only to fall victim to her sword. She knew if she could hold them off long enough, help was on its way, and they would be forced to break their ring.

Several men lunged forward at the same time. She parried, spun, and stabbed. Thick arms reached around her from behind, and she swung her sword over her head and stabbed down behind her back, feeling resistance as the blade penetrated flesh. The arms dropped and crimson droplets sprayed off her sword as she parried another spear thrust. More arms reached through the ring of steel toward her and she spun on her toes; her sword whistled in a deadly arc around her. Paws jerked back behind the spear points. Shouts and the sound of horse hooves grew louder. If only she could hold the men off a little longer, help would arrive; but she was tiring and overwhelmed by too many opponents. Pain suddenly erupted behind her eyes, and Marilana knew no more.

Earek watched helplessly as Marilana faced the hooded man in the meadow, unarmed and proud. The children scrambled up the ridge and he silently urged them to climb faster. Something was about to happen; he could feel the tension in the air. Guardsmen helped the children over the top of the ridge and herded them down to the carriage waiting on the road. Marilana extended the ransom, but the man turned away from her.

"Down!" yelled Earek as hundreds of arrows left the trees and peppered the ridge.

He rolled to his knees and risked looking at the meadow as more arrows arced toward them. His heart sank as he saw Marilana dodging arrows and sprinting straight at the waiting bandits. Turning quickly, he signaled with two fingers at the waiting archers. Two flaming arrows shot high into the sky. Earek ran down the hill and leaped onto his waiting horse. On the road the carriage driver whipped up the horses and pulled off quickly down the road surrounded by an escort. At least the children were safe. Now they faced the daunting task of rescuing Marilana.

On either side of the ridge, horses charged into the trees, racing toward the bandits. Earek turned his horse off the road and joined the stream of men on the south edge of the ridge. As he pushed his horse forward, he suddenly became aware that the bandit archers were no longer firing at them. He felt dread in the pit of his stomach as he heard shouting and crashes over the sound of the charging horses. Looking ahead, he saw a rider racing back along the column toward him. Earek slowed and directed his horse out of the mass charge.

"The bandits are racing into the woods in every direction!" shouted Major Kolt as he drew rein and turned his horse. "It appears that once we charged, the archers dropped out of the trees to waiting horses, and now they are fleeing in every direction. Captain Hayden ordered the men to let the bandits run and is pushing on around the meadow to try to reach Lady Marilana."

Earek nodded and spurred his horse forward. Major Kolt and Guardsman Shaub stayed with him, but he did not push as fast now. Captain Hayden was far ahead.

Earek watched the ground for tracks as he rode around the meadow. Horse tracks were everywhere. Most of the tracks led around the meadow and covered any other signs. Off to the south, horse tracks spread out into the trees. Occasional broken arrows or bows lay where they had been discarded during the bandits' flight. When Earek heard cursing, he looked ahead through the trees. A completely different scene met his gaze. The underbrush was smashed and broken, many bodies littered the ground, and dark red pools glistened in the afternoon sun.

Earek drew rein and dismounted inspecting the carnage. Captain Hayden glowered at the dead creatures, but said nothing as Earek surveyed the area. Horse tracks and boot prints covered the ground. One wolf's throat was cut close to the border of the meadow, and a black bear appeared to have been stabbed down through his neck. Several others had been stabbed under their arms or in the side where the leather armor was weak or the mail did not cover. Nine creatures lay dead and every tree and bush surrounding the area was splattered with blood. Earek inspected the underbrush bordering the meadow and found a section close to the dead wolf that had been broken as if someone had rolled through it. Looking through into the meadow, he studied the pattern of arrows studding the ground. Most of the arrows stood out from the hillside of the ridge opposite where he stood, but a thick line of arrows crossed the meadow from the center directly to where he stood. Turning back, he met Captain Hayden's gaze.

"Marilana," Earek growled.

"I thought so too," agreed Hayden. "She seized someone's sword and slew a few bandits, but there were too many for her to fend off. I cannot tell which direction she was taken; there are too many horse tracks and they often cross each other. Whoever this leader is, he knew how to get away and stop us from following too quickly. Several patrols are following some of the larger trails, but I told them to only go a league and then return to the Estates."

"Good, we will regroup there and determine what they found. While we wait, we need to assemble the best trackers available and devise a plan," said Earek.

"What! And leave M'Lady in the paws of these bandits?" asked Major Kolt in outrage.

"We will go after her as quickly as we can and we will get her back," said Earek placing his paw on Kolt's shoulder, "but if we charge after them blindly, we could spend hours chasing the wrong groups and fall into ambushes set to distract us. Just before Marilana entered the meadow, she told me to think before rushing into action. Heeding her advice will save us time and energy chasing false leads."

"I agree, Master Earek," said Hayden nodding. "Lady Annabella will be arriving in a few hours. We need to have a plan of action to present to her. I will set a detachment to bury these corpses."

Earek nodded and mounted his horse. He surveyed Marilana's destruction once more before spurring his horse back toward the road.

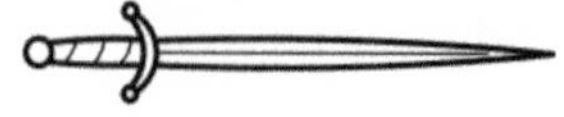

Marquiese frowned as he stood with Master Castant on the steps to Lady Annabella's castle and surveyed the busy stableyard. Everywhere he looked servants and guardsmen hurried about. They seemed to be preparing for something, but no one had exchanged more than demur greetings. Lady Annabella ascended the steps followed closely by Zariff and shook her head.

"No one will say any more than to tell me Master Earek will return soon," she said in a dark undertone.

With the sound of running horses, they glanced toward the gate. Every creature in the yard paused looking fearfully at the gate, but when Earek was seen riding through, everyone resumed working faster than before. The frenzied activity worried Marquiese just as much as the bald fear on the servants' faces. Earek rode directly to the castle steps with his small escort. Marquiese was startled to see a young doe holding tight to Earek with her right arm.

"Mother," said Earek seriously, "I am glad you are home safe. Your Highness, I am not surprised you are here, and I would be grateful for your assistance in an urgent matter. Master Castant, welcome."

"Earek, what is going on?" asked Marquiese as Earek dismounted. "All I have been told was that you would return soon."

"I will explain everything inside after I get Child to the healers," said Earek helping the doe down from his horse.

Marquiese noticed the girl's left arm was tied in a crude sling and bandage. As soon as her hooves hit the ground, however, she ran straight to Lady Annabella and hugged her tightly. Lady Annabella protectively enclosed the slight form in her arms and glared at Earek.

"She should not be here," Lady Annabella said quietly.

"We have no choice; she needs to see a healer and we do not have time to wait," he said gently. "She came to me and bravely agreed to come see the healer here. Come, we must hurry."

Earek ushered them up the stairs and inside the castle. The doe held tightly to Lady Annabella as they rushed to the infirmary. At the door Earek took her good hoof in his paws and bent to look her eye to eye.

"You remember Healer Magus?" he asked gently as the healer hurried to them.

The girl nodded, smiling at the healer.

"Good girl," Earek patted her hoof, "I need to talk with Lady Annabella about Marilana while the healer helps you. Will you stay with him?"

The girl's expression hardened and she nodded more firmly. She looked once at Lady Annabella and then entered the infirmary.

"Healer Magus," Earek called, "do what you can for her and then I need to see both of you as soon as possible."

"Of course, Master Earek," Healer Magus replied with a bow.

Turning, Earek rushed Lady Annabella, Zariff, Castant, and Marquiese down the hallways and into the war room. Guardsmen clustered around maps spread out on the table. Captain Hayden looked up when they entered the room.

"Did you find The Phantom, Master Earek?" he asked seriously.

"Yes, she is with Healer Magus. She was shot in the arm with an arrow, but the wound does not look too serious," Earek replied brusquely. "Please keep the men away from her. Now if you all would excuse us."

The guardsmen saluted with fists to hearts and filed out of the room. Earek closed the doors behind them and turned to face Marquiese, Castant, Zariff, and Lady Annabella. He took a deep breath while studying their faces.

"Marilana has been seized by the bandits," Earek said darkly and proceeded to tell them briefly of the ransom exchange.

"So, you ran back here rather than pursue them!" Marquiese exclaimed angrily.

"I needed the trackers," replied Earek calmly, "There were too many tracks to follow. Some went north and some east and west, but the majority went south. I am reasonably certain that Marilana was taken south as well, but the tracks are difficult to follow, constantly doubling back and crossing each other."

"You have men to use," retorted Marquiese, "and most bandit groups are less than fifty men. How many men do you need to track one bandit group?"

Earek shook his head. "This was not just one bandit group. I think it was the new bandit leader we were warned about. This trap used at least two hundred men, maybe more. I am not wasting my energy tracking every bandit's trail. I sent the trackers to the border to look for where the bandits crossed to the south and follow the trails from there."

"And in the meantime," Marquiese snorted, "you went out to find some girl who was not allowed in the castle."

"That girl is our best chance at finding Marilana quickly," said Lady Annabella softly.

Marquiese frowned at her.

"I know Marilana told you about the family who died in the house where you stayed during your time in hiding," Lady Annabella continued. "This girl is the sole survivor. When her aunt came to take her, the girl ran away. What Marilana did not tell you is that the girl ran back to Marilana and she raised her as best she could. I helped as much as the girl would allow. Her name was Zara, but now she only responds to Child, Marilana's pet name for her. Child is not normal; her family's murder altered her mind. It is not that she was not allowed to come to the castle, but that she cannot mentally cope with being around so many men. Marilana found that the only way to keep Child alive was to give her a reason to live. Marilana taught her everything she could to allow Child to live a life of her own. Like Marilana, Child chose the path of revenge for her family and the protection of others. The bandits call her The Phantom because she has taken up Marilana's bandit hunting, and, like The Ghost, she is very skilled at stealth."

"Next to Marilana, Child is the best tracker in the Southern Tip," said Earek. "She has hunted bandits beyond the border and is our best bet to find Marilana quickly. Marilana introduced me to Child a few months ago so that Child would know I could be trusted. I went out to find her, knowing that she had been nearby when Marilana had been captured. If she had not been wounded, I never would have found her. She wanted to go after Marilana immediately, but I convinced her that I needed more men to take on the bandits. Her impatience is the only reason she consented to come to the castle for help from Healer Magus. Any other time, Magus has had to go to Child to do any healing beyond Marilana's ability. She will not wait for the troops to be marshaled."

"Nor should she," said Lady Annabella firmly. "She needs to get out of this hive of people and return to her solitude."

"Yes," agreed Earek, "and she will be faster alone. She can find us and give us directions once she knows where we need to go."

"The Phantom, Marilana's protégé. I should not be surprised that she is so young, but I am. So will we leave soon?" asked Marquiese hopefully.

"Within a couple of hours, I think," nodded Earek. "I have the men preparing for at least a couple fifnights in the forest, and I will have Healer Magus prepare to follow us at a moment's notice."

"You are expecting casualties?" asked Lady Annabella.

"Our patrols came across six bandits fleeing from the meadow," sighed Earek looking at the map on the table. "They fought fiercely and when they recognized defeat, they slit their own throats rather than be captured. Whoever this leader is, he has strong control of the bandits. Most bandits sell out information to secure their freedom. These did not hesitate to take their own lives, leading me to believe that they feel strongly enough about his secrets to die for him."

Marquiese nodded his head slowly. If this man was one of the Hungdie as Marilana feared, then the bandits had good reason to fear for their lives if they betrayed him. Marquiese feared greatly for Marilana if this man was one of the legendary assassins. He also wondered if she had been his final target, or if she was just bait for another trap. A trap he would have to spring.

"Zariff, what more do we need to do? Will you lead the men south?" Earek asked deferring to the older man.

"No Earek, I will not," Zariff said firmly.

"But you are Lady Annabella's Captain-General. If you do not lead them, who will?" Earek asked frowning.

"You, Major-General Earek, have already taken on that role," Zariff said quietly. "You know what needs to be done. This is what you have been training for. It is time for you to lead. You and Prince Marquiese will lead the armies south. This is not Captain Hayden's first campaign. He can help you. Use his knowledge. I will remain here with Lady Annabella and use the Home Guard to secure the Southern Tip. I do not want any bandits taking advantage of the army's absence to make raids. Send us reports, but do not wait for our response before taking action. Good luck, and may The Goddess favor your campaign."

Earek stood straighter and nodded. Marquiese hoped they were up to the task; the icy fear sinking into his bones told him that they were Marilana's only hope.

17

Marilana's head throbbed. She wanted to groan or move, but she did not know where she was, so she thought it best to remain still. Instead she focused on her breathing and the pain receded to a dull ache. Continuing to regulate her breathing, she tried to determine where she was without revealing she was awake. Her paws were tied above her head, and she assumed she was hanging from the pole that pressed against her back. Aside from her head and a few small muscle aches, she did not seem to be in very bad condition. She concluded from her headache and slow thoughts that she must have been given sedating herbs to make her sleep during her transport. As her thoughts cleared, she heard fires crackling, spoons tapping against kettles, horses whinnying, wagons groaning as they were loaded or unloaded, and a smith hammering on metal. She remembered the events at the meadow and being surrounded by the bandits. She could only conclude, therefore, that she had been captured and was on display in a camp. She heard the drone of voices all around her, so she believed the camp to be large. Suddenly a voice emerged from the din.

"It's too dangerous to hold her here," growled a male with a deep voice. "Most of the men just want to see her die. If she wakes up and escapes, there is no telling how many of us will die before she is stopped. I don't care about your vow to make her scream for us. Most of us would like to see the despair in her eyes when she's beaten and she realizes that all she did was for nothing, but not if it could cost us our lives. When she wakes up, you will have to make sure she cannot escape. It would be far safer just to slit her throat and be done with it."

"First of all, she is not your prisoner," replied a calm baritone voice Marilana recognized as that of the man from the meadow. "She is my prisoner and mine alone. You and the other men agreed to help me capture her in return for the security of knowing that she would no longer hunt you. In addition, I vowed to make her scream for you, to put her pain on display for those who want to hurt her, and to make sure she will never hunt any of you again. Once you and the other men are satisfied with your vengeance against her, I will take her into my personal care and she will never bother you again. Second, if you doubt my skills again, I will demonstrate them on you. I planned her capture, took the same risks you did, and will continue to make my own decisions without consulting you or anyone else. She will not escape on her own."

"We call her The Ghost for good reason," the first man insisted, "we do not understand how she has done the things she has done. She killed nine of our men at the meadow while initially unarmed and dodging arrows. How can you be sure?"

"And third," continued the baritone voice as if there had been no interruption, "if you had wanted to do something to her in her sleep, it is too late."

"What?" squawked the first man in alarm.

"Marilana dear, you might as well open your eyes," said the male with the baritone voice drawing nearer.

Now that one of them had recognized that she was awake, she knew it was pointless to continue to feign sleeping. Marilana slowly lifted her head and opened her eyes. She ignored the two men, and examined her surroundings. The pole she hung from stood alone in a large clearing surrounded by tents. Beyond the tents there was a forest cascading down the slopes of towering mountains on every side. The camp appeared to be situated in a valley of the Great Mountains. Judging by the shadows, they were still on the north face of the mountains and, as long as the camp did not continue to move south, she was not too far from home. It was late afternoon; the sky was a clear cold blue and thankfully showed no signs of the coming winter snows. The air seemed unusually warm for this time of the year, and so she looked closely at the area around her. Melon-sized stones made a ring five paces wide on the ground around her, and inside that ring she found the source of the warmth. Three large braziers formed an even triangle around her at a distance that kept her comfortably warm. Peering down at her dress, Marilana noted that her divided skirts were rumpled and blood splattered, but mostly intact with a few small cuts. She wiggled her feet and found that they were unbound, and her riding boots had been removed.

One of the men stepped closer to her and, careful not to look at the man who had moved, she lifted her eyes. She studied the man furthest from her first. He was a large grizzly bear in a rough brown coat and pants with scuffed boots. Dirty and travel-worn, he snarled at her as she coldly studied his face. She noted that he remained outside the ring of stones as if he had received orders not to get too close to her. After a moment of her scrutiny, he turned and quickly stalked away into the camp. She watched him until he disappeared around a tent.

She looked back at the tent facing her, and noticed another creature. A goat knelt beside the closed tent flaps in dirty brown clothes and worn leather armor. He seemed familiar somehow, but did not look up at her. The tent itself was made of stout brown canvas, a little different than the other tents she could see, and had a large amount of space around it, like a separate camp of its own.

Only then did she turn her attention to the man standing a pace from her. She studied him closely, but was careful to avoid meeting his eyes. He was a lion, probably five or so years older than Marquiese. Unlike Marquiese, though, his growing mane was deep brown, almost black, and he had dark tufts wafting from his ears. He wore clean black woolen pants and coat, and his black boots were polished to a dull shine. He had a black leather belt around his waist and from the belt hung a black-sheathed sword. He waited patiently with an amused smirk and his paws behind his back, letting her study him without interruption. When she was satisfied with her observations, she turned away.

"Will you not meet my eyes, Marilana?" he chuckled softly in the baritone voice she had heard before. "You are everything the fool said you were, and more, so much more. He said you were proud and strong. You are stronger than he knew. He said you had wit, but you are intelligent. He said you would be easily broken, but he was wrong. Yes, I was right to study you and set my trap to capture you. You are the perfect creature for me, and the perfect bait for another."

Marilana had resisted the urge to look at him, but upon the last statement she could not resist any longer. His eyes caught her gaze and she felt as if an iron band had been tightened around her chest. She stared into his black eyes and saw what she had feared. Pain, suffering, longing, and pleasure. She had peered into eyes like his only once before. Terror gripped her.

"Hungdie," she breathed.

His cruel smile bared his sharpened teeth. She shivered reflexively and all her fur bristled. For the first time since she was little, she wanted to flee screaming for help and safety. Yet his eyes held her paralyzed by her own fear, her own nightmare. It would not have mattered if she had been untied with her feet on the ground. She could not take her eyes from his. He stepped closer to her and she pulled her head back breathing fast. He was a predator and she was his trapped prey.

"I am glad you recognize my order," he said quietly. "It means that I was right about you. I was told once about a young lioness who could have led our order to grandeur not seen since before the time of Maebala. But she chose to preserve life instead of embracing pain. Still, I was told that if she could be found as a young woman, she would be invaluable to us. She would be one on whom we could practice the finer arts of pain. She could bear us children to be proud of. And now I have found and trapped you. Your strength of mind and body combined with your knowledge of the old ways will allow us to push you beyond the limits of normal people. The finer arts of pain can only be practiced on one who embraces life yet can endure pain beyond measure. I have caught the rarest mortal flower known to the Hungdie."

He paused and glanced away from her as someone walked by outside the ring of stones. Marilana blinked several times trying to clear her mind and regain control of her fear. She was facing a nightmare come true, yet she reminded herself that she was still Lady Marilana Ranat, Bandit Hunter, and Hero of the Realm. He turned back to her and she forced herself to meet his eyes. She told herself that he was a man, a dangerous, psychotic man, but a man all the same.

"Ah, so beautiful," he said with a hungry smile, "you are so full of fear, and yet your strength prevails. Even now I can see the intelligence pushing through the fear. Such strength you do possess. It will be a shame if I am forced to break your will before I get to enjoy your pain. I see the questions forming in your mind. Ask and I will answer, but be sure you want to hear the answers."

Marilana studied him; she was still breathing fast, but she had to know.

"You did not know I was the girl you sought until I woke, so you must have had another reason for capturing me. You said I was bait for a trap," she whispered. "A trap for whom?"

"Straight to the point," he laughed. "Very well, and since I know you will continue asking questions about the matter, I will tell you everything from the beginning. Wait just a moment."

He turned and called to the goat by the tent. "Saffon, my chair."

The goat jumped and hurried to retrieve a folding camp chair from the tent she faced. Marilana watched the goat closely as he set the chair so that it faced her but the lion would not have to crane his neck back to look at her face. Without so much as a glance at her, the goat returned to his position by the tent. Marilana slowed her breathing while the lion took his seat.

"Ah, better," he sighed, "I would offer you a seat, but you have not been trained yet. Once you obey me without question, then you will sit with me as a decent individual. So, from the beginning, I will spare you some time and give you the brief version. The family of Mercurer has been hunted for several generations. I was chosen to continue their demise when my father was killed. I watched and waited and learned about my subject, King Rylan, for several years before he gave me a great opportunity. He married the woman Prinka without knowing she had a son. Remarkably, I had met the young tiger on my pilgrimage to the Great Rift. He had proven useful on that trip and I had uncharacteristically let him live. I went and found him again, befriended the fool boy, and used him to get into the Palace of Maefair. Through Frishka, I was able to learn much more about Rylan and his family."

"While biding my time, the fool asked me to teach him my skills. He did not know that I was one of the Hungdie, but I told him I was an expert in torture. He was an eager pupil and learned well how to cause pain, but did not care about the pain itself. That was his downfall; he could never grasp the finer details because he was too impatient to cause the pain. Time passed, Frishka grew impatient, he targeted the Castant family, and managed to get me exiled. Given how he blundered the trial later, I probably should have killed him and been done with him, but I did not. After my exile, he was my main source of news from inside the palace.

"When Marquiese went missing, I searched for him for two years with no luck. I was afraid I had lost him when a rumor from a place called Bram's Fen caught my attention. One of my informants overheard a conversation from a merchant son complaining that his visit to the Southern Tip had been ruined by a stupid girl and a couple of merchant sons. He was especially mad at one of the boys named Marquiese who had spoken against him to Lady Annabella."

Marilana gritted her teeth in frustration. Demdrake had not known who Marquiese was, but his vile tongue had still done the damage.

"My informant did not know any more than that. I set about gaining bandits and trackers to scour the Southern Tip. I had suspected he was close to one of his allies, but I had not found any trace of him. I suspected then that Lady Annabella had been helping him hide. I had never been able to gain any informants among her staff. Nearly a year of careful searching of the Southern Tip finally yielded results when one of the bandits reported that a bandit group had caught an important prisoner. However, The Ghost had liberated that prisoner and The Phantom had killed most of the bandit group."

Marilana sneered wickedly at him, but he ignored her.

"I was thrilled to have such a good lead, but then he suddenly turned up at the palace. He had escaped me, but once again I knew where he was. He was different, though. I was told that he was more confident in himself without being arrogant; he was more thoughtful and less impulsive. He also appeared more secretive. My informants could not get the information that I needed to form a plan to kill him. I tried for nearly a year to devise a plan, and then something happened that allowed my goals to come within my reach. You showed up."

He gave her a pointed sneer of his own. Marilana could not stop the hot molten feeling of shame that flooded through her. She knew she had been used by Frishka, but she felt renewed despair to know it had all been part of this creature's plot.

"It was a perfect opportunity to rip Marquiese from Rylan and wound them both. If Marquiese could be exiled for treason, I could kill the son and ruin the father. It would have worked if that fool had not underestimated you. If I had known more about you, I would have kept you out of the trials, but no, the fool used you. He paid for his mistakes. I wish I had been able to see that battle between you and he; my informants were awed by how much you suffered and yet still fought. It sounded amazing."

His eyes locked on to hers with a dreadful hunger. She knew he did not mean the last fight when Frishka lost his head. He wanted to see all the times she had been beaten, and the mental games she had used against the tiger. Marilana snarled with hatred and tried to suppress the shivers of fear that coursed down her back.

"Then the fool decided to forge ahead and attack the palace. If he had taken the throne, he promised that I would be allowed to privately execute Rylan and Marquiese. My goals would have been accomplished, but I said we needed more reinforcements since you had managed to alert the palace of the impending attack. The fool hated the waiting game. He thought he could do it without more men and attacked while I was not with him. He paid for his mistakes with his life. I would have skinned him alive if I ever saw him again," he growled with cold fury. "Anyway, I was once again without a plan or the means to implement Rylan's demise, so again, I have waited and watched.

"As the time for the annual tournament drew near, I knew Marquiese would have to follow tradition and visit each of the noble houses. I arranged to ambush the errand rider bringing messages to the Southern Tip, but the rider outsmarted the bandits and got through—much delayed, but arrived none-the-less—to Lady Annabella's estates. As I did not have the information detailing Marquiese's planned appearance in the Southern Tip, I set ambushes on all the major roads. You thwarted me once again, and Marquiese's visit with you and all the subsequent nobles were too well guarded for me to make any further attempt on his life. I have grown impatient with the continued interferences; however, I once again watched and learned.

"Now, just in the past few days, I received new information and I knew you were again the best bait to catch Marquiese. You see my informants do not know who I am, or what my goal is, so they tell me all kinds of gossip and I pay them well. Over the past month I learned that Marquiese was highly distracted. I was told tidbits of gossip about his visits to the Southern Tip and other provinces as he invited all the eligible maidens to attend the annual tournament. I knew he would be looking for courtship, and so I tried to figure out which of the young maidens would be the best bait. I planned many traps, but did not yet know which one to use. Then, just as I was about to give up on trying to figure out which maiden he would choose before the tournament, an informant sent me a note about Marquiese's behavior the morning of the tournament. They said he was very agitated while getting ready for the tournament, but did not know the reason for his behavior. Then, he was suddenly energetic and focused after the last carriage arrived, the one from the Southern Tip.

"I decided to play upon my suspicion that he still had feelings for you. I implemented a trap for you using the information about you that I had gained from the trials along with what I knew about Marquiese. That information contains some interesting tidbits. For instance, I learned that you are the bandit hunter called

The Ghost and you have dedicated your life to the protection of the innocent. I ask you, who is more innocent and more in need of protection than a child? A quick questioning of the bandit leaders that I had gathered under my leadership, as well as my own observations over the past seven months, told me how you would deal with a large gathering of bandits. I sent out raiders to capture children. I hid close to Maefair to receive information quickly, and when I received a second note that listed all the noble daughters under whose colors Marquiese rode with you as the last, I knew I was right in my suspicions. So, I used the children as bait for you, and now I have the bait to set a trap for Marquiese. I must say I am pleased with the results so far. Not the least of which is eliminating your annoyingly effective interference."

"He will not come for me," Marilana said as calmly as she could, "sorry to disappoint you."

"On the contrary," he laughed, "according to my information he and your persistent brother are already camped on the border of the Southern Tip. I estimate that it will take them at least three more days to follow us with their large force of men. Then I will finally have the satisfaction of killing the younger Mercurer."

Fear and hope twisted Marilana's empty stomach into a painful knot. Redirection was her ally, she had to move the topic away from her weaknesses.

"How could you have thought to let Frishka take the throne," she spat at him, "he would have been the very type of monarch the Hungdie oppose."

He scowled at her for a moment then stood up and paced to her menacingly. His nose nearly touched hers when he stopped.

"The ways of the Hungdie are not for all ears," he growled in a whisper. "You will watch your words carefully or I will cut out your tongue. I had planned to kill the fool and his mother before he could take the throne or soon after. They had been adopted into the Mercurer family, after all. Your barbed wit has reminded me that you can still be dangerous. I have told you enough."

He took a step back from her. Marilana did not hesitate. She lashed out with both feet in a kick to his stomach using the pole at her back for leverage. He was knocked backward and fell in a tangle with his chair. Marilana pulled herself up so that her paws were in front of her face and twisted so that she could hold herself up by wrapping her legs around the pole. Quickly she inspected the ropes binding her paws. He had tied her paws with their backs together and then had wrapped the rope around her fingers so that she could not use her claws on the ropes. Just as she decided she would have to chew the rope with her teeth, pain erupted along her spine and her muscles felt like they turned to jelly. She fell from her perch and slammed face first into the pole. The jolt of her sudden stop at the end of the rope made her shoulders and wrists burn.

"I wondered when you would try that," he hissed over her shoulder. "Now I will bind your feet."

Marilana found that she could move her head and looked down the pole. At the bottom an iron ring waited with a rope. She knew then that he had been testing her by leaving her feet unbound. He knelt and tied her feet together and then tied the rope to the ring. When he finished, he spun her around so that her back was to the pole again. She glared at him.

"A blunt jab to your spine with my fingers temporarily paralyzed your legs. You will regain use of your muscles in a few hours," he said levelly. "That was an impressive display of your skills, but I am curious as to why you did it in front of me."

"How long have I been in your care?" Marilana asked.

He frowned for a moment, then answered flatly, "You were captured yesterday just after noon. A bandit struck you above your left temple with the butt of a spear when he decided that subduing you gently would take too long. I was waiting on my horse when it happened. You were lifted on to my horse with me and I transported you here. It took us the rest of the afternoon, all night, and most of today to reach here. As we traveled, I treated you with remedies for the blow to your head, and gave you something to keep you from waking."

"And in that time, have you ever left me unguarded?" she demanded.

"No," he replied simply.

"So, I could have looked at your knot skill while you were here, or I could have waited until you left me to some bandit guards," she stated. "Those bandit guards are more likely to kill me for such actions because they are afraid I might escape and kill them. You, however, want me alive and mostly whole."

He nodded. "Your assessments are correct. I should have expected as much."

He turned toward his tent, but paused and smiled back at her.

"Enjoy your last pain-free night," he said. "I had intended to leave your skirts alone, but I think I will shorten them as punishment for your actions. Tomorrow your reeducation begins."

With that he picked up his chair and stepped outside the ring of stones. He set the chair in front of his tent and sat watching her as the sun set. Marilana closed her eyes and entered the healing trance.

The sounds of heavy boots approaching her clearing roused her some time later. When she opened her eyes, it was still twilight. Three bandits took up guard positions along the outside of the stone ring and several others refreshed the braziers. Once that was done, her captor disappeared into his tent. The goat, Saffon, curled up at the front of the tent where he had knelt all afternoon. He had no blanket, no cloak, no comfort of any kind. He had eaten only a heel of bread thrown on the ground in front of him and a mug of water. She was not surprised that no one brought her food or water; her captor would likely try to make her beg for every necessity.

She thought about everything he had told her, and was surprised to find that she was no longer so intensely afraid of him. Instead, she found that her fear centered on Marquiese and she was more concerned that he was riding into a trap to try to rescue her than she was about the treatment she would receive. She wondered what she could do to try to disrupt the trap, but she was not sure she would be able to influence anything. Marilana studied her guards as she thought, but when they did not pay her any attention, she closed her eyes and slept.

Earek hurried into the command tent and unfurled a map onto the table next to where Marquiese stood waiting. Marquiese bent over the map and studied the new track that had been added.

"You found her then," he asked looking up at Earek.

"She found me," he said quickly, then pointed to the new line on the map. "She followed this track from the meadow to the border. She said a single horse carrying a heavy burden made the track. She does not know if it was one large man, or two people, but she feels it is the best track to follow for several reasons. First, it was a hard track to follow even for her. She said that whoever directed the horse knew how to hide the tracks and left very few indications of their passing. Second, she found two places where the individual stopped and mixed an herb remedy. She could not tell what the remedy was for. Third, she said the track is consistently directed south. It twists and turns constantly, but over the long distance it is a straight line to the south."

"Is she following it beyond the border?" Marquiese asked.

"She said she found a safe place to sleep for a while, and then she will continue to follow it from this point," replied Earek indicating a point at the border.

"None of the other trackers noticed a horse cross the border there," mused Marquiese.

"She is the better tracker," said Earek.

Someone called at the tent flap asking permission to enter.

"Come," called Earek absently studying the map.

Healer Magus entered bearing a tray of food followed by Master Castant and Captain Hayden.

"Healer Magus, this is not your duty," said Earek frowning at the tray.

"No, it is not, Master Earek," he replied setting the tray down on the table and bowing to Earek and Marquiese.

"You should have stayed with Lady Annabella," said Earek.

"What good could I have done if I had stayed behind?" he asked. "If you need my healing, and I had stayed at the castle, I would have been too far away to be of any use. A summons and return would have taken too long if someone needs me. I have a responsibility to be here."

"Perhaps," said Earek, "but you are not a servant and should not be performing a servant's duty."

"My duty is to make sure people stay healthy or heal from injuries," Magus retorted. "You and His Highness have not eaten or slept since Lady Marilana was captured yesterday afternoon. You won't do her any good if you do not take care of yourselves. I expect this tray to be empty, and for you both to be retiring for the night when I return."

Marquiese frowned at the healer's back as he left the tent. Master Castant smiled when Marquiese looked at him.

"The good healer is right, Marquiese," said Castant gently. "You need to arrive strong if you are going to rescue Marilana; otherwise there is no point in continuing."

Marquiese sighed and picked up a bowl from the tray. Earek ignored the food until Captain Hayden gave him the second bowl. Earek frowned at him and then ate mechanically while continuing to study the map.

"What do you think? Do you have a plan?" Marquiese asked Earek.

"Why ask me?" Earek looked up alarmed. "I do not have the training you do. I was hoping you had a plan."

"I have training, yes," replied Marquiese shaking his head, "but you have grown up with bandit threats, and you have spent the last seven months helping Marilana fight bandits."

"This is when we really need her," Earek sighed. "I keep asking myself what she would do. Captain Hayden, Master Castant, any suggestions?"

"Like His Highness, I have training, but not experience in this type of battle," said Castant shaking his head sadly.

"The only suggestion I have at this point is patience," said Hayden. "You need to know more about what you are up against before you can make any plans of attack."

Marquiese nodded. "We can camp here on the border tonight, but tomorrow we need to push south. I know we do not have a destination yet, but we cannot let the bandits get too far ahead of us."

"I agree," said Earek, "we can safely push ahead as long as we do not move farther than the trackers have followed the trails. We do not want to blunder into a bandit camp or a trap."

"A good plan," agreed Hayden. "Shall I inform the men to rise early and prepare to march?"

"Yes," said Earek, "pass the orders. As soon as the trackers report in the morning, we will march."

Captain Hayden saluted with fist to heart and left the tent.

"I must express my surprise," said Castant as Marquiese and Earek ate, "Marilana's guards are not what I expected. I thought that we might have a bit of trouble restraining them from trying to find her on their own. Instead, they have divided up so that one of them is always on guard close to each of you and this tent."

"Yes," agreed Earek, "I was worried about them at first, but now I think I know what they are up to. First, they are protecting us because they know we will not stop until we find Marilana, and second, we receive the reports, so if they stay close to us, they will be among the first to know what information we get."

Marquiese chuckled, "I am glad they are close. I know they will try just as hard as us to rescue Marilana, and at least I know they can be trusted with her life."

"Very true," said Castant, "but I think I must agree with Healer Magus and insist that we retire for the night."

Marquiese nodded while chewing a last piece of bread. He really did feel better after eating, but tired as he was, he did not think he would have a good night's rest. Earek picked up the empty tray and led the way out of the tent. Marquiese smiled when he emerged from the tent to find Magus taking the tray from a scowling Earek.

"Goodnight, Highness," Earek said with a bow, then turned to his tent next to the command tent.

"Goodnight, Master Earek," he replied.

He walked to his own tent on the opposite side of a cook fire from the command tent. He nodded to Major Kolt who lounged on a stump nearby. Kolt made a seated bow, but did not move from his position. Marquiese stopped in front of his tent, peering up at the clear winter sky. The constellation of the Great Horse shone high above the Great Mountains directing him south. He remembered the bitter cold winter he spent in the Southern Tip, and how Marilana had first told him the legend of the Horse. Silently he prayed that The Goddess would shelter Marilana and send them a miracle Horse to guide them. With a sigh, he entered his tent.

18

Marilana woke with the early morning sun warming her back, the air crisp and cool. The braziers had not been refreshed since midnight, and Marilana welcomed the sunlight. Her neck and shoulders were stiff, and her wrists ached under the rope. The camp was busy with activity, but it seemed the activity of a normal day, not that of packing up the camp. Marilana thought about Marquiese and Earek camping at the border. She wanted them to rescue her, but at the same time hoped they did not get ensnared in the trap for which she was the bait.

Bandits moved around the camp, the smith's hammer started up in the distance again, and wagons were brought in for inspections and repairs. Marilana observed the early morning activity and studied her bandit guards. Like the night guards, they ignored her. Her captor emerged from his tent, and without glancing at her walked off into the camp. She watched him as far as she could. Saffon knelt in his place by the tent and also watched his master, but did not move. Her captor stopped frequently to speak to various groups and was receiving mixed reactions, some excited and others cautious.

Soon after, bandits gathered around the clear area surrounding her. Some watched her with sneers and leers, others with cautious curiosity, and still others pretended she was not there. Marilana maintained a neutral expression despite her growing anxiety. She did not have to wait long to wonder what was happening. An hour after he had left, her captor returned carrying a small wooden crate. He took the box inside his tent and emerged holding a coiled bullwhip. Marilana slowed her breathing and judged the reactions of the gathered crowd. Most of the bandits appeared eager to see what was going to happen. Some of the men leering at her pushed to the front, while others frowned and slipped to the back, but no one left. Marilana returned her attention to her captor as he entered the ring of stones and beckoned for silence.

"I am Newrothen," he called to the assembled bandits, "and I have called you here to see the beginning of pain in accordance with my vow. You helped me capture this creature you call The Ghost. Now I will help you teach her the consequences of her actions against bandits. I begin this morning with humiliation."

The bandits did not cheer, but grew still waiting for something to happen. Newrothen turned his attention to Marilana and she met his hungry gaze with calm. He smirked and uncoiled the whip. With casual ease, he drew back his arm and flicked the whip, which made a resounding crack in the crisp winter air. Marilana did not flinch or look down at where the whip had sliced the front of her skirts just above her knees; she kept her eyes locked on his. He cracked the whip twice more. Many of the bandits laughed and jeered as more of her legs became exposed.

Newrothen walked up to her and turned her to face the pole. Marilana closed her eyes, clenched her teeth, and focused on her breathing. Three more cracks of the whip, this time across the back of her legs and the crowd of bandits whistled and yelled profanities at her as the lower part of her skirts slid down and fluttered around her bound feet. Marilana braced herself; she knew what was coming next. Three more cracks of the whip, and she felt the frigid air brush lightly against her newly exposed back. Some of the bandits cheered with excitement. He was going to whip her, and they were ready to see her blood spilled for them.

The whip cracked and Marilana felt the lash fall across her back like a razor, but she knew it had not cut completely through her skin. At first some of the crowd cheered, but as the lash continued to snap and crack without drawing blood, the cheering subsided, and they muttered sullenly. Marilana did not know exactly what was going to happen, but she felt the pain grow every time the lash kissed her back and made another slight cut. Newrothen was systematic with the whip, first lashing up and down for a count of three, then side to side for another count of three; repeatedly until Marilana lost count of how many times the lash landed across her back. She felt like squirming from the irritation across her back, but she held herself to stillness and silence. After some time, the whip stopped falling. Marilana waited; silence descended around her.

"Behold!" cried Newrothen close behind her, "The beginning of pain has begun. Gone is the cloth covering, gone is the protective hair, and gone too is the tough outer skin. You wonder why I take such delicate strokes with the whip, and I will tell you. This was just the preparation phase; I have awoken every nerve in her back so that every stroke that comes after will be ten times more painful. And as you can see, she can do nothing to stop me. Look how she hangs her head in shame, her clothing is torn, her fur is ragged, she is exposed for you to see what she is. She is not an image to inspire fear, but an image of scorn. You all stand higher than she." Laughter and more jeering came from the crowd. They may have been disappointed that she had not bled, but they liked the state of her predicament. Newrothen waited for quiet before continuing. "She will bleed for you, but not now. However, I did say she would scream for you this morning, and so she shall."

A strong paw gripped her arm and turned her around. Marilana winced as her tender back pressed against the pole.

"Good," Newrothen chuckled quietly. "You are very strong, but I have ways to make you scream whenever I want."

Marilana kept her eyes closed tight and her teeth clenched as she felt his paw press against her right side. The bandit crowd waited expectantly. He pressed and twisted sharply. Marilana felt and heard a snap in her side as he broke her rib. The stinging pain took her breath away. He repeated the motion, the pain even more piercing. Marilana realized she was screaming, but could not stop until the air was drained from her lungs. The bandits cheered as her scream tapered into silence. Marilana gulped shallow breaths, knowing he had broken two ribs. The pain receded slowly to a sharp pang with every breath. She trembled and was weakened from the shock of the pain. She hung limply from the ropes binding her wrists, tears streaming from her closed eyes. Humiliation indeed, she hung here unable to do anything to stop what was going to happen to her. The ache in her chest was not just from the pain, but also from the knowledge that she had been defeated. The crowd of bandits dispersed noisily; several shouted obscenities at her, but most just laughed and talked loudly with their companions.

After a long while the sounds of the camp returned to normal and Marilana's trembling subsided. When

Marilana heard a soft low chuckle, she opened her eyes and lifted her head to see Newrothen. Hatred coursed through her, and she made the choice that even though he had won thus far, she was not going to live for him, she was going to fight with every breath she took. He smiled broadly at her, a malicious light dancing in his eyes. He reached up to her face and gently brushed a tear from her cheek. Marilana bit at his paw and he drew back from her laughing. He licked her tear from his finger and she growled at him.

"Oh, yes!" he exclaimed quietly. "Yes, yes! You are so strong and now I get to see your anger. How wondrous! I have a feeling I am going to enjoy your training very much, very much indeed."

He walked away into his tent, leaving her again with three bandit guards. Marilana dropped her head and entered the healing trance.

*

Marilana opened her eyes when someone entered the ring of stones. Newrothen smiled and stepped close to her.

"The healing trance is such a wonderful thing," he said. "You can survive so much longer with it, yet it has its costs."

"You never taught Frishka about it, did you." Marilana said.

"No, he never had the patience to learn about healing techniques," he mused. "If he had, he might have guessed that you were a lot stronger than you were letting on. Of course, I know you use it, I know the costs of using it, and I know how to force you out of the trance and into normal sleep."

He smiled as he turned and walked back to his tent. She watched as he directed Saffon to move a camp table and chair out in front of his tent where she could easily see. Then he walked off into the camp, leaving the goat kneeling again by the tent. As soon as he disappeared, she stretched her neck and limbs as best she could to ease the stiffness, but it was not enough. Her back itched and twinged with pain as she moved her shoulders. Ignoring the discomfort, she turned her attention to her situation. She studied her guards, watched Saffon, and checked the shadows. It was close to noon. The camp was busy with activity around the cook fires.

Newrothen returned carrying a bowl of steaming stew and a hunk of crusty bread. He sat at his little table and ate slowly watching her the whole time. She watched the activity of the camp, but could not stop her growing hunger pangs. When he had finished eating, he lifted a heavy waterskin from the ground by his chair and took a long drink. She had not had anything to eat or drink since her capture except for the remedies he had given her for the blow to her head. Her mouth was parched, and her stomach grumbled with hunger, but she refused to acknowledge her lack. She did not know what he would do if she asked for something to drink, but she knew he anticipated it.

When he finished his meal, he approached her again. He studied her for a moment, and then motioned to someone behind her. The rope she hung from jerked and shook before she was lowered to the ground. Her legs threatened to collapse under her—weakened as she was from her ill treatment—but she managed to stay standing, and found that the rope binding her feet together had a little slack. She did not take her eyes from Newrothen as the person behind her untied her foot rope from the iron ring.

"You will walk," Newrothen said, "and follow me."

He turned and walked toward his tent. When she did not start walking, the man behind her pushed her shoulder. Glancing over her shoulder, she saw three men waiting for her to move. One, a large black bear, held the ropes to her wrists and feet, while a jackal and gazelle each had crossbows aimed at her. The bear pushed her again and this time, she walked. She was forced to take tiny short steps because of the rope between her feet, but she maintained a calm and unconcerned expression. Newrothen offered to assist her over the ring of stones, however she spotted a place that she could get over on her own and ignored his paw. He frowned, then continued past his tent. Marilana was relieved that he was not taking her to his tent, but still worried about their destination. They passed several more rows of tents and approached the edge of the camp. There, set apart from everything else, sat a small tent. Newrothen opened the tent flap and motioned for her to enter.

Marilana was relieved when she entered and discovered it was a latrine. She frowned at her tied paws pondering how to shift what remained of her divided skirts. The rasp of metal on leather caused Marilana to turn sharply. Newrothen stood just inside the tent flaps studying her and holding his drawn belt knife. They stared at each other for a moment without moving. Finally, he stepped forward and grabbed hold of the rope attached to her paws. Marilana followed the rope with her eyes past Newrothen and out under the tent flaps. She realized that the bear held the end of it outside, and the crossbows were ready to fire at any movement from the tent unless Newrothen gave a signal. Newrothen had her shorter ankle rope looped around one arm. Holding her ropes securely in one paw, he knelt in front of her and raised his knife. Marilana tensed, but did not move. With fluid, quick motions he cut the inseam of her skirt and removed the extra material that would get in her way yet preserved her modesty. He was careful to leave her tail in its pouch, and Marilana wondered why but did not speak.

When he had finished, he stood, his eyes glinting cold and dark. "I control everything in your life," he said coldly, his breath tickling the thin fur of Marilana's face. "Your humiliation, your comfort, your modesty, your health, your sleep, everything. That also means that I must control the emotions directed at you from others. Lust, anger, and greed, are strong motivators for all creatures. It is true that hanging you naked and exposed to the elements would cause you more discomfort, but those brutes out there would not be able to control their emotions if I did. So for now, while I must control their lust for you, you will retain your modesty. That will change when I no longer need them."

He stepped back and motioned for her to go about her business. Marilana did her best to hide the fear coiling in her stomach and ignored him as she relived herself. She had hoped he would allow her this much comfort, although he took his time getting around to it. She realized that he must have dealt with her lack of control while he had kept her unconscious for two days. She swallowed back the bile that rose in her throat, and had a feeling that she needed a bath to wash away more than the dirt that covered her. He whistled once sharply before opening the tent flap for her. She walked carefully back out of the latrine tent to the waiting guards. Newrothen gave the bear her ankle rope, then led the way back to her pole. Marilana was alarmed to find a pile of sticks just inside the ring of stones when they returned. She eyed Newrothen's back suspiciously as he stepped over the stones. He did not offer help over the stones this time, but turned and watched impassively as she worked her way over and continued to watch as she was hoisted back up and tied to her pole. Only after she was secure, and the three bandit guards had retreated did, he approach her again.

"You will probably not need the latrine again until you start to eat and drink again, but if you do, just ask me and I will allow it," he said slyly. "Also, all you have to do to receive food and water from me is to ask for it."

"And what is the cost of my asking for comfort or relief?" she growled at him.

"You already know the answer," he smirked, "but I will say it aloud anyway. Asking politely to fulfill your personal needs is the first step to accepting me as your master."

"Then I will not ask for those things," she replied.

"I did not expect you to," he smiled, "at least not yet, but in time you will. For now, the bandits will get to have some sport."

He turned away from her and waited as the bandits assembled again. Marilana watched their faces closely. Many looked eager and eyed the pile of sticks with glee, others looked skeptical, and still some came and stood at the back of the crowd frowning. It seemed that fewer gathered to watch this time, but Marilana did not know if that was because they had other duties to attend to, or if they had lost the desire to watch.

Newrothen raised his arms into the air and called for silence. He smiled knowingly at the crowd.

"Friends," he called to them, "I promised that those who wanted to avenge their suffering upon this Ghost would have the chance, and this is your first opportunity."

Some of the crowd cheered, but others looked alarmed. Marilana eyed the pile of sticks again. They were mostly willow branches, thin and pliable, and would make excellent switches.

"I only ask that you follow my rules," Newrothen continued. "First, I do not want her to suffer lasting damage, so you will avoid her right side. Second, I do not wish to disfigure her beautiful face, so you will not aim above her shoulders. Lastly, everyone must get a turn that wants one, so stay with a limit of only a few strikes, then let someone else have a turn. If I deem it acceptable, some of you may get a second turn at the end. Now then, three at a time may take a switch and let the fun begin."

Three of the largest bandits leering at her from the front of the crowd leaped forward and grabbed switches from the pile of sticks. Marilana's panic swelled as they approached her. Having no way to escape except to beg for mercy, which she doubted she would be granted and which she refused to utter, she stomped down hard on the panic, took a calming breath and closed her eyes. She knew that she could not survive if she fought the beating, so she forced her muscles to relax but clamped her teeth shut. The first switch struck her across the front of her hips with such force, that she heard the willow branch break. She barely had time to feel the sting of that first blow, before the second and third switches struck. Once again, she relied on her training in the old ways and accepted the pain. She focused on her breathing and drew her mind to thoughts other than the pain. On and on the beating continued. When the pain grew too much, she whimpered through clenched teeth, and tears fell from her closed eyes. She lost track of time as the pain grew, she winced whenever a miss-aimed blow struck close to her broken ribs.

Finally, the switches stopped falling against her. She hung trembling and panting from the pain in her chest, stomach, ribs, and legs. Every inch of her body below her shoulders stung and ached. The crowd laughed and clapped each other on the back, comparing their skills with a switch, as they slowly dispersed into the rest of the camp. Marilana kept her eyes closed, tears still falling down her cheeks, and tried not to listen to the conversations. Long after silence returned to her clearing and she had calmed her breathing, she opened her eyes. Judging by the shadows, a relatively short time had passed, fifteen minutes perhaps, but it had felt so much longer. Newrothen sat at his table in front of his tent sipping from a cup. A clear pitcher of water sat sparkling on the table next to a hunk of dry bread. Saffon ate a similar hunk of bread where he knelt, and had a cup by his knees. Newrothen smiled at her. She closed her eyes to block the sight, but was too aware of his eyes on her to enter the healing trance.

*

Marilana opened her eyes at the sound of someone hurrying into the clearing. She estimated the crowds had been gone for less than an hour. She watched the middle-aged red fox hurry to Newrothen. He carried a bow across his back, but did not move like an archer. His steps were light, and he created much less noise as he moved than most of the men in the camp. He looked at her once before turning his attention to her captor. Marilana was startled to recognize the man.

"Newrothen, sir," he said in clipped tones, "it's the bandit leaders. They are arguing about who should take the prisoner. They have decided that you shouldn't keep her, but can't agree on anything else."

"Keep watch here. Saffon, come," said Newrothen as he sprang to his feet scowling and stormed off into the camp, the goat following quickly at his master's heels.

The fox was jittery as he watched Newrothen round the last tent in the row. After a moment he looked cautiously around the clearing, but avoided looking at her.

"You are Rodan," Marilana said.

He jumped and looked at her. He glanced in the direction Newrothen had gone, then looked back at her and nodded.

"How do you know me?" he asked quickly.

"I have seen you from a distance several times, and I try to know all of the mercenary trackers of high report. It is said that you are one of the best trackers and scouts in these mountains," she said.

"I'm not supposed to talk to you, or even to acknowledge your presence," he said nervously.

"You would not if you did not have something you wanted to say to me," she replied.

"Indeed," he said and took a calming breath. "I want to apologize for joining in the switching. I didn't want to do it, but Newrothen looked into my eyes, and I didn't think I should resist."

"You did well not to make an enemy of him. He is more dangerous than you know. I do not hold a grudge against you," she said.

"It's not right what he's doing to you," he said angrily, "and it's not right what they want to do to you either. You never hunted those that didn't deserve it. You've always protected the innocent. I can't get them to see that, though."

"He has a way of twisting words," she said calmly, "he has convinced them that they are right to do this to me, and they are drunk with the feeling of power he has instilled in them. He will not give me up, though. My fate is sealed."

He studied her for a moment.

"I can't help you escape," he said sadly. "I must think about my wife and daughter."

She smiled and said, "Thank you for the thought, but I cannot escape now. I cannot out-run the scouts and trackers, or fight my way free when I have two broken ribs and am weakened by injury and lack of water. They would easily catch me and bring me back to him. And my punishment would be more extreme."

"I'm sorry," he said. "I also wanted to thank you for opening the food dispensaries along the border. My family wouldn't have survived the winter without the extra food. They've had bad luck this year with storms and plagues of insects. There wasn't much of a harvest."

"You are welcome. I had heard about the hardship; that was part of my reason for giving out the food," she sighed.

"What's the other part?" he asked.

"A man with a hungry family will do what he must to help his family survive," she said with a small smile. "A man with a happy family is content to stay home."

"It decreases the number of bandit raids," he said with a nod. "Is there anything I can do for you? Water, bread?"

"He is too knowledgeable, he would know if you gave me food or water. Do not risk yourself here for me. However, if you see my brother or Prince Marquiese," she said sadly, "tell them I am as good as dead. I will not live to be this man's plaything."

He looked surprised, and then nodded.

"You plan to kill yourself," he said.

"I do not have to," she replied, "I just have to make him think I am stronger than I am, and he will kill me without meaning to."

They lapsed into silence. Rodan watched her for a while, then took his bow from his back and knocked an arrow but did not draw it. He walked continuously around the ring of stones with his bow ready and a serious set to his face. Marilana watched him and wondered what he would decide to do.

Several hours later Newrothen returned alone and relieved Rodan from guarding her. Rodan left hurriedly after glancing at his face. Newrothen scowled at everything and avoided looking at her. She watched him as he retrieved items from his tent and laid them out on his little table. The last item he retrieved was a furled map, which he stretched out and weighted down. He studied the map silently. It was not long before the sounds of approaching boots came from behind Marilana. A hulking grizzly bear, a large black wolf, and a slender gray wolf walked around the stone ring, and gathered around the map. Marilana recognized them as the three bandits who had been most eager to switch her and assumed they were the leaders of the largest groups of bandits. The four men spoke in voices too low for her to overhear. They seemed to be arguing about a position on the map. As the argument continued, Marilana deduced that Newrothen had lost some of his control over the others. They spoke back to him and overrode his objections. Eventually they seemed to come to an agreement of sorts and the grizzly waved his paw to someone behind Marilana. Another bandit trotted up to the group.

"Gather the trackers and scouts, bring them here, and hurry," the bear ordered gruffly.

Marilana watched the four men silently studying the map for another ten minutes as trackers and scouts assembled nearby. Rodan sauntered up to the group and lounged at his ease. Finally, Newrothen nodded and motioned for the trackers to come closer.

"It seems that the Southern Tip encampment has pushed forward without delay," he told them. "I suspect that they have their trackers out searching for us. It has been decided that we should decrease the number of reports they are receiving to slow their progress. You will fan out and comb the woods between our camp and theirs. Eliminate any scouts and trackers that you find. Rodan wait a moment, the rest of you, move out."

The others moved off quickly leaving Rodan waiting for further orders.

"Rodan, I want you to track a specific target," said Newrothen. "I believe that The Phantom is helping lead the Southern Tip forces. I want you to track her and kill her if possible."

"The Phantom is not an easy target," replied Rodan stiffening a little. "I doubt any of us can catch her."

"I understand, but you will try," Newrothen insisted.

"We should find out what she knows before he leaves. It could help him," said the grizzly.

"What do you think she will tell us?" Newrothen asked menacingly without looking at the bear.

"You tell me," the grizzly replied haughtily. "You claim to be a master at torture, yet all we've seen, is that you do not want to damage her too badly. That whipping this morning was nothing compared to other whippings I have seen."

"You know nothing about causing pain," Newrothen replied coldly. "You know nothing about torturing information out of someone."

"I know enough."

The hulking bear drew his dagger and started to cross the stone ring glaring at Marilana. She recognized him as the bear who had wanted to kill her before she woke her first morning in the bandit camp. Apparently Newrothen's humiliation of her had decreased the bear's fear of her, as well as his fear of Newrothen. The black-clad lion moved so fast that the others did not react until it was too late. Newrothen gripped the bear's outstretched paw and twisted it. The man dropped his dagger and fell to the ground on his stomach. He seemed paralyzed as Newrothen twisted his arm behind his back. Marilana recognized the point on the grizzly's paw that Newrothen pressed as one of the major pain centers of the arm. She knew that he was experiencing waves of excruciating pain shooting up his arm and down his back every time Newrothen squeezed.

"The prisoner is mine," growled Newrothen. "No one touches her unless I say so. Do you understand?"

The grizzly shrieked as Newrothen squeezed a little harder. The other two leaders stood rooted to the ground in surprise. Rodan took a step back and watched wide-eyed. Then the gray wolf lifted his paw in a placating gesture.

"We understand," he said cautiously. "Enough now, you have made your point. Continuing this serves no purpose."

Newrothen released the man on the ground then turned to face the three leaders with his back to Marilana. The grizzly lay panting on the ground before he pushed up with his good arm and glared warily at Newrothen.

"You made your point that you can cause pain," he growled. "But I don't understand why you don't do it to her."

"I am only going to explain this once," said Newrothen darkly. "Torture relies on the assumption that the victim wants to live. You start with small pains and work up to more debilitating pains. The victim fears what you will do next and eventually will tell you things in an attempt to prevent more pain. Almost anyone can perform such torture. You understand this."

The three leaders nodded their understanding with impatience.

"This prisoner is different," Newrothen continued. "She knows how to control her pain. It will take much more pain to cause her extreme discomfort, therefore, someone torturing her must take her to the brink of death many times to get any information from her. Her resistance must be worn down a little at a time. It is delicate work. Also, she does not fear death. So, threatening to kill her will do no good. Most importantly, she would rather die than face the future I have promised her. She may try to provoke you so that you push her strength too far and kill her before you mean to."

"Perhaps a different kind of persuasion would work?" asked the black wolf.

"If we had other prisoners," Newrothen replied, "it would be easy, especially if they were young women or children."

"Since we don't have any of those, might I try something else?" asked the black wolf.

"You may try, but I will judge how far you may push."

Marilana glared at the black wolf as he approached her. He studied her a moment. Newrothen frowned as he turned to watch.

"If you tell us what you know about The Phantom," he said in a gentle voice, "I will make sure that you spend the night inside a tent."

Marilana burst out laughing. Newrothen smirked, but the three leaders all frowned.

"What do you find so funny?" demanded the black wolf. "I can't imagine that hanging from a pole all day and night could be comfortable."

"If that is the best offer you can devise," she sneered at him, "then I have my doubts about your leadership skills and your intelligence."

"I can think of another way for you to spend your nights," growled the grizzly.

"By all means untie me," smirked Marilana. "I am sure I could make your tent an interesting place to be."

"I would not agree to that," cautioned the gray wolf. "She means to kill you and then escape."

"I wouldn't need her to be untied," snarled the grizzly.

"That could be avoided if you told us what we want to know," cooed the black wolf. "You could have something to eat and drink. A soft pile of blankets and no one would bother you."

"Do your worst," Marilana sneered again, "I will not tell you anything. There is nothing you can do to me that would make me betray my friends."

"No one can hold out forever. We will find your weakness," the black wolf snarled.

Marilana laughed again. The wolf drew back his fist to strike her, but Newrothen grabbed his arm.

"Enough," he said quietly.

"She needs to be taught a lesson," the black wolf snarled.

"That is exactly what she wants," replied Newrothen. "She has succeeded in making you mad enough to want to hurt her. You could easily kill her."

"You let her get away with too much," snarled the black wolf. "She will never break for you if you coddle her."

"Watch her eyes carefully," interjected the gray wolf quietly studying Marilana's face.

"What do you mean?" growled the grizzly. "I see anger, pride, and resentment, but no fear or any clues to tell me where to push my advantage. I think Newrothen is right. I would kill her before extracting any information from her. What did you see?"

"Yes," said the gray wolf darkly. "Not one of the three of us, nor all three of us together could get any useful information from her. She would anger us, and we would, as he said, push her too far and kill her. The only bargaining chip we have that she wants is her freedom, and she knows we will not let her go."

"So what?" asked the black wolf. "Do we just let him keep her for himself and hope he has better bargaining resources than we do?"

"Yes," replied the gray wolf, "I don't know why, but she's afraid of him. She doesn't show fear in the face of pain or hard use, but when he talks, she is afraid, deeply afraid."

Marilana snarled at him, and Newrothen smiled.

"Well done," Newrothen said applauding lightly, "you have seen clearly one facet of my skills."

"Why does she fear you, torturer," growled the black wolf, "when she doesn't fear pain or death."

"As he said before," commented the gray wolf, "he has promised her a future that she fears and would willingly die to avoid."

"Correct," said Newrothen. "That is a future you do not need to know about. Be satisfied that I have already established a modicum of influence with her because of it. I do not yet have enough influence with her to extract the information you want today, but perhaps in the future I will."

"Rodan," called the gray wolf, "be gone with you, and good hunting."

Rodan gave a slight nod, then turned and hurried into the camp. The three bandit leaders studied her a moment longer. She met their stares with a challenging glare. The grizzly snarled back at her, but refrained from making any aggressive actions. Finally, the black wolf turned away.

"Come, we have men to check on before dinner," he said to the others. "Newrothen, will there be more entertainment after dinner tonight?"

"Not tonight, but tomorrow afternoon," replied Newrothen lightly, "and this time I promise there will be bloodshed."

"Good," growled the grizzly.

The three bandits left the clearing in different directions and Newrothen silently watched them go. Once they had all disappeared around various tents, he turned and snarled at Marilana.

"You will not tempt them again," he growled dangerously.

"I will do as I please," she spat back.

"If you want to entertain them in their tents each night, continue tempting them," he snarled. "It took a lot of persuasion to prevent them from taking you earlier this afternoon. I had to give them certain benefits for their continued cooperation. Those three do not fear you like the rest. They want to control you, to make you their play thing, they do not care if it kills you."

"I would rather they did kill me than be stuck with you," she retorted. "Besides that, you didn't tell them I was bait for a trap. You didn't tell them that it is all part of your plan to lure the Southern Tip forces directly to you, that you don't want their progress stalled. I wonder what they would do if I informed them of it."

"I will make you wish you had never had that thought if you breathe one word of it to them," he snarled.

He reached up to her neck and placed the point of a claw on each side of her throat. Marilana began to tremble at his touch. She raised her chin and swallowed, but did not break eye contact with him. She knew he would not kill her by crushing her windpipe, but he could easily rupture her vocal cords. It would be exceedingly painful and would render her speechless for months while it healed.

"Do I make myself clear?" he asked coldly.

She did not fear the pain, and she did not want to give in to him. However, she also knew that he would never make an idle threat. They both knew that if she called him on a bluff, he would lose some control over her. Instead of risking the loss of control, he would fulfill any threat he made, so he was very careful about what threats he directed at her. She stared at him a long time. Neither blinked.

"Yes," she whispered finally deciding that she could not yet afford to lose her voice.

"Good," he crooned and turned away from her.

She knew she had just given him a very powerful position over her, but she had to be careful when defying him. She could not deny his power over her until after his trap had been sprung. As terrible as the thought was, only after he had killed Marquiese, taken her as his own, and she was beyond all hope of rescue, could she force him to carry through with all his threats until she could die. She glared at his back with pure hatred and blinked back angry tears, knowing that he had just made his first crack in her will.

19

The sun hung low in the western sky when Newrothen finished his supper and came to stand before her. Marilana had ignored her body's hungry and tired urgings for the last few hours. She had not slept or entered the healing trance. She had to appear strong to make him overestimate her condition. She would need to enter the healing trance soon, but she had to push herself beyond her limits.

Marilana glared at Newrothen while waiting for his next move. He seemed amused and smirked back at her. Finally, he spoke, but not to her.

"Saffon, come," he said calmly.

The goat approached earnestly and waited. Marilana studied him in the fading light. His brown clothes were dirtier than before, and his armor was gone. Six inches of one of his horns had been broken off. His eyes never left Newrothen, and Marilana was sickened by the goat's look of terror. Then she looked at his face more carefully and gasped with shock.

"Saffon? You . . . you were Earek's guard at the Royal Palace. You were a member of the palace guards," she looked at Newrothen's smirk and anger washed over her. "What did you do to him?"

"Do not think he is innocent, darling," Newrothen chuckled as his black eyes held hers. Marilana's skin crawled with disgust. "Saffon was one of Frishka's men, tasked with spying on the palace and carrying out tasks among the guards. Weren't you, Saffon?"

"Yes, Master," Saffon said hoarsely.

"He was tasked with knocking out your own guard, Karndel, and then disposing of him. He took Karndel out to the countryside and beat him bloody. That was when you failed, wasn't it, Saffon?"

"Yes, Master," Saffon answered trembling, but did not flinch or move away.

"Saffon left Karndel alive, assuming he would die slowly in the forest, but Saffron was wrong. Karndel was found and nursed back to health, helping you win. Frishka discovered before he attacked the palace that Saffon had failed his task. Frishka gave Saffon to me to punish for his failure. Isn't that right Saffon? Have you been punished enough?"

"That is correct, Master. I failed. No, Master, I can never be punished enough for my failure." Saffon trembled violently, but still did not cower.

Marilana tasted bile in her throat, even though she was dehydrated. Whatever punishment Newrothen had brought to bear on the once proud goat had broken his spirit. She had no doubt that Newrothen wanted to convey that the same fate was planned for her.

"Why, just this afternoon he atoned some more by cleaning the bandit leaders' tents and then serving as their toy for a few hours. It appeased them a little, even though they wanted you to play with. They did manage to damage him a little, but he deserved it. He would muck the horse lines with his bare hooves if I ordered it.

Wouldn't you, Saffon? Did you have fun with the bandits, Saffon?"

"I do what you order, Master. No, Master, tending the bandits was not fun, but you ordered it. I cleaned for them and fought for their amusement, they beat me when I won, and then I cleaned their latrines. I do as you order, Master." Saffon croaked with resignation.

"Very good, Saffon. Go to your place," Newrothen watched Marilana's face.

Saffon gazed adoringly at his master before turning and hurrying to his place by the tent. Marilana swallowed several times feeling nauseated. How could someone who had been so strong and free now be so devoted to one creature? It was disgusting. She looked into Newrothen's hungry eyes and felt doused in ice as dread washed over her. That was what he would do to her. Make her happy to accept torture from his paws. Make her eager to debase herself at his whim.

"I will never succumb to your will," she hissed at him. "You will not break me."

Smiling with pleasure, Newrothen turned away.

Marquiese strolled through the encampment in the evening twilight checking on his and Earek's men. It was important for the men to see him calm and in command. He, Earek, and Castant had discussed many details of this venture as they had ridden south. He and Earek had agreed to share the command decisions, but that he should assume leadership so that the chain of command was clear. Earek and Castant acted together as his seconds, but Earek would assume command if anything happened to Marquiese. They had made camp early in the afternoon, so they would not overtake the trackers. Marquiese longed to press on toward the south. He knew in his heart that Marilana's state worsened with each passing moment. Yet he walked calmly, lifting the men's spirits, and making sure every duty was taken care of. As he rounded the last tent row on his way back to the command tent, he saw Earek and Castant duck through the flaps. He picked up his pace, worried about what new reports had arrived.

Earek was busily marking new information on the map as Marquiese entered the command tent. Marquiese approached the table and studied the new lines. Almost all the trails that the trackers had been following were beginning to converge. They were all still directed south, but now seemed to be pointing in the same direction.

"Any word from The Phantom?" Marquiese asked.

"One of the sentries gave me this," replied Earek holding out a piece of parchment without looking up from his work. "Said he heard a thunk and when he investigated the noise, he found this pinned to a tree with an arrow."

Marquiese took it and realized that it was a crudely drawn map of the area marked with several positions with simple notations. Most of the notes indicated landmarks for reference, but two marks caught his attention. The first was simply labeled "camp," and the second was labeled "next camp." Marquiese compared it to the map Earek was working on, and realized that the "camp" was exactly where their encampment had set up for the night. The "next camp" was not directly south, but angled more to the west. The distance to the next location seemed to be about the same distance as what they had traversed from their previous camp.

"Do you think this is safe to follow? Do you think it is from The Phantom?" he asked quietly.

"I do," the black leopard said firmly. "If you look at the back, you will see that it is addressed to me."

Marquiese turned it over and saw "Brother Blackcat" plainly written on the parchment.

"Blackcat?" asked Marquiese.

"It is the name The Phantom chose for me when Marilana first introduced me to her. She said it was a better name for me," Earek said seriously. "Marilana encouraged the name as a positive identifier of the source of any information. Please keep the name to yourselves."

Marquiese and Castant agreed.

"Should we follow her suggestion for our next camp?" Castant asked. "It is at the outermost edge of where the trackers and scouts have searched. It may not be secured yet."

"Yes," replied Marquiese as he studied the map. "If you look here, the camp will be close to the convergence point of the trails we have been following, but not directly on them. It appears to be in a location that can be easily defended, and will not be directly seen by anyone traversing the lowlands. We can have the scouts secure the area tomorrow as we travel."

"Yes," said Earek, "and I think that the bandits are headed toward this valley. It would be an excellent place for a winter camp. It could conceal a large force of men.

If they do have a camp there, they will not easily see us if we make camp at the place she suggested."

"We will have to warn the men to minimize noise and not light any fires," said Castant.

They discussed the implications of the next camp, and what orders to give to the men until they were satisfied. They called Captain Hayden in to consult with him. He agreed with their decision to trust the information. The burly black bear left eagerly to pass the orders among the men.

"He is too eager," commented Castant.

"I am eager too," replied Marquiese. "I feel the urge to rush toward that valley in the hopes of finding Marilana alive. I trust that he will not let anyone do anything to jeopardize Marilana's life."

"I believe you are right," said Earek, "but we should keep an eye on him and the rest of her guards. I will speak with him and remind him that haste can be deadly."

"Thank you, Earek," said Marquiese, "now I think we should try to get some sleep while we can."

They left for their tents. A cold breeze rippled the tent canvases in the night. Marquiese looked to the sky and was relieved to see a clear night. The winter storms were late this year, and he knew they would come soon, but not tonight. As the young lion prepared for bed, he could not slow his thoughts. He tried to sleep but could not get comfortable. Finally, he took to pacing in his tent. Marilana dominated his thoughts. He could not leave her to the torment of the Hungdie, but he strongly suspected that she had been captured as bait for him. He could see no way to avoid riding into a trap. It struck him that

Marilana must have felt this way before entering the meadow, she had known that putting herself in the most danger was the only way to rescue those children. Now he had to rescue her. She had to still be alive. Yet even as he burned to see her safe, he felt strongly the familiar feeling of betrayal. He knew she had not consciously betrayed him. So what was it that was causing this emotion to persist? He could not find an answer. Hours passed, fatigue set in, and he could no longer concentrate on his thoughts. He lay down and slept fitfully.

A cold breeze woke Marilana from the healing trance; she shivered in the dark. Mild pain in her back and shoulders accompanied the shivering. It appeared to be several hours past midnight. Glancing up at the sky she saw the stars glittering brightly in the clear winter air. She breathed a sigh of relief. She did not fear the snows that would come, but she feared what would happen if Newrothen decided that she could not stay exposed to the cold. After recognizing Saffon, she more than feared what would happen once she was taken inside his tent; she was terrified of that future.

As if the thought had beckoned him, Newrothen emerged from his tent and studied her. He peered at the sky, and then gathered the guards set to watch her. They hurried to do his bidding. An eland began to reposition the braziers closer to her. They had not been refreshed since dusk and had cooled considerably. Soon the other two guards, a weasel and a coyote, returned bringing fresh coals for the braziers. The warmth washed over Marilana as the braziers were refreshed, a welcome relief from her painful shivering. Newrothen watched the men work and gave instructions as needed for the placement of the braziers. When he was satisfied, he nodded.

"Keep her warm," the dark lion said as he turned back toward his tent, "and keep her awake."

Marilana sighed as the men took up their positions. It was going to be a long few hours until dawn.

*

Marilana watched bleary-eyed as the colors changed in the sky and the sun rose. She had entered the healing trance for brief moments throughout the rest of the night when the guards would turn away from her, but inevitably, one of them would turn to check on her and wake her up. Eventually they had decided that one of them should stand facing her at all times to prevent her from stealing short naps. The bandits had also grown weary of approaching her to wake her, so they had devised different means. Now the coyote watching her held a long stick in his paws and every time her eyes closed, he would tap her. It did not hurt, but it was effective at waking her. She was grateful to them though; they had kept the braziers hot, and she had not had to shiver for the rest of the night. Unfortunately, the cold was not the worst of it, her limbs were stiff and aching, she could feel several sore welts left by the switching, and her broken ribs were making breathing difficult.

The camp grew noisier as the sun climbed above the mountains to the east. The smells of cooking and smoke permeated the air, reminding Marilana that she had not eaten or drunk anything substantial in two and a half days. Newrothen emerged from his tent and walked off into the camp. He returned not long after with a steaming bowl of porridge and, as was his want, sat at his little table and ate where she could see him. Saffon received nothing, and remained kneeling in his place. When Newrothen finished, he dismissed the bandit guards with some additional instructions that she could not hear. He approached her and motioned Saffon to come.

"Saffon, bench," he ordered without looking behind him.

Saffon immediately dropped to his hooves and knees. Newrothen sat on Saffon's back, resting his right arm on Saffon's remaining horn. He smirked at her. Saffon held as still and straight as possible. The lion and lioness stared at each other in a silent contest of wills until Saffon began to shake with effort. Marilana wanted Newrothen to stop; she did not know what his purpose was in making her watch Saffon's suffering, but she knew if she interfered, she would suffer next.

Slowly, Newrothen pulled Saffon's horn so that the goat's head was craning back, his nose pointed toward the sky. In a fast strike, Newrothen whipped his dagger around and slammed the hilt into the goat's throat, crushing his windpipe. Marilana gasped with horror as Saffon collapsed to the ground. Newrothen stood calmly, having been braced for the loss of his seat. Tears streamed down Marilana's cheeks as Saffon thrashed on the ground slowly suffocating. Newrothen lovingly caressed her cheek, wiping away her tears. The lioness jerked away from his paw, but he just chuckled darkly. He stood and watched her for a long time. Marilana refused to meet his eyes.

"You have so much love in your heart," he said admiringly. "You could even find pity for an enemy. You know he would have killed you or Earek or Marquiese if ordered to. You should be thanking me for eliminating a traitor to the crown. I will very much enjoy watching you suffer for hours unending."

Marilana's anger surged white hot. She gathered what little moisture was in her mouth and spat in his smiling face. He back-armed her across the right cheek hard enough to make spots erupt across her vision.

"I can see you are not ready to be civil yet," Newrothen growled at her. "You will be allowed two hours of sleep. Use the time wisely."

She watched him march back to his tent and disappear inside. A team of bandits approached and set to work. Three creatures took up guard positions around her, and three others hauled away Saffon's body. Knowing that she was reaching the point where her body needed true sleep, she closed her eyes and forced herself into the healing trance.

*

Marilana woke immediately when Newrothen approached her two hours later. He frowned at her.

"I know what you are doing," he said dangerously. "I am aware that you are preventing your body from getting the sleep it needs. You are wasting energy by forcing the healing trance even though it will prolong your strength. I will not tolerate such behavior forever, and I can force you to sleep properly."

"Do what you will," she growled at him, "I have no reason to stop."

"Perhaps not yet," he replied menacingly.

He turned and strode off into the camp. Marilana sighed as one of the bandit guards took up position facing her with the long stick used to wake her up. She tried to stretch again, but stopped when pain shot through her limbs and made her wince. Instead, Marilana ignored her discomfort and occupied herself by watching the sky and listening to the sounds around her. She played a game with herself, challenging her mind to identify the different sounds of the camp. She was pleased that she was thinking clearly. But she knew that soon her fatigue would take its toll. If she was pushed far enough, she would begin to suffer dementia and hallucinations. She hoped that she could stave off those conditions for a few more days. If Marquiese had not tripped the trap by then, it would be too late for her.

Several hours later, Newrothen returned with his lunch. She watched him eat the stew and bread and wondered if she would be tortured again after lunch. When he retrieved his whip from his tent, her suspicions were confirmed. She scowled as he approached her.

"I see a question in your eyes," he said stopping before her. "Very well, I will give you one last free question. After that, if you ask a question, no matter if it is rhetorical or a phantom of dementia, you will be mine, and I will take you to my tent. So ask carefully."

She hesitated to ask; she thought she knew the answer to the simple question. Her real purpose was to learn how he would answer, and since she knew he would rather watch her suffer her unspoken question rather than to volunteer the information, she decided to go ahead and ask.

"Why did you kill him?" she asked.

"Ah," he smiled at her, "a good question to ask in your circumstances. Very well, the answer has two parts. The simple answer is because it caused you pain. The second is because he was no longer needed. He had done what I wanted, and I did not want to care for him all winter when you will be my primary concern. Did you think he might help you somehow?"

Marilana glared at him without responding, all three parts of the answer were as she expected. She was disappointed to learn that he had indeed thought through each line of reasoning. He was dangerously thorough. He smirked at her, then grabbed her arm and turned her toward the pole. Marilana shuddered from the pain of the movement, but closed her eyes and focused on her breathing as the bandits gathered around. She clenched her teeth and tried to relax her muscles. She blocked all sounds from her mind and waited for the whip to strike. She waited as seconds passed. The seconds stretched into a minute, then two.

Without warning, the whip cracked across her back. The strike was not any deeper than the earlier whipping, but she realized that she was losing layers of skin with every lashing. He was slowly and systematically skinning her alive. The whip strikes came quickly, starting at the top of her back and working down. Then another series of strikes from her left to her right. Her back felt like it was on fire; every nerve burned. She squeezed her eyes closed against the pain. There was a slight pause before the next strike. It landed low on her back and seared like a flame's tongue. The crowd cheered, and she knew the whip had just drawn blood. The lashings continued at a slower pace now. Each strike steadily climbed her back, each making her wince from the agony. She focused on her breathing and clenched her teeth to prevent any sound from escaping her lips. The whip crossed her shoulders and the next strike ran the length of her spine. She trembled violently as the strikes alternated from left to right radiating out from her spine. She could not hear anything but the ragged huffing of her breath passing through her nose and the blood pounding in her ears.

The whip rhythmically bit into her flesh. It slashed diagonally from her right shoulder to her left waist crossing the checkerboard pattern of previous strikes. Marilana winced from the burning that flared across her back. The lashings carved a deeper pattern of diagonal crosshatching across her inflamed back—throbbing pain with every strike of the whip. Marilana panted for air and shuddered with every beat of her heart. Warm, wet, blood tickled her fur, seeping slowly down the back of her legs, and soaked the remaining threads of her skirt. Marilana tried to focus on her breathing by counting breaths, but several times she lost count and had to fight to push back the red haze of torturous pain.

A sudden splash of cold followed instantly by searing pain across her back jolted her mind back to clarity for a moment. She moaned as someone turned her around and her back banged against the rough surface of the pole. The red haze edged her thoughts and blocked comprehension of the sounds around her. Pain flared in her right side and she gasped an involuntary breath. The red haze enveloped her mind as a scream tore through her throat. She screamed until she had no more breath. Black specks appeared through the red haze behind her eyelids as her lungs resisted expanding with a new breath. Sudden pain spiked through the fog in her mind and she became aware of cold air flowing with her renewed breathing.

Marilana could not tell how much time had passed before she opened her eyes. She blinked slowly in the bright afternoon sunlight as her vision cleared. Newrothen stood a pace in front of her watching her critically. He scowled dangerously at her.

"You did not blackout," he growled. "You were still responsive to stimuli. The bandit leaders have declared that I have not yet fulfilled the terms of their cooperation. They want to see more of your blood shed for them. They will not let me take you into my tent until their conditions are met. If you ask any questions of anyone, you will be mine. If you blackout or fall unconscious and cannot be roused within five minutes or no longer respond to external stimuli, you will be mine. I will not push you too far, but you are forcing me to get very close. You will regret angering and tempting them. You will regret pushing me. You will sleep for two hours." He clinched his paws in anger and frustration. Marilana would have smirked to annoy him further, knowing that she was straining his self-control, but she could not even manage to speak at the moment.

Marilana hung limp and weak. She watched Newrothen reach toward her and knew that he was going to try to force her to sleep. Her mind raced; if he made her sleep before she entered the trance, she would not have the control needed to direct her tired body back to the trance. Even if she did successfully enter the trance, there was no guarantee that she could drive her body back to the trance, or that he would not inflict sleep on her again for however many times was necessary until he won. Even so, she knew her body needed to sleep, but she would not let him control her. She closed her eyes and entered the healing trance. She could feel the pressure of his touch and felt her body shift to true sleep. She let her mind drift for a count of ten heartbeats and then forced her body back to the healing trance.

20

The sounds of scurrying and commotion in camp awoke Marilana from the healing trance. Her thoughts slowly made sense of the sounds she detected. When she opened her eyes and looked around blearily, she saw that the camp resembled a kicked anthill. Men were running around preparing weapons and armor as if for battle. Wagons rumbled toward the outer edge of the camp and axes and hammers rang out in every direction. Marilana glanced at the sun and was surprised to discover that she had been asleep for three hours when she had been commanded to sleep for two. She glanced toward the raised voices nearby.

Newrothen and the three bandit leaders strode toward her clearing. The leaders argued and talked over each other. Newrothen peered at her appraisingly as he spread out a rolled parchment on the table. Marilana watched curiously as the four leaders continued to quarrel while pointing to parts of the parchment. She could not make out what they were saying; the clatter of the camp drowned them out. Eventually Newrothen spoke. The others fell silent to listen to his hushed words. The three leaders shook their heads and voiced their complaints when he had finished. His posture stiffened as the bandit leaders pressed him. When the lion spoke again, she detected the undertone of his growl, even at a distance. Whatever they wanted of him, he was not happy about it, which made her think it had something to do with her.

She frowned as Newrothen turned and approached her. He stopped half a pace in front of her and glared at her.

"I suppose it was too much to hope that you might have slept through this ruckus," he growled.

Marilana frowned, glancing over Newrothen's shoulder to where the three bandit leaders watched silently in anger. She returned her gaze to Newrothen's eyes and waited silently for him to continue. He watched her for another few seconds before sighing.

"I know you are still too strong to give in yet," he said more diplomatically. "You are not about to ask a question, so I will fill you in, this time. Two sentries have disappeared, one from the east and one from the west. The disappearances happened on the same shift, so it was not the same person responsible for both. The other sentries did not see or hear anything, and they were positioned within sight of each other. The leaders are convinced that the disappearances are the work of Earek and want me to make you tell them what his strategy is."

"I have no reason to tell you or them anything. Besides I don't know his plan," Marilana said quietly.

"Yes, I know," Newrothen said darkly. "I know you cannot tell them exactly what Earek and Marquiese will do. However, they know you trained with them both. You studied battle strategies with them, and that is what your friends will rely on. So, either I make you tell them what you do know, or they say I have forfeited the right to you and they will take over your care."

"It will take a strong bargain to get me to say anything to them. I would rather they kill me than stay in your possession," Marilana replied.

"Yes, I know that too," Newrothen growled, his frustrations starting to show again. "I have decided on a compromise of sorts."

Marilana frowned more deeply and waited.

"You will answer every question we ask about Earek's strategy and combat knowledge truthfully."

"I will not," she spat.

"You will," he continued, a dangerous glint in his eyes, "or I will ride out as soon as I deem possible to capture your Lady Annabella. I will force you to watch her tortured to death. I can assure you her death will not be quick. If you lie, I will know. I too am well versed in battle tactics. You can be assured that I will recognize any incongruous information."

Marilana looked away from him and watched the bustle in the camp for a moment. She wasn't really surprised at his choice of coercion, but it still filled her with bone deep cold.

"You will leave her alone if I comply," she said darkly.

"Was that a question?" he asked.

"No," she said turning to meet his gaze, "it was a statement."

He smirked at her, then nodded, "Yes, that is the rest of the agreement. If you comply, I will agree to never use Lady Annabella as coercion against you again." After a moment of silence, he mused, "It is a hard decision: your lady and adopted mother, or your adopted brother. Which will I get to torture for you?"

Marilana scowled at him. She could tell them what they wanted to know risking Earek's and Marquiese's defeat and capture while safeguarding Lady Annabella's future, or she could withhold the information and Lady Annabella would become a target of the Hungdie if Earek and Marquiese failed. Refusing would gain Earek and Marquiese nothing since they were already risking their lives for her. She wouldn't even have to try to deliberately mislead the bandits since she really had no idea of the exact layout of the camp, valley, or armies. Agreeing would gain Lady Annabella a small grain of safety. Agreeing, though, would give Newrothen one more victory over her. Too exhausted to restrain her emotions, Marilana closed her eyes and dropped her chin in defeat. Tears welled up in her eyes. He had hit his mark.

"I agree," she whispered.

"What did you say? I couldn't hear you."

"I agree," she said in a loud whisper.

"Good," he crooned at her, "very good, Marilana."

Even with her eyes still closed, she could hear the pleasure in the fiend's voice.

*

Marilana rested her head against the pole, ignoring the pain the motion caused, and studied the pink and purple clouds. Tired and depressed tears flooded her vision as she thought about Marquiese and Earek. The questioning had been thorough and grueling. She had not been able to hold anything back. Newrothen pursued the lines of questioning the bandit leaders overlooked. He had taken full advantage of her agreement to tell what she knew of various attack strategies that could be used against the valley camp. They had finally agreed that she was probably right about Earek's strategy. She had said that since the sentries had disappeared from opposite ends of the camp, that Earek was scouting weaknesses along the flanks of the camp. She said he might be planning to bring most of his force straight into the camp along the valley floor, and send flanking forces to each side to attack from multiple angles. It was a good strategy, and likely one Earek was considering. She just hoped it was not the one he decided to use.

A paw brushed the tears from her cheek and Marilana immediately bit at it. Newrothen chuckled as Marilana lowered her chin and glared at him.

"Such a weak response," he said smiling, "and to think that only a few days ago you were much closer to drawing blood. Come now, gentle heart, surely you can see how much better it would be if you just accepted your destiny as my companion. You could have food and drink, time to heal, and shelter from the cold. Your life would be easier if you would stop resisting the urge to live."

"Sometimes it is better to die," she replied. "I will never stop resisting you, nor will I accept that your vision for my future is the only life I can have."

"Have it your way, Marilana," he shrugged. "The pain of your heart is just as sweet to me as the pain of your body. And remember, you tempted them to want to hurt you, now you have to suffer for them."

She glared at him as he turned and walked away to the front of his tent, the sun dipping below the rim of the mountains. Bandits gathered around her clearing in the twilight. It was the smallest gathering yet to witness her torture. The three leaders stood with Newrothen in front of his tent and watched her hungrily. Marilana wondered sadly what beating he was planning this time. As she watched, the hated lion held a cloth bag out to each of the leaders in turn. They each reached into the bag and withdrew a token of some kind. Newrothen examined each token in turn and seemed to be giving different instructions based on the token.

Marilana tried to take a deep calming breath as the black wolf stepped over the ring of stones, but was reminded sharply of her broken ribs. She took shallow slow breaths instead as he approached her. The small crowd cheered him forward. He raised his fist while smiling at his men. Then he turned a cruel smile on her. Without saying a word, he knelt and seized her right foot. Marilana closed her eyes and suppressed a shudder at his touch. She did not have long to consider his intentions. A sharp blow to her ankle, a loud cracking pop, and pain exploded up her leg. Marilana jerked her head back as she groaned while gritting her teeth. The crowd erupted; broken bones were something they clearly appreciated.

As the pain receded to a throb, Marilana opened her eyes to see the gray wolf step over the stone ring and approach her. Again, the crowd cheered his steps toward her. He did not acknowledge the cheers, but studied her face. Marilana glared hatred at him and tried to slow her breathing. He stopped a pace from her and paused as the crowd hushed in anticipation. She wondered in dread how he would cause her pain. Suddenly he spun, and with a precise kick, his booted heel struck her left kneecap with a loud crack. Marilana jerked and a moan passed through her clenched teeth. She shut her eyes, bracing against the agony. The cheers of the crowd were muffled by the sound of her pulse throbbing in her ears.

A red haze edged her vision as Marilana blinked back tears and reopened her eyes. The third leader stepped over the stone ring. The grizzly cracked his knuckles menacingly as he approached slowly. He bared his teeth at her in a blood-chilling grin. The crowd grew still and silent with anticipation. Marilana could not stop her breathing from growing faster with her fear. He locked eyes with her and his smiled widened. She closed her eyes and trembled uncontrollably as he laid one huge paw firmly on her left hip. Pain exploded with the cheering of the crowd as his other paw slammed into her right hip. She cried out in pain, but it seemed to be a lesser injury than her ankle or knee. She hung her head and panted, the sharp pain receding once again. Hoping the torture session had ended, Marilana opened her eyes and lifted her chin. Terrible pain shot up her spine and down through her legs. She cried out as the raw burning, searing pain caused her muscles to spasm, her back arched and she pulled against the ropes. She sagged back against the pole gasping as the red haze obliterated her sight, and black specks flickered like sparks exploding from a blacksmith's hammer on hot iron.

When she emerged from the haze, Marilana's first sensation, beyond her agony, was an awareness of wild, raucous cheering. She focused on the sound and pulled her thoughts together through the pain coursing through her body with every heartbeat. She hung limp and weak, but someone seemed to be calling her name close by and something tapped her face. Blearily she opened her eyes and looked directly into black eyes full of concern. She blinked slowly trying to make sense of what she was feeling. Newrothen was tapping her cheek and talking to her. Marilana weakly tried to pull back from him. He grimaced and turned away from her. The cheering and laughter faded as the bandits dispersed from the clearing.

Marilana focused on the three bandit leaders as Newrothen addressed them.

"I gave you specific instructions to prevent you from accidentally killing her," he growled at them. "You have no idea how close you came just now!"

"She deserves far worse than a kidney shot, and she still lives. You are overreacting," said the grizzly, wiping blood from his paw.

"The pain I give her is much worse for the length of time it lasts," Newrothen growled exasperatedly. "Yes, a kidney punch is extremely painful, and usually not life threatening, but she is in a weakened state where any extreme shock to her body could easily kill her."

"We would have regretted your loss, but not her death. You should be content that she still lives," replied the gray wolf coldly.

"She is reaching a critical point in her physical condition," said Newrothen in a tight voice. "I cannot afford to let you improvise and accidentally kill her. I must have complete control of her treatment from now on."

"Very well," said the black wolf. The other leaders started to protest, but he continued, "Make her scream for us one last time, and even if her condition has not yet satisfied our terms, she is yours at this time tomorrow. We have lingered here too long. The day after tomorrow, I intend to lead my men to a more secure winter camp. The cloudy sky today warns of the coming winter snows, and I want a good amount of impassable snow between me and Earek's army."

"I must agree with that," sighed the gray wolf, "as much as I dislike your management of the prisoner, she is in no condition to travel, and I, too, want to put distance between my men and the approaching army."

"This camp was to be my winter camp," growled the grizzly, "and I said you could camp with us for the winter. I must agree, though, that I had thought the winter snows would have prevented Earek from catching us here. My men and I will defend our camp if we are attacked, but she is your responsibility."

"It is agreed then," growled Newrothen, "this time tomorrow she is mine, and after that I will not call upon you or your men for any more assistance."

The bandit leaders stalked off into the camp as darkness fell. Newrothen watched them go before returning to Marilana.

"Curse them and their impatience. I'll kill them for this later. I'd kill them now if I didn't still need their bandits," he muttered darkly. "Marilana, do you understand me? Did you understand that conversation?"

"Yes," Marilana mumbled.

"Too much pain all at once and the patient dies. Shock in a weakened state needs careful healing, healing I can't give you yet. You need sleep, but I cannot allow it. I need to be sure you do not lapse into shock and die in the next few hours. Can you stay awake that long?" he asked seriously.

"Not on my own," she replied truthfully.

He nodded and turned to address the three bandit guards that were awaiting instructions. The three took up positions around the stone ring, and Newrothen took up the stick and stood facing her. Marilana sighed, and then winced at the pain. It was going to be another long night. Her last outside to be sure, but she couldn't tell how many she had left in her in any event.

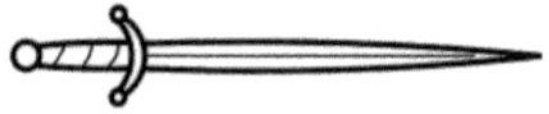

Marquiese rolled out from under his blankets and drew his sword as someone pushed open the flap of his tent.

"Marquiese?" Earek asked quietly.

"Earek, what is it?" Marquiese asked warily.

Light flared inside the tent as Earek partially opened the shutter of the lantern he held. Earek remained standing bent under the tent flap with only his black head and paw inside the tent. He eyed Marquiese's sword cautiously, but did not hesitate.

"Sorry to wake you, but you must come to the command tent right away," said Earek urgently.

"Is it Child?" Marquiese asked as he sheathed his sword and grabbed his shirt.

"In part, but I can tell you no more until we get to the command tent."

"Lead the way," said Marquiese belting on his sword and grabbing his cloak.

Marquiese followed Earek out into the chilly night and noticed guards filling the space around the nearby command tent. Something was happening, and he hoped it was as important as it seemed. Earek held open the flap to the command tent and Marquiese ducked into the well-lit interior. An older red fox stood to one side of the tent. His paws were bound behind his back and Earek's two guards held their swords on him. The fox calmly watched Earek and Castant enter the tent as if he were there by his choice. Marquiese studied him as Earek set the lantern down on the table.

"This man claims to be a mercenary tracker by the name of Rodan," Earek said without preamble. "He says he brings us both a message and an offer, but would say no more until you came. The Phantom caught him sneaking through our sentry line and brought him to me. She says he is who he claims to be, and that he came from the bandit camp."

"How does she know?" asked Marquiese.

"She and Marilana make it their goal to be able to identify any mercenaries or bandits of note. I also recognize his face from a sketch I once saw. The Phantom said she followed him from the valley floor and suggested that we listen to him. It is said that he is an honest tracker."

"Very well," nodded Marquiese, "tell us how you came to be here, then tell us why you have come."

"Thank you, Your Highness, for hearing me out," said Rodan with a small bow. "I came from the bandit camp as The Phantom said. I bring both a message and an offer as Master Earek has said."

"I do not wish to hear any messages from the bandits; I will not negotiate with them. I want Marilana back alive," growled Marquiese.

"I did not say I carried a message from the bandits," Rodan said, "and I want Lady Marilana to live as well."

Marquiese frowned and studied the fox before speaking. "You have deserted the bandits?" he asked carefully.

"I have, and I will tell you everything I know of them," Rodan nodded gravely. "Three bandit leaders direct and control most of the bandit activities in this region. I had accepted a tracking position with one of them for the winter. After the poor harvest this year, my wife and daughter's survival depended on my income. I have since regretted taking part in the events that followed. I was not part of the force that captured Lady Marilana. I was sent to track the movements of Lady Annabella. I returned to the camp just before Lady Marilana and her captor. The lion who captured Lady Marilana is dangerous. He negotiated a deal with the three bandit leaders. In return for their help in capturing Lady Marilana, he made many promises. Most of the promises I do not know, but he made one promise to all the bandits in the camp. He promised that The Ghost would never hunt any of us again. Instead, we would get a chance to see her punished for all the lives she has taken."

"And you were happy about this?" interrupted Marquiese.

"No," said Rodan sadly, "I did not think she deserved punishment, as she was justified in taking every life. She was a protector of her people, and she saved the lives of many families that live south of Redsands. My wife and daughter are comfortable this winter because Lady Marilana distributed food at the border. However, I had already accepted the contract for the winter, and could not back out even though my family no longer needed the extra support. Many bandits, though, believed we were justified in taking revenge on The Ghost. They feared her, and so they wanted to prove to themselves and each other that they were strong, that she was just a girl who could be beaten."

"What has he done to her?" Marquiese asked fearing the answer.

"That creature knows pain. He has her hanging from a pole on display. He has whipped her and let the bandits have a turn at beating her, but her torture is tightly controlled. He has not let her eat or drink. I overheard him say that he does not want her to die because he has plans for her. I shudder to wonder what those plans are, and I am glad I do not know; what I saw before leaving was bad enough. She is not in good condition, and I hope that she will survive."

"But you did not help her escape?" Earek growled.

"You left her there to endure more torture while you slipped away to tell us your tale?" Marquiese added coldly, clenching his paws to stop from striking the fox.

"I would have brought her out of that place if I could have," Rodan hung his head in shame. "She is carefully guarded, but I managed to speak with her privately. She told me that she could not escape, even if I found a way to get her loose and outside the camp. She said she was too weak from her injuries and lack of water to out run the trackers and she would just be captured again. When the leaders tasked me with hunting down The Phantom and killing her, I took the opportunity to come here."

"They sent you out to hunt The Phantom?" asked Earek coldly.

"Yes, some of the bandit scouts who were supposed to be monitoring your movements disappeared and they assumed it was The Phantom. I am the best tracker they had, and so I was given the task to eliminate the threat. I must admit she is better than me. I had a general idea where your camp was, and I was careful not to leave a trail. I had no idea she had been following me, nor did I know she was close by when she caught me."

"She had a good teacher," said Marquiese. "We have listened to your tale, but tell me why have you come here?"

"I want to help you rescue Lady Marilana," said Rodan straightening his back. "I can help you get through the sentry line quickly and lead you to the places you need your men to be so that you can attack the camp directly and quickly with as little advance warning as possible. You must get your men in position by dawn. That will allow us to take the sentries out just after the shift change, and then we can get close to the camp before the next shift change after the morning …uh… entertainment. The morning entertainment is planned to occur just after breakfast and will occupy the attention of most of the bandits in camp."

"What exactly is this entertainment?" Earek asked nervously.

"It, well, if it is still done," Rodan said, "is public torture."

"I see," said Marquiese interrupting any further explanation. "Your plan is a good one, and we will need to move soon to accomplish it, but before we settle the details and get the men moving, you have one more bit to tell us. What is your message and who is it from?"

Rodan studied Marquiese and Earek. His expression softened, and he swallowed nervously.

"The message I carry to you both," he said quietly, "is from her."

Marquiese blinked in surprise. "From Marilana? Did she know you would come to us?"

"I think she suspected I would, but I was not sure when we spoke what I would do. I was still trying to find a way for her to escape. After leaving her, I decided the only way to help her was to come here. But she asked that if I saw either of you to give you a message. She said to tell you that she is as good as dead and that she will not live to be this man's plaything."

The royal lion closed his eyes and turned away from the fox. He knew Marilana would kill herself if she thought she had no other choice. If this beast was a Hungdie as Marilana feared, she would have to work hard to accomplish her own death.

"She will kill herself," whispered Earek sadly.

"I voiced the same assumption, but she said she would not have to," Rodan replied gently. "She said she just has to make him think she is stronger than she really is, and he would kill her by accident."

"Then we must arrive this morning if we have any chance at saving her," said Marquiese turning to face Earek. "I will not give up on her until I hold her in my arms."

Earek nodded and lifted his chin.

"Untie him," Earek barked at his guards.

"Castant, rouse the camp. I want every able man to be mounted and ready to ride as soon as possible. Have our horses brought. But make it quiet, we do not want to alert the bandits with extra noise," Marquiese said firmly. "Come to the map, Rodan. We need to finalize a plan."

Marilana roused herself from the healing trance; it took several minutes for her to become fully aware. She did not feel cold, but she could feel her body trembling slightly and every inch of her body ached from the abuse she had sustained. She knew she could not hold out much longer. She was weak from hunger, pain, and yesterday's blood loss. She knew that she only had until the sunset before she would be claimed by Newrothen and taken to his tent. She had to appear strong, yet she feared she would slip into dementia and he would heal her rather than accidentally killing her. She ignored the protests of her sore neck and raised her head to peer up at the cloudy sky. The clouds spun and tilted. Marilana closed her eyes against the dizziness. At least she would be inside before the snows came.

"Marilana!" Newrothen shook her slightly sending a wave of pain through her body.

Marilana frowned at the clouds as the dizziness passed, then looked down as Newrothen shook her again.

"Are you alright?" he asked frowning. "You did not respond for a few minutes."

"I can ignore you if I want to," she replied still frowning at him to mask her worry. A few minutes of unresponsiveness was not a good sign. She was close to the brink; she had to stay aware of her surroundings.

"So, you can," he said thoughtfully, "perhaps you are too weak. I should not whip you again if you are close to blacking out."

"You are the authority on pain; aren't you?"

"Was that a question?" he asked surprised.

"No, it was a statement," she replied quickly.

"So, it was," he sneered at her. "It does not matter. You belong to me starting tonight and nothing can stop that now." He leered in anticipation.

She glared at him, but he just smiled as he turned her to face the pole. She barely had time to notice that the bandits had already gathered and that he held his whip.

The first strike of the whip felt like liquid fire splashing across her back. She trembled and moaned from the agony. The pain in her legs from the previous night lessened as the whip carved her back again. She could not determine a pattern to the strikes. She imagined that he was striking the last pieces of skin from her back one at a time. She felt a warm trickle of blood down her legs. She tried to focus on the blood and ignore the pain, but she could not hold her concentration. Red filled her vision and she lost count of the lashings she had sustained. She wondered at the black specks that flickered and drifted before her eyes. Ice and fire erupted across her back, clearing her thoughts. She blinked at Newrothen as he turned her to face the crowd. Something was wrong; she could not discern the faces of the bandits and her ears buzzed. She gasped a painful breath at the sharp precise pain in her left side. After a second intense jab, she was screaming without end. Blackness crawled across the red of her vision until there was nothing left but the empty void. Marilana knew no more.

21

Marquiese urged his charger up the back slope of the hill just enough to peer over the crest at the bandit encampment. Everything was going according to plan. The army had ridden out in the darkness trailing Rodan. Child had appeared before them like the phantom of her nickname. She had whispered with Earek and then disappeared into the darkness. They had successfully taken out a group of sentries and replaced some of them without alerting the rest of the sentry line. They would attack the camp at an angle, avoiding the two most anticipated attack lines, straight along the valley floor and from the high ground of the sides. The scouts had indicated that the bandits had concentrated their defenses at those points. Child had directed Earek to this location. The large hill hid their approach from the camp, and provided a straight smooth slope down to the camp directly in line with the clearing where the bandits were gathered. They watched and waited for the right moment to attack. Marquiese had initially wanted to attack during the so-called entertainment, but Rodan pointed out that the last thing they wanted was for the bandits to form a wall between them and Marilana. Glancing down at the large gathering of bandits in the clear area of the camp, Marquiese had to agree that letting the bandits disperse would be better.

Marquiese glanced back at where Earek and Castant waited impatiently behind him, and saw Marilana's six guardsmen waiting just behind them. Marquiese was not sure how those six had managed to get inside the protective ring of his own personal guards, but he decided now was not the time to sort out the arrangements. He admitted that he did feel better having those six where he could see them and know what they were doing. He turned his attention back to the bandit camp. He could not see clearly what was happening, and he was glad he could not; however, he was growing impatient for the gathering to end.

Suddenly a shrill piercing scream echoed through the valley. Marilana's distressed voice was unmistakable. Marquiese did not hesitate. He spurred his mount forward over the hill and charged headlong toward the clearing in the camp. He felt like he had just been kicked in the stomach. Behind him he heard the shouts and cries of the charging army, but he did not slow for them to catch up. He had to reach that clearing.

Marquiese drew his sword and charged into the camp. Surprised men dove out of his way as he rushed past the first tents. One man readied his spear to throw at Marquiese, but a crossbow dart pierced his chest. Marquiese glanced behind him and smiled. Marilana's guardsmen rode in formation behind him, four with drawn swords, and two with crossbows. Marquiese crashed through the confused mass of bandits. Men dispersed from the gathering unaware that they were under attack, while those that had been on watch ran to sound the alarm and meet the attackers in battle. Marquiese quickly knocked aside the small resistance and reached the clear area at the lead of the spear-point formation. He drew rein sharply at the sight that met his eyes.

The lion that Marquiese had come to confront stood next to the pole from which Marilana hung unconscious.

His knife was pressed to Marilana's throat. Marquiese dismounted and stepped over a ring of large stones without taking his eyes from the beast he had known only as Frishka's Confidante. Marilana's guardsmen arrayed themselves in a perimeter around the ring of stones and watched for additional threats from the rest of the bandit camp. Marquiese stopped just inside the ring and waited for the dark lion to speak.

Confidante waited for the sounds of fighting close by to quiet and watched as more soldiers on horses added to the protective perimeter. Marquiese ignored the newcomers and controlled his breathing as he waited. Finally, the man sneered at him.

"The coward Prince has come to me at last," he sneered.

Marquiese refrained from answering and waited silently.

"So, you have changed from the brash young lion I knew from my time in the palace," Confidante jeered. "If we were in different circumstances, I would like to hear everything you learned in your time of hiding. However, you did not come here for pleasantries."

"Listen up all of you," Confidante called loudly. "Prince Marquiese and I are going to enter an agreement. You all are bound by it."

"We do not negotiate with kidnappers," Marquiese growled.

"You will negotiate with me or I will kill the girl right now. You will hear me out, no one will interfere with our deal, and all will abide by our agreement. Or she dies first," the dark lion said pressing his knife into Marilana's neck so that a drop of blood appeared on the blade.

"Very well," snarled Marquiese, "what do you want?"

"Good," Confidant smiled. "I want you, Marquiese. You and I will fight one-on-one. No one will interfere. Whoever wins gets the girl and will be allowed to leave freely. In other words, when I kill you, your men will vacate the area and not try to kill me or take the lioness."

"No," said Marquiese firmly, "they take her now and leave, then we fight."

"You want me to kill her now? Do you?" the beast pressed his knife into Marilana's flesh a little more.

"No!" cried Marquiese then stopped and gathered his emotions. "Fine. We do it your way. On my honor, if you win, my men will leave without harming you or taking the girl."

"But, Highness…!" someone started to protest, but Marquiese raised his paw, cutting off the comment without looking away from the other lion.

"It is agreed; my men will do as I have commanded even should I die," Marquiese said firmly.

"I can ask no more than that," Confidante said. "I will have to deal with Master Earek and his men later."

Marquiese was not surprised that the fiend had seen the loophole in the deal. He knew Confidante was very intelligent and cunning. He also knew that the man was an expert fighter and this duel would not be easy. He wished he had his heavy combat armor rather than his light leather traveling coat, but at least his opponent was not any better armored than he was. He looked at

Marilana once more and focused every fiber of his being on the fight. He could not afford to lose.

Confidante smiled broadly as he lowered his knife and stepped away from Marilana. Marquiese gripped his hilt with both paws and took a ready stance. The man drew his sword and spun his knife into a fighting grip. They began to circle.

The older lion lunged; Marquiese parried the sword and dodged the knife. Without slowing, Marquiese attacked back. For several minutes the world was a blur of motion, he focused solely on motions of his opponent. Slice, jab, spin, and attack again. Confidante was fast and light. He struck with both sword and knife and Marquiese had to work hard to block both. He missed the knife slightly and sustained the first cut to his forearm. Marquiese's sword whistled through the air as he instantly swung in a tight arc, ignoring the cut, and managed to shallowly slice Confidant's upper leg. The dark lion leapt back and then circled to jab at Marquiese's left. Together they struggled against each other, each trying without success to press an advantage, and both taking several minor injuries. Lunge, parry, jump back and spin to the right to block. Back and forth, round and round they fought, neither hesitating; they were in constant motion. Finally, Marquiese nicked the inside of Confidante's knife wrist and caught the blade as the dark lion tried to pull back. The knife flew out of his grip and disappeared into the forest of horse legs outside the stone ring. Confidante backed up a few steps and sneered. Marquiese took advantage of the space to breath.

"You have learned much since I last fought you. My compliments to your trainer," Confidante said.

"She hangs behind you," Marquiese growled without glancing away from him.

"As I thought," Confidante snarled and lunged toward Marquiese again.

Marquiese parried and stabbed at Confidant's shoulder. Even without the knife, the older lion was a formidable fighter. They were a blur of motion, constantly striving to find the other's weakness, pushing their own limits to strike past each other's defenses. Marquiese knew he could not keep this pace much longer. His arms and legs burned from the strain of the contest as well as the small cuts he had sustained. He pressed Confidante hard, and could see the strain in his features as well. The dark lion cleaved down at Marquiese. The younger lion blocked, the swords screeched as they slid against each other.

Marquiese circled back and lunged in again aiming for an upper arm. Then he saw it; Confidante was aiming a swipe for his stomach. Marquiese spun out around the man's sword tip and knocked the sword wide. He continued his spin and whipped his own blade around and across the dark lion's throat. Confidante's eyes widened in surprise as blood sprayed from Marquiese's sword tip. His body slumped to the ground. Marquiese stood over his fallen opponent panting hard. He watched the lion spasm a couple of times and then lay still, blood pooling on the ground from his sliced neck. Marquiese stooped and cleaned his sword on the man's black shirt.

Straightening up Marquiese became aware of the sounds around him again. He had been so focused, that he had completely blocked out everything outside his fight. Now he turned to face the world around him. Across the clearing the marks of the fight could be seen, the ground was pitted and ridged by the passing of their boots and blood was splattered everywhere. Soldiers and guardsmen moved about outside the ring, but only three had entered and approached where Marilana still hung. No one cheered Marquiese's victory, although every creature who met his gaze saluted his win. Fearful expectation hung like a shroud over the camp. Marquiese hurried toward Marilana, fear exploding in his gut.

"What is it?" he asked as he reached the three men. "Why have you not taken her down yet?"

"First of all," replied Castant, "the bandits fled into the hills and rather than pursue them, I ordered a halt to safeguard our retreat. Second, we were not about to step into the ring with you two fighting that way. We would have had our guts spilled before we had time to react. Third," he paused, and his tone softened, "take a look. We are not sure if or how we should move her yet."

Marquiese frowned and studied Marilana and her surroundings. He was relieved to see that she was breathing shallowly, but he was alarmed by everything else he saw. Her legs were covered in bruises and welts. Her left knee and right ankle were swollen and, he assumed, probably broken. Her dress was torn and filthy. The ground under her feet was wet and darkly stained. When he noticed blood dripping from her feet, he walked around the pole and followed the trail of blood up her legs. He clenched his fists in anger as he looked upon what was left of her back. The back of her dress was shredded, and her exposed flesh torn and bloody. It was not the first time he had seen someone who had been whipped, but it was by far the worst. He turned away from her as Earek stepped up next to him.

"What do we do?" Earek whispered hoarsely.

"We get her to Healer Magus as carefully as we can," replied Marquiese.

"Can she be moved?"

"We have no choice. It is not safe to remain here; the bandits could rally and attack us in the night. We must return to our own camp where we have sentries in place. We must risk moving her. Assume she has many broken bones including ribs," replied Marquiese firmly.

He surveyed the camp. A tent made from strange dark brown material seemed out of place. It was not in line with the others, and it was the one Marilana faced from her pole.

"That tent," Marquiese ordered pointing at it, "search it. Bring anything useful, and then use the tent poles and canvas to make a stretcher. Prepare my horse and Earek's to have the stretcher lashed between them. We will ride with Lady Marilana. Rodan, make speed back to Healer Magus and tell him to prepare to tend Our Lady."

Men jumped to obey, and Rodan raced out of the bandit camp. Soon there was a pile of blankets, several canteens of water, a satchel full of medicinal herbs, and a small crate sitting outside the tent. Several men with knives cut long lengths of canvas, while another group used the lengths to tie the tent poles together and make harnesses for the horses. Marquiese peered inside the crate finding an arsenal of grotesque tools whose only purposes could be to cause pain. Disgusted, he ordered it and its contents destroyed. Major Kolt and another guardsman growled that they would see to it personally, and carried it grim-faced into the camp. Not long after, Marquiese heard the ringing of hammers and saw black smoke rising from a nearby traveling forge. He ordered any wounded and most of the army to ride ahead and return to camp. He kept a contingent with him in case the bandits tried to attack them, but the scouts reported that the bandits seemed to be waiting for them to leave and did not wish for a confrontation.

Once the stretcher and harnesses were ready, Marquiese had several layers of blankets lain on the canvas. He, Earek, and four of Marilana's guards took a pair of blankets to where Marilana hung with her feet untied. They slid one blanket between her back and the pole, the other blanket they held in front of her. They twisted the two blankets together around her so that the blankets held Marilana securely between them. Once in position, they carefully lifted her feet as Castant slowly let out the rope keeping her as straight as possible. Gradually the six took her weight and lifted her until she rested fully in the blankets they held tight. Castant cut the ropes from her paws and then positioned her arms carefully along her sides. Together they laid her on the stretcher. More blankets were spread on top of her, and then canvas straps were used to tie Marilana and the blankets securely to the stretcher so she would not slide or roll. They then lifted the stretcher and secured it between Marquiese's and Earek's horses.

Marquiese and Earek mounted to control the horses. They waited while the men gathered and mounted. Marilana's six guards and Earek's two arrayed themselves with Marquiese's guards and as a group they slowly rode back to their camp where Healer Magus waited. The ride was long since Marquiese did not push for speed. He and Earek navigated their mounts carefully around obstacles and tried not to jostle Marilana too much. Marquiese closely monitored Marilana. Her breathing was irregular and she did not stir. When they finally rode into camp, Healer Magus was pacing in front of the infirmary tent.

"I have tended all the wounded men, and reserved this tent for Lady Marilana," Healer Magus called to them as they approached.

Healer Magus fidgeted and chastised the men as Marilana's guards released the stretcher from the horses and gingerly carried her inside. Marquiese and Earek dismounted and let their mounts be led away. They hurried to enter the tent, but were forced to stop as Marilana's guards came back out. Healer Magus stuck his head out and frowned at them all.

"I need to work quickly and carefully. You must remain outside the tent until I say otherwise," Healer Magus said forcefully and closed the tent flap.

Marquiese sighed with frustration and paced. Earek and Castant stood impatiently nearby. Marilana's guardsmen took up positions around the tent. Maids and assistant healers, who had accompanied Healer Magus, entered and left the tent in a steady stream. They carried buckets of clean water in and bloody water out, fetched cloths and clean blankets, removed the blood-soaked blankets from the tent, and brought bowls of steaming water from the nearby cook fire.

After several hours, Healer Magus chased his assistants from the tent and called for Earek and Marquiese. Marquiese hurried into the tent followed by Earek.

Healer Magus sat tiredly on a chair next to where Marilana slept covered in blankets on a cot. He gestured to a pair of stools nearby. Marquiese took a calming breath as he sat on the stool.

"I know you are impatient," said Healer Magus, "so I will give you the full report." He sighed, clearly hesitant to deliver the news. "I have never seen such an extreme case of torture on a still living creature. Our Lady is closer to the brink than I have ever seen her. I had expected her to be in a healing trance, but she is fully unconscious. She has lost a lot of blood. She has six broken ribs, four on her right and two on her left. Her right ankle and left kneecap are broken, her right hip is severely bruised, and it looks like her right kidney is probably bruised as well. Her chest, abdomen, sides, buttocks, and legs are covered with smaller bruises, cuts, and welts. Her paws and wrists are bruised and chafed from her bonds, and her shoulders show signs of damage resulting from being violently pulled. Her back of course is in the worst shape with countless slashes indicating a large number of lashings. Most of the cuts have penetrated through the skin, and the worst ones have shredded the underlying muscle. From what I can tell, the lashings were all precise. The muscles that were carved into were intentionally chosen. I have sewn the cuts as best I can and bandaged and poulticed her wounds."

Marquiese closed his eyes and swallowed. Healer Magus waited while Marquiese and Earek absorbed the information. A question arose in Marquiese's mind and he frowned.

"What would be the purpose of targeting specific muscles?" he asked quietly.

The old cheetah sighed and sadly gazed at Marilana.

"The resulting scarring will limit the range of motion in her arms," Healer Magus replied quietly.

"What does that mean?" asked Earek hoarsely.

"She," Healer Magus hesitated, "she will probably never be able to shoot a bow, and she will have trouble with her sword forms."

A deep sadness overtook Marquiese as he peered down at Marilana. His stomach turned to ice. He knew what those abilities meant to her, how hard she had trained, and how vigilantly she had practiced. He knew that Confidante had done it on purpose; he wanted to rob her of her abilities. Death had been too good an ending for him. Marquiese felt dampness on his cheek and realized he was crying. Healer Magus gave him a kerchief. Marquiese dried his tears and glanced at the black leopard. Earek sat bent forward with his elbows on his knees and his face in his paws. Earek showed no tears, but he too grieved for his sister's loss.

"Is there anything we can do to help her recover?" Marquiese asked quietly, and Earek looked up at the healer.

"There is one thing I would like to try," Healer Magus said cautiously. "I would like to try to replace some of her lost blood. It would help her greatly. We must be careful, however, in choosing a donor."

"You mean you can give her someone else's blood?" Earek asked shocked.

"Yes, but not just anyone's blood," Healer Magus said studying Marquiese. "She is a lion and needs lion blood. There are very few lions in this area, the donor must be healthy and the blood must pass a test before it can be used."

"Is it dangerous to the donor?" Marquiese asked meeting the cheetah's eyes. He felt guilty for thinking of his own safety when Marilana's life hung by a thread, but he reminded himself that Marilana would not want him to forget his duty to his people. He at least needed to know the risks even though he knew in his heart that he would agree to have his blood tested even if the risk was high.

"No, not if proper sterility is maintained and the amount of blood is closely limited," replied Healer Magus.

"Then what do I need to do?" asked Marquiese decisively.

"I need a drop of your blood to test with hers," Healer Magus said quickly standing up and gathering supplies.

Healer Magus directed Marquiese to sit next to Marilana and uncovered her arm. He pricked her finger and squeezed a drop of blood onto a piece of glass, and then repeated the process with Marquiese. Healer Magus tilted the glass back and forth in the lantern light, gently mixing the two drops of blood. After a few moments he smiled and turned to Marquiese.

"It is a match," he said with relief. "You can be a donor to her."

"Let us proceed," Marquiese said nervously.

Healer Magus called for an assistant healer, and together they readied the supplies they needed. Marquiese watched nervously as they laid out syringes, needles, and a thin glass tube that had a bubble towards one end. They arranged his arm next to Marilana's and then tied a cord tightly around Marquiese's upper arm.

"Now you must sit absolutely still," Healer Magus warned.

Marquiese nodded tensely and swallowed. Healer Magus poked a needle into Marilana's arm and tied it down. Marquiese watched a dark drop of blood slowly grow on the open end of the needle. Then he tried not to flinch as Healer Magus poked a needle with the glass tube attached into his arm. He was surprised by how quickly his bright red blood filled the tube. Healer Magus waited until the tube was just ready to drip blood out the end, and then attached the tube to the needle in Marilana's arm. Marquiese watched his blood drip into the bubble, and waited for something to happen.

This was supposed to help Marilana, but as Marquiese watched, he could see no changes. After studying the set-up for a moment, Healer Magus smiled.

"It is working well," he said. "Highness, please tell me immediately if you feel lightheaded, dizzy, or if your vision starts to dim."

Marquiese frowned. It was working well? How could the healer tell anything about how it was going if there was no change? Healer Magus adjusted the cord around his arm and checked his vitals. Marquiese watched his blood dripping in the tube as the healer checked Marilana's vitals.

"Highness, please try to relax," Healer Magus said calmly. "I see you frowning in contemplation of this process, but I assure you I know what I am doing. This will not cause a sudden, drastic improvement to our dear Marilana. It will hopefully give her the strength she needs to begin to heal. She is terribly weak, and I cannot guarantee that she will survive."

Marquiese nodded with a sigh and relaxed his tense posture. None of his thoughts of getting Marilana back had included a long recovery. He resigned himself to the truth that she was not safe yet, and there was nothing he could do but wait. Marquiese lost track of time as he witnessed his blood draining out of his body and into Marilana's. Healer Magus periodically checked his and Marilana's vitals and occasionally adjusted the cord around his arm. Earek paced along the opposite side of the tent. After what felt like hours, Healer Magus removed the cord and extracted the needle from Marquiese's arm. He then pulled the needle from Marilana.

"Thank you, Highness," Healer Magus said quietly as he carefully bandaged them both. "Your gift of blood has probably saved her life, although her condition is still far from stable. You need to sit here and rest for a while."

Healer Magus cleaned and examined Marquiese's remaining cuts, and declared they were not serious. He sent his assistant off with the used supplies, and then left the tent.

"Are you alright?" Earek asked softly touching Marquiese on the shoulder.

"Yes," Marquiese replied, "I am tired. It has been a long hard day, but this blood business has not hurt me."

"Healer Magus is a good healer," Earek said quietly. "He has tended Marilana since she was a child. He is her best hope."

"I know. Thank you," Marquiese replied. "I am just worried that she will never wake again."

"Me too," Earek whispered. "Me too."

22

Not long after Marquiese gave Marilana the gift of blood, Healer Magus returned with Master Castant. Healer Magus set the bowls he carried on his table and mixed remedies.

"I have seen to the men as best as I can," Castant reported. "We lost only five men and nearly twenty are wounded. Not too bad considering we faced around two hundred bandits with only two hundred and fifty. Most of the bandits fled rather than fought. Healer Magus gave Captain Hayden and me a report. I have not spoken to the men yet. It is nearly dark. One of you must let them know if today was a good day. Healer Magus also told me that you need to rest, Marquiese, and that Earek needs to eat."

"I will speak to the men," Earek said meeting Marquiese's eyes, "and then I shall eat."

Marquiese nodded and the two leopards went out. Healer Magus served the young lion a hearty bowl of stew.

"You must eat," he urged. "I have mixed in some healing herbs to help you regain your full strength. You may not feel it, but you gave Marilana a significant amount of blood and it has weakened you."

Marquiese nodded while he ate mechanically. He watched Healer Magus spoon broth into Marilana's mouth and was relieved when she swallowed by reflex. He sat staring at her after he finished his stew.

"I can tell you'd like to stay with her," Healer Magus said when he finished checking her vitals. "I need her to be watched anyway. I am going to check on the wounded men and will return before retiring to my bed. Send one of the guards if she wakes or seems to change in anyway."

Marquiese nodded and the old cheetah took the empty bowls out of the tent with him. Marquiese gently took Marilana's paw in his and reminisced on memories of better times as he watched her in motionless slumber. Suddenly her paw convulsed, and her eyes popped open. Marquiese leaned forward in surprise.

"No, no, no," she whispered weakly shaking her head.

Marquiese was stunned to see that she was crying.

"Marilana," he said cradling her cheek with his paw, "it is ok; you are safe now that I am here."

"Marquiese?" she turned to look at him, and then closed her eyes. "I must be hallucinating."

"No, you are not, I am real. I am here, and you are safe with me," he reassured her.

"It doesn't matter," she whispered opening her eyes. "Real or not, please listen to me."

"I am listening," he said quietly.

"Don't interrupt. I don't have much strength," she whispered. "I am too weak to enter the healing trance. I will sleep deeply. Tell the healer he must change his remedies if I am to wake again."

"I understand," he said when she paused.

"Don't interrupt," she said weakly. "If I don't wake," she hesitated as fresh tears flowed down her cheeks, "I want you to know that everything I did, I did because," she swallowed, "I love you."

Her eyes closed, and her paw relaxed in his. He was stunned by her words.

"Hayden," he called loudly.

"Highness," Captain Hayden stuck his head in the tent flaps.

"Fetch Healer Magus and Earek right away," Marquiese.

Hayden disappeared. A few minutes later, Earek hurried into the tent followed by the healer.

"What happened?" panted Healer Magus moving toward Marilana.

"She woke briefly," Marquiese said urgently. "She thought she was hallucinating, but she said it didn't matter. She told me to tell you that she is too weak to enter the healing trance. She said she was going to sleep deeply, and if there was any chance of her waking, that you must change your remedies.

"Yes, yes I will. One set of healing for the waking patient, a different set for the deep sleeper," Healer Magus said quickly gathering supplies. "Thank you for repeating her words. I am not surprised that she was coherent, but she confirmed my suspicions. If she wakes, she can fill in the details, but I suspected she was using the healing trance to push her body beyond her limits.

She will probably not wake again for many days, if I can keep her alive that long."

"You know a lot about her methods," Marquiese said.

"She had to trust someone to heal her at times," Healer Magus replied as he worked. "I was interested in all kinds of healing, not just the new blood medicines. She taught me about the old ways, we learned much more by working together. I was too old to learn some of her healing practices, but I know enough to tend to her. Using the wrong herbs or the wrong blood medicines can kill her in her serious and unstable condition. I must be very careful if she is to recover. I promise I am doing everything I can to help her, but it will be a long, rocky road."

"Thank you, Healer Magus," Marquiese said.

Healer Magus worked quickly and spooned a new broth into Marilana's mouth. She did not react at first, but then she swallowed by reflex. All three men sighed with relief. She continued to breathe slowly but steadily.

"Only time will tell if the remedies heal her," Healer Magus said and turned to look at Marquiese and Earek. "I doubt either of you will want to leave her. So, you can take turns watching her. Try to get some sleep and send someone to wake me if her condition changes."

He motioned to the cot on the other side of the tent and then left.

Marquiese took Marilana's paw and gazed down upon her. After a moment Earek pulled one of the stools over and sat facing Marquiese.

"I can tell by your face that she said something else, and I think I know what it was," Earek said gently. "Do you want to talk about it, or should I try to get some sleep?"

"You are right, she said something for my ears only," Marquiese replied hesitantly.

Earek looked fondly at Marilana for a moment and then started to get up. Marquiese touched Earek's arm and then indicated the stool. Earek sat and waited.

"You are a good friend, Earek. You are my advisor," Marquiese said blinking tears from his eyes. "You are her Brother and confidante. She said if she did not wake again, she wanted me to know that everything she did, she did because she loved me."

Earek placed his paw on Marquiese's shoulder and squeezed gently.

"I guess I always knew she loved me," Marquiese said haltingly. "However, I let my thoughts be clouded by other events and emotions. Even at the end of the trials, she told me she loved me in the letter she sent me, but I was too angry then to see the full extent of her love. I took it to mean she still thought of me as her friend. I should never have doubted her."

"Marilana taught me that emotions cloud the mind," Earek said gently. "She said that you cannot make logical decisions with emotions controlling your thoughts. She also said that you cannot ignore your emotions; they are part of who you are, and you must be honest with yourself about them. Only then can you be truly honest with others. It took her years to learn that lesson. She was not honest with herself about Lady Annabella for most of her life. She only released those emotions after being named heiress. She also was not completely honest with herself about you. She only started coming to terms with the truth the morning you left the Southern Tip last month."

"That was why she acted differently when she joined me for lunch," Marquiese mused. "Had she finally admitted that she loved me?"

"No," Earek said with a slight laugh, "she admitted she loved you just after she was named heiress. That was only part of the problem. Last summer she admitted that she wanted to be Lady Annabella's Daughter, and then she admitted that she loved you. The deepest injury she sustained during the Frishka ordeal was not dealt by him directly; it was the mistrust you showed her. After killing Frishka, she had not killed anyone until she routed the bandits who ambushed you when you came to the Southern Tip. She had put her bandit hunting skills to use only to train the soldiers and to challenge the scouts to improve their skills. She knew she was leaving a void by not doing the tracking herself. The Phantom was doing what she could, but she is only one girl. In only a few months of training, however, Marilana was able to improve the skill level of the soldiers. I know she and The Phantom are still better than most of the men, but I am confident now that I will not lack for talented trackers in the future. As I watched her turn away from her Bandit Hunting, however, I noticed that there was a void in her life.

"As fall was drawing to a close I saw that she was growing more insecure in her own heart; she was losing her purpose. She finally admitted to me that she did not mind leaving the hunting to others, but she was unsure how to achieve her new goals in life. What took her the longest, all the many months since leaving Maefair, was to admit she loved herself as a beautiful, sophisticated woman. When you visited, she revealed to me her recent dreams of becoming a wife and a mother. The morning you left, she finally let go of the child she had been, the bandit hunter she had become, and embraced the beautiful lady she wanted to be."

Marquiese smiled at Marilana's sleeping face. "So, when she came to the tournament," Marquiese said quietly, "she was playing the game she chose. She was competing with the noble daughters on their turf and making it her own. That explains why she was so confident and in control; she was once again able to be intimately aware of her surroundings and be alerted to others close to her."

"And that was why she was able to cope with both Brittia and Lotal on her own at the ball," Earek added. "She finally accepted that she was the lady we all thought she could be, and was pursuing her own goals."

"I was a fool the whole time she was learning about her own heart," Marquiese shook his head sadly. "I was not being honest with myself any more than she was. I was not listening to my heart. My heart said I loved her, even my actions sometimes revealed that love, but I refused to admit it. I also failed to see the changes in her. I did not want her to risk her life in the pursuits of a bandit hunter. I wanted to protect her, and I see now that I felt betrayed when she put her life before others. I didn't recognize that she was using her skills differently, that she was not as impulsive as she once was. She tried to tell me, but I did not listen. What is more, I refused to acknowledge that she loved me. Every time I got close to accepting the depth of her love, I pushed it away, I told myself that my duty required only the most lady-like, that she was as yet too bold. I hurt her because I was not being honest with myself and I was letting my emotions govern my actions. I was not thinking logically about what I saw. That she is the best partner I could ever want."

They lapsed into silence as their eyes rested on Marilana.

"Thank you, Earek," Marquiese said, "for your counsel. Please try to get some sleep. I need to get my thoughts in order before I can get some rest myself."

They clasped arms for a moment and then Earek crossed the tent and lay down on the cot. Within minutes Marquiese could hear Earek's rhythmic breathing. Marquiese sat vigil most of the night, gently holding Marilana's paw and reflecting on all the time that had passed since their first meeting. It was early morning when he finally woke Earek and then collapsed on the cot.

*

It was mid-morning when Earek gently woke Marquiese. Healer Magus and his assistants were busy around Marilana's cot checking her vitals and changing her bandages. Earek gave Marquiese a bowl of porridge and Marquiese devoured it. When he took his last bite, Earek motioned for him to step outside the tent. Marquiese hesitated, his heart longed to remain with Marilana, but followed out of duty. He was surprised to see a light snow blanketing the ground. Master Castant waited for them.

"It will do you both good to walk," he said without preamble. "Healer Magus said he would be busy changing Marilana's bandages and wanted you both out of his way for a while. It will also hearten the men to see you out and looking healthy."

"You have been doing a good job with the men, Castant," Marquiese said. "I know you are also concerned for Marilana, but you have done well to maintain the men."

"I am glad to hear you say that, Highness," Castant said. "I was worried you would continue to neglect them."

"I know," Marquiese said. "I did a lot of thinking last night. I am going to try to do better."

"Good," nodded Castant. "I think you both need to see something."

Marquiese and Earek exchanged a curious glance and then followed Castant east through the tents. The camp was divided with the men from the Southern Tip on the east side of the command tent, and the men from Maefair on the west. Not that the two groups held any animosity toward each other, but it was easier to maintain the chain of command if all were kept in order. The mood in the Southern Tip part of the camp was grim. Men saluted Earek as he passed, and he acknowledged them proudly. Marquiese could feel Earek's pride spread among the men. They were no less worried, but at least they knew Earek was proud of them and firmly in command of the situation. Marquiese knew he needed to do the same for the men from Maefair.

Eventually, they reached the edge of the camp and Castant motioned toward something set at the edge of the forest. Marquiese and Earek stepped closer. A piece of dead wood sat in the snow with a bouquet of green and red foliage stuck in a hole on the top. Mementos were carefully placed around the piece of wood—coins, kerchiefs, bouquets of dried flowers, and many smaller bouquets of the red and green foliage sat in the snow. Marquiese frowned at the display, wondering what it was.

"A patrol reported seeing The Phantom place the piece of wood and large bouquet. None of the men from the Southern Tip have said anything about it. The mementos keep appearing with no explanation," Castant said under his breath. "They act like they don't know what I'm talking about if I ask, but I get dirty looks when I come over here."

Marquiese looked past Castant and caught several men watching them darkly. He looked at Earek and was surprised to see him smiling with tears in his eyes. Earek pulled a small green and silver kerchief from his cloak and knelt down in the snow. Carefully he wrapped the cloth around the piece of wood on the right side of the foliage bouquet and secured it tightly. He knelt there a moment and then without a word got up and walked back into camp saluting men as he passed as if nothing had happened. Marquiese shared a look with Castant and then glanced back at the display. He smiled as an idea occurred to him. He knelt down as Earek had and removed one of his own red and blue kerchiefs. He wrapped it around the wood on the left side of the foliage and secured it tightly. Standing he walked back into the tents without looking back. Castant caught up to him after a moment and started to say something, but Marquiese shook his head. Castant refrained from speaking and they continued through the camp.

Marquiese did not go directly back to Marilana's tent, but made his way through the Maefair side of the camp. He spoke to the men and proudly returned salutes. Several officers asked how things stood, and Marquiese said that they had done well but he was unsure when they would be returning home. They saluted and set about the chores of camp. It was nearly noon when Marquiese returned to Marilana's tent. He motioned Castant inside and then followed.

Earek sat in the chair next to Marilana and glanced at them as they entered. Three bowls of stew sat on the table and Earek motioned for them to join him. Marquiese and Castant took the stools. Marquiese picked up a bowl and began to eat.

"Are you going to tell us what that display is all about?" growled Castant.

"It is not something that is to be discussed in the open," Earek said quietly. "The foliage is called Hope Leaf. It is one of the few plants that keeps its color throughout the winter, even in deep snow. It is commonly given as a winter bouquet to those who need cheering up. When set in dead wood by a loved one, it is called a Hope Altar. It is believed that the altar will hold the wishes of those who leave mementos and help the loved one heal. It is a very personal act to leave a memento and it is believed that if spoken about it decreases the healing effects. Everyone knows that it must be spoken about sometimes, to explain to children or the naive, but it should be done quietly in private so as to cause as little disruption of the hope of healing as possible. The people of the Southern Tip would have seen your inquiries as rude and as a disruption of the healing. It would be best to act as if it does not exist. The Phantom placed the altar, and so it is her right to touch the mementos. I am sure she will collect it when we move and set it up again at every camp site."

"I understand," Castant said. "I will quietly pass the word among the men from Maefair and I will not openly speak of it again."

"That would be good. I suspected its purpose. I left my own colors opposite yours Earek," Marquiese said quietly.

"Marilana will be pleased to see it when she wakes up," Earek smiled.

Castant picked up the bowls left on the table and gave one to Earek. They ate their lunch in quiet company.

*

Healer Magus entered the tent to find the three of them quietly discussing the route back to Lady Annabella's castle. He evaluated Marilana and fed her more broth and remedies.

Earek sat on the empty cot and gave the healer the chair.

"Our Lady's condition has not changed much," Healer Magus reported. "She is breathing well, her heartbeat is strong, and her bleeding has mostly stopped. Her bandages must still be replaced regularly, but the wounds look healthy. The new poultices should help the tissues start to repair."

"When can she be moved?" Marquiese asked. "We are lucky that last night's snow was light and that the ground is still frozen and not turning to mud, but if a worse storm comes in or the temperature rises, we could be stuck here for fifnights. I would rather return to Lady Annabella's estate."

"I understand, Highness," Healer Magus nodded. "I ask that you wait one more day before moving her, and when we do move, to not push hard. She should not be jostled too much. The stretcher that you brought her on should work for moving her to Lady Annabella's castle."

"Very well," nodded Marquiese, "we will leave at first light the day after tomorrow and we will travel slowly. If we travel from sunup to sundown, we should make the trip in three days. We will pass the orders to the men, and we should send a messenger to Lady Annabella with an update on our position."

"I will spread the orders," Earek volunteered. "You can take the afternoon watch here."

Marquiese glanced at Castant. Castant smiled and nodded. Together Earek and Healer Magus left the tent.

"I really am impressed with how well you are coping with this situation," Castant said quietly.

"I have been doing a lot of truth finding. Earek and I had a discussion last night after Marilana woke briefly. He helped me see a bit further into the murky depths of my heart," Marquiese smiled.

"Healer Magus said she had spoken to you," Castant said. "He said her condition was grave. You, however, seem to have found an answer you were seeking."

"Yes," Marquiese answered openly, "she told me she loves me, and Earek shared one of her lessons with me. He told me how she has learned to embrace the beautiful lady that she can be. I have realized that I had been refusing to see the changes within her and within myself. I know now what path I want to take. The first step, though, is to get her safely back to Annabella, then she must heal. I pushed her away last summer. I kept that wound between us open. Now I almost lost her, and may yet. I cannot lose her, Castant. I do not think I would ever recover from that."

"You know I do not make close friends easily; but Marilana has earned her place as my trusted ally. I have put my hopes on Magus, he will pull her through this. However, Marquiese, even if she survives, the Royal Courtship Dance was supposed to happen at the Winter Council," Castant reminded him. "I doubt she will be ready to dance by then."

"I will find a way to delay the dance until she is ready," Marquiese said firmly.

"I will support you in this, as I always have. I will leave you for now and start spreading word of the altar through the men," Castant said standing up and giving Marquiese a knowing smile. "I am glad you have come to that conclusion, my friend, she is a good match for you."

Marquiese returned his smile and watched Castant leave. He stood up and performed the stretching exercises Marilana taught him to remove stiffness. When he finished, he sat in the chair and took Marilana's paw in his, wishing with all his heart for her to awaken, that she might dance with him again.

23

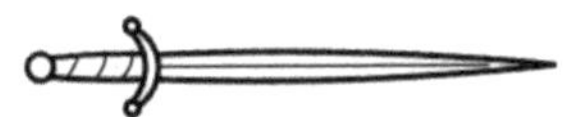

One fifnight after Marquiese had rescued Marilana, he and Earek guided their horses carefully through the gates of Lady Annabella's estates. The sun was sinking below the horizon behind them. The courtyard was blanketed with a fresh layer of snow, yet stablemen and servants stood waiting to assist the new arrivals. Lady Annabella anxiously waited at the bottom of the stairs to her castle. Marquiese and Earek stopped in front of her and held their mounts steady as Marilana's six guards moved in to unhook the stretcher. Lady Annabella led them into the castle. Marquiese had sent Healer Magus on ahead once they reached Mystillion. He knew the healer was anxious to settle Marilana into a real bed. He and Earek dismounted as their mounts were led off to the stables.

"If it pleases you to follow me, Your Highness," said a serving man with a bow.

"I will go to see Lady Marilana settled in," Marquiese said firmly.

"My Lady Annabella requested that you and Master Earek and Master Castant go to your rooms first. Hot baths have been drawn for you and fresh clothes laid out. Lady Annabella said to tell you that she will not allow you to see Lady Marilana until you are presentable. When you are ready, you may join her for dinner in Lady Marilana's rooms," the servant replied apologetically.

Marquiese exchanged looks with Earek and Castant and then laughed.

"Lady Annabella can always make me feel like a child again," Marquiese said. "A hot bath and clean clothes sound good. Please lead the way."

Laughing Earek and Castant followed Marquiese into the castle.

*

An hour later, feeling much better for being clean, Marquiese hurried to Marilana's rooms. He nodded to three of Marilana's guards as they headed toward the stairs. A freshly washed Major Kolt admitted him into Marilana's rooms. Marquiese crossed the study and sitting room and entered Marilana's bedroom. He was not surprised to find Earek speaking quietly with Lady Annabella next to Marilana's bed while Captain Hayden stood guard by the foot post. Annabella and Earek both smiled as he approached. He bowed to Lady Annabella and then turned to check on Marilana. She lay sleeping peacefully in her bed. She had not woken since she spoke to him the first night.

"Healer Magus said she is beginning to show signs of improvement," Lady Annabella said stepping up next to him. "He said she is not as dehydrated as she was, and her color is returning to normal."

"I am pleased to hear that," Marquiese replied softly.

"Earek was telling me about his part in rescuing her. Would you join me at the table and tell me your story?" she asked.

"Of course, My Lady," Marquiese turned and smiled as Castant entered.

"Master Castant, good to see you again," Lady Annabella greeted him. "Please come and join us for some supper. I would like to hear about your part in Marilana's rescue as well."

They sat at the table and took turns sharing tales of Marilana's rescue as they ate supper. Marquiese noticed that Lady Annabella barely touched her food. Mostly she listened, asked questions, and sipped her tea. Finally, they had eaten their fill and finished the telling of events. Lady Annabella stood and looked toward Marilana for a long moment.

"Thank you all for dining with me and thank you most of all for bringing my daughter back to me," Lady Annabella said quietly turning back to them. "I wish to stay with her for a while, and so I ask that you please retire for the night and get a good night's rest. You have all had some difficult fifnights."

They wished her goodnight and left her alone with Marilana and Captain Hayden. Marquiese wished the others goodnight and entered his rooms. He fell asleep quickly on the first real bed he had lain on in two fifnights.

*

The next morning Marquiese woke early. He felt refreshed after sleeping all night without having camp activity disturb his rest. He dressed quickly and went back to Marilana's room. The guard at the door nodded to him and knocked lightly once before opening the door to let him in. He nodded to Captain Hayden standing at the foot of Marilana's bed and then smiled warmly at the scene before him. Lady Annabella sat in the chair next to the bed grasping Marilana's paw, her gaze resting on Marilana's peaceful face. She looked up at him when he leaned against the foot post.

"You are up early, Marquiese," she said.

"And you have not yet gone to bed," he replied. "You need to get your sleep, My Lady. You will do no one any good if you do not get some sleep, least of all Marilana. If she wakes up someone can fetch you immediately."

"How many sleepless nights have you had in the last fifnight?" Annabella asked slyly.

"I had many, but I decided that I could trust others to watch her sleep just as well. Those others love her just as much if not quite in the same way."

"When she came back from the bandits as a child," Annabella reminisced, "I stayed with her until she woke. I was afraid that she would wake up when I was not there, and that she would panic. It took her a fifnight and a half to wake that time."

"This time there are others here that she knows well and trusts," Marquiese said gently. "She would not panic if I or Earek were with her."

"Marquiese, I do not wish to offend, but you and she have not gotten on so well lately."

"That was my fault, not Marilana's," he replied. "I have spent a lot of time thinking next to her bedside. I know now that I was wrong and have chosen a better path."

"Please do not hurt her again," Annabella said meeting his eyes. "Her heart has been broken and her emotions fragile since the trials, and I do not think she would survive another encounter like the last one in my garden."

"I know I hurt her." Marquiese grimaced at the reminder. "I know how hard it has been for her. It has also been hard for me. I have had many months of unease and restless nights. With Marilana's and Earek's help I have finally addressed the base cause of the problem, and when she wakes I want to set our relationship on a path towards a happier future. I cannot even contemplate a future without her. I cannot promise that we will not have arguments, but I can say that I would be the happiest man alive if she would be my wife. If I propose a courtship, would you agree to it?"

Lady Annabella blinked in surprise and then studied him thoughtfully. "You no longer feel betrayed by her?" she asked cautiously.

"No, I do not, and when she wakes I intend to beg her forgiveness for my betrayal of her trust," he replied.

"Yes, if she wishes the courtship, I will agree to it," Lady Annabella smiled with relief. "I had hoped that you would sort out the problem and that you would realize that you both love each other."

"I took too long to figure it out. And in the end, I needed Earek to tell me of a lesson Marilana also had trouble learning, but I know what future I want to pursue and how I want to achieve it," he said returning her smile.

"Relationships are never a smooth path, they are full of ups and downs, but they are the sustenance of the soul, we cannot be strong without love in our lives. You and she both needed to learn that." Annabella stifled a yawn behind her paw. "You are right, I can trust my daughter to those she loves, and I need to sleep," she said standing up. "We shall take turns watching over her."

*

The next fifnight passed slowly. The Hope Altar had appeared the first night on the practice yard, and had continued to gain mementos. It could be seen clearly from Marilana's windows. Marquiese, Earek, Lady Annabella, and Marilana's personal guards took turns watching Marilana so there were always two people in the room. Marilana's condition continued to slowly improve. Her wounds were healing and the bruises fading, she had stopped losing weight, and her color was back to normal. Still Healer Magus cautioned that unless she woke from the deep sleep, she would die.

It was the morning of the eleventh day since Marilana's rescue and Marquiese dressed and headed for Marilana's rooms to take his turn sitting by the bed. When he arrived, he was surprised to find the rooms filled with servants and assistant healers.

"It is not time for her bandages to be changed," Marquiese said to Major Kolt, who stood by the door. "What has happened?"

"She woke briefly," Major Kolt answered quietly. "Captain Hayden and I were with her. We were whispering when she called our names. She asked where we were, and Captain told her she was in her bed in Lady Annabella's castle. She smiled and went back to sleep. I ran for Lady Annabella and Healer Magus, but she has not woken since. I would have woken you as well, but Lady Annabella told me to let you sleep."

"I am sorry I was not here, but I would not have gotten to see her awake if you had woken me," Marquiese said honestly. "Lady Annabella was right to let me sleep."

Marquiese waited in the sitting room watching the activity around the bed through the open doors. He paced, not wanting to get in the healer's way. It was not long before Earek, Castant, and Captain-General Zariff had joined him. Together they waited and watched. Finally, the assistant healers and servants left, and Lady Annabella motioned them forward. Zariff took up a position next to the chair where Lady Annabella greeted them, and the three young men brought chairs from the table and sat facing the bed and Annabella. Healer Magus was taking Marilana's vitals again.

"She woke up and spoke very briefly with Major Kolt and Captain Hayden," Annabella said quietly. "Since then Healer Magus has been working hard."

"She has entered the next stage of healing," said Healer Magus. "I had to change my remedies and while I was here, I went ahead and changed her bandages. She is no longer in the deep sleep nor is she in the healing trance. She is sleeping normally like any of you would. She will wake more often and begin to finally recover from her ordeal. She still needs to be watched. I would like one of you to always be here with her in case she does wake. I do not need to be fetched if she wakes unless something is wrong."

"With time she will be strong and healthy again, but I do not want any of you to talk to her about her scarring and what it will mean until I say she is ready. It will not be easy for her to hear," he said regretfully. "In the meantime, she can have sips of water when she wakes. I will leave you now."

The relief they all felt was strong. Marquiese felt slightly light headed as the knowledge that she was truly going to wake spread through him. That he would once again see her smile, hear her laughter, and walk the garden paths with her. Looking around at every face, he felt the warmth and love of his closest friends, the family of his heart. Together they gazed down at Marilana as she slept. She twitched and made small movements as if she were dreaming, instead of the lifeless sleep of the past fifnights. They sat in silence for a long while, simply finding comfort in each other's company.

"Shall I have some breakfast brought up, My Lady?" asked Zariff gruffly breaking the silence.

"What? Oh, no, thank you, Zariff," Annabella replied looking away from Marilana. "Earek and I have some business to attend to; we shall have breakfast in my study."

She and Earek stood and Zariff followed them out.

"I should go check the men," Castant said standing.

He moved the extra chairs back to the table and saluted as he left. Marquiese returned the salute and settled into the chair Lady Annabella had occupied. He clutched Marilana's paw gently and watched her sleep. After half an hour, Captain Hayden checked the door and then returned to his position by the foot of the bed. Marquiese looked away from Marilana and realized the Captain was watching him closely.

"Captain, do you need something?"

"I beg your pardon, Highness," he said nervously with a slight bow, "I was wondering if I could speak my mind to you for a few moments."

"Of course, Captain Hayden," Marquiese replied, "I was impressed by the way you and your men comported yourselves during Our Lady's rescue."

"Thank you for saying so, Highness. I will pass your words on to the others." He took another bow. "Your Highness, the others and I hold our Lady Marilana close to our hearts. We serve her with honor and pride, loyalty, and fealty. I know I should not speak of it, but I want you to know we were all impressed with how you dealt with the Hope Altar situation. Tension was high in the camp when Master Castant pressed for answers; the regular men felt that your men needed to leave. The men honor Master Earek for his actions, and you remained respectful and left your own memento. When you had word quietly passed among the Maefair troops, it not only kept the peace, but it prompted your men to leave their own mementos. That your men, the men of distant Maefair, would hope for Our Lady's healing, well, let's just say that if you call for aid, the soldiers of the Southern Tip will march with haste to your side."

"I appreciate that, thank you. Every man with me volunteered to come to Lady Marilana's aid," Marquiese said. "Most were either part of the palace garrison or stationed on the walls the night the traitor attacked last summer. They recognize her efforts in defeating the traitor, and many of them feel she saved their lives."

"I was with Lady Annabella's troops that night," Captain Hayden nodded. "I saw the palace guards praising her for saving them. She will be touched that they chose to come to her aid." He paused, then continued, "I don't know if you knew it at the time you left your memento, and I know I should not mention it, but I think you should be told that the left side of the altar bouquet, where you left your mark, is traditionally reserved for a husband or lover."

"I suspected as much," said Marquiese.

"Well," Captain Hayden hesitated, "I was here and heard what you said to Lady Annabella, so I know your wish to court M'Lady, but I wanted you to know that when you left your memento, the men took it as a proclamation of your intentions. They are holding their tongues, of course, but they are pleased to think that she could become Queen."

"I am glad to hear that," Marquiese smiled. "I want the people of the Southern Tip to support her as queen. She cares greatly for them."

"Yes, she does," Captain Hayden nodded. "I . . . um . . . wanted to ask that if she does become Queen, would you accept me into the King's Guard?"

Marquiese smiled but shook his head, "No, Captain, I would not accept you into the King's Guard."

Captain Hayden's face fell with disappointment.

"I have a much better position for you and any of your men who wish it," said Marquiese. "You see, Captain," Marquiese continued, "the King's Guard is a regiment within the Royal Family Guard. Currently they serve only my father and myself, so all of the Royal Family Guard is the King's Guard. Once I have a future queen, however, the Royal Family Guard will have an additional regiment within it. I would be pleased if you would accept command of that new regiment and if your men would form the core of the regiment."

Captain Hayden smiled with growing understanding.

"The Queen's Guard," Marquiese continued, "would be called upon to defend any member of the Royal Family, but they would primarily be responsible for protecting the Queen. They would be allowed to enter her sanctuary and her court where men are traditionally not allowed. The King can enter these places, but they are her domain and therefore he would default to her in those places. The Queen must still be protected, and so the Queen's Guard is allowed to serve her in her domain. The Queen's Guard answers first to the Queen and then to the King. Are you still interested in joining the Royal Family Guard?"

"If M'Lady becomes Queen, I would be honored to assume command of the Queen's Guard," Captain Hayden saluted with a smile.

Marquiese thought it was the first real smile he had seen from the bear.

"May I pass your offer to the others of M'Lady's personal guard?" Captain Hayden asked.

"Yes," Marquiese nodded, "I will need a core of men that I can trust with Marilana's life. She chose you, and I have come to trust you as well."

"Marquiese?"

Marquiese turned quickly to the soft whisper. Marilana's eyes were open, but she frowned in concentration.

"Marilana, I am here," he said quietly as he gently squeezed her paw.

"Am I dead or dreaming?" she whispered trying to focus on his face.

"No, dear heart, you are alive and at Lady Annabella's castle," he replied.

"Then I am having a good dream," she sighed and went back to sleep.

Marquiese watched her fondly until Healer Magus and Earek came in just after noon. Marquiese told Healer Magus that she had woken briefly and then left Earek to watch her. He went to the kitchen for a quick meal and then went to check on the men in the barracks. He was greeted with salutes from both the men of Maefair and the men of the Southern Tip.

24

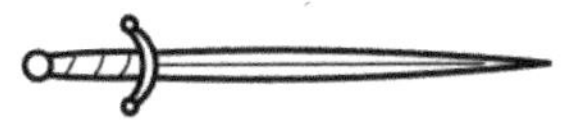

The next morning when Marquiese entered Marilana's rooms to sit with her, he found Captain-General Zariff gently laying Marilana back on her bed. He smiled to see her eyes open. Marilana whispered to Zariff and he smiled fondly as he replied to her. Lady Annabella embraced her daughter lovingly before leaving. They nodded to Marquiese as they left the rooms. Marilana smiled tiredly at him as he approached her. He sat on the edge of the bed where she could see him without turning her head. She lifted her paw feebly toward him and he cradled it between his paws.

"How are you?" he asked.

"I've been better," she whispered with a faint smile.

He smiled and gently squeezed her paw.

"They showed me the Hope Altar," she whispered. "Thank you for understanding how important it is to the people."

"It is a good tradition, and I think it helps you to see that they care," he said.

"I saw the blue and red," she whispered studying his face.

"I am glad," he said. "I was told later the significance of that placement. I have no wish to change it."

"I thought I was dreaming," she whispered with tears beginning to trickle down her cheeks. "I remember telling you that the healer had to change his remedies."

"It was not a dream," he said, "I heard what you wanted to tell me, and I know the truth of your words."

She sighed weakly. Marquiese lifted his paw to her face and brushed away her tears. She pressed her cheek to his paw and fell asleep. He remained there until his back was sore from the awkward position. Carefully, he lifted his paw from her cheek and shifted to sit in the chair. He continued to hold her paw as he watched her sleep the rest of the morning.

Marquiese stayed away from Marilana's room for the rest of the day so she could rest. The next morning, he headed toward her room full of hope to see her awake again but found Lady Annabella, Earek, Zariff, Healer Magus, and all six of Marilana's guards gathered in the hall outside her door.

"What is going on?" he asked suddenly filled with dread.

"She ordered everyone out of her rooms," Lady Annabella replied sadly. "Healer Magus talked to her about her condition and what it means for her future. I let her speak with him alone, and now she has ordered her doors closed to everyone."

"She should not be left alone," Healer Magus said firmly.

"I will brave her anger," Earek said turning toward the door.

"No," Marquiese said firmly laying his paw on Earek's arm, "let me go in."

"Are you sure?" asked Lady Annabella.

"If nothing else," replied Marquiese, "she cannot order me to leave; I out-rank her."

Marilana's guardsmen exchanged worried glances and then let him approach the doors.

Marquiese entered Marilana's study quietly and took a deep breath before crossing the sitting room to the open bedroom doors. He paused and watched her for a moment. She sat propped up on her pillows, staring out her windows.

"I said I wanted to be alone," she said hoarsely without looking at him.

"So, I was informed, but unfortunately for you, Healer Magus said someone should be with you. It is my turn to watch you, henceforth here I am," he said lightly.

"I do not need to be watched," she frowned.

"Well, since I do not have to take your orders, I chose to side with the healer, and besides, there is nothing I like better than to watch a beautiful girl."

"Marquiese," she said in exasperation.

Smiling gently, he walked to her and sat on the edge of the bed. Her eyes were bloodshot and swollen. Gently he brushed a tear from her cheek. She closed her eyes at his touch and took a shaky breath.

"Healer Magus told me about the gift of blood," she said quietly blinking her eyes open and gazing at her paws, "thank you."

"I was glad I could do something," he said gently. "I felt so helpless watching you sleep, and Healer Magus said sharing my blood with you could possibly save your life."

"It did," she replied. "I had pushed my body as close to death as I could. Without careful advanced healing, I would not have survived."

They paused for a moment, Marilana still staring at her paws. Marquiese broke the silence.

"Do you want to talk about what is really bothering you?" he asked gently.

She closed her eyes and trembled as she breathed. "Newrothen achieved one of his goals," she whispered sadly, "and you should be happy to get your wish too."

"What do you mean and who is Newrothen?" he frowned.

"Newrothen was an assassin of the Hungdie. You knew him as Frishka's Confidante," she opened her eyes and studied his face. "He promised the bandits that he would make sure I never hunted them again. Healer Magus told me I would probably never be able to draw a bow again or raise a sword in certain directions. He took my abilities from me."

She hesitated to say more, and closely watched his eyes. "You did not want me to hunt anymore, so you got your wish," she accused him, tears filling her eyes.

His heart ached at the hurt in her voice. He closed his eyes and took a calming breath. "I never meant for you to be hurt this way," he said softly meeting her eyes again. "I know how much your abilities mean to you. When Healer Magus told me, I grieved for your loss."

"But you are still glad that I will not be able to hunt again." Tears poured down her cheeks and her body shuddered as she wept.

"No, I was wrong," he cupped her cheek in his paw. "I was wrong about a lot of things." She closed her eyes and swallowed but did not turn away from him, so he continued. "I was not honest with myself. I was furious with the lordlings who thought you needed to be tamed, and yet I did not realize that I was acting like them. I thought once you were a lady you would give up being a bandit hunter because it was not lady-like. When you did not, I felt betrayed. When you risked your life for mine and others, I again felt betrayed. Even as I rode to your rescue, I felt betrayed because you had put your life before others. I was always proud of your skills—I even praised you for them—but it angered me when you used them. After I killed that man and got you back to a safe camp, I spent a lot of time thinking. You woke briefly and said that you had done everything because you love me."

Marilana opened her eyes and studied his face, tears still streaming down her cheeks.

"Earek shared one of your lessons with me," he continued with a grin, "he said that you taught him that you have to be honest with yourself if you are to be truly honest with those you love. I realized that I had not been honest with myself. I realized that I had always known you loved me, and that I had loved you too. I saw that I had been ignoring the fact that I loved you because you were not yet lady enough for me. When I was honest with myself, I realized that I loved all of you, not just the lady. I love the innocent child, the servant, the tutor, the lady, and the bandit hunter. I love you—all of you—just the way you are.

"After I admitted my love, I realized that you had not betrayed me; instead I was the one betraying you by not trusting you to make your own choices. I should have been content to let you learn your own way and not try to force you to act the way I thought you should. I know I have treated you poorly, and I hurt you in ways that no one else could. I beg your forgiveness for being slow to come to my senses. I have hurt you in my betrayal, and I do not feel worthy of your affection. For that I do not deserve your forgiveness for my actions. You are not a prize; you are a free spirit who makes her own choices. You are wiser and more intelligent than me, and I see now that it is your right to use your skills and act as you see fit."

Weakly Marilana pushed herself off the pillows and placed her arms around his neck. She rested her head on his shoulder and sobbed. Careful of her wounded back, he wrapped his arms around her and held her to him, letting her cry. Marquiese had yearned for this moment so many times—to hold her in his arms, to feel so close to her. He had imagined she would throw herself into his arms, maybe happy, smiling, or laughing, sometimes crying or relieved. Never had he thought that she would be battered and fragile, seeking comfort from him in a moment of such intense sorrow. Yet because of that sorrow, this moment was both more intimate and real than he had ever believed possible between two individuals. He poured his love for her into his embrace and grieved with her, giving her as much comfort as he could. He felt his own tears building, but they did not spill from his eyes.

"Of course, I forgive you," she whispered through her tears. "I love you."

He held her a silent moment to compose himself before speaking again.

"That man may have taken your physical abilities," he said softly, "but he did not take your knowledge. As Lady Annabella says, knowledge is power. Your abilities still exist inside you. Once you are fully healed, you will be just as formidable as you once were. You may not shoot a bow or wield a sword, but I owe my life to your ability to throw knives and I know your dagger skill is excellent. For that matter you do not need a weapon to kill someone. Your greatest weapon is your exquisite intelligence. That is why you are so good at politics and law. That is why Lady Annabella named you her heiress. That is why you will make a good leader and ruler. And that is why I love you. Maybe someday you will teach our children how to be excellent with bow and sword and knife and dagger, as well as the best strategists and leaders."

Marilana lifted her head and gazed into his eyes. "Our future, our children . . . . Thank you, my love," she whispered weakly with a smile.

"You have expended your energy, and now you must sleep," he said gently laying her back on her pillows.

"Stay with me . . . until I wake, . . . please," she whispered.

He smiled and kissed her forehead. She closed her eyes and drifted to sleep. He settled into the chair and clasped her paw, smiling more broadly as he fully acknowledged his own pleasure from sharing his vision of their future as a family.

25

Several hours later Marquiese heard the sound of the door opening. He glanced over his shoulder and motioned for Lady Annabella to approach.

"She is sleeping," he said in a near-whisper. "She was exhausted by our conversation. She has been sleeping for a few hours."

"She is smiling," Lady Annabella said with relief. "Thank you, Marquiese."

"I told her the truth and helped her see that she has not lost as much as she feared," he said.

"You told her you love her," Lady Annabella said.

He smiled.

"Your coat was wet," she said with concern.

Marquiese looked down at his shoulder to see a discolored spot where Marilana had leaned on him.

"Marilana's tears."

"I trust you were gentle," Lady Annabella smiled.

"Of course," he smiled in return.

"A messenger arrived for you," she said turning serious. "He asked me to tell you that your father wants you to return as soon as possible."

"I will leave tomorrow," he sighed. "Will you let Master Castant know to prepare the men for a mid-morning departure?"

"I will. Do you need anything else? I could sit with her if you want a break," Lady Annabella offered.

"No, thank you, but she asked me to be here when she wakes," he replied.

She gently squeezed his shoulder and left him alone with Marilana.

*

It was evening before Marilana awoke. Healer Magus had arrived to give her broth and remedies, and change her bandages. She woke slowly as the assistant healers manipulated her limbs. Healer Magus shot Marquiese a dark look as he stubbornly refused to move from her bedside. Marilana's eyes darted from person to person as she became aware of her surroundings, her movements stiffening with concern.

"I am here," Marquiese said softly.

Marilana turned towards his voice and smiled gazing up at him. She relaxed and let the healers go about their work. She ate the broth and remedies, and answered Healer Magus' questions. Throughout it all Marquiese kept his eyes locked on Marilana and smiled. She frequently glanced at him and met his eyes. Finally, the healers' work was done, and they left. Marquiese sat on the edge of the bed so Marilana could see him better. Her face lit up when she met his eyes.

"I was worried that I had been dreaming," she whispered.

"Nay, my beauty, I am here, and it was not a dream," he replied gently.

"Now that you want to court me," she whispered, "you are bound by tradition to dance the Royal Courtship Dance. What will you do? The dance was supposed to happen at the Winter Council. I will not be fit to dance by then."

"I know," he said frowning, "I will have to delay the dance to give you time to heal."

"You will not be able to delay long. Letting me heal is not a good enough reason for the noble daughters. They would rather push for sooner so that I cannot have the chance to out-dance them."

"I know," he agreed. "I have not yet chosen who is to dance with me, so I could suggest that two fifnights' notice is not enough time for the Daughters to prepare and the seamstresses to make the gowns. I should be able to buy a month with that excuse."

"I must be ready by then. I will make my own reputation in their games. I will proceed in this as they do, with politics and intrigue. I must gain their respect with my own skill and not be seen as your peasant friend or Lady Annabella's puppet."

He smiled at her determination. "You will make your own mark, but do not push yourself too hard," he chided gently. "I do not want to have to court someone else because you reinjure yourself and cannot dance."

"What if I can't out-dance them? I cannot risk speeding this healing; there is too much damage to be repaired," she whispered with tears brimming in her eyes.

He smiled gently and took her paw in his.

"You will out-dance them, and besides you were able to chase Master Arndt off in just one fifnight. How long could it take for me to chase off some sensitive girl?"

"You are too charming, and these girls are too power hungry for you to chase off," she whispered smiling back at him.

"I will not have to chase off these girls, you will find ways to do it for me and they will learn to respect your mastery of politics and intrigue just as I have," he chuckled for a moment and then his smile faded. "Marilana," he said sadly, "I have to return to Maefair."

"You have to prepare for the Winter Council and eventually the Royal Courtship Dance," she whispered. "When will you go?"

"I leave tomorrow morning," he replied. "There is little over two fifnights before the Council, and my father needs my help. I would like you to come to Maefair as soon as you are able. I want you to attend the Council and show the court your strength and loyalty."

"You also want me close by so that you can protect me," she sighed.

"No," he shook his head, "I want you close, so I can see your beautiful face and the love in your eyes."

"Will I see you again before you leave?" she asked tearfully.

"I will check on you in the morning, dear heart," he smiled and kissed her paw gently. "Now you need to sleep."

She smiled as she drifted off to sleep.

*

The next morning Marquiese made sure his men were ready before he and Master Castant went to Marilana's rooms. Lady Annabella sat talking in hushed tones with Marilana when they entered. Marilana was propped up by pillows and looked stronger. She beamed when they entered her bedroom.

"Healer Magus says I am healing well," Marilana whispered when they were close enough to hear her. "He said that the wounds on my back are closing cleanly. Another fifnight and I should be able to remove the bandages. My bruises and welts are almost completely gone. My broken ribs are still in good alignment and I did not cause any damage with yesterday's tantrum, as he called it."

"That is good to hear," Castant said gently, "I am glad you are recovering well. I must take my leave of you, My Lady Marilana, My Lady Annabella."

"The Blessings of The Goddess on you, Enton; and I thank you for your part in rescuing me. Words cannot express how happy I am to have been rescued." Marilana's eyes sparkled.

"The pleasure was mine, Marilana," he said taking her paw and kissing it gently. "Lady Annabella, your hospitality was as refreshing as always."

"Thank you for all of your assistance, Master Castant. I wish you a fair journey," Lady Annabella replied with a smile.

"Thank you as well, Prince Marquiese," Lady Annabella turned to him. "Thank you for bringing my Daughter back to me."

"It was my pleasure," Marquiese said bowing to her. "I hope to see you at the Winter Council."

"Time will tell, but I think I shall be able to attend," Lady Annabella replied.

"I will miss you," Marquiese said softly, turning to Marilana and gazing into her eyes.

"Until we meet again, My Prince," she whispered.

He wanted to say more, he wanted to stay with his beautiful lioness, but he knew he could not. He had to do his duty, she of all people knew the importance of his position and expected greatness of him. He knew he had to trust her family to care for her, and knew in his heart that they would see each other again. He took her paw and kissed it gently, lingering just a moment, but then quickly released it. He bowed to Lady Annabella and walked briskly from the room. Castant followed him down to the entrance hall and out to the front steps. Earek waited for them.

"Master Earek, farewell," Castant said simply as they clasped arms.

"Fair journey, Master Castant," replied Earek.

"Earek, my friend, I trust you to take care of your Sister, and I hope to see you at the Winter Council," Marquiese said and clasped arms with Earek as well.

"I will do my best, Highness, and I will try to arrive in time for the Council. Until then, farewell," Earek said with a bow.

Marquiese descended the steps, mounted, and led his men out the gate. Once they were on the road, Castant reined his horse close to Marquiese.

"I was expecting your farewell to take longer," he mused.

"If I had lingered longer, we would not be leaving," Marquiese replied quietly. "My heart is back in that castle, and if I were not forcing my steps forward to do my duty, I would turn around and return to my heart."

"I feel the same way every time Ailse and I part," Castant said.

Together they led their men north on the snow-covered road toward Maefair.

26

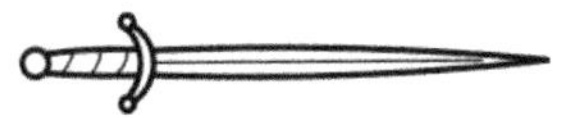

After dinner, Marquiese stood on the balcony overlooking the entrance hall speaking with Lord Castant and Lord Ruberic. It had been two fifnights since he had left Marilana in the Southern Tip. There was only one day left before the Winter Council and he had not heard anything from Lady Annabella or Earek. The other nobles and their entourages had arrived during the past fifnight, and winter storm clouds had rolled up from the south during the day. It had started snowing during dinner. Marquiese worried that the Southern Tip delegation had been caught in the winter storms and would not make it to the Council.

"It is getting late. Lady Annabella has never missed a Council," Lord Ruberic said, echoing Marquiese's thoughts.

"I hope they were not on the road when this storm blew in," added Lord Castant. "They could be stuck for days in snow like this."

The front doors of the palace flew open with an icy blast of swirling snow. The men shielded their eyes with raised arms as they looked to see who was entering the palace. Marquiese held his breath as a lady entered wrapped in heavy traveling robes followed by several guardsmen. She turned to look behind her once she was inside, and Marquiese felt relieved as a man entered carrying another lady wrapped snugly in blankets followed by several more guardsmen. The first lady shook off her robes and lowered her hood as the doors were closed. She led the group up the west stairs and off toward the guest rooms. Palace servants scrambled to catch up and assist the new arrivals.

"Leave it to Lady Annabella to push the limits and arrive in spectacular fashion," Lord Ruberic chuckled.

"Yes, at least they arrived safely," Lord Castant smiled at Marquiese, "and unless I am mistaken that was Master Earek carrying Lady Marilana."

"I had heard she had an encounter with bandits," Lord Ruberic said studying Marquiese, "and that you helped resolve the situation, Highness."

"You heard true, Lord Ruberic," he nodded. "She was captured in a clever trap and gravely injured. Master Earek, Master Castant and I rescued her when she was near death. I am sure the journey to Maefair was taxing for her."

"I hope she recovers well. I was quite impressed with her at the tournament ball," Lord Ruberic said. "I had better retire for the night; I wish to reach my house before the storm gets worse. Good night to you both, Prince Marquiese, Lord Castant."

He bowed to them and made his way down the east stairs to his waiting escort.

"I need to be going as well, Highness," Lord Castant said quietly with a bow. "Please pass my pleasure to Lady Annabella that she and her heirs arrived safely."

"I will. Farewell until tomorrow, Lord Castant," Marquiese replied.

Marquiese turned toward the Royal Family apartments and strolled at his ease down the hallway. Many noble daughters shot disappointed glances at him as he left the entrance hall. He entered the Royal Family apartments and stopped at the door to his father's study. King Rylan called for him to enter when he knocked.

"Lady Annabella and her heirs just arrived," Marquiese said when he saw his father was alone.

King Rylan looked up and smiled.

"We will give them an hour to settle in and then go greet our new arrivals," Rylan said happily.

An hour later, Marquiese followed Rylan to Lady Annabella's door. He nodded to Major Kolt and the other three guards standing around the door. He knew that Earek and Marilana were with Lady Annabella. A guardsman knocked three times and then opened it so they could enter. Marquiese smiled to see Earek and Captain-General Zariff discussing plans while pouring over a map spread on the desk. They cut off their discussion and bowed to Rylan. Earek approached and clasped arms with Marquiese. Earek tipped his head toward the couch with a knowing smile, and Marquiese continued further into the room. Lady Annabella rose from her chair and greeted them with warm smiles.

"King Rylan, Prince Marquiese, I am so glad to see you both," Lady Annabella curtseyed.

"Annabella, I am pleased you made it," Rylan rumbled and kissed her paw. "We were starting to get concerned when the snows arrived. I hope your journey was not too troublesome."

Marquiese smiled and acknowledged Lady Annabella's greeting with a slight bow, but continued past her to the couch Earek had indicated. Marilana lay upon it covered in several blankets. She beamed at him. He dropped to one knee and took her paw. She weakly squeezed his paw.

"Are you alright?" he asked with a furrowed brow, "You seem weaker than when I last saw you."

"The journey took its toll," she sighed. "Healer Magus was not pleased with my insistence to come. He was probably right; I should not have traveled so soon."

"Did you reinjure anything or did your wounds break open?" he pressed.

"No, my back is healing well; I no longer have bandages, only a lot of angry red lines across my back. My knee is almost completely healed as well, but my ankle and ribs need more time to get stronger. I was well-cushioned lying on the floor of the carriage, but it was strenuous bouncing along with the wind rocking us sideways and snow pelting the windows. We pressed harder than we should have for my comfort in order to beat the worst of the storm. Mostly, I am just tired."

"I was relieved to see you finally arrive. It was hard to wait before coming to greet you."

"I am glad to see you, too," Rylan said from behind Marquiese.

Marilana raised her eyes and smiled at the King.

"Forgive me for not rising, Majesty, I am glad to see you again," she said softly.

"No forgiveness necessary, you need to rest and regain your strength," Rylan replied warmly.

"Lord Castant asked me to pass on his pleasure that you all arrived safely," Marquiese said looking up at Lady Annabella.

"Thank you for passing on his words. I look forward to seeing him tomorrow," Annabella said gently. "As for tonight, however, Marilana needs to sleep."

"Of course," Marquiese smiled at Marilana and then released her paw as he stood to go. "Is there anything you need?"

"No, thank you, Highness," Lady Annabella replied. "We are pleased to see you and hope you have a good night."

"We will see you tomorrow," Marquiese smiled at Marilana and then bowed to Lady Annabella.

King Rylan kissed Lady Annabella's paw and then led the way out of the rooms.

Marilana was propped up by pillows on the couch in Lady Annabella's rooms. Lady Annabella had decided that she was well enough to continue her studies of history and law. The elder lioness said that there was still much for Marilana to learn, and that engaging her mind was better than lying in bed bored. Sir Libor had happily sent up several volumes from the Royal Library that he thought she might like, along with a note expressing his pleasure in her return to the palace. Marilana had chosen to attempt to study the large history book perched on the stand next to her, but instead she gazed out the window watching the snow swirl across the balcony. It was a decent snowstorm by Southern Tip standards, but here in Maefair it was one of the worst storms in memory. She smiled remembering the snowball fights she had participated in with the children of Mystillion. Usually she had refrained from joining in because she had better aim than the other children, but Marquiese had always insisted on targeting her if she did not defend herself. She had to admit it had been fun, he at least had been able to occasionally hit her and sometimes dodge her throws. She longed to be able to go out and run in the snow, but she could barely walk.

The door opened behind her and her attention shifted to her surroundings. Lady Annabella and Earek had gone out to the library to study the Family Annuals. Sir Libor would not let the Annuals out of his study, so she would have to wait to study them when she was up and moving around better. She held her eyes steady on the open book. She usually loved to study the histories, but today she was having difficulty focusing. She was nervous about the Council the next day. She was not sure how the nobles would react to her injuries, but expected that they would need more proof than the rumors that circulated. Altia glanced up from her mending toward the door as the quiet tread of booted feet approached. She quickly picked up her mending, stood, curtseyed, and headed toward the other end of the room. Marilana idly reached out and turned the page of the history book even though she had not read the page. Hearing a familiar chuckle from behind her made her stomach flutter and her heartbeat quicken.

"I can see you are studying hard," Marquiese said leaning over her to read the page she had turned to.

"Sir Libor thought I might enjoy some light reading," she replied.

"Yes, I see, and you seem to be engaging in your studies with less enthusiasm than normal. Here, I brought you something to brighten your mood," he said and dropped a snowball in her lap.

She laughed in glee as he moved the book stand and pulled a chair up next to her. She grinned at the snow and raked her claws across it, furrowing the surface.

"I wanted to take you outside to enjoy the snow, but Healer Magus flat refused," he said. "I cannot say I blame him, you need to rest, and do not need me carrying you out into the frigid wind."

She tossed the snowball at him and he caught it easily. He set it in a bowl on the table, and then studied her face. She dropped her eyes away from his intense look. He reached up and gently cupped her cheek with his paw. She looked up and met his fond smile.

"I am worried about you," he said quietly dropping his paw from her cheek and laying it on her paws in her lap. "What that beast did to you was more than physical. He hurt your soul and mind too."

She sighed and gently smoothed the fur of his paw. "I have had nightmares my whole life. First Victon and Brute, then the old Hungdie priest, later Frishka, and now Newrothen. They have all left scars on my soul, parts of my past I will never be able to escape. Four of them are dead, three by my own paws, one by yours. I cannot say that I have not been changed by what happened. On the contrary, the course of my life has changed, my thoughts, hopes, dreams have altered because of each of those individuals."

"You are stronger than any of them, better, braver. You saved others, and put other lives first. That is no small thing," Marquiese reassured her.

"Humph," Marilana sniffed derisively. "I know those words are supposed to make me feel better, but they are meaningless unless I choose to give them meaning for me."

Marquiese shifted uneasily, unsure what to say or do next. Marilana squeezed his paw and looked up into his eyes with the focus of the hunter.

"I will go on with my life as I choose," she said firmly. "I have always chosen life, even when you had to help me see that not every battle ends the way we want and sometimes lives are lost. Life is the most important thing. The lives of those children, Lady Annabella, Earek, King Rylan, Enton, your life, and yes, my life too, are worth every ounce of pain those men gave to me. I will get better, I will be strong again, I will face other opponents who wish to harm others, and I will stop as many as I can. That is my purpose; that is why I live."

Marquiese smiled proudly at her declaration and her determination. Marilana knew she was not past the nightmares, she knew she would always have thoughts and dreams of those terrible days. Looking up at Marquiese however, she also knew that as long as he was with her, she would not face those dark moments alone.

"You sound stronger this morning, but you spent the night here in Lady Annabella's rooms," he commented to shift the flow of the conversation.

"Lady Annabella and Healer Magus are still insisting that I be watched constantly," she replied quietly. "I have to admit that last night I needed to be watched; I was exhausted by the trip. I am much better after a good night's sleep. I think they are having me watched as I am getting stronger, so they can stop me from trying to do more than I should," she added ruefully.

"I happen to agree with them," he chuckled. "As much as I want you to be able to dance and go for walks with me, I do not want you to push yourself too fast. Do not try to deny that you would not. You need to be protected from yourself," he laughed.

"Here, give me that snowball again," she said with a grimace.

"Oh no, I know better than to arm you when you have that mischievous twinkle in your eyes. I have no wish to have that snowball in places that will make me dance for your amusement."

"Speaking of dancing," she said smiling brightly, "we received a proclamation this morning. Let me see if I remember the wording. I believe it said, 'Do to His Highness' recent involvement with a military campaign, he was unable to select partners for the Royal Courtship Dance in a reasonable amount of time. We have decided therefore to give the subsequently selected partners and seamstresses additional time to prepare. The Royal Courtship Dance shall be performed one month following the Winter Council.' It was signed by King Rylan and Prince Marquiese."

"Yes," he laughed lightly, "that was what it said."

"So, you have chosen partners?" Marilana asked.

"Yes," he smiled. "I am not supposed to discuss my selections with anyone, but I will tell you anyway. I have sent invitations to nine noble daughters. They will have their measurements taken by the royal seamstresses during the next fifnight, but they will not see the dresses or the cloth for the dresses until the day of the dance. They know that two of them will be chosen to direct the dance and wear black, but again they will not know who until the day of the dance. They are all busy learning the protocols and pattern of the dance. They are not aware of the other selections, as the invitations were secret, and the families have been sworn to secrecy. I chose seven noble daughters who have shown that they want the courtship, rather than the ones who want to marry someone else. I realized that I made those girls very nervous and frantic by riding for their honor during the tournament. The men they love were also annoyed by my show of interest in their girls. Although at a certain point during the ball they all calmed down; I think they had finally figured out what I had done. I believe that was your doing."

"I just pointed out that they were overreacting," she replied. "They are smart girls. They just needed someone to point out that they were all in the same shoes. Once they figured out that you did not want to court them, they agreed with me that they should enjoy dancing with the best dancer in court."

He smiled broadly at her, and she laughed.

"I sent two of the invitations to Lorlina and Ailse," he said. "By tradition the two that direct the dance become the first of the future Queen's Ladies-in-Waiting. I thought they would be good choices. They are intelligent, and I want to keep them close since they want to marry Enton and Timral."

"Only nine invitations?" she asked. "I thought you were to choose ten maidens."

"I am delivering the last one in person. Of course, she already knows I want her to dance with me," he grinned.

"Oh, really and how would she know that?" she asked.

Laughing he leaned forward, cupped her face gently in his paws, and kissed her forehead. She grasped one of his paws as he sat down and pressed it to her cheek. She closed her eyes and savored the sensation of his touch. Tenderly he brushed the tears from her cheeks.

"It was not my intention to make you cry," he said.

"Sometimes I still find it hard to believe that after everything that has happened in my life, I love a lion and he returns my love for who I am," she whispered. "I was never interested in the young men around Mystillion; they were only interested in my beauty and womanly charms. I hated being treated as a prize. I was embarrassed by my looks and took refuge in my skills. Only in my deepest most secret dreams did I ever dare to hope that someday you would show me such tenderness."

"I know, dear heart," he whispered.

She closed her eyes for a moment and when she opened them, she was surprised by his tears.

"I never dreamed that I would ever feel this way about someone, or that she would love me for who I am and not for my power or crown," he said. "I was never interested in the noble daughters because they only wanted the prize."

They smiled at each other and Marilana turned her head to kiss the palm of his paw.

"Thank you for mending my heart," Marilana whispered releasing his paw.

"Thank you for protecting mine," he replied giving her his kerchief.

She dried her eyes while he slipped his paw into his coat and removed a gold embossed envelope. He offered it to her, and replaced his kerchief. Her heart beat faster as she broke the royal crest sealing the envelope and removed a letter on heavy paper also embossed with gold.

Lady Marilana Ranat,

It would give me great pleasure if you would agree to participate in the Royal Courtship Dance. The purpose of this dance is to help me choose a noble daughter to propose a suit to. If you accept to dance, and subsequently receive the suit proposal, you may choose to accept to enter courtship with me lasting until reason has been found to terminate the courtship, or until the end of one year at which time a marriage proposal may be offered. The procedure of this traditional dance is outlined in this letter. Please note that you and your family are hereby sworn to secrecy. There shall be no mention to anyone that you have received this invitation or any part of the procedures of this tradition. Please send your acceptance or refusal to me personally.

Awaiting your reply,

Prince Marquiese Mercurer

Marilana smiled at his strong clear writing and turned to the next page. She read a few lines talking about the procedure to be followed for the traditional Royal Courtship Dance. She replaced the top page and read it again. She gazed up at him letting her smile fade to seriousness.

"This seems rather formal and intimidating. I have a feeling that I will not be able to perform as I once was able."

"Marilana, I have to go through with this. I wish I had seen the truth sooner, but I did not. Tradition dictates this dance, there is no other way now. I cannot . . . if you do not . . . ," he hesitated, his confident smile vanished. She could almost see his fear wrapping around his heart. She took pity on him and smiled mischievously.

"Of course, I accept," she said. "Do you need me to put it in writing?"

"That was not funny," he glared accusingly at her. "And yes, I do need your formal acceptance in writing." He motioned across the room to Altia as Marilana chuckled quietly.

Altia hurried to him and curtseyed.

"Bring the lap desk, pen, ink, and parchment, please," he said.

The maid curtseyed and hurried to Lady Annabella's desk. She returned with the requested items. Together Marquiese and Altia held the lap desk steady while Marilana wrote. She kept the reply letter simple and formal.

Prince Marquiese Mercurer,

I would be honored to participate in the tradition of the Royal Courtship Dance. I acknowledge the requirement of secrecy and my family and I will refrain from mentioning my participation to anyone.

Yours in service,

Lady Marilana Ranat

After she sanded the ink and pressed her seal into a pool of green wax, she held it carefully aside while Altia removed the lap desk, and then gave it to Marquiese. He smiled as he read it over.

"I am now in possession of ten acceptance letters," he said meeting her eyes. "The seamstress will stop by sometime during the next fifnight to get your measurements. I have agreed to the fabrics of the dresses, but I gave them free rein within the limits of the traditional requirements to design the gowns. Each gown will be different, and I will not see the results until the dance begins."

"I am sure they will be wonderful," she beamed. "Your royal seamstress does beautiful work."

"I need to tell you that the Royal Courtship Ceremony requires me to spend time with each noble daughter, those I have asked to participate, and those I have not. I have been going on walks and rides one-by-one since I returned to Maefair," he said.

"You make it sound like heavy duty," she said. "You should enjoy your freedom to spend time with a variety of young women."

"It is far from freedom," he replied ruefully. "The Daughters have accepted the challenge whole-heartedly. They are going to great lengths to disrupt the time I spend with the other women. I have been making public show of spending time with each one, and on each ride or walk, I have seen at least five or six of the others. Their goal is to be seen by me as much as possible, while at the same time, they are trying to block the others from being seen. It has become an intrigue war. Unfortunately, I will have to involve you when you are strong enough."

"The unfortunate part is that I have not been involved before now," Marilana said. "I said I would play the game, and they will learn that I am a serious contender. I will not stand aside and let them play their intrigue games without me."

"I think they will be surprised by how well you play the game," he smiled, "but not until you are stronger."

"I do not have to get out of bed or be seen in public to play the game," she said ominously.

They shared a smile, gazing into each other's eyes.

"I am afraid I have to leave you now," he said sadly. "I must appear at a number of parties this afternoon and finish the final preparations for tomorrow. I must go do my duty."

"I understand," she replied squeezing his paw. "Thank you for the snowball."

"It was my pleasure," he said and gently kissed her paw.

After Marquiese left, Altia brought her mending over by the couch and smiled at Marilana through glistening tears.

"I am so happy to see you two derive so much pleasure from each other," Altia said weeping softly. "I would love to serve you as my queen."

"I am happy too, and would like to have you as my own chambermaid," Marilana smiled and hugged the girl gently. "However, right now we have work to do. What do you know about the activities of the noble daughters?"

"What do you mean?" Altia asked.

"The noble daughters have had the past two fifnights to hound his footsteps. I need to interrupt their games of intrigue. They must see that I will not sit aside as a bystander. I need to make my own reputation," Marilana replied.

"I understand," Altia smiled. "The Daughters have been swarming the areas where His Highness goes. They ambush him and his partner as they walk or ride. Some are content to just be seen, but others try to stop him for a short conversation. At the same time, they send accomplices to block the other Daughters from being able to get positioned along his path."

"Then the first thing I need is to gain some accomplices," Marilana nodded. "You and Commander Lorne are doing well together?"

"Yes," Altia blushed, "we have published our courtship. He is the kindest man I know."

"I am glad for you," Marilana smiled. "I would like to ask him to help me. Are you comfortable with my request?"

"Of course!" Altia beamed.

"Good, I need to write some letters," Marilana said. "To start, I will contact Commander Lorne, Guardsman Karndel, Master Castant, and Master Roana. I know I can count on your help. I think gaining some of the other servants would be good and I think the stable master will be willing. I cannot interfere with the parties tonight, or any other private invitations that he receives, but I can make sure his walks and rides are no longer interrupted by swarms of eager ladies with batting lashes."

Altia hurried to retrieve the lap desk with pen, ink, and plenty of parchment. Marilana spent the next several hours plotting with Altia's help and writing many letters. Altia also introduced Marilana to several members of the staff who were eager to assist in her intrigues. Protecting their Prince from unnecessary annoyances was not only agreeable, but was also going to be the source of great amusement for the palace servants.

27

Marquiese had been disappointed when he had arrived at the Castant Manor the previous night and found that Marilana had chosen to remain at the palace instead of attending the parties. He was pleased that Lord Castant had sent her his regrets and a gift of supper. The palace kitchens had not served anyone at the palace while they prepared for the Council Feast. He had understood that she had wanted to reserve her strength for attending the Council, and he had refrained from visiting her when he had returned to the palace. Now at mid-morning, he stood at King Rylan's left upon the dais and watched as the nobles and their entourages filed in and gathered along both sides of the great hall for the Winter Council.

The Winter Council was actually an oath ceremony. It marked the start of the New Year and all the high-nobles and great-nobles of Redsands along with the nobles and landed-gentry of Maefair came to the Council to pledge their fealty to the King and royal family. Marquiese enjoyed the parties the night before and the feast after the ceremony, but standing on the dais while nobles repeated the same words all day was hardly the highlight of his year. The Southern Tip was the furthest province from Maefair, and so Lady Annabella and her heirs would be the last of the great-nobles to swear their oaths of allegiance. After the great-nobles came the high-nobles from each province, and then finally the nobles and landed-gentry of Maefair. Marquiese clinched his teeth to stop a yawn.

The room was almost completely filled when Lady Annabella entered and glided slowly to the right side of the room, half-way between the dais and the door. Zariff followed her carrying a chair. Marquiese sighed softly as he watched Earek assist Marilana into the great hall following Zariff. Marilana looked stunning in a gown and veil of Southern Tip green. She wore a silver shawl about her shoulders and used a short staff to help her walk. She sat carefully on the chair Zariff had placed with Earek on one side and Lady Annabella on the other. Lord Castant tipped his head and spoke quietly with Lady Annabella. Master Castant nodded to Marquiese from his place next to his father, all was ready.

The hum of conversation rose as the nobles noticed the chair. Marquiese gritted his teeth in annoyance. The only nobles allowed to sit during the ceremony were the elderly or those who had some condition that prevented them from being able to stand all day. He had made sure to spread rumors of Marilana's injuries—which should have been enough to quell any protests—but from the din of the crowd, it seemed the rumors had been dismissed as false or exaggeration. Marilana met his eyes and shook her head slightly.

He realized his fists were clinched and he had started to step forward. He met her eyes and could see that she had been expecting this reaction. Taking a deep breath, he forced himself to calm down. He would not help her if he stepped in now. He had to let her deal with the situation.

His eyes tracked Zariff as he left the great hall while the herald entered formally bearing the scroll of nobles' names and his staff of office. Conversations died as the herald approached the dais and the palace guards closed the doors. In unison the gathered nobles followed the herald's lead and bowed to King Rylan. The herald took his position to the King's right at the foot of the dais and unfurled his list of names.

"Marquiese Mercurer, Crown Prince of Redsands," the herald called clearly to the assembly.

Marquiese stepped down from the dais and went to one knee before his father.

"I, Marquiese Mercurer, Crown Prince of Redsands, pledge my life with fealty and honor to the service of Rylan, King of Redsands. I pledge my life to uphold the laws of Redsands and to guard against threats from inside and abroad. My life for my king and kingdom."

Rylan smiled at him. "Rise Marquiese Mercurer, Crown Prince of Redsands," Rylan intoned. "I accept your oath of allegiance and will hold it for truth."

Marquiese rose and returned to his place on the dais. Next, the herald read off the names of the nobles who were unable to attend. Most were elderly nobles who were gravely ill or too frail to travel. Marquiese glanced at Timral and Lord Roana when the herald spoke the name of Lady Nya Roana of Mira's Plateau. Timral's mother had been bedridden for many years and Marquiese felt a pang of pity for the Roana family. He had not seen Lady Nya in person since before he had hidden in the Southern Tip. She was a kind-hearted bear with a ready smile and a quick laugh.

Finally done with the list of nobles who had sent their oath in writing, the herald read off the first name of the great-nobles in attendance. The named nobles approached with their families, and each member spoke their oath. Some families, like Roana and Castant, only had two members present, while other families were much larger. Lord Ruberic led his clan of twelve members forward, all of whom gave their oaths. Marquiese shifted his weight subtly from one foot to the other and wiggled his toes in his boots, trying to hide his impatience with the proceedings.

"Annabella Ranat, Great-Lady of the Southern Tip and her heirs Marilana Ranat and Earek Ranat," the herald called out.

Marquiese watched Lady Annabella approach the dais with Earek on her left. Marilana would speak her oath from her chair like the few others in attendance who also needed assistance to walk. The King could only be approached without potential weapons, like staffs or canes. Angry murmurings swept through the crowds. Annabella and Earek ignored the crowd and pledged their oaths. Marilana opened her mouth to speak when a cold voice interrupted from the left side of the hall.

"Lady Marilana is young and strong; she shows dishonor by not approaching the King."

Marquiese's fists clenched in anger again. He thought he recognized Master Lotal's voice. He ground his teeth as he forced himself to remain by the King's side.

"Lady Marilana's injuries are known to me," King Rylan proclaimed. "She need not approach the dais."

Angry protests from nobles erupted on both sides of the hall. King Rylan tried to speak, but the chorus of protests and those arguing with them drowned out his words. Marquiese could restrain his anger no longer and started to step forward when three sharp cracks echoed through the hall. The protests died immediately as everyone turned their attention to the herald, who look stunned. Marquiese then realized that Marilana had used her own staff to signal the herald's silence.

"I shall approach the dais," she announced standing and clutching her short staff.

"Lady Marilana, that is not necessary," King Rylan said, but she stopped him with a cold glance.

"My honor has been questioned. I shall approach," she declared.

She gave her staff to Master Castant and dropped her shawl on her chair. Marquiese frowned as both Master Castant and Lord Castant winced and looked away from her. Murmurs spread behind her as she limped forward. Several ladies behind Marilana urgently fanned themselves as if they were feeling faint. Her face set with determination. Marilana carefully hobbled toward the dais. Marquiese yearned to go to her, but he knew he could not. When she met his gaze, he could see her jaw was set and her strained eyes registered agony. Whispers swept through the hall hissing like a dank winter wind. Finally, she reached the dais and with a grimace of pain knelt on one knee next to Lady Annabella who had remained kneeling.

"I, Marilana Ranat, Lady of the Southern Tip, heir of Lady Annabella Ranat, pledge my life with fealty and honor to the service of Rylan, King of Redsands. I pledge my life to uphold the laws of Redsands and to guard against threat from inside and abroad. My life for my king and kingdom," she spoke her oath with a clear strong voice.

"Rise Annabella Ranat, Lady of the Southern Tip. I accept your oath of allegiance and will hold it for truth. Rise Marilana Ranat, Lady of the Southern Tip, heir of Lady Annabella Ranat. I accept your oath of allegiance and will hold it for truth. Rise Earek Ranat, Master of the Southern Tip, second heir of Lady Annabella Ranat. I accept your oath of allegiance and will hold it for truth," Rylan intoned smoothly.

Lady Annabella and Earek rose smoothly to their feet, and before anyone could react, King Rylan stepped off the dais. He gently lifted Marilana to her feet and held her steady until she gave a slight nod. Rylan released her and returned to his place on the dais. Lady Annabella turned and slowly led the way back to Marilana's chair. As Marilana turned and haltingly followed Lady Annabella, Marquiese could see what had triggered the whispers and near-fainting spells.

The back of Marilana's gown dipped low to expose the angry red lines carved by her torturer.

Marquiese closed his eyes and took several deep breaths to calm his temper. Next to him he heard his father's soft growl. He realized that Marilana had intentionally worn that gown to reveal her wounds, anticipating protests to her remaining in her chair. He opened his eyes to see Marilana limp the last few steps toward her chair and sit stiffly. Master Castant returned the staff, and Lady Annabella draped the silver shawl around her shoulders. Marilana whispered her thanks but let the shawl droop off her shoulders so her back was still exposed. As the ceremony continued, Marquiese wondered why Marilana would so blatantly invite the nobles to gawk at her scars. Marquiese studied her posture and face, she was still determined, but also clearly exhausted from the effort to approach the dais. She met his gaze and blinked slowly. His level of concern rose phenomenally, he hoped she would be all right.

The herald read more names and the ceremony continued as expected. The last of the landed-gentry of Maefair returned to the crowd of nobles in the late afternoon. Marquiese glanced at Marilana and was worried by her drawn face.

"My Nobles of Redsands," Rylan said spreading his paws wide and smiling, "the oaths have been given and accepted. May we stand together and prosper in the next year."

The guards stationed around the hall opened the doors and servants poured in carrying trays of food and drink. The nobles cheered and spread out to speak with each other. Marquiese wanted to go check on Marilana but was swarmed by nobles as he stepped off the dais. He greeted and spoke with them while subtly stretching his stiff muscles. Glancing away, he saw his father was likewise beleaguered. Gradually he managed to position himself, so he could see Marilana from a distance. She spoke quietly with nobles who bent towards her to hear her responses. He also noticed that nobles strolled behind her chair, looking at her back as they passed. Marquiese struggled to control his anger at the insensitive nobles, but had to marvel at Marilana's forethought. She had intentionally left her back exposed to provide the doubting and nosy nobles the chance to see her scars close and clear, saving herself, and them, from awkward questions and spying attempts. He also realized that by refusing to cover her wounds, Marilana was declaring to everyone that she was not ashamed or hiding from the results of her ordeal. Forcing a pleasant smile, Marquiese returned his attention to the noble talking to him.

Half an hour after the ceremony had ended, Marquiese had still been unable to reach Marilana. Time and again various nobles asked for details about his recent military campaign, stalling his progress toward her. He had repeated the same answers to everyone who inquired—that he had found and ended the traitor

Frishka's Confidante. He searched for Marilana again, but she was gone, even her chair was gone. He glanced quickly toward the doors and sighed. Earek carried her from the hall while Master Castant hefted her chair. Both young men returned to the great hall shortly after. Marquiese continued to answer yet another question about his foray beyond the Sothern Tip, but was halted as the herald's staff interrupted the din of conversation. Marquiese turned his attention to the dais and frowned to see his father calling for everyone's attention.

"I have been asked repeatedly about the recent military campaign," Rylan said into the silence. "I have grown tired of repeating myself, so I will make an explanation to the assembly."

Marquiese glanced around and saw that Rylan had everyone's attention.

"During the tournament ball," Rylan spoke clearly, "Lady Marilana received a ransom request." He continued to inform the assembled nobles the details of the trap that lead to Marilana's capture. "I had previously received information that led me to theorize that the lion known to many of us as the traitor Frishka's Confidante was gathering an army of bandits beyond the Southern border. My Generals were in the process of trying to confirm the information and to determine the best course of action. Of course we had previous evidence that Confidante had been gathering and directing the traitor's army last summer and I had not forgotten that the traitor Frishka had cursed us just before his death, promising long painful deaths at the paws of his second in command. This threat to the Southern Tip seemed like the type of trap Confidante would use, and since Frishka's death was dealt by the Lady Marilana, I was not surprised that she would be the first targeted to suffer his wrath. I told Prince Marquiese and Master Castant of my theory of a greater threat and ordered them to take whatever action was necessary."

"Prince Marquiese joined forces with Master Earek and led the combined army against the bandits who had captured Lady Marilana. In the ensuing battle, Prince Marquiese came face to face with Frishka's Confidante, engaged the fiend in personal combat, and slew him. In doing so, he ending the last major threat stemming from the traitor Frishka. Lady Marilana was rescued, but having spent almost a fifnight in the fiend's custody, she was grievously injured and near death. She is obviously still recovering from her terrible ordeal."

When King Rylan paused, the nobles exchanged stunned looks. The rumors had not detailed the events that Rylan had just revealed. Marquiese was surprised by the depth of his father's explanation but kept his features serious. The King's explanation of the threat was a good touch that made the story sound less like he ran off after his friend and more like a serious military campaign. Dread still lingered in his thoughts of the dead Hungdie. He and Marilana had not discussed the matter of the Hungdie with King Rylan, but this explanation was logical enough to allow him to continue to hide the fact that the man Marilana called Newrothen was one of the legendary assassins. He and Marilana had not spoken about the details, but he had decided it would be best to keep that information secret, especially as most people viewed the Hungdie as a childish superstition.

"I propose a toast," Rylan said into the silence and raised his glass, "to Prince Marquiese, Master Castant, and Master Earek, for ending the threat to the peace of Redsands. I hereby name them Champions of Justice."

"Champions of Justice," the nobles echoed.

Marquiese cringed as the nobles around him congratulated him and pressed him for more details. He was glad King Rylan had made the explanation and presented the cause of the events, but he was not pleased to have been cast as a hero.

For the rest of the night, the three young heroes were surrounded by the curious, doubters, and admirers. Marquiese had never been so happy for a feast to end. When he finally stumbled into his rooms, dawn was just a few hours away. He wanted to go check on Marilana, but he did not want to disturb her rest. Deciding he would go to her when he woke, the young lion collapsed on his bed and fell asleep in minutes.

28

It was mid-morning by the time Marquiese was washed, dressed, and had eaten breakfast. He smiled as he strolled toward Major Kolt standing guard outside Marilana's room. Major Kolt nodded to him and knocked twice on the door.

"She's been expecting you," Major Kolt said opening the door.

Marquiese grinned to see Marilana propped up on pillows on her bed.

"Ah," she smiled, "my hero has come to see me."

"You heard about my father's speech," he said rolling his eyes and sitting on the edge of her bed.

"Earek was ranting about it over breakfast," she laughed. "He said it was bad enough being named Hero of the Realm last summer, but to be named Champion of Justice just six months later is tiresome. I told him that if he keeps earning titles, he would start getting more interest from the noble daughters. I could not stop from smiling when he shot me an appalled glare."

Marquiese laughed and looked down at his paws imagining Earek's indignation.

"Of course, it does not matter how many tittles you get," she said with a hint of contempt. "You cannot take a step out your door without gathering a swarm of daughters batting their lashes at you."

He froze frantically trying to think of something to say that might soothe the hurt in her voice. He looked up at her forming an apology. A smile lit up her face and she laughed.

"That is not fair," he complained, "I am required to spend time with each of the noble daughters until the Royal Courtship Ceremony. I do not want their attention."

"Of course, you do not want their attention. That is why I can laugh about it. I would be hurt if you encouraged their behavior," she said.

"While we are talking about courtships, I don't know if you heard or not, but Master Arndt called off his courtship with Brittia," Marquiese said more brightly. "Lord Arndt was not pleased with her displays at the Tournament Ball. He said that Brittia's behavior toward you was unacceptable, but not necessarily unexpected. Her disrespect to me however, could not be easily excused. He said her lack of remorse when he spoke to her about it later pushed him past his tolerance. He forced the end of the courtship. Brittia's family has moved out of Redsands to seek their fortunes elsewhere. And judging by Master Arndt's behavior with the noble daughters last night, he is not too upset by the developments."

"I am not surprised," Marilana said. "Master Arndt has no respect for women, and Brittia has never been good at giving proper respect to her superiors. I do pity her, though; she had finally found someone to care about other than herself."

"You have such a gentle heart," Marquiese said smiling at her. "Most people would be pleased by her loss of position and the fall of her family's honor. You give her pity and forgiveness."

She returned his smile for a moment before he became more serious.

"I have not asked you to relate the details of your ordeal," he said. Marilana dropped her eyes. "I know you will tell me when you are ready, but I want you to know that I have not told anyone that the man you call Newrothen was one of the Hungdie. I think it would be best to keep that information between us."

She glanced up and nodded.

"You, Earek, and Lady Annabella are the only people who have ever believed me about them," Marilana said. "It should not be hard to maintain the pretense that he was a master of torture and was simply avenging Frishka's death. I have told Lady Annabella and Earek much of what happened to me, but they have promised not to tell anyone unless I give my permission. They are simply saying that the ordeal was terrible, and that I do not have much memory of it. I want to spare you the details of what he did and said, but there are a few things he said that you should know."

She took a deep breath and told him about her talks with Newrothen. She told him about the Hungdie, the treatment of Saffon, and the plans for killing Marquiese and Rylan. He listened carefully and noticed that she seemed less afraid of the Hungdie. She told him about the information Newrothen had received from Bram's Fen.

"Demdrake," he said shaking his head in disgust. "I did not take as much care with him as I should have. It nearly cost me my life. You and Earek warned me to be careful of my actions and words. He did not know who I was, but he was mad enough at me to rant about it when he got home."

"Yes, it explained the timing of the strange bandit raids," Marilana nodded. "I wondered why it had taken two years for your pursuer to start systematically combing the Southern Tip. I do not think taking more caution with Demdrake would have made much difference though. The longer you stayed in hiding, the more likely it became that someone was going to recognize you."

"You are probably correct, and there is nothing we can do about it now," he smiled. "Besides I do not think I would have changed what I chose to do. I had no intentions of letting him get his lustful claws on you, even if it cost me my secret."

"You did very well with that situation. I could not have asked for a better friend," Marilana beamed. "I did not ever think you would be hunted by the Hungdie, however. They are relentless. If I had known, I may not have been so willing to be your friend for fear of my own secret threat."

"You do not seem to fear the Hungdie like you did before," he said gently.

"I discovered that fearing them gave them power," she said sadly. "To fight him, I overcame my fear; it was a battle unlike any I have faced. I focused every fiber of my being on prolonging my strength so that I would die. I actually wanted to die. Even my slight hope that you would rescue me helped me push my limits. When I woke the night you rescued me, and I recognized that I was in a tent, the first thought I had was that he was healing me and that I would live to be his plaything. I was terrified.

When you spoke to me, I thought I was hallucinating, but I took the chance to tell you to have the healer change his remedies because of that slim hope of rescue." Marilana shivered slightly and grimaced sourly. "If it had been a hallucination, it would not have changed how Newrothen treated me. He knew enough that he would have noticed the change in my sleeping patterns. He would have known what to do. Without the gift of blood, however, I think I would have died. Newrothen may not have been able to pull me back with only herbal remedies, but it is possible that his knowledge of the old ways might have allowed him to bring me back from the brink."

She paused and closed her eyes. He watched as she took several deep calming breaths, pushing down her residual terror. "When I finally became aware of my surroundings, and I knew I was not dreaming, I was so relieved to be home that all I could do was cry. Lady Annabella and Zariff were there, they told me how I had been rescued and showed me the Hope Altar. Seeing all the mementos had the desired effect and I was able to regain my composure. Knowing that all those people wanted me to recover helped to dispel my fear. And seeing the red and blue in the lover's place made me want to live again."

She closed her eyes and tears streamed down her cheeks. He reached up and cupped her cheek with his paw and then gently brushed her tears off her cheek with his thumb.

"When Rodan gave me your message that you were as good as dead, and not to try to rescue you," he said quietly, "I felt like someone was crushing my heart. My world was on the verge of collapsing, but I refused to give up on you. I do not know what I would have done if you had died, but I know I would not be the person I am now. When I tied the red and blue on the Hope Altar, I hoped you would see it and know I loved you."

She blinked open her eyes and beamed at him, leaning her head into his palm still cradling her cheek. They gazed into each other's eyes. Finally, he dropped his paw from her face, and rested it on her paws in her lap.

"What did Healer Magus say this morning? What damage did your display of determination yesterday cause?" he asked gently changing the topic.

"Nothing major," she replied dropping her gaze to her paws. "Healer Magus was furious, though. He had me brought in here so that Lady Annabella would not wake me when she retired for the night. He said I should not have stressed my knee and ankle so much. They are both swollen this morning, and he wrapped them with cold poultices. He restricted me to bed for a few days."

"That is not too bad," Marquiese said. "You could have done worse damage. Where are Lady Annabella and Earek now?"

"In the library," she sighed.

He smiled at her frustration. She did not like being confined to her bed for so long and yearned to be in the library with the others.

"Well on the bright side," he said smiling, "I have nowhere to go today until dinner, and so you may order me to assist you in any way you need."

"I could use some entertainment," she mused, "a song and dance perhaps."

He threw his head back laughing heartily.

29

The next few fifnights were frustrating for Marilana. She was frustrated by her confinement, by her invalid body, by her slow healing, and even by her isolation. She was happy to be back in the Royal Palace and close to Marquiese. He came to see her every day as his duties allowed and they spent many happy hours together playing chess or backgammon, and talking. When he was not with her, she plotted to interfere with the noble daughters. Commander Lorne and Guardsman Karndel proved invaluable in her efforts as they were frequently with Marquiese on his rides or walks and could share his plans for venturing out in public. It wasn't enough though, she needed to be seen by the other Daughters. She wanted them to know who was interrupting their intrigues, but she had to be content with Marquiese saying that the ambushes had inexplicably stopped. She did not disclose her actions, but his looks revealed he suspected it was by her design.

She was also acutely aware that she only had six fifnights from the Winter Council to be ready for the Royal Courtship Dance and she was not gaining her strength back as quickly as she had hoped. She tried to be patient, carefully following Healer Magus' instructions and restrictions. He kept her restricted to bed for the first three days after the Winter Council, and only let her stand up on the fourth day just long enough for the seamstress to take her measurements. He did allow her to stretch her arms and back, though. She was careful not to push her back muscles too far, but she did practice the arm motions for the High Style Courtship Dance. At first she struggled to hold the fan in her paw at full extension of her arms. Many times she gritted her teeth as her muscles reached the point of pain before completing a full sweep. Gradually, with a great deal of resolute patience and a few bouts of frustrated tears, the motions became easier and more fluid.

What really bothered her, though she was loath to admit it, was her isolation. She had always taken comfort in her privacy and the quiet times of her life. Now however, all her other frustrations would be more bearable if only she could leave her confinement, have something different to see or do. With so many nobles in the city, Marquiese and Annabella were receiving invitations for dinner parties every few days. Annabella and Earek were enjoying pleasant evenings visiting with the nobles in the palace and in the city. Marquiese and King Rylan received so many invitations, they sometimes attended two or three parties a night. Lord Castant and Lord Roana took turns hosting parties at their manor houses in the city. Marilana regretted missing those parties, as she suspected she would have savored the festivities and enjoyed the company. Being tucked away in the same boring room was wearing thin.

As Marilana continued to improve, Healer Magus approved some gentle strength-building exercises. Marilana began a daily routine of stretches and simple balancing poses. She also counted her steps around the room. At first, she could only walk short distances using her staff before tiring. As the fifnight wore on, she made it further without her staff and without needing rest. By the start of the third fifnight Healer Magus was cautiously optimistic. She was healing fast, even without using the healing trance, and Healer Magus declared that her ankle and knee were mostly healed. With intense scrutiny he allowed her to move up to more complex balancing poses but reminded her not to push too hard too fast and forbade her from dancing. He did not want any twisting on her ankle and knee. Marilana agreed begrudgingly; she was anxious to do more than arm motions.

Marilana was careful to hide her frustration and worry from Marquiese. He was always positive when with her and always reminded her that he did not want to court anyone but her. As Marilana's frustration with her slow healing continued, she became increasingly aware that the other noble daughters who were going to dance the Royal Courtship Ceremony were playing for keeps. If one of them out danced her, Marquiese would be forced to enter a courtship with someone else. She knew Marquiese would want to end any other courtship after a reasonable amount of time, but the other daughters wanted to be crowned queen. If any of them entered courtship with Marquiese, Marilana knew they would do everything possible to prevent the courtship from ending. The young lioness was determined to protect Marquiese from any deeper deceit. The easiest way to stop the noble daughters was to be the last dancer remaining in the Royal Courtship Dance. If she were at her best, she was sure she would out dance them all, but those other seven were determined. She knew they were practicing hard and were more fit than she was. Even so, she restrained her exercises to Healer Magus' instructions, knowing he was trying his best to prevent her from injuring herself. An injury now would mean she could not dance at all. It would guarantee that Marquiese would court another.

On the last day of the third fifnight Marilana stood on her left foot breathing and balancing carefully as she swept her arms through the complex motions of High Style. She was not practicing the twists to make the flourishes grand and smooth, but she was pleased that she was able to finally reach the full extension of each motion without pain. Marilana brought her left arm around in a full sweep, keeping her fan at full extension, blocking her imaginary dance partner from seeing her face. She reached back and caught the fan in her right paw to continue the circle around her. She caught the fan, but wobbled in her balance. Gritting her teeth in annoyance, she started back at the beginning of the motion. If she could not do the motions flawlessly at a slow pace, she knew she would miss the motion as the pace increased throughout the dance. A knock sounded on the door behind her, breaking into her concentration. She placed her right foot back on the floor and turned to see Mistresses Lorlina and Ailse entering. She collapsed the pure white fan she had been practicing with and greeted them with a smile.

"Mistress Lorlina, Mistress Ailse, please come in and sit with me," she said indicating the couch and chairs next to her. "To what do I owe the pleasure of your visit?"

They smiled and curtsied before sitting together on her couch. She did not miss their glances at the fan in her paw.

"We wished to speak with you," Lorlina began hesitantly. "You were very helpful at the Tournament Ball and we thought we should like to get to know you better. His Highness speaks fondly of you at his little gatherings."

"You mentioned these gatherings at the Tournament Ball, but I am afraid that I have not heard about them," Marilana said curiously.

"His Highness has been holding small gatherings once or twice a month since the end of summer," said

Ailse. "He invites a few of the lordlings and noble daughters to join him in a palace sitting room after dinner. Lorlina and I have attended all of them, but the other attendees vary depending on who His Highness speaks with. Before the Tournament Ball, we thought he was trying to learn more about us so that he could choose who to enter courtship with. After you spoke to us and he did not choose anyone to court, we reanalyzed what we could remember of his parties."

"We concluded," said Lorlina taking up the explanation, "that he had already chosen someone he would like to court, but that person was rebuffing his attentions."

Marilana waited and both girls watched her intently. She raised her eyebrows in a simulacrum of surprise.

"Are you suggesting that I am this person?" Marilana gasped acting intrigued. Inwardly, she was pleased that these two had boldly brought the conversation straight to the point they wished to discuss.

"Well, yes," Ailse said fidgeting. "His Highness tells stories about his time with you in the Southern Tip or he might mention something you told him. When he thinks about what he said, he becomes sad and distracted. It is obvious that there is something between you two."

"And you feel strongly enough to confront me about it?" Marilana asked cautiously.

The girls exchanged nervous glances.

"Timral told me that you are a good person, that you are intelligent and care about others," Lorlina said quietly. "His Highness has been kind to us, and we want to try to help him."

"You feel you owe him something in return for allowing you to spend time with Timral and Enton at his gatherings without parental intervention," Marilana said shrewdly.

"Yes," said Ailse firmly.

"I suggest you trust His Highness to take care of his own heart," Marilana replied.

The girls blushed but did not turn away.

"You told Timral that bravery comes in all forms," said Lorlina narrowing her eyes in suspicion. "I do not feel brave, but I know how to read people. You are hiding something."

"You are just as intelligent as I suspected," said Marilana smiling broadly. "I trust Master Timral's judgment, so I will tell you something. Before I left for the Southern Tip last summer, I suggested to His Highness that he should get to know some of the noble daughters better. I suggested he start with you two."

"Why?" asked Ailse frowning in confusion.

"Because you love his friends," Marilana replied. "I wanted him to determine if he could trust you. You will both be in positions where you could overhear important conversations, or influence decisions Enton and Timral make. His Highness must know from whom and when to censor his words. I am glad he took my advice."

Lorlina and Ailse exchanged an alert look, but both relaxed again and turned back to her.

"You would make a very good partner for His Highness," Lorlina said. "You have not been a noble for long, but you are a match for any I have encountered."

Marilana laughed softly. "I may have only been a noble in name for nearly eight months, but I have been a noble in training with Lady Annabella since I was three years old. His Highness has added his own tutelage as well."

"You are dancing the Royal Courtship Dance," Lorlina stated frankly indicating the fan. "I think, Ailse, we arrived a little late to our conclusions."

"You and His Highness have reconciled your differences," Ailse said nodding.

"So much has happened in the past two months," Marilana said somberly before returning to a brighter tone. "I will correct your conclusions on one point, however. I was not refusing his advances. We had differing opinions and needed time to resolve our feelings."

"Will you be well enough to dance?" Lorlina asked concerned. "You seem stronger than you were at the Winter Council, but are you strong enough to out-dance the other Daughters? Whoever they are, I doubt they will give up quickly."

"It is a valid concern. I am healing well and regaining my strength and skill. I am hopeful that events will be resolved in my favor," Marilana said.

A double knock sounded loudly on the door, Marilana looked up with a smile. Lorlina and Ailse jumped in surprise at the sudden interruption.

The door opened, and Marquiese strode in. He smiled as Lorlina and Ailse stood and curtseyed to him.

"Ah, here is my rescuer, come to check on the invalid," Marilana said lightly.

"Mistress Lorlina, Mistress Ailse, I am surprised to see you here, although I am glad that Lady Marilana has some company other than myself," he said grinning and ignoring Marilana's comment.

"We thought she might like to hear some news since she has been confined to her rooms for so long, Highness," Ailse said with a curtsey.

"Good, good," he said, "she needs to hear some news from a lady's view. I think she tires of my talk about manly goings on."

Marilana rolled her eyes and Ailse raised her paw to hide her smile. Lorlina smiled knowingly at Marilana.

"At least they can help me decide on what to wear to watch you chose a courtship," Marilana said. "The only thing you say about dresses is that they look nice."

"Well, they do look nice," he said in exasperation. "What do I know about lace and trim and other frills? Now if you wanted to know about sword length and balance, or the best stance for throwing knives I could be much more informative."

Lorlina and Ailse giggled behind their paws. Even Marilana could not stop from laughing lightly. Marquiese smiled and gestured to the fan in Marilana's lap.

"It looks like you were practicing dancing, Lady Marilana," he said lightly. "Did Healer Magus allow you more strenuous exercises?"

"Dancing is too strenuous, but the motions can be done separately and if done slowly are good for stretching the muscles. Healer Magus said that I am still restricted to my rooms," Marilana said with a sigh.

Marquiese nodded with slight disappointment of his own.

"Well it is nearly time for dinner," said Marquiese. "Mistress Lorlina, Mistress Ailse, will I have the pleasure of your company for my little gathering after dinner?"

"Yes, Your Highness," replied Ailse with a curtsey.

"I would not miss it," smiled Lorlina also curtseying.

Marquiese bowed to them in return.

"Lady Marilana, until I see you again," he said quietly.

"I hope you have a pleasant evening, Your Highness," Marilana replied hiding her increased frustration with a seated bow.

Marquiese gave her a commiserating smile as he returned her bow and left. Lorlina and Ailse remained standing and started to step away from their seats.

"Mistress Lorlina, Mistress Ailse, might I request a moment more of your time?"

"Is there something else you require of us, Lady Marilana?" Lorlina asked frowning.

"Is there something we can do to help you out-dance the other Daughters?" Ailse asked hopefully.

"There is unfortunately nothing you can do to help my healing, but there is something else I think you might do for me. I wanted to tell you that I have heard it said that the two who wear black during the Royal Courtship Dance are asked to become the future Queen's first Ladies-in-Waiting," Marilana said. "I also wanted to thank you for coming here with your concerns for His Highness."

"We did not come primarily out of concern for His Highness," Lorlina confessed. "That was a secondary consideration."

"I know," Marilana replied. "You came here to further your own interests regarding your young gentlemen. I understand your priorities. Nevertheless, during our conversation, you have shown concern for His Highness and demonstrated that you are willing to place your own interests above those of your parents."

Both girls blushed and sat down again warily.

"I want to know if I can trust you to keep my priorities secret. I trust Enton and Timral to be honest with me and I expect they will gladly give me their loyalty. Will I be able to trust you as much?"

"You are talking about in the future, as our queen," Lorlina said cautiously, "and with us as your Ladies-in-Waiting."

"That is another reason he wants to get to know us," Ailse said with comprehension. "He wants to know if we can be trusted to serve you."

Marilana studied them in silence as they thought about the situation.

"Yes," Lorlina said finally, "I would be honored to give you my loyalty and service as my queen."

"I, too, would be pleased and honored to give you my loyalty and service as my queen," Ailse said nodding firmly. "You have Enton's trust. He and Lord Castant speak highly of you, and in the few times we have spoken, I have also been impressed by your intelligence and behavior, especially the way you dealt with Master Lotal at the Tournament ball. My father does not interfere lightly, but he told me later that he did it with pleasure. He was pleased that I wanted to come and speak with you today, although my mother was less enthusiastic."

"Your mother is more ambitious, your father is more practical. Thank you both for beginning this path of loyalty," Marilana said with slight relief. "I am hoping you will also join me in an alliance of sorts until I become queen. Would you be willing to be my accomplices in this intrigue war between the noble daughters? I know you are doing as your parents wish and trying to interrupt His Highness' walks and rides with the other Daughters."

"We have been working together and taking turns being seen," Ailse nodded.

"Although lately we have been having trouble getting close to His Highness on his walks and rides," Lorlina studied Marilana thoughtfully. "In fact, I think the trouble started after you arrived."

"Yes," Marilana acknowledged, "I have been interrupting as much intrigue as possible. As I grow stronger, I will be able to make my presence felt, and I will need more accomplices to achieve my goals."

"What are your goals?" Lorlina asked shrewdly.

"We saw the looks that passed between you and His Highness a moment ago," Ailse added, "and we know you want to become queen. What are you accomplishing with your interruptions?"

"I know he is required to spend time with all the noble daughters during this time leading up to the Royal Courtship Dance, and I cannot change that. My goal instead is to stop the ambushing of His Highness and let him have some peace while he performs this duty of tradition," Marilana said simply.

"He did seem annoyed by the constant interruptions," Ailse smiled. "I would be happy to help achieve that goal."

"I agree," Lorlina nodded, "Interrupting the other Daughters' intrigue is part of what my parents want, and we have been devoting most of our efforts to that anyway since we do not want to enter courtship with His Highness."

"We have not had near as much success with it, however," added Ailse.

"Thank you both for accepting," Marilana smiled and rose to embrace the gray clouded leopard and slender yellow leopard, "I will send my requests to you directly as I know what is needed for each situation. Thank you also for coming to speak with me; I enjoyed the break of monotony to my solitude. I hope you both have a pleasant evening with your dear gentlemen."

"I wish you were joining us," Ailse said. "Enton speaks fondly of your company and I would like to get to know you better myself."

"We will have plenty of time very soon," Marilana smiled. "Now off to dinner, both of you."

Smiling, they curtseyed and left.

Marilana sighed. She had enjoyed having company for a while. She knew she would not truly trust Ailse and Lorlina until she became better acquainted with them, but it was a start. And speaking with her had helped to alleviate their nervousness regarding the upcoming dance. With fatigue setting in, she moved to her bed and lay down to sleep.

30

Marquiese was concerned about Marilana. She had been confined to her rooms for nearly four fifnights, and while she was healing well, he could see she was increasingly frustrated by her isolation. She tried to hide it from him, but he knew her too well to not see her tension and regret. She had always enjoyed solitude and quiet, but she had also grown to relish the social life of a lady. There had been so many gatherings over the past four fifnights, and she was missing out on them all. Marquiese breathed a small sigh of relief as he trailed Rylan up the steps of Castant Manor. They had attended two other parties that day, and he was ready to relax with good company. A servant took their gloves and cloaks in the entrance hall, and they followed the sounds of laughter to the sitting room. Another servant offered them glasses of mulled cider as they entered the well-lit room.

Lord Roana and Lady Annabella greeted them. Marquiese sat on the couch and rested his feet on a low stool. He grinned, watching Enton and Timral teach Earek the finer techniques of darts. The three acknowledged their arrival with smiles and nods as they continued their game. Rylan sat next to Lady Annabella and joined in her discussion with Lord Roana.

Marquiese frowned when he heard voices coming from the inner hall of the manor. He wondered who would be intruding on this gathering of friends. He assumed the deep and masculine voice was Lord Castant's. The other voice with a higher lilt was harder to distinguish. He twisted around when the door opened and beamed as Lord Castant led Marilana into the room. Her eyes twinkled when she noticed him.

"Wonderful," smiled Lord Castant, "our last guests have arrived. I have just treated our dear Marilana to a tour of the house. She was interested in seeing the hidden treasures."

"I simply wanted to see some of the works of Draukshar. I had not previously had the privilege," Marilana smiled. "Thank you for showing me your beautiful manor."

"Perhaps someday I will have the pleasure to have you visit my castle in Draukshar. My late wife was fond of roses, and I think you would enjoy seeing her rose arbor," Lord Castant said happily.

"I would love to visit you in Draukshar and see the roses. I have roses growing in my garden in the Southern Tip. Oh, how I love their sweet aroma," Marilana beamed.

"Come now, Withers," called Lord Roana, "you have kept Marilana to yourself long enough. Let the rest of us have a chance to enjoy her charming company."

"If you had wanted to spend time with her you could have joined us on our walk, Ames," Lord Castant laughed, leading Marilana over to the sitting area.

Marilana sat down on the couch next to Marquiese with a sigh.

"I am pleased to see you out of your rooms, Marilana," Rylan said. "Are you recovering well enough?"

"I am recovering very well. Thank you," Marilana replied. "I am not yet back to my full strength, but I am very pleased to be able to leave my rooms at last."

"We are all delighted that you can grace our gathering again as well," Master Castant said flopping into a chair facing her.

Timral took a chair next to Marquiese and Earek leaned against the wall next to Lady Annabella.

"We have had to suffer the absence of your beauty and put up with a despondent Marquiese," Master Castant continued.

"Enton," Lord Castant growled in warning.

"I am sorry to have caused you discomfort, Enton," Marilana said with mock concern. "Next time someone asks if I want to be injured, I shall dutifully inform them that your happiness would be better served with a treatise on why their actions are wrong, and a written apology for inconveniencing you."

The room erupted in laughter. Master Castant failed to find an appropriate response and so joined in the laughter. Marquiese smiled to see the sparkle of mischief in Marilana's eyes. This was a sure sign that her recovery was well on its way. She met his gaze and winked.

The rest of the evening passed in amiable companionship. Marquiese was pleased with Marilana's vitality. She sat most of the time but occasionally walked around. She did not need support as she moved around, and she walked with poise and grace. He could not help but think that maybe she would miraculously recover in time to out dance the other girls in the Royal Courtship Dance. He fervently hoped for it.

As the visit wore on, Marilana couldn't suppress her yawns. She tried unsuccessfully to hide behind her paw. Everyone smiled fondly at her and Lady Annabella declared it was time to return to the palace. King Rylan said they should retire for the night as well; they all said their goodbyes.

"Marquiese, a moment, if you please," Lord Castant called to Marquiese before he followed his father out to their carriage.

"Sir?" Marquiese asked turning around.

Lord Castant and Lord Roana stood watching him flanked by Timral and Enton.

"You did not hide your emotions tonight, Marquiese," Lord Roana said quietly. "Your eyes hardly left her. Your intentions are obvious."

"My Lord Roana, I—" Marquiese began but Lord Castant held up a paw interrupting him.

"We have all been in your position," Lord Castant said. "We want you to know that we approve of your choice. She will make an excellent Queen. We just hope she is able to perform well for the Royal Courtship Dance."

"Thank you, My Lords, my friends. I greatly value your words," Marquiese replied. "I also hope for the best performance possible. Goodnight."

They bowed to him, and he turned and left Castant Manor.

*

"There was one time I got in trouble for hiding from Sir Libor. I did not want to study that day, the tournament was the next day, and I just wanted to watch the knights practice. As punishment, Father had me help the cook prepare the evening meal. I tried to do what the cook asked, but I did not know the difference between sage and mint. The mint sauce was totally ruined, but the cook had a sense of humor and was on very good terms with Father. He made up a fresh mint sauce for the general assembly, but served my sage sauce to the head table. He brought it out himself calling it 'Marquiese's Special Lamb Sauce.' Father nearly choked on the first bite. I thought he was going to be furious. Instead, he started laughing and arranged for me to start a regular rotation in the kitchens. He claimed he did not wish to be poisoned every time I got in trouble."

Marquiese smiled as he watched Marilana riding on his left and laughing merrily. He loved telling her stories from his past. He had been careful to talk only about the city life in Maefair when he had been hiding in the Southern Tip, but those stories had not been personal. She had enjoyed hearing stories from far away, but she seemed to enjoy stories about him even more. It was the end of the fifth fifnight after the Winter Council, and he had taken her on a horseback tour of Maefair. There was still much of the city she had not had the chance to see, and he had not wanted to take her too far from the Palace. She was relaxed and seemed as strong as ever as she easily directed Storm along the streets. The only sign that she had not fully recovered was that she had let the stable master assist her into the saddle rather than vaulting to mount her white stallion, Storm.

He checked the guardsmen that surrounded them, and Commander Lorne nodded, indicating no problems or interruptions. They crossed a market square and turned down a street lined with shops on their return to the palace. Smiling, he studied Marilana as she exchanged paw signals with Captain Hayden.

"I wanted to thank you for what you have done, My Lady," Marquiese said quietly.

"What have I done that has earned your notice and thanks, Your Highness?" Marilana asked coyly.

"You know perfectly well what I am talking about. The first two fifnights I was back from the Southern Tip I was hounded whenever I went on a ride or walk. Since the Council, I have not had to endure the persistent interruptions. In fact, I have not even seen any of the other Daughters except the one I was entertaining until just this last fifnight when I started to see you out and about," he replied. "I am not complaining. I have enjoyed the uninterrupted conversations. I have noticed, however, that you have been much more successful than the others. Also, judging by the fact that I have twice seen you accompanied by Mistresses Lorlina and Ailse in the gardens, I gather you have found some willing accomplices."

"I said I would not sit idle while the other Daughters wove their intrigues around you. My intentions were not to capture your interest but to let the others know that I would not let them have their way. Lorlina and Ailse were willing to join forces to interfere with the others' intrigues," Marilana said. "Lorlina and Ailse were especially pleased to be seen by you. Their parents were not happy about them not being seen for all their efforts, and they told me that their parents regard me more favorably now for helping them."

"Yes, and the others are livid with the three of you," Marquiese chuckled. "My sources have told me that the Daughters and their families were flummoxed in the first couple of fifnights after the Council. No one could determine who was behind the seemingly random interference. Then you were seen walking alone and unhindered in the garden where I was strolling in the snow with Mistress Serina. No one can figure out how you are able to prevent the others, but small mishaps are reported, or messages delivered, or conversations entered that keep the Daughters from making their ambushes. They were not sure it was you even after that first sighting, because you did not lie in wait for me. Reports say you simply walked at your ease and took the path at random that led you to cross my path so that I saw you from a distance."

"Your reaction to seeing me strolling alone in the garden did help them figure it out," Marilana laughed. "If you had not been so startled and concerned, Serina probably would have thought nothing of it. As it was, she told Lorlina that you nearly jumped out of your boots and almost pulled her down the path to get a second look to confirm it was me."

"Probably not the best of reactions," he chuckled, "and I am sure you wanted to remain in the shadows a while longer."

"On the contrary," Marilana smiled, "I wanted them to know I was behind it all. I want the nobles to recognize that I achieved more success from my sick bed than they could with all their experience. It makes them question my abilities and connections. I have begun solidifying my reputation, and I have made some good connections."

"I know Lorlina and Ailse are conspirators, but most of the reports say the interruptions are coming from sources other than the Southern Tip including palace staff. I am sure you have Altia helping you, but who else?" Marquiese asked.

"Well, if you must know," Marilana chuckled, "the Castant family, the Roana household, Lorlina and Ailse, and all the resources of the Southern Tip of course."

"Naturally, and who else?" Marquiese persisted.

"Oh, just a pawful of palace servants, your stable master, and several of your guardsmen," Marilana said lightly.

"My household!" Marquiese said surprised and flashed Commander Lorne a suspicious glance.

Commander Lorne gave him an amused smirk in return.

"I am staying at the palace and you are the center of the intrigues," laughed Marilana. "Who would know the palace and your habits better than your own staff?"

"How can I trust my staff now knowing that they can be bought?" Marquiese asked frustrated.

"The members of your staff who are helping me are the most loyal to you," Marilana said. "You do not need to fear that they can be bought. I did not buy their help with money or wealth, but something much more important to them—you. They help me, because I am helping you. They all wanted to help you find some peace but did not know how. I gave them direction. Also, they all know I make you happy; they like that and trust me."

"I suppose you are right, and I trust you too. It reminds me though that not all the staff can be trusted," Marquiese mused.

"You are correct," Marilana said. "Your privacy is a valuable commodity that some are willing to sell to the highest bidder. You cannot disregard the staff in matters of security."

"The nobles have good reason to consider you a threat to their plans," Marquiese said. "I am glad that your endeavor has met success. Those are skills you will need to use for the rest of your life."

"I know," Marilana nodded, "I needed to make my mark now before the Ceremony so that they know I am skilled in my own right. I—"

She broke off and glanced left down the side street they passed, suddenly alert. Marquiese nudged his horse faster to match Storm's pace and the guards around them adjusted as well. Marilana motioned quickly with her paws as they approached the next crossing street. Storm's ears flickered in irritation. One of Marilana's guards, a slender wolf, casually left the group and trotted down the side street. Marquiese reined in his mount as Storm slowed his pace, and the guards smoothly adjusted again. Marquiese waited silently for Marilana to assess the situation. He trusted her to deal with it without his interference and he knew she would fill him in when she could.

As they began to cross the next side street, Marilana's left paw suddenly shot forward next to Storm's neck. A second later there was a commotion on the corner of the side street. Marquiese glanced over and spotted the wolf dragging a short weasel away. Marquiese kept pace with Storm and Commander Lorne raised no questions.

"Apparently, I have made someone mad enough to raise the stakes of the game," Marilana said amused and held her paw toward him.

He took the small sling stone from her and studied it for a moment before slipping it into his coat pocket. It was not big enough to have seriously injured horse or rider, but it would have been enough to make most horses shy or jump. A relaxed and unprepared rider could have been unseated and fallen. The rider would not have been badly hurt, but for Marilana's current state, it could have slowed her healing enough to prevent her from dancing well in the ceremony. He studied Marilana for a moment. To all observers, she would appear relaxed and slightly amused, but he could see the bandit hunter intensity was still there. She was not nervous or afraid, but calm, alert, and aware.

"So, tell me fully what just occurred. Why did you vary our pace?"

"Storm shivered slightly from an irritation," Marilana stated. "I suspected a projectile of some kind had hit him. I did not see where it came from, but it hit Storm on the left. I assumed that the culprit thought he had missed, so I sped up our pace so that he would have to act fast at the next street. I sent the guardsman off to take the side street and watch for the culprit. The culprit tried a second time and again received an unexpected reaction from Storm. I expect he would have hurried to reach the third street ahead of us. I slowed our pace to give my guardsman time to get into position. When I caught the third stone, the culprit realized I knew about the attempts and tried to scurry away. My guardsman was ready for him."

"Lucky for us that they underestimated Storm's training, and your reflexes," Marquiese said. "Your guardsman did not kill that weasel, did he?"

"No, he will be taken to Castant Manor and interrogated," Marilana said. "Getting thrown from a horse would have been a rather large interruption to my plans. It was a good try, they think of Storm as high-spirited, and think he overreacts to stimuli. If he were a docile ladies horse, they would have had to use a much stronger stimulus to try to get me thrown, but that could have risked you and the guards as well. As it is, they have not yet realized that he is a war horse and is trained to never throw his rider. This attempt failed to slow our ride even a little. Such a spectacular failure should prevent other such attempts unless they decide to try something more drastic. I think I shall be very careful of what I eat and drink from now on, someone might think to slip herbs into my food."

"They have no idea how to contend with someone of your skills," Marquiese chuckled, knowing full well that she could detect most herbs and was in very little danger from such an attempt.

"Thank you for trusting me," Marilana said quietly, "both with the intrigues and with the situation just now."

"I do trust you and your skills," he nodded seriously, "with my life and yours."

Marilana smiled at him with true amusement and he returned her smile as they continued their leisurely ride back to the palace.

Marilana paced in her rooms. The seamstress had come for a final fitting before the Dance the next day. Tomorrow everything would be unalterable—the dress would be donned, the dance performed, the courtship begun—and she hoped she was up to the challenge. She had to be the one, she just had to. The seamstress and her assistants arranged their tools and then motioned for Marilana to approach. Marilana took a calming breath and stepped up onto the low stool. Since the real gown was to be kept secret until just before the Ceremony, the seamstress had made a mock gown called a form. Marilana stood motionless as the seamstress and her assistants dressed her in the white muslin form and marked it where adjustments needed to be made. Lady Annabella was smiling as she watched from a chair. Marilana took another calming breath, but it did not still the wild fluttering of her stomach. After about a half an hour, the seamstress removed the form, packed up all the tools and led her assistants out.

"I am proud of you, Daughter," Lady Annabella said quietly.

"Mother?" Marilana asked confused. "You are proud that I will be Queen?"

"Are you afraid of being Queen?" Lady Annabella replied in her way that meant they were discussing a tangent and would return to the topic in a moment.

Marilana smiled fondly and shook her head. "No, I am not afraid to be Queen. I know it will be difficult. I know that my patience, understanding, and temper will be tested again and again. I know I will face hard choices, and that people—good people—will die for my choices."

Marilana paused for a moment to let the wash of sadness dissipate from the thought of innocent deaths caused by her future choices.

"I know that there will be times of grief. Mother, I know I am strong enough to face the bad along with the good. Alone, if I must. However, I also know that no monarch stands alone. I already have trusted helpers that I can rely on. You, Zariff, Earek, Family Roana, Family Castant, Altia, many of the servants and staff here at the palace, as well as Rylan and Marquiese are available for advice, opinions, and sometimes guidance. That will be my duty, and I am willing to take up that burden."

"Are you afraid then, of becoming a wife and mother?"

"I like children and I have tutored young children, but I have never helped raise normal children. I raised Child—but she was a special case—and look what happened, I turned her into a hermit bandit hunter. Also, I have never really thought about being with a male without any inhibitions keeping us within the bounds of propriety. I have no knowledge to guide me. So, yes, that does frighten me, but I am also excited to get to be a wife and mother. There was a time I believed those roles were unsuitable for me. I will try my best."

"Do not try too hard on that score, daughter," Annabella laughed. "Those things will come with time. Instinct will guide you through as long as you relax and listen to your body and heart."

"I think the biggest thing that worries me at present, is being in the social eye," Marilana admitted. "I was never in the fashionable circles, and I still get nervous when surrounded by so many people."

"That is an aspect you will have lots of time to learn how best to navigate for yourself. Even at my age, I still prefer small gatherings, intimate settings, and solitude. You and Marquiese will have to learn together how to balance your public and private times. And that bring me to why I am so proud of you. I am proud that you are following your heart," Annabella smiled. "I am proud of the woman you are, and I am pleased with the leader you are becoming. You are in love with a good lion, and you are not afraid to take on the enormous responsibility that will become yours if you marry Marquiese. Most of those other girls that try to catch his eye want the power of the position and do not think about the responsibility that goes along with it. Unlike you, they do not have the temperament or the skills to cope with it. You have managed the intrigues expertly. You have become every bit the lioness I hoped you would."

"I could not have come this far without your love and guidance," Marilana replied smiling.

"Thank you, but I cannot take credit for your heart, determination, and strength. Those are all yours."

Marilana walked over and embraced her Mother.

"Come now," said Lady Annabella breaking the embrace, "let us put that nervous energy to use; time to dance."

Marilana flowed smoothly through the forms of the Royal Courtship Dance. She hoped she would be able to perform the dance well in front of an audience, she still did not have the stamina she was used to and tired quickly as the pace got faster.

31

Marilana stood in her rooms with her eyes closed and meditated. She wanted to pace, to move, to do something other than stand still. She knew she should have been resting, but she was too nervous and could only manage to meditate to conserve her energy. She had put all her efforts for the past fifnights into building up her stamina and conditioning her body to perform this one dance, but she was doubtful if it had been enough. She still tired much sooner than she liked, and her knee ached if she danced too long. She had spent most of the day meditating with only mild stretching and walking to warm her muscles.

The gown arrived during dinner when the guests would not see. It was beautiful. It reminded her of the dresses Marquiese had ordered for her when she first arrived in Maefair last summer. Only nine months had passed since then, but it seemed a lifetime ago. It had been four and a half years since she first met Marquiese, and she could not even imagine going back to that simple, and dark, life. She had to believe that she would go forward with him. The dress was royal blue with a hem ruffle, belt, and loose sleeves in royal red. It was accompanied by pure white gloves, slippers, and a large lace fan. To conceal her face and head, was a multi-layered royal red lace veil and royal blue circlet. She smiled fondly at it and allowed Altia and a seamstress assistant to dress her. Tradition required that they had to leave her alone for an hour of contemplation until it was time to emerge.

It was late evening and Marilana was meditating again when the seamstress assistant returned to her. It was difficult to see through the veil, but once she was dancing, she would not need to see much anyway.

"It is time," the girl said excitedly.

Marilana followed the girl alone to the entrance hall. Her guards had been forbidden from accompanying her so that no one would be able to identify her. When she approached the doors to the great hall, she could make out two women in identical black gowns with black veils and a woman in a royal blue gown with inset royal red skirt panels and veil. Marilana took a deep calming breath and focused on the ceremony ahead. Soon after she arrived, the doors opened a little and Master Castant stuck his head out. He motioned, and the two women in black entered. The doors closed behind them. Inside the great hall the music changed. It sounded like the courtship dance, but with playful additional stanzas. After a few minutes, the doors opened wide.

The nobles gathered around the room, but Marilana had difficulty distinguishing their faces. Squinting, she realized that the nobles were wearing masks. She smiled with understanding. Marquiese had turned the ball into a masquerade so it would be harder to figure out who of the daughters were missing. Looking further into the hall, she saw King Rylan standing alone on the dais looking regal in a royal blue suit.

The two women in black curtseyed to her and the other woman waiting in the entrance hall. Then one of them took Marilana by her paws and danced her forward. Marilana turned her attention to the dance area in the middle of the room. Six women knelt in a ring facing the watching crowd of nobles. Like Marilana, each wore a unique gown in royal blue and royal red with her face concealed behind a royal red veil. Each woman clutched a large white lace fan. In the center of the ring, Marquiese stood facing the dais wearing royal blue pants and a royal red coat embroidered with gold. Marilana smiled at his back as she danced with the woman in black and took her place in the ring around him.

She inhaled deeply and focused on the dance. The two women in black danced past her around the ring. When they danced past again, they had Marquiese by the paws and danced him around the ring of kneeling women. There was a pause in the music followed by the proper strains signaling the start of the courtship dance. Marilana focused on the sound of dancing and waited. Soon one of women in black stepped in front of her and gently touched her shoulder. Marilana raised her fan as Marquiese danced with the woman on her right. The woman in black moved to the left, and Marquiese stepped in front of her. She rose immediately and flowed into the motions of the dance smoothly following Marquiese's lead while keeping the fan between them in High Style. He turned away from her and she froze in place. He danced with the woman on her left and then moved around the ring guided by the second woman in black. Marilana waited, controlling her breathing, and did not move. The music picked up to a slightly faster pace. The first woman in black touched her shoulder, alerting her that her turn was next. Marquiese spun to her and she flowed with him in the proper steps of the dance before he moved on again.

In the pause between her turns, Marilana wondered briefly if Marquiese could somehow recognized her. She knew he was honest and would not have cheated by sneaking a peak at her dress in the seamstress' work rooms, but they had danced together many times before. Then again, all of the daughters had been chosen because they were good dancers. Even if there were some quality that allowed him to recognize her, he could not indicate it to her. Nor could she somehow tell him who she was. According to the rules she had read and agreed to, any variation to the dance from her—whether to gain attention or to sabotage another—would lead to her dismissal. Likewise, if Marquiese were to add something special for only one of the dancers, that girl would be immediately removed. The rules were harsh to prevent cheating, and were probably one of the reasons the Dance was unpopular among the young royals. It gave the participants very little freedom as everything was proscribed. There was one thing Marilana could control––she could dance her very best. She returned her focus to the music as her turn came again.

The dance continued the same way with each round speeding up, pushing the dancers to keep up. In between her turns, Marilana steadied her breathing and conserved her strength. In the sixth round the woman to her left stumbled slightly. The second woman in black took her by the paws and danced her out of the ring. Marilana's turn to dance came faster now; she had less time to slow her breathing. In the twelfth round the woman on her right bowed her head while gasping for breath and was danced out of the ring. She could not see any of the others and had no idea how many of the women had been removed from the ring. She was beginning to lose control of her breathing and by the fourteenth round her knee was throbbing. She gritted her teeth and moved into the fast steps of the fifteenth round. It seemed Marquiese had barely spun away when he stepped back in front of her again. She focused and flowed with the music. He spun away again, and this time there was a gasp from the nobles.

Marilana did not have time to wonder what had happened. Marquiese was back and she was dancing again. This time he did not spin away. Together they danced faster and faster until he faltered slightly, and she realized that she was about to out-dance him. She had been able to rest in between her turns, while he had been dancing the whole time and was tired from his efforts. With a flourish of her fan, she dropped to one knee and placed the fan on the floor at his feet. The music ended in a crescendo. She remained where she knelt breathing hard and waiting for something to happen. Marquiese knelt in front of her and, taking her paw in his, encouraged her to stand. He heaved deep breaths as he bowed to her. Her knee was trembling so much, she wasn't sure it would hold her as she curtseyed in reply.

Holding tightly to his paw for support, Marilana followed his lead and turned to the nobles. Marilana squinted through the veil and watched as the two women in black moved from woman to woman and replaced the heavy red veils with white lace veils revealing the identity of each participant in turn and indicating that they were available for courtship. The crowd graciously clapped for each of the young women, but there was a tension in the crowd as everyone wanted to know who stood holding the Prince's paw. Finally, the two women in black approached Marquiese. He reached out with one paw and lifted each of their black veils in turn without releasing Marilana's paw. He bowed to each of them in thanks for directing the Dance. Marilana smiled as Ailse and Lorlina curtseyed to him.

Marquiese turned to her and Marilana lowered her eyes. The silent air was thick with expectation as Ailse and

Lorlina approached her. A hiss of muttering broke out but was quickly lost in applause as the veil was lifted from her face and left to hang down around her head. Marilana raised her eyes to meet Marquiese's proud gaze and any sound from the crowd became a dim hum in her awareness. He was all that mattered. She curtseyed to him again and he bowed as the musicians struck the beginning chords of a waltz. With a smile he swept her into the slower dance.

The gentle dance eased away the tension in her mind, and cooled her over used muscles, allowing them both the chance to recover slightly from the strain of the Ceremony. They ended the waltz in front of the dais and together they turned to face King Rylan. Marquiese bowed as Marilana curtseyed. Without a word King Rylan stepped to them and tied a blue and red cord around their joined paws. Marilana curtseyed with a small smile as Marquiese bowed again. They repeated the show of respect in front of Lady Annabella and her green and silver cord was also tied firmly around their paws signaling that the royal courtship was accepted by both families. Marquiese turned and bowed to the assembly and Marilana curtseyed beside him. The nobles clapped in appreciation of the show, some more enthusiastically than others. The musicians signaled the end of the ceremony with a trumpet salute and started playing a reel.

Marilana smiled as the lordlings descended upon the women in blue and red gowns. Many of the women who had participated in the Royal Courtship Dance had frustrated tears in their eyes and shot her dark looks. The lordlings soon gave them other concerns to think about as they pulled them out to the floor to dance. As a condition of the Dance, no bans now restricted the participants from courtships and the lordlings appeared to be taking full advantage of the openings. Marquiese led her around the room by their joined paws. Together they greeted the nobles and received many congratulations. Marilana glanced to the dance floor when the musicians struck the beginning notes of the courtship dance. She smiled as she spotted two black gowned figures flourishing pure white fans. She looked at Marquiese and found him watching the dancers as well. He met her gaze with a twinkle of mirth in his eyes.

Looking at his handsome face in that moment of shared understanding she realized that they were truly bound together. Giddy relief swept through her making her sway slightly. She had healed, had danced her best, and had won the right to hold his paw in public, but it was more than just achieving this courtship. She had a secure future. For the first time in her life, she had a path firmly under her feet that she wanted and had gained for herself. A road to travel that had its dangers and threats, but that could not be traded at someone else's whim. She was mistress of her own fate and she had grasped a future with a handsome lion who deeply loved her.

The masquerade ball continued well into the early morning hours. Marquiese felt happier than he had for fifnights. He could relax now that Marilana had managed to out-dance the other Daughters. He was full of energy but could see that behind Marilana's smile and poise, she was drained. He had been carefully steadying her occasional swaying and bouts of trembling ever since the end of the Dance, but she was beginning to lean on him more fully. Marquiese felt they had stayed long enough and led Marilana to King Rylan. Together they retired from the hall.

"I know you are tired," Marquiese said quietly as they followed King Rylan, "but there is something I want to show you."

Marilana squeezed his paw and glanced at him curiously as he led her through the doors to the Royal Family Apartments.

King Rylan stopped at the door to his rooms and turned to them. He untied the cords joining their paws.

"I could not be prouder of both of you," he said smiling at them. "You have gained much during this past year. You saved the kingdom, you protected my life. You have suffered and sacrificed to stand together. Tonight, you have officially gained the right to show your affection for each other."

King Rylan gave Marquiese the green and silver cord. "I still have the blue and yellow cord that bound my paw and your Mother's when she accepted my courtship. My father told me some advice that night, and I will now pass on that advice to you."

"Keep this cord in remembrance of where Marilana comes from. You have a duty to her to remember her past and her loyalties. Do not put her in a position where she has to pick you over her family, or you will regret every moment that follows."

"I hear and understand, Father," Marquiese replied quietly.

King Rylan turned to Marilana and gave her the red and blue cord.

"Keep this cord as a reminder of where your duty lies," he said gently. "You have chosen to leave your home and family behind. You have accepted the responsibility of helping Marquiese rule the kingdom. Do not force him to choose you over his duty, or you will regret every moment that follows."

"I understand, Sire. Thank you," Marilana replied.

King Rylan smiled and kissed Marilana on the forehead.

"I am looking forward to having you here as part of our family," he smiled at her. "I never allowed Prinka or Frishka to enter these apartments. I never felt comfortable enough, like it was a betrayal of Sahry's love. You have just accepted Marquiese's courtship, and already I want you to be here. You are the first woman other than servants to be allowed past the doors since Marquiese's mother died. Welcome, dear heart, I hope you can come to feel at home here with us."

"Thank you," Marilana smiled, her eyes brimming with tears.

King Rylan cupped her cheek and looked at Marquiese.

"Do not keep her up too long," he said opening the door behind him and leaving them alone.

"Come," Marquiese smiled at Marilana and again took her paw in his. "I have wanted to bring you here since my time in the Southern Tip. You shared your secret places with me, and I want to share mine with you."

He led her up several flights of stairs before turning to her.

"Close your eyes," he said gently.

She smiled ruefully at him but closed her eyes. He took both her paws and led her up the last steps and into the highest tower room. He guided her past the low furniture and released her paws. He shuttered the lamp so the light from the fireplace was the only light in the room. He leaned on the low back of a couch and watched her.

"Open your eyes," he said softly.

Marilana scanned her surroundings in open unfiltered awe. She turned and slowly walked around the room investigating the low furniture and tall stand lamps as well as the endless star-filled blackness high above the lantern dotted gardens. She walked past the windows three times before she stopped and looked north, toward the constellation of The Goddess, the symbol of peace and hope. The very spot that had been his mother's favorite. His heart raced as he gazed at Marilana silhouetted by the stars. His Marilana. Quietly he stood and nestled up behind her. She leaned back against him and he wrapped his arms around her. She sighed and rested her head on his chest. It felt so good to hold her, to feel her warmth against him.

"I played here as a child," he whispered. "This was my mother's favorite view, the unassuming night and uncountable stars, and it is mine as well. I frequently come here to think, as does my father. No distractions, only possibilities. I am so happy that you have finally seen it."

"It is amazing," she whispered. "Thank you for sharing it with me."

"I will enjoy sharing it with you in the years to come, my love," he whispered.

She twisted around in his arms and looked up at him beaming. He gazed into her eyes and kissed her long and lovingly.

Epilogue

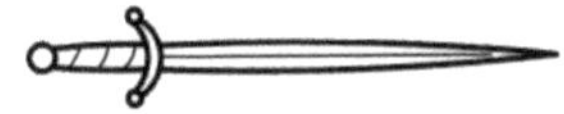

Marquiese scooped Marilana up in his arms and carried her up the lantern-lit steps of Mercurer Manor, a half-hour drive into the country south of Maefair. Her laughter rang out warm and sweet as she wrapped her arms around his neck.

"Welcome, Marilana Mercurer, to our home for the next three months," he said strolling into the entrance hall. "My father and I have not spent much time here since my mother died. She loved to come here in the late summer just to spend time with her family. The manor felt empty to me as I grew up. I am so happy we can give it new life."

She scanned the manor with interest as Marquiese carried her up the stairs to the second floor. Marquiese was pleased to see that the staff had prepared well for their arrival. The skillfully carved wooden tables were freshly polished and the ancient tapestries were clean. The candelabra were free of cobwebs and every available surface had a porcelain or crystal vase with fresh spring flowers scenting the air with the smells of new life. It was not as opulent as some of the castles and manors they had visited during the past year-—there was very little gold or silver to be seen—but it was regally beautiful.

It had been a very busy time since the Royal Courtship Dance, it hardly seemed like over a full year had passed. They had traveled to all the provinces, visiting the great-noble families. He was very pleased with how well Marilana had comported herself. It had been pleasant to visit the Roana and Castant estates, and the visits to the Southern Tip had afforded them some time to relax. He smiled fondly remembering how Marilana had engaged Lorlina and Lady Nya in a lively debate over a rare old book at the Roana castle. Lady Nya had been impressed with the young girls' scholarly insights. At the Castant estates Marilana had been elated to see the extensive rose arbor Lord Castant treasured, and Lord Castant had been thrilled when Ailse had enlisted Marilana's advice on growing and caring for roses. Marilana had even enhanced her reputation during the less than amiable visits to the Arndt and Lotal Estates. She had cordially joined Lady Arndt in discussing the newest fashions, and as a result had been invited to visit whenever she needed to. At the Lotal Estates, she quickly developed a positive rapport with Lady Lotal, who had unceremoniously dismissed Master Lotal for interrupting their conversation. Marquiese knew Master Lotal would cause them problems, but Marilana had taken steps to limit the scope of those problems for a time by earning Lady Lotal's respect.

Then there had been the Royal visits. Many of the Royals from the allied kingdoms had visited Maefair to meet his potential bride. King Carloth and Prince Dansho had congratulated him on finding such a worthy woman after spending several hours talking with Marilana. Marquiese had been worried when Princess Clara and Marilana had taken a long walk in the gardens since their first encounter had been so disastrous, but Clara had surprised him by threatening him with her wrath if he mistreated Marilana. Even Prince Zandor had made an appearance. Marquiese had gained a new respect for Zandor after the three of them had spent a day in the library discussing topics ranging from law to jousting and battle tactics. Marilana had laughed easily after dinner that night when Zandor had told her that he would gladly marry her if Marquiese let her go. Marquiese had glared in mock anger when Zandor winked mischievously at him. Marquiese had completely agreed when Marilana had said Zandor would be a good ally, but she also cautioned that he was too cunning to trust explicitly. Most of the royals had approved of his choice; some had even said Marilana reminded them of his mother, or that Sahry would have liked her. He cherished the thought that his mother would have loved to have Marilana join her family.

The last month of winter had been the busiest month yet. They had been fitted for many sets of clothes and had gone to many dances. They had attended the wedding of Commander Lorne and Palace Maid Altia as guests of honor to the humble proceedings. Then they had traveled to the Roana Castle, where they stood with Ailse and Enton as witnesses to the union of Lorlina and Timral. The party that followed was a grand event equally matched the next fifnight when they had stood with Lorlina and Timral as witnesses to the union of Ailse and Enton at the Castant Castle. They had enjoyed celebrating with their friends and at the same time had been preparing for the highlight of the new year taking place in Maefair on the first day of spring.

That very day, Earek had joined Enton, Ailse, Timral, and Lorlina for the privilege of standing as witnesses to their union. Marquiese glanced at Marilana and smiled broadly as he remembered watching her glide toward him in the great hall of the palace. She had smiled nervously as she had joined him and faced Father Iscoot. The marriage ceremony had been perfect. King Rylan even placed the Princess' circlet of carved silver flowers on Marilana's head and kissed her on the cheek. The nobles had been respectful, but the people of the city were overjoyed. The people celebrated extravagantly in the streets, enjoying the warm, and unusually dry weather of the early spring.

Marquiese entered the large sitting room and set Marilana gently on her feet. She brushed his cheek with her paw and studied the room. A train of servants entered with their luggage and Marquiese went to the sideboard to pour two glasses of white wine. He sipped his wine and smiled with amusement as Marilana investigated the windows, walls, and furnishings. She moved regally in her gold-embroidered white gown. The circlet of silver flowers on her head glittered in the light of the lamps. If their children took after their mother in looks and intelligence, he would be the happiest lion alive. She caught him staring at her and beamed in return. The serving women giggled as the head maid chivied them out of the room. Marquiese sighed with relief when they were finally alone.

Marilana opened the doors to the next room. "What is this about?" she asked.

Marquiese picked up the second glass of wine and joined Marilana in the bedroom. He chuckled at the large pile of blankets and pillows on the floor where the bed should have been. Marilana frowned at his lack of response and watched him set the glasses on a side table. He opened a cabinet and slid open a hidden wooden panel reveling a metal mechanism that when manipulated correctly unlocked the doors of a small blue velvet cushioned compartment. Marilana approached him and peered over his shoulder. He turned to her and lifted the silver circlet from her head. He placed it carefully inside the compartment next to his gold circlet and then relocked the cabinet. Marilana shot him a mischievous glance and turned away. He watched her slip off her white gloves and turned to take another sip of wine. He removed his gold coat and draped it over a chair, then sat down and pulled off his white boots.

"Marquiese," Marilana inquired innocently, "can you help me with this?"

Marquiese frowned, suspicious at the tone of her voice, and looked up. He blushed upon seeing her standing by the pillows and blankets unbuttoning the back of her gown. His stomach flipped over, and his heart raced as he stepped up behind her.

"What can I help you with?" he asked suddenly nervous.

"Why these buttons, of course. I cannot reach them all," she said with that innocent lilt.

He fumbled with the rows of tiny pearl buttons. After he undid the last one, he gently slid his paws up her back tracing the scars that crisscrossed her skin. She trembled slightly at his touch and he realized she was just as nervously excited as he was.

"It is called a love nest," he whispered softly. "The servants remove the bed and leave the nest of blankets as a way of showing their happiness for the newlyweds; it's a playful prank."

He slid the gown off her shoulders, and the dress dropped to the floor. Marquiese's breathing quickened as he gazed down at her lovely figure and watched transfixed as her tail swished back and forth. She turned, smiled at him, and slid her paws up under his shirt.

"How do you know about this love nest?" she asked lifting his white shirt over his head.

"My father and the northern lords teased me about it," he replied wrapping his arms around her and pulling her close. "They also warned me that the wardrobes and luggage are probably empty."

"I hope you do not need their advice on what to do with the love nest," she teased.

"We will just have to find out together," he smiled and kissed her.

*

"Good morning, Husband," Marilana said when Marquiese opened his eyes.

"Good morning, Princess Marilana," he replied. "It is truly wonderful to wake up next to you, Wife."

He smiled, rolled on top of her, and kissed her. She returned his kiss and then suddenly flipped them over so that she straddled his stomach.

"Come on," she said thumping his chest, "I smell breakfast."

He reached for her, but she sprang away and landed on her feet, laughing in glee. He flashed her a rueful smile and then rolled up onto his knees. He approached the wardrobe and flung the door open. As expected, it was empty; the servants had made their luggage disappear. Marilana opened the bedroom door and smiled. He followed her out to the sitting room, chuckling as he went.

A large copper tub sat next to a heavily-laden breakfast table. There were no chairs by the table. The tub was filled with steaming water and two fluffy white towels were neatly folded on the table next to the food. Marilana gestured for him to go first. He gave her a small bow and stepped into the water. The hot water felt good, and he leaned back with a sigh. He laughed heartily when Marilana stepped into the tub and plopped onto his lap facing him. She wrapped her legs around his waist and then grabbed a pawful of grapes from the table.

"This is what the servants of the Southern Tip call a breakfast bath," she smiled and delicately fed him a grape.

They took turns feeding each other a breakfast consisting of warm breads and jam, fresh fruits, and rolled meats until the bathwater cooled. Just as they were about to climb out of the tub, there was a knock on the door. Frowning Marilana leaned forward against Marquiese. He wrapped his arms around her. The door opened a little and a serving man backed into the room.

"Please forgive the intrusion, Highnesses," the goat said. "There is a man here who claims to be a priest. He wishes to speak with you. He says it is of utmost importance, and it would be in your best interest to see him immediately. Here are some clothes for you."

The goat set the pile of clothes on the sideboard and retreated back to the door. Marquiese felt Marilana stiffen in his arms and he saw anger rising in her eyes. She nodded in resignation and he sighed.

"Very well," he said with a slight growl, "give us a few moments to make ourselves presentable."

"Yes, Highness," the serving man bowed to the door and scurried out of the room.

They dried themselves and gathered the clothes left for them. Marquiese pulled on white pants and shirt. He retrieved his sword belt from the bedroom and glanced at Marilana; she looked beautiful in the simple white dress. She returned a tight smile and he noticed she grasped the hilt of a dagger in one paw. He wondered how many weapons she had managed to hide in their rooms while he had been sleeping. After the disastrous encounter with Frishka when she had trusted Lady Annabella's insistence to leave her weapons in the Southern Tip, she concealed weapons wherever she went. He did not mind; he always had his sword with him for his own protection. He grasped the bell cord hanging above the sideboard and rang it before moving to stand a few paces from Marilana, giving them both room to maneuver if necessary. A few seconds later the door opened, and an ancient tiger was escorted in by two of Marilana's men wearing their new Queen's Guard uniforms.

"We will speak privately," the tiger growled.

When Marquiese glanced at Marilana, he was not surprised to see hatred written on her face. He had suspected the "priest" was one of the Hungdie. Now he knew it was the priest who had spoken with Marilana as a child. Marilana gave a slight nod without taking her eyes off the tiger. Marquiese suppressed a sigh and motioned for the guards to leave. They went reluctantly.

"So, it is true," the Hungdie said leering at Marilana. "You are the one that he almost got to keep."

"I should kill you where you stand," Marilana growled.

"I am here under a flag of truce," he flashed a sinister smile.

"Then speak your business and be gone," Marquiese commanded.

When the tiger turned his eyes on Marquiese, he could see the pain and greed glinting there. The Hungdie smiled menacingly at him. Marquiese's hackles stood on end and he understood why Marilana had spoken of the man with such fear and loathing.

"I have come, Marquiese Mercurer," the man said darkly, "because you slew one of my order, one of the Hungdie. We are an order of talented assassins. We place great value on individual ability and accordingly acknowledge your skill. Normally the defeat of one of the Hungdie by a target secures the target family three generations of peace; however, as this was the fourth attempt on the family Mercurer to have been defeated in twelve successive generations, the name of Mercurer has been added to the *Book of the Painless*."

Just then a knock sounded on the door. The tiger frowned darkly. Without waiting for a reply, the door opened, and King Rylan stood on the threshold. He surveyed the room and scowled at Marilana's threatening expression focused on the stranger.

"Please join us, Rylan Mercurer," the tiger said and waited.

Marquiese saw his father bristle at the lack of respect. Rylan glanced at the dagger in Marilana's grip and closed the door. He walked over to join Marquiese and faced the stranger.

"What is this about?" Rylan asked quietly.

"I was informing your son that the name of Mercurer has been added to the *Book of the Painless*," the Hungdie said in irritation. "The *Book of the Painless* is where we record the names of the families that have been deemed our peers outside of the Realm of Pain. We do not hunt our peers. From now until the lineage of your blood is broken, all members of the family Mercurer are deemed beyond our interference."

"That includes your new wife, much to our regret," the tiger added darkly without looking at Marilana. "These letters outline our forbearance from hunting your descendants and are marked with the Seal of Blood and Pain. I will leave you now."

The Hungdie placed the letters on the table and turned toward the door. Rylan started to speak, but Marquiese touched his arm stopping him. They let him leave in peace. Marquiese walked to Marilana and gently rested his paw on her shoulder. She trembled as she set the dagger on the table, and then buried her face in his shoulder and wept quietly. He held her protectively and looked at his father.

"The servants said you had received a visit from a man calling himself a priest and suggested that I enter immediately. I take it he was a priest of the Hungdie," Rylan said darkly.

Marquiese nodded with surprise that Rylan acknowledged the assassin's order.

"It seems I need to apologize to you both," Rylan said seriously. "I came here today to confirm that our family was in danger from the Hungdie, and that I have known about it since my father died. From your reaction, Marilana, this man was not a stranger to you, and you knew the danger he posed.

"You knew about the Hungdie hunting us?" Marquiese asked as Marilana dried her tears.

"Yes, my father told me that he was the third generation, and that the Hungdie would hunt me and my family after he passed away. I have letters very much like those on the table indicating which generations have previously been protected. For years I have been watching for them to make an attempt on my life."

"Newrothen was Hungdie," Marilana said shakily.

"Who?" Rylan looked puzzled.

"The man we knew as Frishka's Confidante," Marquiese said. "He told Marilana his plans and how he had been attempting to get to us all those years he was in the palace. His death at my paws is what caused this encounter today. We did not mention his identity to you because of your disdain for the subject. I suspected you knew more than you were telling but chose not to pursue the issue. Marilana unfortunately has previously encountered the man who just left. She told me everything she knew about the Hungdie shortly after she killed Frishka."

Marilana stood straighter, focusing on Rylan. Marquiese kept his arm around her waist as she related her previous experience and all the things Newrothen had told her. She made no attempt to pull away from him. When she was finished, they watched Rylan pace.

"I was a fool to think I knew what I was facing," Rylan said darkly. "I should have learned more, and I should have pursued a better answer from you, Marilana, instead of trying to block the topic. I realize now that I could have learned much from your investigations. I am sorry you both had to face these terrors." He turned to face them. "I cannot express how proud I am of the strength you have shown. Can you forgive me for not warning you sooner?"

"Of course," they said together, and each embraced him.

"Even if you had warned us," Marilana said more calmly, "we may not have been able to stop the events that happened. I had my suspicions about Newrothen before I met him, and still walked right into his trap."

"You did as you felt necessary, and no good can come from holding on to your feelings of shame. We all learned lessons from that time and we have moved on with our lives," King Rylan said gently.

He smiled at them as he placed one large paw on Marquiese's shoulder and cupped Marilana's cheek with fondness. They returned his smile warmly. Marquiese was heartened by his father's affection for them.

"On a more encouraging topic, Lady Annabella did not wish to intrude upon your mood yesterday, so she asked me to let you know that Master Earek, or Master Ranat as we should call him now, received word yesterday morning that the farmers beyond the southern border have accepted the trade treaty. They have chosen to call themselves the Farmers Union and have chosen a tracker by the name of Rodan to lead them. Master Ranat seemed pleased by the choice," Rylan said.

Marilana smiled. Marquiese could detect tension in her eyes, but also pride for her Brother and pleasure at Rodan's elevation to leadership. He was glad that Earek was continuing Marilana's work to decrease the bandit presence in the Southern Tip. Earek would make an excellent lord and ally.

"I also wanted to tell you that last night during the festivities, many nobles approached me and told me that they have chosen to support the new laws you both proposed," Rylan said. "The one most easily accepted has been the change to the treason law stating that individuals charged with treason are placed in the custody of the magistrates' court not any one individual. The lords and ladies have said that it is much less likely to be abused that way. The other law is not so well-liked. Most of them see the positive effects of protecting the lower castes from being abused by the upper castes, but they also do not like that the upper castes can be called to account for their actions. Some think the possible loss of rank for taking an individual against their will is too extreme. You were correct though, Marilana, by presenting your arguments the way you did this last year, the majority have decided to support the law. You both have done very well with these new laws. I am proud of you."

"I will return to the palace now and put these letters in a secure location," he said becoming serious again, "but remember that the protection these letters represent are only good as long as the blood lineage is unbroken. You cannot forget to be watchful."

"The Hungdie are only one group of assassins," Marilana said gravely. "While they are probably the most dangerous and cruel, there are other assassins. I will not forget that Frishka was not Hungdie, he was just power hungry and others like him will try to gain power at all costs. I will continue to be vigilant against all threats to my family and I intend to teach my offspring vigilance and strategy."

"Your words lighten my heart," Rylan smiled and kissed her forehead.

Rylan picked up the letters and Marquiese walked him to the door.

"And speaking of offspring," Rylan winked at them, "I think you need to find some more inventive ways to get the most out of your love nest."

Marquiese's face flushed as his father closed the door. He glanced at Marilana and she grinned, color high in her cheeks.

"Our children. I like the sound of that," Marilana said quietly. "They will be a bit stubborn and proud, I am sure, just like their father."

"As beautiful and deadly as their mother," Marquiese replied.

They relaxed as they gazed at each other, and then with a mischievous twinkle in her eyes, Marilana grasped her skirt and dashed toward the bedroom.

"Only if you can catch me," Marilana laughed over her shoulder.

Marquiese beamed and pulled his shirt off, chasing after her.

Appendix

Note on Time

The world in which Redsands is located varies slightly from our own planet of Earth. In Redsands, they have 24 hours in a day, but as most people cannot afford to own a clock, the daily schedule is based on the position of the sun in the sky. This system works fairly well as the difference in amount of daylight between summer and winter is only two hours. The clocks are therefore calibrated at High Noon when the sun reaches its highest point in the sky, also called its zenith. So the difference between High Noon and the common noon, is only a difference in language. However, how a person uses language can give clues about the individual. Most of the population uses dawn, dusk, and noon as references for the time of day. Those who are accustomed to clocks will measure in hours before or after these references. When compared to a clock, the exact time of dawn and dusk changes throughout the year, but the daily schedule still uses these points as references since many activities require light. Candles, lanterns, and oil lamps can provide light for some activities, but candles and lamp oil are considered luxuries due to their expense, and are used sparingly by most. Other time-of-day references used to indicate passage of time include mid-morning, mid-afternoon, and midnight. Trackers, scouts, bandits, peasants, and others who spend much of their time in the outdoors can learn to measure the passage of time by watching the change of the length and direction of shadows or the movement of the stars and moon.

Note on Calendar

Redsands has a year consisting of 390 days. The year is broken into 13 months of 30 days each. Each month has 6 fifnights of 5 days, making 78 fifnights per year. The first day of the fifnight is called Restday, and every month starts on a Restday. The other days of the fifnight are indicated by counting from Restday. School is held for the local children four days a fifnight for ten months, excluding three months of summer break and two fifnights for the New Year. Children attending school may also indicate the day of fifnight by indicating the day of the school fifnight. So the third day of the fifnight could also be indicated as the second day after Restday, or the second day of the school fifnight. Calendars, like clocks are a luxury not found in most homes. Months are indicated in reference to important annual events and the changing of the seasons. Each season is three months plus seven days with an equinox day at the beginning of spring and fall. Specific events are indicated by telling what day of the fifnight and how many fifnights or months before or after a reference day.

List of Important Days

*All days referenced by month from New Year for consistency of this list.

New Year—1st day of 1st month (start of 2nd month of winter)

School resumes after New Year break—2nd day of 3rd fifnight after New Year

Spring Equinox—8th day of 3rd month

First day of Spring—day after Spring Equinox

Last day of school year (Exhibition Dance)—last day of 5th month

First day of Summer—Restday of 4th fifnight of 6th month

National Day of Worship—Restday of 2nd fifnight of 7th month

First day of school year—2nd day of 1st fifnight of 9th month

Fall Equinox—3rd day of 5th fifnight of 9th month

First day of Fall—day after Fall Equinox

Annual Tournament in Maefair—4th day of 6th fifnight of 12th month

Tournament Ball—day after tournament, last day of 12th month

First day of Winter—1st day of 13th month

Winter Council in Maefair—last day of year, last day of 13th month

Last day of school for New Year break—last day of year

Note on Rank

Rank in Redsands is determined by birth and by merit. Birth determines caste: peasant, low-class merchant, mid-class merchant, high-class merchant, landed-gentry, noble, high-noble, great-noble, royal. Adoption and marriage are the primary ways to gain a higher caste. Disowning from family and abdication of duty will result in a drop in caste. When a non-heir child comes of age, they drop in caste unless they marry an heir to a caste title. Marriage grants the rights of the higher caste heir; these rights remain if widowed, but are lost in cases of divorce.

Rank within caste is determined by merit. Respect and common consensus are the currency of rank. In the peasant caste there is very little change in rank from orphans at the lowest to upper servants at the highest. Peasant rank is determined by wealth and hired position; these can be very fluid, causing drastic shifts in very short time. Successful farmers who own lots of land and upper servants who oversee other servants garnering the highest wages are granted the highest rank. With the merchant caste, the rank is a reflection of wealth and position on the Merchant Council. Possession of a Family Name is a token of respect from the royal family and grants higher rank. The ability to maintain financial wealth influences the respect of the community and can grant higher rank as well. With the noble castes, from landed-gentry to great-noble, rank is granted by size of land governed and by respect from other nobles and the royal family.

The soldier class works within and outside the caste system. Soldiers are treated with respect according to rank, but are not granted the rights of the castes. For example, an officer (Lieutenant, Major, Captain, etc.) may speak up in public and attend gatherings as an equal to the merchant caste. However, an officer is only granted the rights of land ownership equal to a peasant and are not able to speak to the Merchant Council regarding laws or leadership. All of the children of soldiers of any rank are considered peasants.

Rank among soldiers is granted by merit alone. All soldier recruits start out as simple guardsmen. As they prove themselves worthy, they can be promoted. Officers are treated with the respect granted to the merchant castes. Knights of the Realm are treated with the respect granted to the noble castes. Soldiers must have a liege to whom they owe allegiance and from whom they take orders. Knights of the Realm can be soldiers or can be individuals of any caste, but they must accept the leadership and regulations of the Brotherhood of Knights to claim the title of Knight. Those who have proven themselves through competition of arms are granted the highest ranks. For example, Zariff is a Knight of the Realm who won many competitions and who has proven himself a very capable officer by gaining the position of Captain-General, he is therefore treated with respect equal to a great-noble, but is only granted the rights of property ownership equal to a peasant.

Characters Around Redsands

Maefair:

The kingdom of Redsands and the province of Maefair (mā-fair) are ruled by the royal family Mercurer.

Rylan Mercurer—rī-lan mər-kyər-ər—[lion] King of Redsands. Son of Coryan, father of Marquiese, descendant of the ancient queen Maebala (mā-bah-lah). Rank: royal leader of Redsands, none stand higher within the kingdom.

Marquiese Mercurer—mär-kwēs mər-kyər-ər —[lion] Crown Prince of Redsands. Son of King Rylan and Queen Sahry. Posed as first son to Merchant Colbran, with his wife Adealy and daughter Lida in Mystillion for nearly three years. Friend of Marilana and Earek. Rank: royal heir to the throne of Redsands, second only to King Rylan.

Sahry Mercurer—sah-rē mər-kyər-ər—[lioness] deceased Queen of Redsands. Wife of King Rylan until death, mother of Marquiese. Rank: second to king, equal to crown heir.

Others of Maefair:

Lord Threine—threyn—[oryx] high-noble ruler of the city of Maefair under King Rylan. Rank: high-noble.

Katrine Applurn—kah-treen ap-lurn—[gazelle] noble daughter of Orchard Plain, a township in Brecan county in the province of Maefair. Rank: noble non-heir daughter.

Gwina—gwin-ah—[caracal] Herb Mother, lives and deals herbs in northwestern part of city of Maefair. Great Aunt to Palace Maid Altia. Rank: peasant.

Soldiers of Maefair:

Lorne—lȯrn—[cheetah] captain in the Royal Palace Guards. Rank: solider class equal to noble

Ranold—ran-ald—[leopard] lieutenant in the Royal Palace Guards. Rank: solider class equal to high-class merchant.

Bordou—bohr-doo—[weasel] Errand Rider for the Crown of Redsands. Rank: solider class equal to landed-gentry.

Urdan—ər-dan—[caribou] guardsman of the King's Guard assigned to Marquiese. Rank: solider class equal to high-class merchant.

Karndel—kärn-del—[cheetah] guardsman of the King's Guard assigned to protect Marilana. Rank: solider class equal to high-class merchant.

Royal Palace staff:

Refrona—ree-fr-ō-nah—[grey wolf] Head Maid of the Royal Palace, in charge of all the servants in the palace. Rank: high-class merchant.

Altia—al-tē-ah—[caracal] Royal Palace Maid assigned to help Marilana. Rank: peasant.

Father Iscoot—iz-koot—[leopard] Royal Priest of The Goddess, Head Priest of the Royal Chapel in the Royal Palace of Maefair. Rank: high-class merchant.

Sir Libor—li-bȯr—[snow leopard] Royal Librarian, King's advisor, royal family tutor, rode with the Knights of the Realm. Rank: knight, equal to high-noble.

Strunt—struhnt—[giant anteater] Royal Head Healer, oversees all healers, assistant healers, and novice healers at the Royal Palace Infirmary. Rank: high-class merchant.

Jonwin—jon-win—[reindeer] assistant healer to Healer Strunt. Rank: mid-class merchant.

Others known in Maefair:

Prinka Ebnic—priŋk-ah eb-nik—[tigress] traitor to the throne of Redsands. Former Lady-wife of King Rylan. Mother of Frishka Ebnic. Former non-heir princess of Ankenhun (ahn-kin-hoon). Rank: peasant, traitor, sentenced to banishment from Redsands.

Frishka Ebnic—frish-kah eb-nik—[tiger] traitor to the throne of Redsands. Former Lord of Redsands, second heir to throne of Redsands. Son of Lady Prinka Ebnic, former adopted son of King Rylan, stepbrother of Marquiese. Disowned by royal family of Ankenhun. Rank: peasant, traitor, sentenced to banishment from Redsands.

Confidant/Newrothen—con-fi-dahnt/noo-rawth-en—[lion] assassin of the Hungdie, former second-in-command and companion to Frishka. Banished from Redsands for violence against royalty and nobility. Rank: Adapt of the Hungdie, below Priest but above Initiate, treated as outlaw peasant in continent of Maen.

Saffon—saf-ohn—[goat] former guardsman of the Royal Palace Guards assigned to protect Earek. Rank: peasant.

Southern Tip:

The province of the Southern Tip is ruled by the Great-Noble Family Ranat.

Annabella Ranat—ann-ah-bell-ah ra-nat—[lioness] great-noble ruler of the Southern Tip. Adopted mother to Marilana and Earek. Rank: great-noble, highest of noble caste.

Marilana Ranat—mair-ih-lain-ah—[lioness] bandit hunter known as The Ghost and heiress of Lady Annabella Ranat. Formerly a noble ward equal to landed-gentry but treated as orphan, lowest of peasant caste. Adopted by Lady Annabella Ranat and named as heiress to the Southern Tip. Rank: great-noble heiress.

Earek Ranat—air-ik—[rare black leopard] second heir of Lady Annabella Ranat. Formerly disowned second son of merchant Yulan. Rank: non-heir great-noble son.

Others of the Southern Tip:

Zara—zar-ah—[deer] also called Child and The Phantom, orphan trained to become a bandit hunter by Marilana. Rank: orphan peasant.

Hosten—hōs-ten—[cheetah] Lady Annabella's Head Horse Trainer. Rank: mid-class merchant.

Magus - ma-gəs - [cheetah] Lady Annabella's Head Healer. Rank: mid-class merchant.

Soldiers of the Southern Tip:

Zariff—zär-əf—[lion] commander of all Southern Tip troops in service to Lady Annabella, and a Knight of the Realm. Marilana's and Earek's trainer and mentor. Rank: Captain-General in soldier class, equal to great-noble.

Hayden—hā-den—[black bear] captain of Marilana's personal guardsmen. Rank: captain in soldier class, equal to noble.

Kolt—kohlt—[coyote] one of Marilana's personal guardsmen. Rank: major in soldier class, equal to high-class merchant.

Shaub—shob—[grey wolf] one of Earek's personal guardsmen. Rank: lieutenant in soldier class, equal to mid-class merchant.

Others known in Mystillion:

Brittia—brit-tē-ah—[lynx] daughter heir of merchant Sleater. Rank: high-class merchant heir.

Demdrake—dem-drāke—[lynx] first son of former high-class merchant Branish, cousin to Brittia, Branish's and family's rank and caste lost due to Demdrake's crimes. Rank: peasant.

Working Animals:

Storm—Marilana's white stallion war horse trained by her own paw, only accepts Annabella and Marilana as riders.

Other Provinces of Redsands:

Abdshar:

The province of Abdshar (abd-shär) is ruled by the Great-Noble Family Clain.

Master Clain—clān—[puma] hier of Clain family, rides with the Knights of the Realm, purchased a war horse from Lady Annabella trained by Marilana. Rank: great-noble heir.

Others from Abdshar:

Lord Bostwik—bas-twik—[zebra] elderly head of the High-Noble Family Bostwik, rulers of Pracbar (præk-bar) county in Abdshar province, spend most of his time in Maefair leaving the ruling of Pracbar to his heiress, Marthina. Rank: high-noble.

Lady Bostwik—bas-twik—[zebra] elderly wife of Lord Bostwik, mother of Marthina. Rank: high-noble.

Marthina Bostwik—mahr-thē-nah bas-tiwk—[zebra] only living child of Lord and Lady Bostwik, mother of Phoebe and four more daughters. Rank: high-noble heiress.

Phoebe Bostwik—fee-bee bas-tiwk—[zebra] second daughter of Marthina. Rank: high-noble non-heir daughter.

Draukshar:

The province of Draukshar (drak-shär) is ruled by the Great-Noble Family Castant.

Withers Castant—with-ərs cas-tənt—[leopard] great-noble, rode with Knights of the Realm, former advisor to King Rylan, strong ally to Families Mercurer, Ranat, and Roana. Rank: great-noble.

Enton Castant—en-tən cas-tənt—[leopard] great-noble heir, Noble-Commander of the Royal Palace Garrison, rode with Knights of the Realm, current advisor to King Rylan, strong ally to Prince Marquiese. Rank: great-noble heir.

Cheylotta Castant—shī-lah-tah cas-tənt—[leopard] deceased, mother of Enton, adopted sister of Queen Sahry. Rank: great-noble.

Eastridge:

The province of Eastridge (ēst-ridg) is ruled by the Great-Noble Family Lotal.

Lady Lotal—loh-tawl—[grey fox] head of family Lotal, mother of Master Lotal. Rank: great-noble.

Master Lotal—loh-tawl—[grey fox] rides with the Knights of the Realm. Rank: great-noble heir.

Glancenar:

The province of Glancenar (glahns-nahr) is ruled by the Great-Noble Family Quway.

Lorlina Quway—lohr-lēn-ah kwā—[clouded leopard] one of six adopted daughters of the Quway family, sweetheart of Timral Roana. Rank: great-noble non-heir daughter.

Others from Glancenar:

Graduin—gra-doo-en—[red wolf] former merchant son from Glancenar province, rides with the Knights of the Realm, purchased a war horse from Lady Annabella trained by Marilana. Rank: Knight, equal to high-noble.

Grudent:

The province of Grudent (grü-dent) is ruled by the Great-Noble Family Arndt.

Armen Arndt—är-men ärnt—[jaguar] head of family Arndt, father of Frederick, Warhaim, and Graita. Rank: great-noble.

Frena Arndt—frē-nah ärnt—[jaguar] wife of Armen Arndt, mother of Frederick, Warhaim, and Graita. Rank: great-noble.

Frederick Arndt—fre-drik ärnt—[jaguar] heir of Arndt Family, rides with Knights of the Realm. Rank: great-noble heir.

Warhaim Arndt—wȯr-hām ärnt—[jaguar] rides with Knights of the Realm. Rank: great-noble non-heir son.

Graita Arndt—gra-ē-tah ärnt—[jaguar] only daughter of Armen and Frena. Rank: great-noble non-heir daughter.

Herinsford:

The province of Herinsford (hair-ins-ford) is ruled by the Great-Noble Family Ruberic.

Masod Ruberic—mæs-ad rūb-ər-ik—[leopard] head of Ruberic family (12 members in all), rode with the Knights of the Realm, cousin to Withers Castant. Rank: great-noble.

Ophelia Ruberic—ō-feel-ē-ah rūb-ər-ik—[leopard] eldest child of Masod Ruberic. Rank: great-noble heiress.

Heledia Ruberic—hah-lēdē-ah rūb-ər-ik—[leopard] fourth child of Masod Ruberic, second daughter. Rank: great-noble non-heir daughter.

Mira's Plateau:

The province of Mira's Plateau (mahy-rahs pla-toh) is ruled by the Great-Noble Family Roana.

Amos Roana—ey-muhs rohn-ah—[brown bear] head of Roana Family, rode with the Knights of the Realm, strong ally of Families Mercurer, Castant, and Ranat. Rank: great-noble.

Nya Roana—nī-ah roahn-ah—[brown bear] wife of Amos, mother of Timral, bedridden due to long illness, cannot travel. Rank: great-noble.

Timral Roana—tim-rawl rohn-ah—[brown bear] only child of Amos and Nya, rides with the Knights of the Realm, strong friendship with Enton Castant and Marquiese Mercurer. Rank: great-noble heir.

Others from Mira's Plateau:

Glain—gleyn—[white tiger] farmer of northern forests of Mira's Plateau. Rank: peasant.

Pavlatach:

The province of Pavlatach (pav-lah-tach) is ruled by the Great-Noble Family Inclond.

Clidan Inclond—kli-deyn ingk-lohnd—[elk] only daughter of Lady Inclond, has two older brothers. Rank: great-noble non-heir daughter.

Reine's Crossing:

The province of Reine's Crossing (rens cross-ing) is ruled by the Great-Noble Family Kenhol.

Ianto Kenhol—yan-tō keen-hōl—[leopard] head of Family Kenhol, rode with the Knights of the Realm, father of Banol and Ailse. Rank: great-noble.

Valencia Kenhol—vuh-len-see-ah keen-hōl—[leopard] wife of Ianto, mother of Banol and Ailse. Rank: great-noble.

Banol Kenhol—bān-al keen-hōl—[leopard] son of Ianto and Valencia, rode with Knights of the Realm. Rank: great-noble heir.

Naseema Kenhol—nay-see-mah keen-hōl—[leopard] wife of Banol, mother of Banol's son. Rank: great-noble non-heir daughter.

Ailse Kenhol—ālz keen-hōl—[leopard] daughter of Ianto and Valencia, secret sweetheart of Enton Castant. Rank: great-noble non-heir daughter.

Versith:

The province Versith (vur-sith) is ruled by the Great-Noble Family Doquib.

Serina Doquib—suh-reen-ah doh-kwib—[caribou] adopted daughter of Lord Doquib, has one adopted sister and three adopted brothers. Rank: great-noble non-heir daughter.

Others from Versith:

Master Roatal—roh-tahl—[jaguar] oldest son of High-Noble Family Roatal, rulers of Pandensy county in Versith province, rides with the Knights of the Realm, purchased a war horse from Lady Annabella trained by Marilana. Rank: high-noble heir.

Orthan Roatal—ohr-theyn roh-tahl—[jaguar] second son of High-Noble Family Roatal, rulers of Pandensy county in Versith province, rides with the Knights of the Realm, purchased a war horse from Lady Annabella trained by Marilana. Rank: high-noble non-heir son.

Frauh—frou—[antelope] rides with the Knights of the Realm, serves Great-Noble Family Doquib as Captain of Versith Home Guard. Rank: captain in soldier class and Knight, equal to high-noble.

West Cove:

The province of West Cove is ruled by the Great-Noble Family Flaznek.

Lord Flaznek—flaz-nek—[elk] head of Great-Noble Family Flaznek, owns the largest fishing fleet in Redsands. Rank: great-noble.

Others from West Cove:

Tavin Breltic—tav-in brel-tik—[eland] third child of High-Noble Family Breltic, rulers of Coal Bend county in West Cove province, rides with the Knights of the Realm, purchased a war horse from Lady Annabella trained by Marilana. Rank: high-noble heir.

From Outside Redsands:

Carloth—kär-lawth—[lion] King of Precinlia (pre-sin-lē-ah), close ally of Redsands, border north of Maefair.

Considered friend to King Rylan and Lady Annabella. Father of Clara. Rank: royal, equal to King Rylan, none stand higher in Precinlia.

Clara—klair-ah—[lioness] Crown Princess of Precinlia. Daughter of Carloth. Grew up in friendship with Marquiese and Dansho. Rank: royal heiress to throne of Precinlia, equal to Marquiese, second only to Carloth in Precinlia.

Dansho—dan-shō—[lion] Prince of Lentier (len-tē-ər), close ally of Redsands, border farthest west of Redsands. Grew up in friendly rivalry with Marquiese. Rank: second prince, royal standing below heir but above great-noble.

Zandor—zan-dȯr—[lion] Crown Prince of Coandor (cō-andȯr), member of allied kingdoms with Redsands, but has strained relations with Precinlia. Grew up in strong rivalry with Marquiese and Dansho. Rank: royal heir to throne of Coandor, equal to Marquiese, second only to Queen of Coandor.

Akadine—ah-kā-dē-in—[oryx] Prince of Rucdign (rūc-dyn), member of allied kingdoms with Redsands, situated north of Precinlia. Fierce personal rivalry with Dansho. Rank: fourth prince, royal standing below heir but above great-noble, slightly lower than Dansho.

Rodan—roh-dan—[red fox] mercenary tracker of the Great Mountains south of the Southern Tip. Rank: peasant outlaw.

Haspar Lapidis—hahs-pahr lap-ih-dis—[lion] scholar of the Great Mountains south of the Southern Tip, granted Family name Lapidis in order to expedite communication with King Rylan, blood father of Marilana. Rank: peasant.

Priest of the Hungdie—[tiger] assassin and teacher of the Hungdie, met with Marilana as a child. Rank: Priest of the Hungdie, above Adapt but below High Priest, treated as outlaw peasant in continent of Maen.

Acknowledgments

This book would not have been possible without the help and support of so many people. As always, I must mention my wonderful husband who has supported and encouraged me and has been my most solid sounding board, as well as my sons, for always reminding me that there is more life to live. I must also thank all the fans who have read Mystillion and Maefair and are quietly, or not so quietly, demanding this third part of Marilana's and Marquiese's journey. You all are my encouragement without which I would fail to write such epic tales.

I am thankful for my editors, Mark and Ann, for finding all the places in my story that needed changes to make it better, and for supporting my choices in regards to those changes. My thanks to Deanna for all her encouragement and exacting attention to detail; and to Kathy for giving my world color and shape.

I cannot leave out my most important helpers, Ryanne, Andy, Dani, David, and Kim, my wonderful beta readers. Without whose help I could not have seen this book from a reader's perspective. Thank you all for all you have done to help bring this piece of the journey into existence.

About IA Mullin

IA Mullin grew up on a farm in rural Colorado. She helped raise crops and cattle. She learned the value of hard work and fostered a love of animals. She went to Colorado State University to further her interests in animals and science. She graduated with a Bachelor's degree in Zoology. Next, she attended Front Range Community College and attained the status of Certified Veterinary Technician with an Associate's degree in Veterinary Technology. She has worked as a kennel cleaner, vet assistant, and vet tech with various veterinary offices, the Larimer Humane Society, and volunteered with the Rocky Mountain Raptor Program, a rehabilitation center. She has raised cattle and pygmy goats. She loves all kinds of pets as well as nature and the outdoors.

In 2010, she chose to leave the veterinary field in order to raise her family. She began to write in earnest at that time. She had started her first manuscript in 1997 as a freshman in high school, but had only written in her spare time as a hobby. Now as a mother of two active boys, she has founded Avio Publishing, LLC and is very excited about the future as an independent publisher and author.

"It's been a long journey to this point, but I don't regret any step of it. It has lead me to understand that imagination is the substance of creation. If I can imagine it, I can create it, at least on paper." ~IA Mullin

Forthcoming Works

IA Mullin has a lot more stories yet to write. The journey of Marilana and Marquiese is at an end, but the world of Redsands is vast. More stories from Redsands and other worlds may come to light as time moves on. IA Mullin has two future lines of exploration planned that will lead readers into the vast cosmos. One will take readers along on the adventures of a space salvage crew seeking to find more than junk floating in the void, while the other will delve deep into the mysteries of magic where the Magewood Tree is key. Please keep an eye out for updates on these and other projects on IA Mullin's website Magewood.com.

Learn More

The world of Redsands and other worlds yet to be explored are waiting to interact with visitors at Magewood.com, the internet home of IA Mullin. Come learn more about IA Mullin, her worlds, and upcoming projects. See color maps, read short stories, and join other fans on the Mages of Magewood forum. Sign up for the Mages of Magewood email notifications for future releases, events, and special deals. If you enjoyed this story, please leave a review or comments on Goodreads.com or wherever you purchased your book. And please encourage other readers to join your experience.

You, the readers, make these worlds come to life and sustain them.

Thank You.